TERROR GALLICUS

TERROR GALLICUS

BRENNUS-CONQUEROR OF ROME

C. R. MAY

COPYRIGHT

ISBN-10: 150314352X
ISBN-13: 978-1503143524

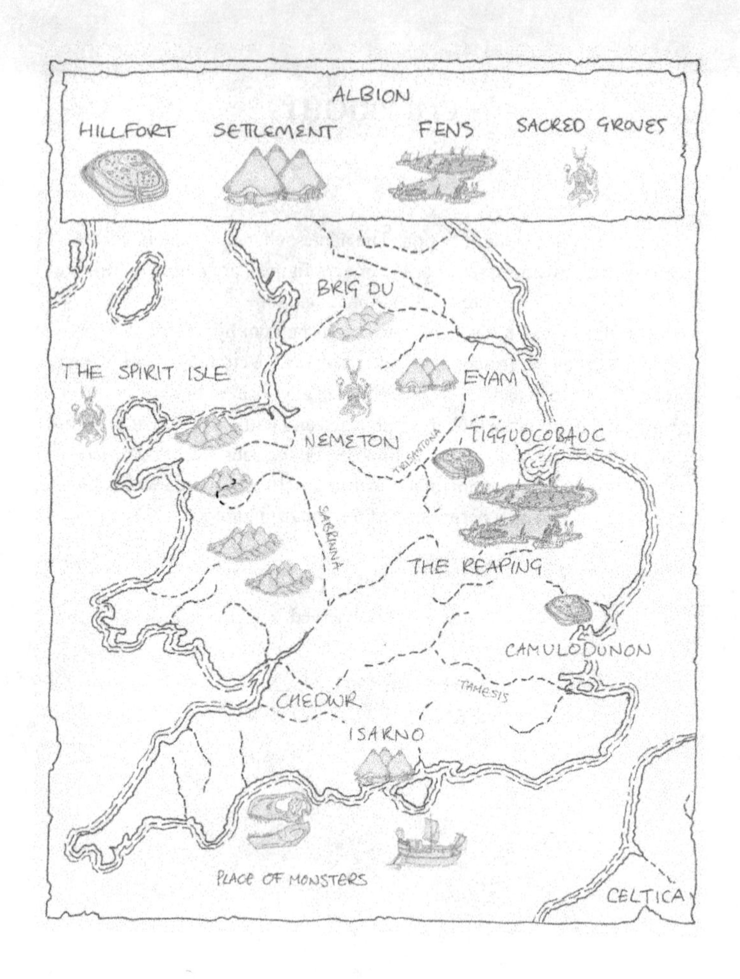

ALBION
HILLFORT
SETTLEMENT
FENS
SACRED GROVES
BRIG DU
THE SPIRIT ISLE
EYAM
NEMETON
TRISANTONA
TIGGUOCOBAUC
SABRINNA
THE REAPING
CAMULODUNON
TAMESIS
CHEDWR
ISARNO
PLACE OF MONSTERS
CELTICA

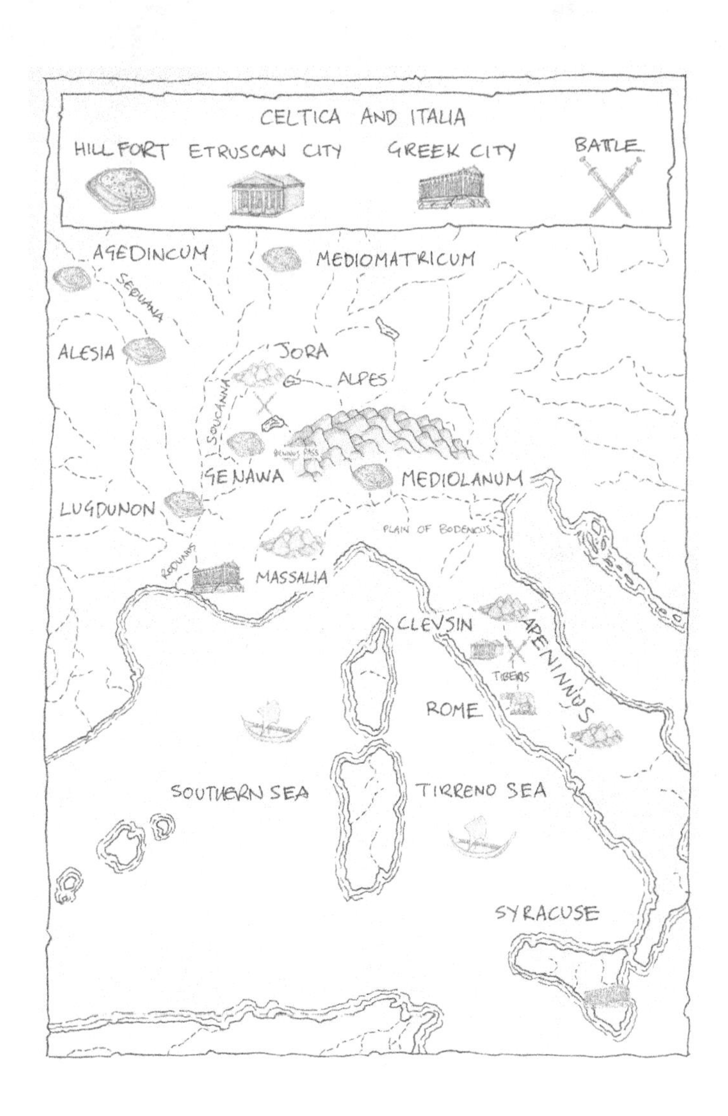
CELTICA AND ITALIA
HILLFORT
ETRUSCAN CITY
GREEK CITY
BATTLE
AGEDINCUM
MEDIOMATRICUM
SEQUANA
ALESIA
JORA
ALPES
SOUCANNA
GENAWA
MEDIOLANUM
LUGDUNON
PLAIN OF BODENCUS
MASSALIA
CLEVSIN
APENINNUS
TIBERIS
ROME
SOUTHERN SEA
TIRRENO SEA
SYRACUSE

At the time when Dionysius of Syracuse was besieging Rhegium, the Celts who lived in the regions beyond the Alps streamed through the passes in great strength...

Diodorus Sikeliotes-Bibliotheca historica

PROLOGUE

Camulodunon, late Summer 401BC

DOUBLED OVER, the trio ran across to the boundary ditch and threw themselves over the lip; sliding down the grassy embankment they cocked their heads, listening. Panting hard from a heady mix of fear and excitement, Catumanda made the mistake of glancing across to the boy at her side and instantly regretted it. Her friend was holding his nose, his cheeks full and ruddy as he fought what was about to become a losing battle with the air within him. Balling his fist he made a last desperate attempt to delay the inevitable by biting down on the whitened knuckle of his forefinger, but her look had only hastened the end. The air erupted in a spray of spittle, and Catumanda chewed anxiously at her lip and listened hard. Nothing but the soft sounds of summer: bird song: the drowsy hubbub of insects.

Her gaze flicked back to her companions, and the shorter

boy indicated that she check the field above them with a sweep of his eyes.

Catumanda rolled onto her front and scurried lizard-like through the tall grass. Reaching the lip she cautiously raised her head, only to let out a gasp of horror as she found herself staring at the damp brown leather of a man's boots. Her mouth agape, she slowly raised her eyes until she was staring straight into the face of Andalos, but a heartbeat later the man's look of triumph was swept away as a whoop cut the air, and a blur of green raced in from the side to strike his temple with a meaty *thud!*

"Quick, run!"

Andalos reeled away and the spell was broken. Catumanda slithered back down the bank, scooped up the sack and tore up the opposite slope after her companions.

Even though they were helpless with laughter and weighed down by their booty the gang quickly outpaced their victim, and they were several fields away before they came to a halt and fell to the ground in a brawl of arms and legs.

Catumanda lifted her head and looked back but there was no sign of their irate pursuer, and the children lay on their backs and choked on their laughter as they gulped down air.

High above them, iron grey clouds hurried away to the East as the season of gales approached. The leaves were already beginning to lose the waxy pallor of high summer, and a murmuration of starlings swept the sky in waves as the seasons rolled on as they had for all time.

Suddenly Acco rolled onto his side and began choking and wheezing. As his friends looked nonchalantly across, he pulled a large oak leaf from his mouth and held it up to them. "Thanks for helping. I could have died!"

The others laughed at his histrionics. Although he was the youngest among them, he was already a hand's width taller with the build to match. Catumanda made an ostentatious sweep with her arm. "The mighty Acco; slain by a leaf!"

Acco hawked and spat out the last traces of foliage as his friends chuckled beside him. Looking down at the leaf he paled. "That is the biggest oak leaf that I have ever seen!"

Catumanda shrugged. "So? It's a big leaf."

Acco stared back. "Can you see an oak tree here? It is the sign!"

The children looked around them: they *were* far from any sacred oaks and the winds were light in the shelter of the valley. Perhaps their big friend was right. It *was* the sign they had sought all summer.

Acco drew his knife and closed his palm around the blade. His friends caught the mood, and the grins washed from their faces as they recognised the importance of the moment. "If we are going to do it, it must be now. I travel tomorrow and we may never see one another again."

They shared a look of confirmation and each gave a solemn nod. There were no doubts.

The ends of Acco's mouth twitched for a heartbeat as he drew the sharp edge of the blade slowly across his palm. Passing the knife across he cupped the leaf in a small hollow; making a fist he watched as a steady flow of darkening blood dripped into its folds. Within moments the lifeblood of all three friends was collecting together and Catumanda, the eldest, stirred the mixture with her finger as they looked on. Catumanda and Acco listened as Solemis spoke the pledge:

"Let us be joined for all days.
One blood...
One bone...
One clan...
Steadfast and true."

Catumanda sipped from the leaf, passing it carefully around the circle for each boy to drink in turn. Folding the leaf in on itself, she scooped a shallow bowl in the earth and placed it carefully inside. As the girl swept the dark earth back across, they looked to one another and smiled nervously at the sight of their crimson rimmed teeth. Finally they clasped their bloodied hands together and made a ball as Catumanda made the dedication:

"Erecura, earth mother, accept our sacrifice.
Watch over your children, keep us true."

They embraced for the first time as *blood genos,* and slumped back to the grass with a sigh. Pulling the sack open she tossed an apple to each of her friends, and they lay back and bit through the rough green skin of their plunder with a loud crunch.

Acco's voice was the first to rise above the sound of munching. "If you are studying the clouds again, I don't want to know what they tell you."

Catumanda turned her head and squinted. "I have told you before, I have not reached that stage of my training yet."

She raised herself onto her elbow and looked earnestly at her friends. Acco frowned and threw Catumanda a look of warning. "If you have had a dream about us I don't want to know that either, especially if it involves storms at sea. You know that I am leaving for Celtica in the morning."

Catumanda took another bite of her apple and sighed. "I *have* dreamed about us, but it is a good dream...*I think!* I dreamt that we were adults, and we were wandering among a forest of tall trees. The trees were perfectly straight and equally spaced, but that was not the strangest thing." She looked across at her new genos who, despite their protestations, were staring at her with rapt attention. Everyone in the tribe knew that Catumanda's dreams were a gift to her from the gods. That was why the druid Abaris had brought her from the distant lands of the Coritani the previous summer, and although both boys had accepted her as their genos, she had always known that there was an indescribable aura about her which marked her apart. She grinned reassuringly as she noticed the concern etched onto their features. "The trees," she continued, "were a creamy colour, but so too was the ground, and looking up we noticed that the sky was the same hue."

Acco's arm shot out, and Catumanda flinched as an apple core rebounded from her forehead. "You hag! You could have told us all this before we bound ourselves to you. I told you that I didn't want to hear about any of your dreams, especially today of all days!"

Catumanda rubbed her forehead, but smiled happily all the same. She had always loved that her friends treated her exactly the same as they treated each other, despite the fact that she was not only a girl but a girl who had been touched by the gods, and she was overcome with pride that they had finally accepted her as blood genos. Although they had frequently swum together in the river which ran below the oppida during the hot summer months, there were moments when she had begun to feel just, well, *awkward* doing certain things before them, and she realised with a pang of sadness that this day was in many ways to be the last of her childhood. Acco was leaving in the morning, maybe for good: soon her moon cycle would begin and she would become a woman. Shaking off the sudden sense of melancholy she rallied to the defence of her dream. "What is wrong with that? It is good news. Not only will we all survive into adulthood, but we meet up again in a wondrous place." She grinned. "Anyway, you should be grateful."

Acco pulled a face. "Why?"

Catumanda snatched up the core and sent it spinning back at the young Trinobante. "Because at least you know that Andalos doesn't kill you for braining him with that apple. Whether you are going to foster in the morning or not, I don't think that many boy's fathers would be so forgiving."

1

Kyriakos of Syracuse was worried. He had always made it his business to mark all that happened around him, even the small seemingly insignificant details which would pass most other men by combined to build a picture of the whole, and the picture which was beginning to form in his mind was unnerving.

This was the fifth and final journey he would make to the wild lands beyond the North winds on behalf of the shadowy figure he knew only as Sebastos. Kyriakos snorted in derision, and an image of the man entered his mind as he recalled the name. To think that he had expected to fool a trader of his experiencc. Only a true Greek could speak the mother tongue of civilisation as she should be spoken, and Kyriakos had placed the man as a barbarian from the city of Rome within moments of their first meeting.

He neither knew nor cared why the leaders of the upstart republic would wish to encourage these barbarous Keltoi to cross the Alpes at the apparent behest of his own people and settle among their cousins there. He was a merchant and worshipped at the altar of Ploutos, god of wealth, such affairs did not concern him. As a man of experience Kyriakos knew that all men had their price, and his had been met.

The gold had been welcome of course, and the Greek merchant had quickly calculated that the summers spent plying the River Rodonus, shepherding huge shaggy Keltoi to the slave markets in Massalia, would at last be at an end. Now he was desperate to return south to the island of Sikelia and, Zeus willing, see out the remainder of his days among the sprawling vineyards which he had purchased on the slopes of mighty Aetna. He would pay those taxes which he could not avoid to the Basileus Dionysius, grease a few palms, and live the life of ease and self indulgence which seemed to be the lot of wealthy and important men the world over.

His lip curled into an involuntary smile as he wondered for the thousandth time on the naivety of these Keltoi, a quality which was only matched by their complete lack of sophistication. People at home had simply refused to believe that he could exchange a single amphora of wine here for a fit healthy slave, but he had grown rich beyond his wildest dreams on the process. The fact that they guzzled vast quantities at every gathering had helped, he smirked, and not even watered down! Now, he thought happily, with the addition of the gold deposited into his vault by 'Sebastos,' his days of bartering in the northern forests were drawing to an end.

A cry of acclamation broke his reverie, and his mind drew back to the present. Kyriakos smiled warmly and his mental discipline reasserted itself as the chieftain swept through the grove, a party of druids hastening along in his wake like a gaggle of strange geese. The Greek's gaze drank in the image of the man as he advanced towards him, hailing individuals and smiling broadly at the chosen warriors which lined the path.

Catubaros, chieftain of the Senones, was naked save for the heavy gold torc which circled his neck and the long Celtic sword which hung suspended from the belt at his waist. The chieftain was armed with a heavy stabbing spear, a *lancea*, and a bronze shield of exquisite craftsmanship; the Greek watched in admiration as the watery light of spring filtered through the surrounding oaks, flickering and dancing from the red and blue enamelled details on shield, scabbard and pommel. Flaxen hair hung in sturdy plaits, while a long flowing moustache of a redder hue graced his features in the fashion of the Celtic nobility as the man came on.

Although Kyriakos had come to like and, in a strange way which surprised him, admire the simple ways of the huge northerners, their unpredictability had interfered with his digestion almost as much as the vast hunks of roasted meats which he had been forced to ingest here on a daily basis. They were, he reflected, almost the physical embodiment of the volcanoes which lay strewn around his home lands. Benign and magnificent one moment they could suddenly explode into mind-numbing violence the next, completely without warning and for little apparent reason. To a man the warriors in Keltica appeared as tall and broad as the oak trees which surrounded him, and Kyriakos sighed inwardly as he felt the old familiar pang of regret at the absurd morals of these northern giants. Such bodies really were wasted on pleasuring women alone.

The sunlight slashed down through the ancient boughs as the chieftain came to a halt only feet away from the admiring Greek, illuminating every curve and detail of his powerful frame. The hard, milk-white torso was made even more alluring by the angry red scars of battle and the puckered swirl which adorned his shoulder like one of the heavy, grotesque, brooches favoured by these barbarians. Kyriakos had heard the tale of how in his youth Catubaros had defended the door to the hall alone against all attackers, allowing the women and children to escape even as the burning building collapsed about him. The bravery displayed by the young warrior had caused the enemy to rescue the unconscious boy from the flaming debris and return him to his clan. It had been the fight which had first drawn him to the notice of the tribal elders, and the Celt had always displayed the scar with pride.

Catubaros held his arms wide as the druids moved forward to anoint his body with the sacred swirls and patterns whose meaning were known only to those of their craft. Unusually, Kyriakos had been present when the dark blue paste had been mixed by the druids that morning at the chieftain's hall in his oppidum of Agedincum, and the Greek dimly began to become aware that the feelings of disquiet which had slowly built within him over the course of the day had begun at that time. The rituals and rites performed by the holy men were closely guarded secrets, and his sense of unease had increased when the chieftain had requested that he accompany them to the sacred grove of oak trees which they called the *nemeton* for the final ceremonies that afternoon.

The chieftain glanced across to him and smiled disarmingly. “You are sure that all is prepared?”

Kyriakos nodded as he attempted to overcome his rising sense of dread. “Yes, basileus, the payments were made which will ensure the safe passage of your people across the lands through which they will travel. You have my word.”

Catubaros nodded thoughtfully. “And the boats?”

“All has been arranged and paid for as we agreed. They are assembling even as we speak.”

The chieftain smiled happily and nodded to the druids who were hovering nearby. Kyriakos caught the look which passed between the Keltoi and was suddenly gripped by the icy realisation that he was no longer of use to these barbarians. He cast about in fear as he sought a way out of the sacred grove, but of course there was none. Turning back towards the chieftain, he had just opened his mouth to plead for his life as the lancea punched in to liquidise his innards.

THE CHIEFTAIN SMILED WARMLY at the grizzled warriors as they clashed their spears against their shields and roared out their love for their leader. Calling out to each man as he came up, recalling his lineage and recognising his bravery in raids and battles, Catubaros led the procession between the ranks of proud men, through the oak grove and on down to the riverbank. Spring had forced its way into the northern lands early this year, and the pathway which had been slick with mud only a few weeks before was now dry and firm underfoot. He inhaled deeply, looking out across the bed of the river to the distant tree line and the haze of green which lay indistinct, dreamlike almost, beneath the warm evening air. Reaching out a hand as he passed by, the chieftain ran his fingertips lightly across the rough ridges and valleys of the holy oaks and walked free of their embrace.

Catubaros, chieftain of the Senones, paused at the bank as a shaft of golden sunlight forced its way between the clouds and slid across his body. He recognised it as the mark of approval from the god Bel, the Shining One, and thrusting his arms out wide he smiled as the druid moved forward to decorate his torso with the magic patterns which could be read only by the most powerful druids and the goddess Sequana herself. They had sacrificed a fierce boar that very morning, and the dark blood of the animal had been mixed with woad to constitute the paste with which the druids were now anointing his body. It would add to the power of the spells and ensure that his spirit fly swiftly to the river goddess' watery realm.

He turned to the squat, swarthy man at his side and smiled, thankful that it would be the last time that he would have to conceal his contempt for the grasping little Greek. From their conversations over the previous five years he had come to the conclusion that this Kyriakos regarded himself as a wealthy man of some importance, yet he had not once seen him distribute so much as a cup of wine to one of his followers, much less gold or silver. It was a chieftain's duty to reward his followers with riches, as much as it was their duty to take *potlach* in return. If the people in the South were all as feeble and grasping as this oily bastard he reflected happily, a bright future lay before his people, and he would live forever in the tales of the bards as the great chieftain whose spirit and foresight had led them to the new lands. As the druids moved swiftly around him, daubing his body and mumbling their spells, he turned to the Greek and threw him a final, cold hearted, smile. "You are sure that all is prepared?"

The Greek rolled the fingers of his hands together in the ingratiating way that had disgusted the chieftain for so long as he replied. "Yes, basileus, the payments were made which will ensure the safe passage of your people across the lands through which they will travel. You have my word."

Catubaros nodded, satisfied. "And the boats?"

"All has been arranged and paid for as we agreed. They are assembling even as we speak."

The chieftain glanced across to Devorix, the chief druid, and exchanged a look which both men understood without the need for spoken words. To Catubaros' amusement, he saw that the Greek was at last beginning to understand why his presence at the ceremony had been ordered but, he knew, he was far too late to alter his fate.

As Kyriakos, panic stricken, cast about for a means of escape from the nemeton the chieftain lowered the tip of his lancea and prepared to strike. The instant the Greek turned back Catubaros drove the spear forward, the leaf shaped blade sliding effortlessly into his soft, plump belly. Years of experience on the battlefields of Celtica had taught him which wounds resulted in quick kills and which were merely debilitating and, unfortunately for Kyriakos, the chieftain had inflicted one of the most painful wounds of all. The weapon slid easily into the soft tissue of the Greek's lower abdomen and sliced down into the groin. Catubaros withdrew the weapon with a slick sucking sound and stood back as the man instinctively clutched the wound, gasping with shock and surprise as he tumbled forward onto the dusty ground.

Moving forward, Devorix stood in the soft warm sunlight and silently studied the agonised thrashings of the man at his feet. Crouching, scurrying around the clearing like a monstrous crab, the druid listened to the gasps and whimpers of the dying man as he rolled and tossed before them. Suddenly the Greek's leg kicked out in a series of involuntary spasms, and Devorix grinned up at his chieftain. "The signs are fortuitous brother. The gods have blessed our great undertaking."

The chieftain nodded earnestly. "You are sure?"

"The gods speak through him. He is calling for his home and family and they of course lay to the South. Also, you see," he continued, pointing at Kyriakos' agonised kicks, "the gods are drawing his legs down and pointing to the South. The signs could not be clearer!"

Catubaros' features relaxed into a relieved smile. To have had to come so far on this journey before they could be permitted by the gods to ask for their consent had always troubled him but, it would seem, nothing could now bar the Senones from the path he had beaten for them.

The chieftain indicated that his servant hand him his favourite battle helm, and he studied it for a moment as he recalled every detail on its golden surface. The swirls and patterns on its lower edges were as familiar to him as the lines on the backs of his own hands, each nick and graze on its bronze surface spoke to him of a successful raid or a fight won. The helm had been a gift from his own father, the day that he had returned from foster, and it had been handed down from father to son within his family for generations. It was right that it would now accompany the greatest of his clan to the home of Sequana. Placing it slowly and deliberately upon his head the chieftain turned and, raising his lancea and shield for the last time, bathed in the roar of acclamation from his warriors as it rolled around the wooded bowl. A final glance skyward, and he turned to take the timber steps into the underground chamber.

Catubaros crossed the boarded floor and took his place on the royal seat at its far end; sweeping the chamber with his gaze he smiled with satisfaction.

Ahead of him stood the enormous cauldron which had always been the centrepiece of every feast, ever since the Basileus Dionysius had sent it north four summers ago. Chest height even to him, the cauldron held enough wine or *cervesia,* a brew fermented from barley and the warriors' favourite, to satiate the thirst of even the largest gathering, and it had been the gift which had caused Catubaros to first give serious thought to the Greek entreaties to invade and settle the lands of the Etruscans.

Along the left hand wall of the chamber dozens of amphorae stood in ordered rows, each containing the finest wines from the South, alongside tables piled high with joints of roasted meats, fine bread, fish and cheeses. Bowls and cups of the finest quality had been stacked, ready for the feast he would soon provide for the river goddess.

Looking across to the opposite wall Catubaros was pleased to see that his war chariot had been disassembled and now lay in pieces, surrounded by scores of ritually bent and twisted sword blades. A series of wrestling matches had been organised at the feast the previous evening, and the prevailing warriors had been allowed to supply personally marked shields to accompany the chieftain on his final journey. The familiar designs helped greatly in recreating his hall in miniature, as had been intended.

A shadow fell across the chieftain, and he glanced up to see the smiling face of Devorix standing before him. The druid held forward a golden cup, its surface a brawl of swirling pattern, and Catubaros reached out and took it from him. To his surprise the chieftain felt the first pangs of anxiety pick at him as he swilled the dark liquid. It had been many years since he had felt this way he recognised with a twinge of nostalgia, and his mind drifted back to the fights which had taken place with the older boys during his childhood. No, he smiled proudly to himself, even then there had been no fear. Most of them had in time become good friends and trusted companions, the others, well, they had died he smirked.

Throwing back his head, the chieftain sank the bitter tasting liquid in one deep draught. Once ingested he knew, the mistletoe would react with the porridge of herbs and grains with which Devorix had fed him earlier and death would be only a matter of time.

The druid nodded in respect as he took back the cup and, in a final display of empathy, grasped the forearm of

Catubaros for the final time. Many winters had passed since they had tumbled and played in the family hall, but even the long years which they had spent apart at foster had vanished like smoke in a gale the moment that they had returned. Devorix had travelled far beyond the lands of the Senones as he learned the ways of his calling, and when he had returned he had been unsurprised to discover that his brother had risen to the rank of chieftain of their people. With a final squeeze the brothers parted; without a backwards glance Devorix stepped across the still squirming form of Kyriakos and ascended the rough wooden steps, back into the full light of day.

Immediately several slaves began to fix oak planking to the post heads of the underground chamber, forming a rough roof over the whole. As the roofing neared completion Devorix turned to face upriver and raised his staff in the agreed signal. The action was answered by the young druid at the barrier, and his master watched as he turned and gave the order for the bindings to be cut through. Stout ropes had been attached to the trunks which had so expertly diverted the waters of the River Sequana back along an old course earlier that week, and now men on each bank dug in their heels and grunted with effort as they pulled the loose timbers free.

With a roar the waters of the river crashed through the remains of the barrier and swept back along their original course, a dark brown soup edged with white which rolled and tumbled at breakneck speed towards the entombed chieftain. With a look of horror the slaves completing the roof of the vault recognised the wall of water for the death it was and attempted to scramble back onto the bank, but the party of druids moved forward and, drawing their distinctive moon shaped blades, hacked down at them until they were still.

. . .

CATUBAROS HEARD the cracking of timbers as he sat in the half light and closed his eyes briefly as he awaited the deluge which would soon engulf him. The chieftain pulled a face as his mind alighted on the fate of his only son as he sat and prepared to set out on his own great journey. Maros was, he had to admit to himself, a disappointment, and he wondered if he had done the right thing in nominating the boy to succeed him. Even his name had become a thing of scorn among some of the warriors, he knew. Maros, Big Man, had seemed a good choice when he was younger, but on his return from foster he seemed to have hardly grown at all. Naturally he had extinguished the lives of the entire client family for their failings, and if lack of size had been the only problem with the boy, that had been quickly rectified. Maros had inherited his ancestors' massive frame, and a diet of meat coupled with a year or two of hard physical work had covered those bones in layers of hard muscle.

He sighed, annoyed with himself that his final thoughts in the world of men had been allowed to drift in this direction, but there was no doubt in his mind that his son's character did not sit well with the qualities required to be chieftain of the Clans. He was as brave as a boar, but the boy seemed to combine a dangerous mix of bravado and impetuosity which would likely as not do for him sooner rather than later.

A cry of alarm carried to him from above and he recognised the panicked actions of the slaves as they attempted to scurry to safety. It would do them no good, they were fated to serve him in the afterlife. Their bodies would be carried away by Sequana and their spirits would serve his meal this evening.

As the slaves cleared away, strips of light cut across the gloomy chamber, illuminating the golden forms of the offerings which he hoped would placate the goddess. The Senones were moving away from the goddess' protection, and it was important that the chieftain obtain her blessing on their great adventure.

A pathetic mewing sound came from the mortally wounded Kyriakos, but Catubaros ignored him as his eyes drank in the life and beauty represented by the strips of blue above. The Greek would need to accompany him to the goddess to explain their reasons for leaving her divine protection. He had brought his end upon himself.

The small grey form of a dove flashed across the serried lines of sky above the chieftain as the waters reached them, gone in the blink of an eye. Catubaros, chieftain of the Senones, gripped his sword a little tighter still and clenched his jaw as the waters of the river, the very body of the goddess Sequana herself, cascaded in to carry his soul away.

THE WAR BAND stood in the cover of the tree line and peered across at the dim lights of the farmstead. All was reassuringly quiet and the leader's *gaesum*, his short throwing spear, flicked out to left and right. Immediately two groups of three melted into the gloom as they made their way to opposite ends of the Belgic settlement. Once in position they would sweep in, silencing anyone foolish enough to be abroad at this time of night and reassemble outside the door of the main hall, ready to eliminate any opposition which might emerge.

Maros glanced again at the lone guard which paced apathetically to and fro before the corral and snorted. The fool was yawning and scratching his balls as if he had years left to live. The Senone knew better, and he turned his head to one side and whispered to the man beside him. “Crixos. What is the name that the Germans use for fate?”

The dark shadow smiled, obviously guessing his leader's

thoughts. Pale moonlight reflected dully from a line of stained, crooked teeth. "Wyrd."

Maros nodded. "Wyrd, that's it! I wonder how many other men have been led to this place by their wyrd tonight?"

Crixos shot his chieftain a look which caused Maros to narrow his eyes in suspicion. He opened his mouth to question him but the warrior seemed to sense his mistake and recovered quickly. Hissing a warning he began to move back into the position allotted him for the attack. "The boys are in position, Maros. Time to strike."

Snapping his head back to the front, Maros squinted and tried to pick out the warriors in the darkness. High above, a cloud, its grey outline edged in white, slid slowly from the face of the moon.

There!

As the silvered light washed across the settlement, Maros caught the tell-tale flicker made by the heavy blade of a lancea. Lowering his gaze, he picked out the crouching forms of men on either side of the heavy door posts which framed the entrance to the main hall and smiled. It was where the Belgic chieftain and his retainers would sleep, and there was only one doorway. They were trapped like rats and would be cut down as they tried to emerge. A thought flitted into his mind like a bat in the night, recognised for an instant before it disappeared back into the gloom. Other men, more astute men, might have recognised it as a warning sent by the gods, but Maros discounted it. He already knew why the Belgae had allowed themselves to become trapped in their own hall as their prized herds were driven off. The Germans were tough fighters but not the cleverest of men, it was common knowledge among the tribes of the south.

A quick glance to left and right confirmed that his men were ready, their faces turned towards him as they awaited his charge. Pride welled in Maros' breast as he prepared to lead the men against their hated foe. Gripping his spear and shield tightly he inhaled deeply and burst from cover. Catubaros' son tore across the clearing at the head of his men. Legs pumping like bellows, he emerged from the shadows and began to cross the slick grass of the meadow which separated the forest from the corral, carefully shifting the weight of the spear in his hand as he sought the point of perfect balance. He was not the biggest or strongest warrior in the tribe he knew, but his eye for a target was second to none and he drew back his arm as he prepared to hurl the weapon at the unfortunate guard.

Sighting along its shaft the Senone leader was shocked and bewildered to find that his intended target had simply disappeared. No man could recover his wits that quickly, and the first seeds of doubt caused Maros to check his pace. Arrayed in a shallow arrowhead to either side of him the other members of his war band were beginning to slow their own runs, their battle cries trailing away to nothing as they began to cast looks of horror about them.

A glance across to the tree line confirmed the worst, as a mass of shadowy outlines slowly solidified into scores of heavily armed men. The sound of fighting carried from the direction of the Belgic hall, and Maros looked across just as his men there were engulfed beneath a wave of stabbing spears and slashing sword blades.

"Form on me. If any man can see a way out of this, now would be a good time to share it with us."

As the ragged line of warriors drew themselves into a tight circle, Maros was struck again by the look which Crixos had given him in the tree line moments ago. He called over his shoulder, fearing that the reasons for his sudden unease would be confirmed. "Crixos?"

The men around him looked about as the enemy closed in around them. "He is not with us, Maros."

The Senone leader spat in disgust as the truth became obvious. It had been Crixos who had first raised the idea of a last, final, raid on their enemy before they left these lands for good and it had been Crixos who had persuaded him to lead the raid in person. He called out again. "Crixos has betrayed us. If any of you can see a way out take it quickly before they arrive. I will remain here and cover you for as long as I can."

The familiar sound of long swords being drawn from their scabbards confirmed to Maros what he knew already. No Celt would desert his chieftain in the face of the enemy. Death will reach out and snatch away the lives of all men, but shame can live forever.

A long line of torches approached them from the direction of the hall, like a flickering wave as it wend its way past the corral and crossed the meadow. As they came up the torch bearers threw the brands to the ground between the opposing forces, and slowly the area came aglow with a spectral light.

Maros drew his own sword, hefting his heavy rectangular shield as he walked clear of the knot of Celtic warriors. Pacing the ground between the opposing bands he began to search the front ranks for the Belgic leader, when suddenly he was there before him. The man was unmistakeable. While most of his leading men still wore a large disc of bronze suspended across their chest to protect their vital organs, the man before him was dressed in the finest quality mail shirt which shone a dull red in the light from the flames. Mail shirts were the latest gift from the gods to the Celtic people, and Maros knew that the man before him must be the Belgic king, Cynobelin himself.

The king stepped forward and addressed him with an amused smile. "Welcome to Belgica, Maros of the Senones."

Reaching across, he withdrew his own sword with a purposeful sweep. “Although you may find it hard to believe at the moment, your gods are smiling on you this night.”

Cynobelin raised his sword and examined the blade in the wan light thrown down by the moon, turning it this way and that as he admired the dull reflections. Finally he looked back to the Senone chieftain with a cold smile. “I need you alive...for now.” The king described a small arc in the air with the point of his blade, before continuing with a menacing scowl. “Listen carefully. This is what is going to happen.”

2

The young man held the brand beneath the overhanging eaves of the building and waited patiently for the flames to take hold. Despite the generally dry start to the spring the days were still short enough to allow the aged thatch to retain the winter's dampness, and the process was taking far longer than the leaders had anticipated. Finally, after what had seemed like an age, the drier layers caught and thick dark smoke began to curl from the upper surface. Moving around the base of the building Solemis repeated the process until he was certain that the fire had taken hold, before tossing the brand inside the open doorway.

The previous evening had witnessed a riot of drunken destruction as the people had broken up the many items which would be too cumbersome for the great journey ahead, and the interior of the buildings were now crammed full of combustible material. The tinder dry wood and straw flickered and caught immediately, and moments later a great whoosh rent the air as the building finally erupted.

Dancing back from the scorching heat, Solemis turned to the line of expectant children and called them forward with an amused flick of his head. "Come on then, not too close. And be careful where you swing those sticks." He let out a delighted chuckle. "We will need young people with both eyes in the new lands."

The children scampered excitedly forward, raising their makeshift weapons in anticipation as the first of their quarry came squealing from the now roaring thatch. Peels of laughter erupted from the crowd as they watched their young running in a chaotic teeming mass, swinging and kicking at the flood of mice which were suddenly spewing forth from the burning building. A scream came from the line of watching women as a mouse arced through the air to land among them and soon the crowd were bellowing with laughter. As the terror stricken rodents began to overwhelm the children's defensive line through sheer weight of numbers and scurry to safety through the line of hopping, stamping adults, Solemis walked clear of the chaos and stood to one side.

Albiomaros jogged across with a grin, pausing only to aim a kick at a particularly large rodent which disappeared back into the conflagration with a squeak. "If we had known it was going to be this much fun we would have left years ago. Flying mice," the big man laughed. "A house is not a home without a hundred of them!"

They stood together and looked on as the last of the mice scurried away into the grass which surrounded the homestead. Solemis cast a last long look around the collection of huts and barns which had been a home to his extended family for generations. With the exception of Albiomaros every man, woman and child here were part of his clan. Several families, each tracing their descent from a common ancestor, shared the settlement whose head man, Solemis' father, Connos, was the very embodiment of that long dead man, the continuation of his line made flesh and bone.

Raising his gaze the young Senone noted the lines of oily smoke which were beginning to climb into the warm spring air nearby. The neighbouring clans were doing likewise, firing their farms and outbuildings as they prepared to leave the lands of their ancestors for the final time. Soon the clans would come together on the road which led south and the tribe would move away.

As the adults gathered the children together and began to drift back towards the waiting wagons, Solemis walked across to the horse which was waiting patiently nearby. Taking hold of the reins he paused and looked about him. "Let's get this done and be gone," he murmured to his big friend. "There are too many ghosts watching us do this work."

Albiomaros trotted across and gripped the rope which led back from the horns on the big stallion's saddle. With a tug of his powerful arms he watched as, freeing itself from the sandy ground, the line grew taut under the forward pressure from the mount. One final heave was enough. The central post which supported the roof of the hut snapped under the pressure as, already weakened by axes, it proved unequal to the task of withstanding the combined effects of the conflagration which surrounded it and the efforts of beast and man. Freed from its support, the entire structure crashed in on itself in a welter of sparks and flames. As the ruin began to settle a cry drifted across from the direction of the main hall at the centre of the farm, and the two friends glanced across as a similar fate befell the communal building. It was here that the people of the clan had gathered together to feast and celebrate the yearly cycles taken by man and nature. Births and deaths had been celebrated with equal gusto, thanks given to the gods for good harvests and successful raids on neighbouring tribes. It was the place where the heart and soul of the clan resided, and the involuntary moan which escaped from the watching crowd at its destruction marked the symbolic moment when the clan detached themselves from their ancestral home and cast themselves adrift.

Albiomaros glanced across and threw Solemis a wry smile. Although he was not of the clan his people held similar beliefs and traditions, and he understood as completely as any of them the gravity of the moment as he murmured a sentence at the scene spread out before him. "The cord's been cut."

Solemis dragged his thoughts reluctantly back to the present. Like most of the people, he suspected, his mind had wandered away to recall long forgotten episodes played out within the walls which they had all just witnessed come crashing down. He looked across, furrowing his brow at his big friend's comment.

Albiomaros explained. "The cord which connects a bairn to its mother. It has been cut." Walking around he laid a hand on Solemis' shoulder and sauntered towards the now reflective crowd which had gathered at the limit of the settlement, the earlier jollity driven away by the smoke of memories. Turning his head he threw a parting comment back across his shoulder. "Just like the bairn, you are on your own now. It's time to fend for yourselves."

Solemis' father and the senior warriors were leaving the flaming pile now and making their way across to rejoin their families. A great crash rent the air as the last remaining wall of the building collapsed into the conflagration in an eruption of smoke and flames.

Gathering up his weapons, the young Celt tagged onto them without a backward glance.

. . .

If confirmation had been needed that the old chieftain, Catubaros, had been successful in persuading the goddess of the tribe that their future lay in distant lands, it had been provided a few days after the sacrifice at the river.

A party of warriors had looked on excitedly as a huge heron had circled the spot where the chieftain had passed into the underworld before, with a graceful dip of its wing, it had flown away to the South. Hastening back to Agedincum they had described the event to the druid Devorix who had confirmed that, as the bird of death and the underworld, the heron must have been sent by Sequana to indicate her approval of the migration of her people. The bird's actions had clearly indicated that the clans of the Senones gather and head south, and the preparations for the journey had been completed.

The morning was beginning to grow warmer as the sun rose higher, driving away the earlier covering of fine mist which had flowed across the land and collected in the gullies and hollows like so much spilled milk.

Solemis and Albiomaros had been sent on ahead by Connos, and they chatted happily as they rode south. The track hugged the banks of the Sequana as the sacred river crossed the heavy clay soils from its source near the meeting place. There the body of Sequana left mother earth in a series of springs to flow westwards, bringing life and protection for the Senones and others. The spring was one of the most sacred places for the tribe and Devorix would make a final sacrifice to their deity there before the tribe left her protection forever.

A kingfisher, its chest the colour of the most perfect summer sky, darted from a low branch and slipped beneath the surface of the river with a barely discernible splash, before emerging moments later with a fat brown trout held tightly within its dagger-like bill.

Despite the uncertainties which lay ahead of them, the people of the clan had been in high spirits when the pair had trotted out that morning. Even the weather had turned fine, and Solemis was in no doubt that Toranos, the sky god, had added his own blessings to their great undertaking.

As the sun climbed to its zenith the forest cover began to grow thinner, steadily drawing back from the roadway as the great meeting place of the tribe grew ever nearer. The staccato beat of a woodpecker sounded from the shadows of the deeper forest while, closer to hand, the familiar call of a cuckoo announced that spring was finally here.

Albiomaros was the first to break the silence between them. "You never see one, do you?"

Solemis glanced across. "See a what?"

"A cuckoo, you never see one."

Solemis took another bite of the roast pork which they carried with them. While the cattle were being driven south to supply the tribe with fresh meat and milk on the journey, the hogs' well deserved reputation for the special kind of obstinance which men aptly called pig-headedness had caused them to be culled to the last animal. Glancing down at the dogs which trotted happily at their side, Solemis indicated the direction from which the distinctive call had come. "Tarvos, Suros: fetch the cuckoo!"

The dogs loped off into the tree line without a sound, and Albiomaros chuckled as he watched them disappear into the shadows. "That is the last we will see of them today, Solemis. Nobody can see a cuckoo, a druid told me that years ago."

Solemis gave a nonchalant shrug. Although the dogs belonged to the clan as a whole, everybody knew that they were devoted to the young tribesman. They had been inseparable since Solemis had returned from foster with the Trinobantes in far off Albion, and they had grown into full adulthood together. Solemis had taken on the task of training the big animals when all others had lacked the patience or will required, and he had been rewarded with the unswerving loyalty of the big dogs who clearly regarded him as the leader of their own little pack.

They had been brought to the tribe by the Greek, Kyriakos, as a gift for Catubaros, but the chieftain had given little thought to their training and he had been more than happy to dispose of them as *potlach*. Wide of muzzle and solidly built they were of a type known by the Greeks as molossus and were used by them and others for protection, hunting and even in war. Kyriakos' judgement had proven to be sound in this instance at least, and they had developed into excellent hunters. Suros, the runner, possessed what seemed to be almost unlimited stamina. Able to easily outpace a horse over some distance, he was used by the clan to bring game to bay. Tarvos, the bull, was stockier and less fleet of foot than his brother, but made up for a lack of pace with a ferocity and apparent disdain for the effects of pain which had drawn widespread admiration from the older warriors in the tribe.

Solemis and Albiomaros walked their mounts forward as they awaited the return of the hunters. The other members of the clan would move at the pace of the slowest wagon or cart and there was no need to hurry. The day was fine, and they were looking ahead to renewing friendships among the other clans which together constituted the tribe of the Senones. Ahead of them the roadway slowly widened until, doubling a final bend, the wide expanse of grassland where the clans were to congregate came into view.

At that moment, the dogs finally crashed from cover and ran excitedly over to the place where the young riders had reined in their stallions. Carefully placing the limp grey body of the bird on the track next to Solemis' horse, Tarvos and Suros eagerly awaited the praise which they expected would be forthcoming; they were to be disappointed.

Solemis' eyes swept the grassland, and he pursed his lips and spoke. "Something is wrong, genos."

Albiomaros nodded his agreement as a group of warriors caught sight of them on the edge of the tree line. Peeling off from the milling group on the far side of the plain they galloped across. Solemis quickly scanned the faces of the oncoming riders and was pleased to discover that he recognised several of the men from a raid he had undertaken the previous year, and he was gratified when their leader slowed his mount and raised an arm in recognition as they came up. The warriors looked magnificent in their war finery, and Solemis wondered that he had not been told to dress likewise. The man hailed them as his horse trotted up. "How far behind you are your people?"

Solemis caught the note of anxiety in the warrior's voice and his mind raced. In truth he had no idea. They had been enjoying a morning's ride in the warm sunshine, completely oblivious to the progress of the rest of the clan, but he knew that he needed to supply a definitive answer or look at best incompetent or worse, a fool. Almost before he had time to think he found that he was volunteering the first answer which flashed into his mind. "They are no more than half a mile behind. They will be up with us soon."

The leader nodded, satisfied. "Ride back and tell them to get here as quickly as they can, and tell the warriors to arm." Pulling the head of his mount around the rider glanced back, grim faced. "Tell Connos that the army of the Belgae are blocking our path."

. . .

THE CLANS of the Senones were streaming into the clearing now as the appointed time for the great gathering of the tribe approached. Solemis had sent Albiomaros hurrying back to inform his father and the elders of his own clan of the dire reports which had reached them as they had gained the meeting place and, his dogs in tow, he had trotted his mount across in search of more information.

The discipline shown by the clans in the face of this, the first of what could well turn out to be many setbacks and confrontations they would face before their great journey was completed bode well for the future, and Solemis was quietly proud of the fortitude displayed by his people. Swinging himself down from his horse, he made his way across to the centre of the plain where the warriors were gathering. Clearly, a meeting was in progress to discuss what response the potential threat formed by this German force would draw from the tribe. Despite his youth it was obvious even to Solemis that a potential disaster lay before them. Whether the tribe fought or not, the fact that they were facing a confrontation of any sort before they had even assembled, much less left their own borders, was an ominous sign of what could lay ahead for them. Even the strongest tribe could not hope to fight their way down the length of Celtica encumbered as they were by their young and old.

Ahead of him a man was attempting to persuade a magnificent warrior to take the leadership of the tribe, and Solemis halted at the edge of the large group and listened as the advocate attempted to whip up support for his proposal. "I tell you brothers, there is only one clear choice open to us. As I look around me now I see many faces which are familiar to me from feasts, raids and battles against our common enemies." The man pointed out individuals for particular praise, showing them honour and delighting their followers.

The power of flattery was beginning to have its desired effect, and several of those who had been chosen began to add their voices to the clamour. The support for what in truth seemed to be the sole contender for the leadership of the tribe was growing by the moment, and Solemis studied the man carefully. It was not difficult to see why he was so highly thought of, the man really did look magnificent. Easily a head taller than almost any other man in the clearing and built like a bull, the warrior shone in a highly burnished shirt of mail. It was the first time that the young Celt had seen such a war shirt and he studied it closely. Formed from hundreds of interlocking iron rings, the mail reached down past the warrior's waist. The shoulders were protected by a further pair of shaped panels which were laced together by leather strips; edged in red rawhide the contrast between the almost liquid silver of the mail and the blood red leather detail, the war shirt was simply breathtaking. A heavy golden torc of exquisite workmanship encircled the big warrior's neck, its delicately cast terminals a writhing mass of pattern. Plain trews of an earthy colour added an air of practicality, and the contrast between them and the finely worked brilliance which adorned the upper body of the man sent out a powerful message to all.

Around him it would seem that the entreaties of the crowd were growing by the moment, and Solemis looked on in excitement as the big warrior held up a hand to quieten them. Stepping forward, the hero fixed his countenance to reflect the gravity of the moment and began to address the throng. "Men, warriors, fellow Senones," he began. "You do me a great honour by asking that I lead our people at this anxious time, but I fear that I cannot."

The crowd yelled as one for him to accept their leadership, but the big man shook his head sadly. "You all know that I cannot lead our people, for I am not of royal blood. Only one man has the right to our oath of loyalty and that man is the beloved son of our chieftain, Catubaros."

A voice cried out from the rear of the crowd, as the clamour grew for the big warrior to lead them in the coming confrontation. "Where is Maros then? Why is he not here to lead us?"

The warrior opened his mouth to make a reply, but only a gasp escaped as he held his arms wide in a gesture which seemed to say that he knew as little of the whereabouts of their new leader as any other man. He turned to the man who had led the proposals for his acclamation as war leader, and done so much to garner the support of the crowd. "Crixos, they tell me that you came to us from Maros' hall. Where is the man who would be our chieftain?"

The man lowered his gaze and looked at the ground as if struggling with his conscience. The mass of warriors turned to him and began to demand that he share what he knew. Finally Crixos looked up and reluctantly addressed them. "I don't know for sure what happened at Maros' hall, as I left early and spent the night elsewhere." The warriors shrugged knowingly. All men took female slaves for the night if they were away from home, it was expected, but he clearly knew more than he had so far shared with them and the crowd grew quiet as they turned their faces to him. Solemis glanced back at the big warrior and felt a momentary pang of fear as the man's piercing gaze met his own for a heartbeat. He spoke quietly, but his voice carried an unmistakable air of authority. "Crixos, tell us all you know."

A warrior cried out as Crixos hesitated. "Yes, Crixos, this is no time for misguided loyalty. Our families are here and we are milling around like sheep. Tell us what you know."

The cry was taken up, and soon the meeting was in

uproar. Eventually the big warrior stepped forward and, raising his arms, called for silence. Slowly the clamour abated as the men craned forward to hear Crixos' explanation. Solemis watched as Crixos sighed and reluctantly looked up at the throng. "Maros and those closest to him were talking about going on one last raid before we left our lands for good." There was a collective gasp of astonishment as the words sank in, and Crixos raised his voice as he added an apparent defence of his chieftain. "I don't know if they actually went. I left before the morning, but that seemed to be the plan which was being hatched over their cervesia the night before."

The meeting descended into uproar as the apparent irresponsibility of their appointed leader was revealed. Solemis found that he was as outraged as any at the unsuitability of a man who would abandon his people at such a time for vain personal glory, and found that he was swept up by the fast growing cult of the man who had been proposed by the man Crixos.

The warriors crashed their lancea against the rear of their shields as they chanted the name of the mail clad giant who had come to save them in their time of greatest need. It was the first time that Solemis would hear the name of the man who would play so great a part in his own life story.

Bren-nus!... Bren-nus!... Bren-nus!

Brennus fought to mask the sense of triumph which coursed through his blood like fire, as he held up a hand to quieten the crowd. Slowly the chanting lessened as men waited anxiously to see if their champion would lead them to safety and Solemis listened as desperately as any. Brennus held his arm out to one side, and they watched as one of Brennus' war band passed him his battle helm. Solemis gasped in wonder as the man ostentatiously raised his helm and lowered it onto his head. The helm was a thing of wonder, totally in keeping with the dignity and bearing of the man. Fashioned not from bronze but iron, the base of the helm was decorated in writhing scrolls of red and blue enamel. Solemis could see that a similar design adorned the iron neck guard which protruded from the rear of the helm while above, a swirling pattern of loops and whorls rose up to a fantastically crafted raven. As large as a jackdaw, the raven figure perched atop the very apex of the helm, and Solemis was astonished to see that the wings of the bird had been cunningly worked by the craftsman so that they moved in time with the man's own movements. The crowd were suitably cowed by the appearance of Brennus in his battle finery, and Solemis watched in awe as he addressed them once more. "My friends, I am not worthy of this honour which you press upon me."

Cries of dismay greeted the announcement, and Brennus waited calmly for the pleas to subside before speaking again. "However," he continued, "our need is great. If there truly are Belgae ahead of us our people are in great danger. I would be dishonouring the oath to my chieftain and people if I did not do as you ask and lead this fight now."

Solemis was swept up by the great outpouring of relief as the warriors acclaimed their new leader, and Brennus smiled as he waited to complete his address. Finally men calmed as they craned forward to hear his final words. "However, I want every man here to know that I only do this thing on behalf of my chieftain. I will pray to the gods that Maros returns soon to lead us in our great journey, and the moment that he does you have my word that I will stand aside and become again as you are now, a freeborn warrior, a man of honour and loyalty to his chieftain and people."

The cheering intensified and the loud braying of the

Celtic battle horn, the *carnyx*, swept across the heads of the crowd as the men hailed their saviour. Solemis watched as Brennus and Crixos shared a momentary look of triumph before they led the warriors across to the camp of Devorix and his druids for his blessing on their enterprise. No man, however popular or suited for the role could hope to survive without the support of the druids, but Solemis felt sure that the holy man would, despite his family ties to Maros, have no objections to Brennus taking over leadership of the people. They were faced with an immediate and tangible threat to the very existence of the entire tribe and were desperate for the type of experienced leadership which only a man of battle experience like Brennus could supply. Besides, he reflected, the man had stated his intention to relinquish any authority the moment that Catubaros' son returned, what possible objection could he raise?

His dogs had sat patiently at his side as the events had played out before them, but now they yelped in excitement as a familiar voice spoke at his ear. "Men are sheep."

Solemis turned to see the solemn face of Connos standing behind him, his head slowly shaking in apparent dismay. He began to explain to his father about the disappearance of Maros and the appointment of Brennus as war leader, but Connos only pulled the same face which he remembered from his childhood when he was struggling to master a skill. He had clearly been unimpressed by the whole thing. "I saw what happened, son. The whole thing stinks worse than a midden." He shook his head sadly and turned to go. Solemis gathered up his reins and hurried after him, the dogs trotting happily at his side. "But Brennus is going to lead the army against the Belgae. As soon as Maros returns he has promised to stand aside."

Connos placed an arm around his son's shoulder and

threw him a sympathetic smile. “I arrived too late to hear the beginning of the fun. Tell me; who proposed that Brennus should become war leader, 'just until Maros returns?'”

Solemis cast his mind back and answered truthfully. “Crixos.”

Connos snorted and stared straight ahead. His warriors were just leading the families of the clan safely out onto the plain. Albiomaros saw Solemis and Connos and waved happily from the flank. Solemis was about to return the gesture when his father asked another question. “And who was stood closest to Brennus when he went to have his acclamation approved by Devorix?”

Solemis' cheeks flushed as he realised that he had been as easily manipulated as the others. He sighed but answered truthfully. “Crixos.”

At his side Connos hawked and spat. “As I said. Men are sheep.”

3

He was still questioning his father as he slid the thick leather battle shirt over his head. "But it makes no sense. Why would the Belgae wish to fight against the combined might of the whole tribe, when we are already vacating our lands? All they have to do is move south and take them. They will need to conserve their strength to fix the new border with the Carnutes and Tricasses when we are gone."

Connos glanced up as he fixed his sword belt, instinctively sliding the weapon out a short distance and clipping it back as he readied for battle. "Trust me, we won't fight, but we need to be prepared for anything. Many men like to say that the Germans are mindless fools, who trust to their strength to extricate them from the trouble which they blunder into but believe me," he smiled, "most men who think that way end their days impaled on a German sword or spear."

Connos swung up into the saddle, unhooking his helm from the saddle horn as the remaining clansmen urged their stallions to his side. Solemis watched with pride as his father fixed the headgear into place and wondered if it would ever grace his own head. A high dome of polished bronze, the helm was crowned by a plume of horse hair which streamed behind Connos as he rode. It marked the wearer as the clan Chieftain and had given them their name, the Horsetails, the headgear serving both as a rallying point in the chaos of battle and as a mark of rank in the tribal councils. The warriors of the clan carried similar plumes attached near the tips of their spears, both the heavy bladed lancea and the lighter shafted gaesum, which streamed in their wake as they rode into battle beneath a black, sinuous storm cloud.

Connos glanced down and smiled as Solemis fastened his own sword belt and tucked the strap end safely away. "Shall we wait here for you, or shall I go and ask the Belgae if they can wait a little longer until you are ready to join us?"

The warriors laughed as Connos urged his mount into a gentle trot. He turned and called back across his shoulder as the riders moved away. "Hurry and catch us up. And leave those dogs behind!"

Albiomaros had waited for his friend, and he leaned forward and stroked his horse's neck as it skipped sideways in excitement. Solemis called down to the dogs as he mounted his own stallion. "Tarvo, Suros: stay here!" He pointed to the families crowded on the wagons to emphasise his command, struggling to suppress a smile at the abject disappointment which the dogs' body language betrayed as they realised that they had no part to play in whatever was exciting their masters.

Solemis hauled the head of his mount around and urged it forward with a squeeze from his knees. As Albiomaros came abreast of him, he glanced across and laughed aloud as he recognised the look of joy on his big friend's features at the prospect of a fight. They had fought together on several raids and, although the man was usually full of good humour and difficult to provoke, when he was moved to anger there were very few men who could match him in strength, despite his youth. Solemis picked out his father's helm on the far side of the milling mass of horsemen and made his way across to join his clan.

A great roar of acclamation rolled across the clearing from Solemis' left, as a wave of warriors swept back down towards the place where the road led away to the South. At their head rode the metal clad figure of Brennus, the raven figure surmounting his helm giving the illusion that it was beating down the meadow mere inches above his head with long, lazy strokes of its wings.

Connos urged his mount across and threw Solemis a wry smile. "It would seem that your man was an acceptable leader to Devorix. Let us see what he intends to do."

The men of the Horsetails shuffled into line as Brennus swept around the mass of mounted warriors and curbed his mount facing them. Alongside the men of his cantref, Solemis was no longer surprised to see that Crixos had taken his place. Brennus waited at the head of his men, and the very ground shook as thousands of mounted warriors ringed him in a crescent of bronze, iron and muscle. As the clans settled into position, Solemis watched as Brennus' features shone with pride and triumph. Soon the clans were gathered beneath their banners and totems, and a silence descended on the plain broken only by the occasional snort and whicker from the excited war horses.

Brennus urged his stallion forward, pausing until he was certain that all eyes were upon him. Drawing a deep breath he began to address the army of the Senones. "Brothers; let each and every man here be aware that I would gladly lay down this duty if it were not thrust upon me out of dire necessity." He paused once more and scanned the arc of grim faced warriors for any signs of dissent but found none. Satisfied, he continued. "I took the liberty of sending trusted men to scout the valley which lies ahead of us before I met with Devorix, and they have returned with confirmation that a Belgic army has taken up a position barring our way south."

A murmur ran along the line of mounted men, and Brennus waited until it had died away before continuing his address. "I propose that we divide our own army into two equal parts. I will lead the first contingent of warriors into the pass followed by our families. The remaining warriors will then bring up the rear to guard against treachery." Brennus thrust his lancea straight ahead and made a sweeping gesture to his right. "Those men to this side will follow me into the valley, those to my left will bring up our rear."

The first mutterings of discontent arose from the lips of those who would form the rearguard, but Brennus had anticipated their disappointment and moved to placate them. He held up his spear for silence before continuing with the details of his plan. "Brothers, this is no mere raid we are embarked upon. The gods have chosen us to be responsible for the continued existence of the Senone people. We have never been, nor will we ever again be more vulnerable than this summer."

Brennus paused to allow the warriors to reflect on his words.

"If we win through and carve ourselves a new home in the South, the reputation of each and every man here will shine like a Bel Fire when future bards recount the deeds of his clan. We are a brotherhood of warriors, and to prove this is so the warriors of my own cantref, men who are dearer to me than life itself, have volunteered to be the very last warriors in the column."

Solemis and Albiomaros shared a smile as the men of Brennus' cantref exchanged looks of surprise at the news. Albiomaros leaned across and dug his friend playfully in the ribs. "It looks as though the 'volunteers' were unaware that they had volunteered!"

They were not alone in noticing the looks of surprise and bewilderment which swept across the faces of Brennus' closest companions, and a ripple of laughter ran through the ranks of horsemen at the sight of the crestfallen warriors.

Brennus smiled and waited for the laughter to subside before concluding his rallying call. "As your appointed war chief, I will go ahead alone and challenge the king or champion of the Belgae to fight for the honour of our people, as is our custom." Brennus, the Raven, raised his shield and lancea and cried out to the assembled host. "That is my plan. What say you to it?"

A roar shook the clearing as thousands of warriors voiced their approval, and Solemis was surprised to see that Connos had added his voice to the general acclamation. Ahead of them Brennus' stallion was moving in skittish circles, but the new leader of the Senones brought it expertly back under control with practised body movements. The horse's movement had drawn Brennus across to the place where the Horsetails were gathered, and Solemis was now close enough to the man to see the light of triumph shining in his eyes. Brennus thrust his shield and spear higher into the air and roared out once again. *"What say you to it?"*

The field erupted as men called out and beat their own shields with their spears. A forest of carnyx rippled upwards, and soon the low wail of the Celtic war horn added its doleful note to the rising crescendo of noise.

Brennus leapt lightly from his horse and trotted across to the rear as a fine war chariot drew to a halt, its heavily tattooed charioteer balanced expertly between the leading horses. Mounting the fighting platform, Brennus waved his warriors on as the chariot rumbled away and took the road which disappeared back into the tree line to the South. The exit had obviously been planned in advance, but nobody seemed to notice or care. They were all Brennus' subjects now.

As the Senones, warriors and people alike, crowded the way south and funnelled themselves in his wake, Connos edged his stallion through the press and leaned across to his son. "Baa." Solemis looked at his father and was gratified to see that the man was smiling happily. Connos nodded and laid a hand on his shoulder. "That was impressive: this Brennus will make a fine chieftain of the clans." Solemis raised a brow in surprise at his change of heart. Connos shrugged and threw his son a wry smile. "We are all sheep now!

THE ROADWAY SOUTH hugged the main channel of the Sequana as it snaked away towards its distant source. It was here, gods willing, that the chief druid, Devorix, would make his final sacrifice to the goddess as the mass of her people left her protection for the final time.

The Horsetails had been among the first of the clans to negotiate the press of warriors as they left the wide expanse of the plain, and they now found themselves little more than a hundred paces behind the raven capped helm of Brennus as he led his people towards the enemy.

The valley of the Sequana was wide and shallow here, enabling the leading column to advance on a wide front as they approached the position which the scouts had indicated contained the Belgic army blocking their path.

The day had warmed, and the sun had passed beyond its high point as the warriors rode to battle under a sky of deepest blue. High above, the returning swallows and swifts scythed the air as they chased down the first insects of the year. It was the sign that the long, hot, summer months of central Celtica had finally arrived and the Senones thundered south in high spirits.

Solemis turned in his saddle and looked back at the mass of warriors which trailed away in their wake, and felt a surge of pride that he was a member of such a mighty people. As he turned back Solemis saw that the valley ahead took a gentle turn to the right. Across the river a narrow finger of bare rock came down almost to the water's edge. At its centre stood a taller dome capped by a knot of wispy trees which swayed gently in the fitful breeze, and Solemis and Albiomaros exchanged a grin as Connos pointed out the similarity of the formation to his own helm. It was clearly a sign that the clan spirits were with them this day, and the Horsetail warriors grinned happily as they walked their mounts on. Soon they were abreast the rocks, and they reined in their horses and marked time to allow the clans immediately to their left to trot on, swinging the Senone formation around like an immense door. The manoeuvre was expertly accomplished and the army swept on.

As the line reordered itself a mighty roar filled the valley ahead, and Solemis looked up and saw the Germans for the first time. The road still hugged the bank of the river, rising gently as it ran away from them until it crested a small rise a half mile or so ahead. The water meadow narrowed at this point where a small ridge of bone coloured rock snaked down through the tree line towards the Sequana, mirroring the 'Horsetails Rock' which they had just passed on the opposite bank. As they drew closer Solemis could see that the waters of the goddess had cut steeply through the ridge, forming a sharp drop down to the stony bank below. It was the perfect place to bar their passage, narrow and virtually impossible to outflank. Solemis nodded to himself as his respect for the tactical acumen of the Germans increased a little more, and he found himself agreeing with his father's opinion of the men from the North. He would do all that he could to ensure that he did not end the day *'impaled on a German sword or spear.'*

The rising ground allowed those to the rear of the Celtic war host to gain a glimpse of the Belgic battle line as soon as they negotiated the river bend, and soon the valley was filled with the war cries made by thousands of warriors as the rival armies converged.

As Brennus came within a long bow shot of the German line, Solemis watched as he ordered his charioteer to halt before turning back to face his host. It would have been impossible for the Senone leader to address his people, strung out as they were over several miles, even if they had been travelling in complete silence, and the young warrior watched as the big man held his arms out wide and motioned for them to halt where they were. Solemis and his clan were close enough to the front ranks to see that Brennus was addressing those within earshot but, having already included them in his plans, they knew that he was preparing to go forward alone to challenge the king or his appointed champion to single combat. It was a tradition shared by both the Celtic peoples and those of the German tribes, that a fight of heroes between the opposing armies was acknowledged as an honourable way to decide the outcome of a contest between them. Both peoples lived for war, but the continual conflicts between them would quickly drain the armies of their stock of seasoned warriors if large scale engagements continually swept the lands, leaving even the victors of such conflict weakened and vulnerable to cattle and slave raids, even conquest by their neighbours.

As Brennus finished his address the front ranks roared their approval, and the cry rolled back through the host like an ocean breaker. Senone carnyx were thrust into the air, and soon the very trees which lined the valley of the Sequana seemed to shiver and haze in a solid wall of noise as the war chariot containing their leader rolled forward up the incline.

BRENNUS CHEWED his lip as the chariot rode the uneven ground. Unknown to any other, the simple ride forward between the massed armies was the most nerve shredding moment of the day for the great war leader. Brennus planted his feet against the sides of the chariot, fighting against the urge to grasp the side rail as the charioteer whipped the horses up the slope towards the heaving mass of Germans. He had told the men of the clans that his great size and weight had barred him from learning of the war chariots and their distinctive ways of fighting but, in truth, his upbringing had not included taking instruction in this most aristocratic form of warfare.

He had arrived at the hall of Catubaros a seasoned and experienced killer of men and had risen to lead the Senones over the bodies of friends and enemies alike. The secrets of his upbringing in the forests of the East were unknown here and that was where he intended they should remain.

The chariot lurched suddenly as a wheel crashed across a

small rut and Brennus cursed as he reached out a hand to steady himself. Angry for allowing his concentration to ebb, he sent a silent plea to the great war god Camulos that his balance did not fail him again during the short journey. The horned god's very name meant champion, the personification of the deed which he was about to undertake, and Brennus dedicated the coming victory to his chosen deity as the charioteer hauled his charges around in a sweeping circle midway between the battle lines.

Brennus stepped down from the back of the chariot and watched gratefully as the charioteer withdrew. Alone now in the place of honour, Brennus basked briefly in the glory of the moment and waited patiently as an expectant hush fell upon the rival hosts. Inhaling deeply as he fought to suppress the battle frenzy which was building within him, Brennus swept the German warriors with his gaze as he launched into his ritual challenge.

"I am Brennus, Raven of the Longsword.
A foundling placed upon the earth by the great war god Camulos.
Too wild for human clansmen, a she wolf suckled me, I grew powerful on her milk.
You will know my reputation.
Gesatorix of the Parisii and Urogenos of the Bellovaci fell to my sword along with others too numerous to recount here.
A midden of skulls rose alongside my hall as high as the gable, each fell to my sword alone.
Hear me now, men of the Belgae.
Clear the path for my people for we wish to fulfil the will of our gods and settle a new land.
Clear a path now or send forth your champion that the gods shall decide the matter between us!"

Brennus planted his legs foursquare and awaited the response from the Belgic war lord. Within moments the centre of the line began to draw apart, and the mailed figure of King Cynobelin emerged and strode purposefully down the slope. The king came to a halt several paces from the Senone leader, and a heavy silence fell as the rival armies awaited the outcome of their leaders' confrontation.

Cynobelin smiled thinly and regarded Brennus for a moment, before answering the challenge in a voice which was calm and deliberate. "I remember Gesatorix of the Parisii. He came to me once, trying to arrange a betrothal between his daughter to my son. The whole party were haughty and aloof, they acted like it was beneath them to eat my food and drink my ale!"

Brennus could not help but smile as he listened to the king, despite the gravity of the moment. The Germans had a well deserved reputation for plain-speaking and Brennus found that he liked them all the more for it. "The Parisii are well known for their rudeness," he replied. "How did you respond to their request?"

Cynobelin grinned. "I kept their gifts and told them to piss off." Brennus struggled to retain his composure as the king continued. "Mind you, his daughter was as sweet as a honey pot. I had a mind to marry her myself."

Brennus snorted and indicated his baggage train with a flick of his head. "Gesatorix may have been an arse in life, but his skull makes a fine drinking bowl. Perhaps you would like to have it? I could arrange for it to find its way to your hall in Mediomatricum."

The Belgic king shook his head and smiled. "We leave head hunting to the Celts. We Germans set more store in gold and weapons." He placed his hand on the hilt of his own sword to add emphasis to his words. “I presume that all the arrangements are in place?”

Brennus nodded. “The payment lies beneath the midden which I just described. A cow hide filled with gold, and another filled with sword blades.”

Cynobelin nodded, satisfied. “I will send my 'champion' down to you then. Have fun.”

As the king turned and retraced his steps the German war line opened again, and a large warrior emerged as Cynobelin passed him without a glance. A low murmur arose from the Celtic army at the sight of the German champion as he descended the slope towards Brennus. Clad only in a pair of buff coloured trews, a sword belt hung at his waist, and the man carried the heavy hunting spear which the Germans called a *framea* in his right hand. Although the warrior carried no shield his entire head was encased in a full faced helm of iron, and the watching warriors found that the expressionless stare of the mask added greatly to the sense of menace which hung about the man like a winter cloak.

Brennus unsheathed his sword and rolled his shoulders as he waited for his opponent to reach him. He would be at a slight disadvantage due to the run of the slope, but he trusted to his ability. Camulos had not brought him this far to abandon him now. He grinned as the helmeted warrior came within speaking distance. “Welcome back, Maros. I trust that you enjoyed your time among our German friends?”

Maros grunted angrily in reply and swung his framea in wide slashing arcs as he came on.

“Forgive me, I forgot,” Brennus continued, “I asked my friends to cut out your tongue before they sent you to me.” He shrugged apologetically. “We could not have you calling out to your clansmen below, could we? They have a new leader now, a man who will ensure that they reach the new land without going off on wasteful cattle raids for personal glory."

Maros exploded in anger and rushed at Brennus, lunging wildly with his spear as he did so. Brennus slipped inside the strike and brought his blade up and across Maros' unguarded side. A great cheer rose from the ranks of the Senones as the first blood sprayed from the gash in Maros' side to spatter the grass. Brennus, despite his heavy armour, skipped lightly around Maros as he continued to taunt his opponent. "Feeling a bit weak? That would be because I asked my friends not to feed you. Of course," he went on, "being the son of a chieftain you have never experienced hunger before. I have; it gnaws at your every waking moment, all you can think about is food, food, food."

Maros took his chance as Brennus allowed his concentration to wander momentarily, deftly switched the framea to his left hand, swinging it in a backhanded sweep as he drew his sword with his right. Brennus, caught unawares, managed to withdraw his head a heartbeat before the blade cut the air before it. He laughed and instinctively felt his throat after the point had whistled by, flicking a glance down at his fingertips. A roar of support came from the watching Belgae, and Brennus wondered for a moment whether the support was genuine or to maintain the illusion of conflict between their peoples. Satisfied that there had been no contact with the wickedly honed blade he gave his opponent a curt nod of respect. "That was good! I see that I shall have to end this quickly."

A series of guttural cries came from within the iron helm and Brennus, seizing on his opponent's moment of distraction struck out, snake fast. Feinting low, he waited until Maros dropped his blade to parry and brought his own crashing back upwards with a flick of his wrist. His downward vision restricted by the full faced helm, Maros seemed to sense the onrushing blade and tore his head to one side but he was too late. Brennus powered the blade up and under the chin of his opponent. The point of the sword slipped easily through the soft tissue and on upwards, pulping the brain and crushing the teeth and jaw as the widening blade scythed through muscle, sinew and bone alike.

As the roars of the Belgae trailed away in disappointment, the Celtic horde erupted into wild celebration as Brennus withdrew the gore spattered blade and stepped deftly aside. The lifeless form of Maros began to tumble forward at his side and Brennus spun a complete circle, decapitating his luckless opponent with a great sweep of his longsword as he fell.

Brennus tossed his blade aside and, stooping, grasped the still helmeted head of Maros with both hands. Rising slowly he turned back to the North and raised the gruesome trophy in the direction of his own people. A great cry of triumph rent the air as the Senones acclaimed their victorious chieftain, and the braying bark of hundreds of carnyx filled the valley once more. Walking across to the edge of the drop, Brennus hurled the head out into the centre of the Sequana where, still encased in the covering of iron, it immediately sank from sight.

As the sounds of victory continued to carry from downstream, Brennus sighed and directed a few words towards the disturbed patch of water midstream. "Goodbye Maros my old friend, may Sequana carry your spirit away to rejoin your father, my chieftain. Tell him that I did what I did for the good of his people. They have a long trek ahead of them, a journey which only the strongest and ablest will survive. Go, tell Catubaros that Brennus, Raven of the Longsword guides them now. He will understand."

Brennus pulled a wry smile and turned back towards the Belgae, but to his surprise he found that they had already departed.

Retracing his steps back to the centre of the valley, he painted his face with a grin and waved his people onward.

4

The young woman gazed idly out across the wide expanse of flatlands and sighed with contentment. Reaching down she unstopped the goatskin flask and swigged the drink within as she contemplated the events of the previous week.

Catumanda was perched atop the great earthwork which marked the western boundary of the lands of the Eceni, the northern neighbours of the Trinobantes, enjoying the last of the mutton which she had brought with her for the trip to the distant Spirit Isle. The ancient trackway swung to the south-west as soon as it cut through the man made ridge, arrowing away across the island of Albion as far as the great southern sea. It was the route which she had been instructed to take by her old master, the druid Abaris, to avoid the vast area of wetlands which straddled the heart of the island, but as her journey had progressed and she had been left alone with her thoughts, she had slowly come to the realisation that she had become her own master now. She need follow instructions no longer. She was a full druid, the master of her own destiny.

The day which she had awaited for so long had finally arrived at the feast of Beltaine. Abaris had been in the oppidum to oversea the regeneration of the cleansing fires that dawn, and he had taken the girl aside and confirmed that her ordination was at hand. She had, he had said, a great work to undertake on behalf of all the people, he had always known it to be so, ever since he had first set eyes upon her in the home of her family among the distant Coritani. The hearth fires relit by the sacred flame throughout Camulodunum, she had been stripped and dressed in the characteristic clothing of the full druid, dark brown trews, tunic and a cloak fastened at the shoulder by a large silver brooch depicting the full face of the moon. A matching solid silver pendant of the heavenly body had been placed around her neck, and she had been presented with a druid's distinctive weapon, the moon blade.

Catumanda felt inside her tunic and pulled the blade clear as she pondered the journey ahead. She may not have been the most punctual or attentive of the initiates she knew, but she had studied hard to become proficient with the blade ever since the first lesson she had received in its use. She was, by common consent, the fastest and deadliest user of the blade among the druids who practised among the lands of the Trinobantes, and she had greatly enjoyed the added respect with which she had been regarded by the warriors of the tribe. She ran her fingers lovingly along the smooth curve of the blade, sweeping it through the series of cuts and slices which she knew so well. Each blade was unique to its owner, perfectly balanced and honed almost to the point where the weapon became an extension of the user rather than an inanimate object. Unlike more conventional blades, the moon blade had no handle or point. The druid's fingers passed through a series of holes at the rear of the crescent, the leading edge curving back at either end in a finely honed cutting edge.

A small leather bag made from the skin of a crane had been produced, and Catumanda had looped it proudly around her neck. Each druid possessed their own crane skin bag which was used to store their unique magical tools, herbs and any other things pertaining to their craft. The original crane skin bag had been made from the skin of Aoife, a deity who had taken the form of the majestic bird, and Mannanan the sea god had crafted the bag on her death to hold the great treasures of the land, the tools of the soul.

Finally Abaris had ritually shaven the forward part of Catumanda's scalp with his own moon blade and plaited the remainder. It was the window to the soul, the most obvious characteristic of the druidic order, and the hairstyle was jealously guarded by them.

Finally that day the great Bel fires had been lit, and Catumanda had taken her place among the druids for the first time as the herds of the Trinobantes were driven between them, cleansing and purifying the valuable animals in the light of the shining god.

A crow cawed, and Catumanda craned her neck as she followed the flight of the bird until it became little more than a speck on the western horizon. The gods were calling her on she knew, on to the Spirit Isle, where Abaris had assured her help would be found which would guide her on the next stage in her quest to discover the meaning behind the strange recurring dreams which had plagued her for her entire life.

The sun was approaching its high point in the southerly sky, she would have to continue her journey soon if she was to find shelter that night. Ahead of her, the meadows and coppices familiar to her from her passage across the Eceni lands slowly transformed themselves into the watery waste men knew as the Reaping. Marching away beyond the horizon, the vast area formed an almost impenetrable barrier between the lands ruled by the chieftain of the Eceni and his western neighbours, the Coritani. Inhabited by spirits, desperate men and their families, the Reaping was said to be more water than land. The great northern sea which lapped against the coast of Albion smothered the earth here, thousands of watercourses penetrating deeply into the body of the island like the boughs of an enormous tree.

Hauling herself back to her feet Catumanda scooped up her staff and gambolled down the bank. Pausing at the bottom she hesitated for a moment, her foot poised to leave eastern lands for the first time since she had been a child. She had arrived little more than a frightened bairn, cursing the dreams which had caused her parents to send her away, but she would soon return to them full grown, a druid. Not every man there would welcome her return. Some would fear her, or at least she hoped that they would. They would have good reason.

SHE REACHED the edge of the water world within the hour. With every step taken, the flatlands slowly changed from the fine grassy glades and dense woodland typical of the lands beyond the earthworks, becoming coarser and more scrub like as the deepening runnels carried increasing amounts of bracken water to the land. Very soon the pathway drew in on itself and the spindly, stunted trees, alder, willow and sycamore, began to crowd in on her. As the path dipped and grew wetter underfoot, the hand of man began to show itself in the otherwise wild and untamed land. A corduroy of logs laid by the hands of men long since gone to the ancestors, marched away into the depths of the marsh. The sun had passed its zenith and the day grew hot as Catumanda made her way deeper into the Reaping along the rustic roadway. Soon the trees drew back and retreated to higher ground, their place taken by tall stands of sedge and reed. Spring was the time for bulrushes to seed, and the downy heads of the spear-like plants sent wispy clouds tumbling and falling through the air with every gasp of wind. A damselfly, its brilliant blue body shining with the lustre of burnished enamel, darted across the path before it banked and disappeared with a flick of its gossamer-like wings.

A trusted man and several guards had been stationed where the road cut through the earthwork by the chieftain of the Eceni, to collect tribute from traders and travellers entering and leaving his lands. A small settlement had in time developed there to supply their needs, and Catumanda had been amused to see the look of fear and dread which had crossed the faces of those who discovered that she intended to cross the Reaping alone. It was, apparently, 'the home of wraiths, spirits and wild men.' One wide-eyed herder told her of a spectral light which had followed him through the swamp as he had desperately searched for a missing ram, and the druid allowed herself a chuckle of amusement as she realised just how far removed she had become from the fears and superstitions of ordinary folk.

Catumanda soon began to enjoy the day. Above and all around the bowl of the sky, huge and blue, lay over her. The path ahead rose to cross a small island, and she stopped at its highest point and drank in the view. Turning full circle Catumanda marvelled at the view as the horizon fell away on all sides, her gaze unimpeded by anything greater than an occasional carr of alder clinging precariously to spots of higher ground. Below her a brace of swans beat their way majestically across a wider expanse of water, their reflections moving in harmony on the flint coloured surface below.

All was serene, and then suddenly she saw that she had arrived at her destination for the day. Ahead of her the path approached a wide water channel, on the far side of which she recognised the long, low island. Stakes had been driven crosswise into the silty bottom of the mere on which a series of logs, worked flat on the upper surface, had been laid to carry the traveller across.

She inhaled and nodded to herself. *Yes. This is the place.*

For once the spirits had sent her a dream which she could clearly recognise. There was no doubt in her mind, she was to wait here. The end of that day's journey clearly in sight she suddenly felt weary. The oppressive heat of the day combined with the soft going underfoot had sapped her strength, and Catumanda moved into the shade of a small goat willow tree which hugged the shoreline. Settling herself, she watched as a pair of otters tail chased through a knot of alder roots further along the bank. The South facing slope was a drugget of small flowers, marsh pea, milk parsley and a blue mist of fen violet. It was a haven of calm, and the druid lay back and closed her eyes as the myriad sounds of the Reaping washed over her.

THE AIR FELT different when she finally awoke, cooler, and although nothing else seemed to have changed since she closed her eyes in this place, she knew instinctively that she was being closely watched. Climbing to her feet she shook the grass from her clothes and, without turning her head, called out in what she hoped was her friendliest voice. "Am I going in the right direction to cross the Reaping in the shortest possible time?"

Straightening her clothing she turned and flashed a smile. At the point which would pass for high ground in these parts two men were leaning against their spears, unsmiling, as they watched her walk towards them. Catumanda pressed on. "Out hunting?"

The shorter of the pair glanced quickly at his companion. It was a clear act of deference, so Catumanda made eye contact with the man and addressed the following question directly to him. "What do you hunt?" she asked, breezily. "Maybe I can be of help to you?"

The druid ran her gaze across the men as she waited for a reply. Both were dressed in clothing made from the skins of animals, and although they were barefoot there was no doubt that these were not poor wretches, eking out a life from the wild lands. At each shoulder both men wore what appeared to be pins of solid gold to fasten their russet coloured cloaks and their weapons seemed as fine as any, save those of the very highest classes, which she had seen during her time living among the Trinobantes.

A thin watery smile passed across the lips of the leading man. He glanced down at the slender shaft of his gaesum and nodded almost imperceptibly. "Could be."

Catumanda smiled to herself and repeated her question. "What do you hunt?"

The leader barely raised a brow as he replied: "the usual."

It was all that the young druid could do not to laugh. These were obviously two examples of the 'wild men' that she had been warned about in such hushed tones back at the border. Despite their lack of communication skills, Catumanda felt drawn to their laconic style. She had no doubts that these men had been sent by the gods to guide her through the wilderness which was the Reaping. She found that she was pleased with their choice. If she was to share the following few days with these men, it would allow her to enjoy her time in this magical place all the more. She tried again to strike up a conversation with the reluctant pair. “Let me guess. The usual would be fish, fowl, swans and the odd beaver?”

Again, the taller hunter, his face deadpan, sniffed and replied: “aye.”

The shorter man cocked his head and flashed a lopsided grin as he finally decided to join what Catumanda concluded must pass for a conversation in these parts. “They be the usual.” Both men chuckled as he continued. “Unless you can see a nice fat deer for us.”

The harsh *prrrk* of a raven call drew the druid's attention, and Catumanda looked past the hunters and along the reed lined shore. A young doe had come down to drink and, its thirst satiated, stood watching them from the shadows. The beast's dappled coat blended in perfectly with its surroundings, and without the intervention of the gods she knew that she would never have noticed it there. Catumanda indicated along the bank with a gentle flick of her head. “Would that one be fat enough for all three of us do you think?”

CATUMANDA STRETCHED and twisted her back again as she watched the forest of reeds march by on either side. Ahead she could see that the channel was at last beginning to open out onto a wider expanse of water, and she was looking forward to regaining the ability to see further than her own nose.

She had spent the previous evening at the home of the men she now knew as Attis and Dorros, the hunters who had finally agreed to guide her across the Reaping. They had travelled to the settlement in the same reed boat in which she now sat and, although rather primitive looking, Catumanda had to admit that it seemed sturdy enough and was certainly in keeping with the place.

The people of the settlement had lived together in a solitary roundhouse which sat atop a small island in one of the less accessible parts of the mere. Approachable only by boat, and surrounded by an earth bank topped by a sturdy palisade, the dozen men in the community would be able to defend their island against all but the most determined attack. Naturally visitors were rare, and Catumanda had been amazed to discover that very few of the inhabitants had ever heard of druids, much less seen one. Attis had explained that each midsummer a party would attend The Gathering, a meeting of the many disparate communities who inhabited this wild place, on the largest island which men knew as the Isle of Eels. Here the communities could barter among themselves and with the traders who travelled there from outside. It was a time of merriment and games, a time when old friendships were rekindled and alliances forged or strengthened through foster and matchmaking.

Catumanda sat alone with her thoughts as the reed boat swept along the channel. Far from being the haunt of malevolent spirits and savage wild men, she had found both the environment and the people who lived their lives beneath its vast skies to be almost an echo of a time which had already passed in what they called the Hardlands. It seemed as if the tide of time had swept past the Reaping, leaving the land and the people marooned in a simpler time and place, one without tribal obligations, without duties to be performed for distant, unseen rulers.

A sudden splash drew her attention, and she smiled as a small black coot ushered its brood of chicks back into the safety of the reed bed at their approach. The weather had turned overnight and the bowl of the sky, so deep and blue the previous day, had reacquired its more familiar patchwork of greys. The breeze began to tease the tops of the reeds as it carried the distinctive boom of a bittern to them. The call was answered by another, so close that it could have been alongside them, and Catumanda searched the reeds for the elusive bird. Dorros chuckled as he poled the boat forward. "You'll not see a bittern unless he wants to be seen, especially you being a Hardlander and all."

Attis glanced back with a smile. Once the ice had been broken, Catumanda had found the pair to be open and friendly, perfect companions for the journey which lay before her. "Dorros is right, druid. A bittern is very picky who he appears to. They stand with their heads pointed up at the sky and the brown lines on their chest make them blend into the reed bed. We saw one swallow a water snake whole once, didn't we Dorros."

Dorros nodded enthusiastically. "Aye, we did that. I dare say that it was not as good as that deer meat last night though."

The trio laughed together, and Catumanda reflected on the providence of the gift which the gods had provided for her. Once Attis had described the power of the druid to them and the fact that her gods had provided the deer as a willing sacrifice for their needs, any mistrust about the newcomer had soon evaporated. Deer meat was rare and highly prized in the settlements and the large doe had provided the centrepiece of a celebration that evening. As the hunter who had brought down the animal, Attis had been allowed to distribute the roasted flesh among the people and he had, following a barely perceptible nod of the elder's head, come forward and presented the doe's brain to Catumanda. All the tribes in Albion, and even, Catumanda knew, among their cousins across the sea in Celtica, believed that the life-spirit of every living creature resided within the head, and the young druid knew instinctively that she was being shown honour by the chieftain. Catumanda had taken the platter containing the brawn and carefully divided it into two equal portions with the ledge of her hand. As an intrigued silence had descended upon the inhabitants of the hall, Catumanda had approached the high table and presented them to the chieftain and his eldest son. The man had been delighted at the gesture, and a murmur of appreciation had rippled around those watching from the side tables. Catumanda could almost hear their thoughts as she returned to her place at the benches.

Whoever this Hardlander is, she has impeccable manners!

Fully accepted as an honoured guest, Catumanda had spent an enjoyable evening filled with feasting and laughter before the chieftain had delighted her by confirming that the hunters would convey her safely through their lands.

A slight choppiness caused the boat to buck and fall, and Catumanda's thoughts drifted back to the present. The reed boat had left the narrow channel, and she looked beyond the creamy yellow upsweep of the prow to find that they had entered a large expanse of open water. The swell here was greater, and the surface of the mere was a crinkled field of white flecked waves. The first spots of rain began to patter the surface of the water as the men poled them forward, and they pulled their cloaks tighter as Dorros guided the rear of the boat around until they were running parallel to the bank. Attis studied the sky and glanced back. "Looks like this is settling in druid. There is a suitable place where we can hole up for the night a little way ahead. If we make an early start we should be through the Reaping sometime tomorrow."

Catumanda narrowed her eyes and nodded as the rain

redoubled in intensity. The wind swept the rain across in waves; away to the West ramparts of dark grey clouds were tumbling down upon them.

Catumanda knew that they would soon pass, the ways of Toranos, god of the sky, were an open secret to her as they were to all druids, but she was happy to make camp early and enjoy the company provided by these men awhile longer. The frosty, reserved, exterior they presented to 'Hardlanders' like herself she now realised, was in fact the people of the wetlands first line of defence. By preserving the sense of fear and dread which most men from outside harboured for their lands, they were in fact consciously making them as unattractive as possible to the powerful tribes which surrounded them. Despite the fact that they had yet to discover the way of the true gods, she found to her surprise that she hoped that they would succeed.

THE LAZY CRACKLE of a fire and the smell of roasting fish dragged Catumanda back into the world of men. The dreams were still coming, nightly now, but with no more lucidity than before, and she hoped that the gods would forgive her the small diversion which she had undertaken on her route to the Spirit Isle. Although she had been little more than a bairn and it sometimes seemed a lifetime ago, the physical and mental squalor in which the people of her home settlement lived out their days had seared itself into her memory. Unfortunately for the men who inflicted such misery on their own people she was now no longer a defenceless girl but a woman, and a woman in possession of powers which they could not even begin to comprehend. No, she smiled, as she realised the truth. The gods were all around us and saw all. If she felt so strongly about righting the wrongs of her birthplace, it was likely that she was doing their work.

Catumanda raised the edge of the upturned boat beneath which she had spent the night and looked out. Away to the East a thin pink line hung suspended above the iron grey waters of the mere, and she sighed as she remembered that she had agreed to make an early start this day. She was never at her best until she had eaten a good, late, breakfast and she struggled to understand those who were.

The tall silhouette of Attis appeared from the left bank, two fingers hooked into the gills of a brace of fish as he sauntered across to rejoin his companion at the fireside. Catching the movement from the boat he glanced across and called out sarcastically. "Druid's up…"

Dorros looked up and smiled, his teeth flashing pink in the early dawn light as he expertly gutted a fish with a flick of his knife. "Had to happen sometime, sun'll be up soon." They both chuckled as Dorros continued with a light-hearted wink. "Not even a Hardlander can sleep through the smell of roasting perch at breakfast time."

Catumanda levered up the side of the boat and rolled out. As she stood and stretched in the pale light she reflected on the usefulness of the primitive looking craft. Light and easily lifted by a pair of men, the reed boat had been alternatively poled and carried across the tangled knots of twisting channels and grass topped banks which led to the island. Safe behind their natural defences, Attis had shown Catumanda how to make fish traps using the long thin strips of willow from the tree which grew there while Dorros had gathered reeds from a nearby bed to make small repairs to the boat. Far from being a remnant from the distant past, the reed boats used in the Reaping were ideally suited for the environment in which they were used.

Toranos had soon moved the squall on, as the druid had known that he would, and they had spent a relaxed evening under a clear, star studded sky. The pair had entertained Catumanda with tales of the spirits who inhabited their world and of the great warriors and hunters who had come before them. The druid in turn had begun to explain to them the dreams which were the reason for her journey but her tales of dimly glimpsed monsters, mountains of fire and magical clouds had unnerved the men to such a degree that she had soon resorted to descriptions of the lands which bordered their own for her contribution to the evening's tale telling. They had listened in wonder as she had described forests which took men days to cross, and she had smiled at their good mannered attempts to conceal their doubts when she had described the number of warriors who owed their allegiance to the Chieftain of the Trinobantes.

All too soon the fish was eaten, and they broke camp and carried the reed boat back across to the wide waters of the mere. Above them now the light from the East had chased all but the brightest stars from the sky. Over to the West the moon still hung, its milky light fading almost as they watched. Hovering near its lower edge the pale red glimmer which men called the blood star was now barely discernible.

Dorros exclaimed and pointed to the North. Low to the slate grey waters, a brown and cream bird was crossing to the north-west, its huge wings and curious bent necked appearance unmistakably marking it to Catumanda as a type of heron. “A bittern, druid,” he laughed. “It is a sign from the spirits of the Reaping, they must like you.”

It *was* a sign Catumanda knew, a sign that the gods had confirmed her conclusion of the previous day. The bittern, the very symbol of the Reaping, was moving away from the place towards her childhood home in far away *Brig Gwyn*, the

White Peak. She watched the bird as it cleared the mere before, with a dip of its wing, it flew south and disappeared behind the heavy fringe of an old willow. The druid smiled to herself and nodded that she understood as the boat began to move north.

5

The Senone encampment stretched away for a mile to either side of the road as the party of warriors appeared from the South. People stood and stared as a flicker of alarm ran through the tired travellers and the guard hauled the heads of their mounts around and cantered away to intercept the newcomers in a curtain of fine, pale dust.

It had taken the tribe a further two days to wend their way through the forest after the departure of the Germans, and the road had finally fetched them up on a wide rolling plain. Here at least the mounted men could spread out and exercise their mounts, shadowing their charges on either flank as they advanced through a sea of grass. Spring was turning to full summer now, and the grasslands through which they passed were scattered with clusters of mauves and whites as butter-wort and saxifrage flowered in the hot sun.

Solemis and Albiomaros retrieved their spears from the weapons stand and strolled towards the edge of the camp.

Albiomaros pointed with a strip of dried pork. “Shouldn't we be hurrying? We could be under attack.”

Solemis laughed. “What, by all twenty of them? I think

that I will finish my pork and wait until they cut their way through to me. Besides," he added, with a flick of his head, "our scouts are already bringing up their rear."

The best part of a week had now passed since Brennus had dispatched the Belgic champion with such power and grace and the huge column was nearing its first destination, Alesia, the oppidum of their cousins the Mandubii. Here they would rest their tired mounts, and their numbers would swell as those warriors of the tribe who were to accompany them to the new lands joined them. In a very few days they would need to move on. The summer months were short, and the journey which they had embarked upon was long and arduous. Even if all went well, not all would survive to see the new land: there was little time for rest.

At first there had been disagreement between the tribes as to which of them would undertake the great adventure. As was customary in the Celtic nations the druids had convened at the nemeton, and Devorix had finally returned with the news that the spirits had indicated that the Senones would be the people to leave their ancestral lands.

A remnant population had been left behind in Agedincum and the outlying settlements to preserve the tribal name in their ancestral home, and negotiations had been ongoing for several years between the leaders of the tribe and those of their neighbours the Mandubii, the Carnutes and the Lingones as preparations had been made for the great trek. Rivers of wine and cervesia had flowed before agreements were reached, and it had been a wonder among the warriors and leaders alike at the generosity displayed by the Greek basileus in the South, as shipload after shipload of wine and gifts came north along the River Souconna.

It had finally been confirmed at a great council of the tribes that Catubaros' people would make the journey, while their neighbours would undertake to protect those few Senones who did not wish to leave the old lands. In return each of the three tribes in the alliance would add five thousand warriors to the undertaking. The act would increase the proportion of warriors available to the Senones and help to alleviate the overpopulation which was plaguing their lands. The gods had provided food in abundance to the peoples of Celtica for their devotions, but good farmland was becoming scarce. The offer of resettlement in the South was seen by most as the work of these gods, for the people would move into the foreign lands and sow the seeds of their worship in virgin soil.

Solemis watched as the mounted party was escorted through the camp to the tent of Brennus. The Mandubii warriors were resplendent in full war gear, but their shields remained covered and stowed at their sides and they carried their lancea blades downwards as a mark of their peaceful intent.

The winter months had seen the women of each clan busily weaving and stitching the woollen tents which would accommodate their men and families until the halls could be constructed in the new land. The surface of the roofs had been coated in a layer of pig fat in an attempt at waterproofing the porous material, and it had become a common joke among them all that if the buzzing of the flies were not announcing their presence for tens of miles around the smell which the roofs were giving off in the baking heat would certainly do so.

The riders dismounted before the tent of Brennus and were ushered inside as Solemis and Albiomaros turned away and strolled through the encampment. As ever Tarvos and Suros trotted at his side, and Solemis had become a popular member of the camp once the people had seen how friendly the dogs were towards them. Children in particular always loved to pet the animals and the friends had discovered that the dogs had many other uses than fighting and hunting alone. Albiomaros nudged his friend and threw him a mischievous wink. "Let's wander across to the South. You never know, we may see something you like."

Solemis pulled a wry smile. "I wish that I had kept my thoughts to myself. She is lovely, but you know as well as I do that a woman like that will already be betrothed to a successful warrior. I have only been on a few raids and have no reputation among the clans."

Albiomaros shrugged. "So what? We are on a long journey, many things will happen and many things will change. Let her recognise your face in the crowd and trust to the gods. If you like her that much, it can do no harm to let her family see that you are interested in her."

Solemis sighed and pulled a face. "I don't know. I don't wish to appear to be a fool. I can't just turn up at her tent and start speaking to her in front of a group of sniggering women."

Albiomaros placed his hand on his friend's shoulder and hugged him affectionately. "Of course you don't. Come on, leave everything to me. Before we reach the boats she will be calling on you."

A PEEL of laughter rolled around the clearing as the boy splashed noisily to the bank. Albiomaros reached down with his huge arm, lifted the spluttering victim up by the scruff of his neck and deposited him in an untidy heap on the grass. Solemis choked back his laughter and called out to the good natured crowd which had gathered to watch the contests. "Who's next?"

Albiomaros' idea had been wickedly simple, as Solemis knew that all the best plans tended to be, and now after more than a dozen soakings the pair had whittled their way through the bigger and more confident boys and the remainder began to look to each other, hoping that another would step forward to accept the challenge. The moment had arrived, and Solemis stepped forward to seize it. Ordering Tarvos to remain on the far bank, he waded into the stream and trotted across to the expectant families which had crowded there to watch the fun. Solemis tugged at his moustache as he walked the line as if in deliberation, chuckling to himself as the smaller or wiser boys shrank back into the hoped-for anonymity of the crowd. Finally she stood before him, her young brother at her side, and Solemis smiled as he announced his choice.

"Here, this is the one," he called, as the crowd cheered; "we have our next vict..." He paused for effect as the crowd roared again, "volunteer!"

Solemis smiled encouragingly as the boy was pushed forward by his friends and flicked a look up to gaze at the face of the woman he hoped would become his own. She smiled coyly in return, and his heart leapt as he thought that he recognised a mutual attraction in her eyes. He broadened his smile and spoke reassuringly to her. "Don't worry, we will take good care of him." He grinned as he led the boy away, calling back across his shoulder, "I have a feeling he may win."

Solemis tousled the boy's hair as they walked to the bank. "I am Solemis and my friend is Albiomaros. He can sound a bit strange sometimes because he comes from across the sea in Albion, but he has already eaten today so you are quite safe." The crowd nearby laughed as he continued. "Do as he says and give your best. I think that Tarvos is beginning to tire." He winked at the boy: "you could become a hero."

Albiomaros grinned in welcome and led the boy to the riverbank as Solemis splashed back into the shallows and waded across to the far bank. Tarvos wagged his tail excitedly at his master's return and drew more laughter from the crowd, slobbering all around Solemis' ear as he heaved himself up onto the grass.

Albiomaros called across from the opposite bank, and Solemis looked up to see that the boy had taken up the rope and now stood with his left foot braced against the root of an old willow. He chuckled to himself as he pictured the results which the other boys had had using that method before him. Although it was the obvious thing to do, it had the effect of suddenly launching the hapless boy through the air and depositing him into the centre of the watercourse once Tarvos had the bit between his teeth and really began to tug. Most of the boys had ended the contest that way and Solemis had to agree that it did look far more spectacular, and funnier, than the alternative which was a bone jarring slide into the shallows.

Solemis ruffled the dog's ears and offered up the horsehair rope as Tarvos bit down and began to pull. Solemis had learnt long ago that every dog loves a game, and Tarvos clearly knew that he was good at this one. The dog took up the slack and, scrabbling once more for a grip in the now bare patch of earth, hauled away. The rope rose dripping from the surface of the river, growing taut as the dog dug in and heaved himself up the bank with a swaying motion.

Solemis stole a quick look towards the boy's sister on the far bank and was gratified to see that she was standing with her hands cupped anxiously to her face as she waited for her brother to follow the now familiar trajectory, face-first towards the bright green tendrils of pondweed which combed the surface midstream.

Glancing back he noticed the first signs that the contest was beginning to draw to its inevitable end. As the boy grimaced with effort and struggled against the power of the dog, Solemis concentrated on the boy's legs as he braced his feet against the now polished tree root. Suddenly his legs began to tremble as they reached the limit of their ability to resist the muscular pull of Tarvos, and Solemis knew that he must act quickly if his plan was to succeed. Tarvos had now drawn level with his master and was concentrating hard on the contest as Solemis reached across and tugged the dog's tail up with one hand, exposing the shiny pink sac containing the dog's balls which dangled beneath. As Tarvos single-mindedly struggled on, Solemis cupped the dog's balls in his hand and gave them a squeeze. Taken unawares the results were all that the young Senone had hoped. Tarvos dropped the rope and let out a high pitched squeal of pain as cable and boy shot backwards into the waiting arms of Albiomaros. The dog had had its back to the crowd lining the far bank and they had all clearly seen the cause of its distress. As Solemis acknowledged the catcalls and laughter which carried from the opposite bank, he became aware that Tarvos was beginning to recover and search for the cause of his agony. It quickly became obvious that the dog knew full well that his master was the only ball crusher close by. The dog let out a low menacing growl, and Solemis added to the moment as he took to his heels and leapt into the water as the dog plunged in after him. Luckily a dip in the cold water seemed to calm the dog's anger, and as they both rose dripping from the opposite bank all seemed forgiven. Solemis threw himself onto the bank, cradling the dog and ruffling his ears playfully. Looking across he squinted up at the boy who was still holding the now limp rope. "You *are* a hero, well done!" The boy dropped the cable and smiled as Solemis continued. "What is your name?"

The lad smiled proudly. "Matunos: it means bear."

Solemis and Albiomaros laughed aloud. "Well, Matunos the bear, it would seem that you were well named!" He rose to his feet as Suros came across and nuzzled his brother sympathetically. "Let us return the bear to his clan," he laughed. "I think that Tarvos has had enough fun for today."

The pair raised the boy onto their shoulders and called out as they walked him over to his waiting family. "We give you the new champion: Matunos!"

The crowd smiled and applauded as they began to move away. The day was drawing on and meals would need to be prepared. Another long day beckoned them all on the morrow followed by another, and Solemis was pleased to have provided a small moment of entertainment to lighten this day.

The men of Matunos' clan were absent when they reached the tent, and the friends deposited the boy at the feet of his women with a smile. "Your champion, ladies, unharmed as promised."

A middle-aged woman wearing a shift of fine green linen stepped forward and welcomed the boy back with a hug. Solemis admired the necklace of pale amber beads which hung at her neck as she did so. Amber came from the far north and such necklaces were rarely seen among the clans. The woman gave off an aura of understated wealth which was unusual among the Celts who were usually far more ostentatious. The cut of her accent reinforced the impression that she also may have originated much further north as did her pale skin, a trait she had passed on to her daughter. It had been one of the first things that had attracted Solemis to the young woman, and he exchanged a small smile with her as she followed the other women inside.

Solemis and Albiomaros turned and called the dogs to them as they made their way back towards the place where the Horsetails had pitched their own tent. Solemis was downcast and, surprised at his demeanour, his big friend asked what troubled him. "I had every opportunity, and I did not even think to ask her name. How is she ever going to notice me if I can't even speak and think at the same time?"

Albiomaros laughed, and throwing an arm around Solemis' shoulder drew his friend to him. "Are you mad?"

Solemis glanced across. "Why?"

Albiomaros chuckled. "Every woman who saw you today will already be talking about the pair of you, whether you know her name or not."

Solemis was still unconvinced, and he screwed up his face as he questioned his big friend further. "How do you know?"

Albiomaros gave his friend another squeeze and shook his head in exasperation. "You know so little about women," he sighed. "You could sit in a crowded room for an entire night, and if you so much as glance at a woman with a smidgeon of desire, even for a heartbeat, every woman there will immediately know."

"How?"

Albiomaros shrugged. "I don't know; they just do."

THE MEN and women sang and beat the tables with their fists as the spitted calf was carried in by the two slaves and placed on the low table before Connos. It was the tradition among the members of the Horsetail clan that the welcoming song be chanted in honour of the sacrifice made by the animal for the common good, and the moment was always a highlight of any gathering.

Connos rose from his position of honour at the head of the benches and made his way to the carcass, as the clan members belted out the ending of the song in a final, deafening, crescendo of noise. The people laughed and joked among their neighbours as the final notes reverberated around the woollen walls of the tent, and Connos smiled broadly as he waited for his people to settle once more.

Solemis, Connos' sole surviving child, grinned across to his friend Albiomaros from his seat at the side of his father. Across the gap vacated by Connos the chieftain's champion, Cauros, stood and, reaching across the front of his battle shirt, placed his hand upon the hilt of his sword as he waited for his leader to apportion the choicest cuts of meat. The very best, most succulent cut of meat, was always reserved at such gatherings for the greatest warrior among them after the chieftain himself. As Connos began to carve through the thigh of the beast Solemis smiled as a silence descended on the men, women and children present. It had been weeks now since they had tasted fresh meat and he was sure that most were as tired of the diet of salted pork or porridge which had been their staple since the last of the hogs had been culled in the spring. The cattle were just too valuable to eat on a regular basis on the great journey south. Not only would they provide fresh milk and cheese for the duration of the journey itself, they would be needed to form the basis of the clan's wealth when they finally reached their destination.

This evening though was a special occasion for all the clans who comprised the people of the Senones. Tomorrow they would strike their tents once again and take the road to Alesia. Around the middle of the day the path would slowly rise once again as it entered the foothills of the higher ground to the South. As it did so, it would lead them past the coloured stones which were carved in the image of the boar, and as they passed by, the wagons and mounted warriors would leave the ancestral lands of the Senones for the last time.

The fats and juices glistened the flanks of the calf as Connos removed the hind quarter and transferred it to Cauros' platter. The big warrior scanned the gathering for a moment before, satisfied that no challenge to his position was forthcoming, he regained his seat and took the first bite of the evening. The heavy silence which had accompanied the moment broke immediately, and conversations were restarted as Connos regained his seat between them. The chieftain clapped his champion on the shoulder as he passed and grinned. "No challenge tonight then? Good, I am starving!"

Solemis raised his cup of cervesia to the pair and they joined him happily. It was always a moment of tension at any feast when the leading warrior took the hind quarters. Custom dictated that any man could challenge for the right to become the chieftain's leading warrior, and an immediate fight to the death between the pair would follow within the confines of the building which held the feast. Unusually, the chances that such a challenge would be forthcoming this night were high. All three knew that several of the men were having second thoughts about the long trip south. To die in combat before your family and friends, challenging for the right to be held as the clan's champion, would be a very public and honourable way to travel on to the world of the ancestors.

Soon such thoughts were forgotten, as wine and cervesia flowed like the waters of the nearby Sequana herself and the people gorged themselves on the food provided by their chieftain. Men's bodies glistened as they wrestled inches from the flickering flames of the hearth, and a bard held the people spellbound as he recounted the great deeds of the past. It was a moment of melancholy as they remembered family members and ancestors who had not lived to see the day when the Horsetails moved away to a richer, softer land.

Albiomaros had immediately lightened the mood by recounting the events at the riverside earlier that day. Tarvos was happily scrounging for scraps between the benches and he seemed both surprised and delighted when the tale of his sore balls resulted in a cascade of meat from the sympathetic listeners.

To Solemis' discomfort Albiomaros had included the details of his infatuation with the mystery woman into his tale, and this had not only drawn forth many catcalls and ribald words of advice from the now drunken gathering, but had resulted in a raised eyebrow from Connos at his side. Solemis had hoped that the effects of wine and cervesia would dull his father's memory of the tale but, in truth, he held out little hope. His father could to drink flagon upon flagon without any noticeable affects on his abilities or memory, either at the feast or the following day.

As the evening reached its climax, a warrior rose from his place on the benches and approached the top table. The warriors rose and greeted him in turn as he passed along them. He paused before Connos and smiled happily as his chieftain rose to reach across, drawing him close as he planted a kiss on each cheek. Connos signalled that the moment had arrived; gifts were brought forward, and a murmur passed along the benches as the chieftain showed the grizzled veteran great honour by their number and value. The man gasped in surprise at the generosity of his chief, and Solemis watched as he inhaled deeply in an effort to control his emotions.

Solemis too reached out to embrace the man as he passed

down the top table, before crossing back to his own bench to share the *potlach* among his friends and relatives. As he did so one of his brothers placed the warrior's distinctive shield on the floor at the centre of the gathering and, with a tender kiss for his woman and children, the man laid down upon it and fixed his stare at the sagging roof of the tent. As the clan watched in awed silence, his brother drew his sword and reached forward to cut the warrior's throat slowly and deliberately from ear to ear. Twin founts of bright arterial blood pulsed out to darken the soil, and a voice filled the tent as the deeds of the warrior were recounted for all to hear. As the doors of Anwnn swung open to receive the hero's spirit, the Horsetails resumed their drinking.

6

Squatting on the fallen trunk, Catumanda picked at the last of the fish as she watched the reed boat carrying her new friends navigate the channel. Attis at the rear of the boat turned to wave a final farewell, and as she raised her hand in reply a gusting breeze threw the bulrushes which lined the lakeside to one side, hiding him from view.

As the gush of air passed through and the rushes settled slowly back, the druid prepared to smile in farewell, but found to her disappointment that the men were no longer in sight. It was, she mused, as though the spirits of the Reaping had reclaimed their own and gathered them safely in. With a sigh, Catumanda reflected on the day's journey which she had just undertaken with the men.

They had followed one of the main channels which led to the northern sea for most of the morning as it twisted and turned erratically. The waters in the northern part of the Reaping were tidal, and for most of the morning they had made good time as the ebb tide had carried them swiftly along. Attis and Dorros had hummed contentedly as they poled the reed boat along with long lazy sweeps beneath a sky filled with soft grey clouds. Catumanda had watched as Attis expertly judged the moment when the waters hesitated and then began to turn. Soon the water would flow back, deep into the land, and with such force that the light craft in which they travelled would be swept up and carried with it however hard they struggled to overcome its power. As the moment arrived when the waters stilled, on the very cusp of the turn, the men had brought the head of the boat round and plunged into the reed beds. The water was at its highest level now, and the experienced watermen had grabbed their opportunity to cut straight across the flooded lands before the ebbing tide once again uncovered the myriad channels and salt marshes which were so typical of the country here.

They had made good time, and by early afternoon the boat was wending its way through the last few miles of twisting channels before a low grassy ridge told them that the edge of their world had been reached. Catumanda had practised her newly acquired fishing skills on the journey and, to the surprise and delight of all, had managed to catch a reasonable haul without any obvious signs of divine help. Several fat roach and bream lay in the bottom of the boat by the time that they were hauling it ashore and soon the fire had been lit for the parting meal.

Catumanda looked out into the Reaping one last time as she rose to her feet and turned to go. Even at this higher elevation the boat containing her new friends was no longer in view. It seemed to have simply melted away, back into the watery fastness which lay stretched out before her as an indistinct haze of blues and warm yellows, shimmering in the heat of the afternoon sun.

Fixing the sight in her memory, the druid scooped up her crane skin bag and crested the ridge.

. . .

"TIGGUOCOBAUC, DRUID!"

Catumanda levered herself up from the floor of the cart and peered around the great bulk of the driver. She placed her hand on the man's shoulder and ran her gaze across the oppidum of the Coritani and sighed. Unlike most women who originated from the smaller settlements, she had spent a great deal of time in such places and knew them for what they were. The wind gusted directly into her face, and she grimaced as she recalled the musty odour from her years in Camulodunum. She squinted at the driver and nodded mischievously, drawing a deep rumble of laughter from the barrel chested man. "Yes, it certainly smells like we are close."

She remembered that she had always regarded the name with awe during her childhood. Compared to the ramshackle collection of roundhouses huddled together like sheep in a rainstorm which was Eyam, she had imagined then the great centre of Coritani power to be a place of fine roundhouses, swept roads and happy smiling people. Older and wiser now, she had still been disappointed by the reality which lay before her.

The oppidum nestled hard against the waters of the River Trisantona which, from her elevated vantage point, she could see curving away gently northwards. A thick haze hung over the settlement from the scores of fires which were burning unseen in the hearths of the roundhouses, the fog no doubt added to by the stench of the population of the town and their coterie of livestock. It was she reflected, the main reason why she had implored Abaris to find her a lodging on the outskirts of Camulodunon. She made a face, sucking in air with an audible whistle as she contemplated whether or not she should seek shelter there. There would be druids like herself in Tigguocobauc who would be delighted to welcome a brother, or she could simply demand quarters from the chieftain. The realisation made her smile and she was almost tempted to do so. She glanced at the driver and noticed that he too was smiling.

Ruffos was aptly named. As large as an ox, the man had a shock of the reddest hair which tumbled half way down his back. Unlike the Celtic nobility whose custom it was to shave their cheeks and chins leaving only a long flowing moustache to grace their faces, the carter sported a full beard made from bristles as thick as pins.

"Don't fancy a night in Tigguocobauc after all, druid?" Catumanda grinned as she began to sense that an alternative offer was about to make itself known. She raised an eyebrow and waited for the man to continue. "Plenty of room at my place."

Catumanda smiled and raised a brow in question. "Cheese?"

Ruffos nodded happily. "My woman makes her own with her own special fixings, best for miles around." He paused, before adding with a smirk, "she brews the best cervesia too."

The druid clapped him on the shoulder and vaulted onto the bench at his side. "It looks as though you have a guest for the night."

IT WAS late in the evening as the cart left the main track and descended down into the valley. Ahead of her Catumanda could see a small but well constructed roundhouse nestling at the head of a small burn. Before it lay a wide courtyard and off to one side a smaller rectangular building which was obviously the stabling and hay loft, the whole enclosed by a sturdy wattle fence. The sun was setting directly behind the roundhouse at the valley head in a magnificent cordage of reds and blues, and Catumanda shielded her eyes as Ruffos goaded the horses carefully down the final incline and through the gateway.

A cry drew her attention to the waterside, and Catumanda smiled as she recognised the sight of what could only be the carter's daughter managing to wave happily as she returned from the burn with a full pail of water. The hair colouring was unmistakeable, and the druid chuckled happily as she watched the young girl struggling to walk normally with the heavy pail swinging before her like a mad thing.

The shout of recognition brought another into the yard, as the large door of the stables swung open to reveal a boy of about ten winters. The boy stood framed by the heavy oak posts, and he beamed and waved at his returning father as Ruffos shot a grin in return before turning his face to Catumanda. "Culwych and Nia, my sun and moon," he explained proudly.

Nia left the pail by the doorway of the roundhouse and skipped across to welcome them, and Catumanda looked on as Ruffos jumped down from the cart and swept her up in his arms. The boy Culwych tossed his hayfork aside and came across, and the druid was saddened to see that although fit and healthy looking, he carried a pronounced limp as he walked. Ruffos extended an arm and drew the boy into a great family bear hug as he reached them. Finally he released his grip and the children stood back, grinning happily. Culwych was the first to speak. "Welcome home da, you were gone longer this time."

Ruffos tousled the boy's hair affectionately. "Aye, I went as far as the Reaping this trip and brought back a load of salt from the pans there. It will fetch a good price in Tigguocobauc, you can come with me this time and I will introduce you to a few of my contacts."

The boy's face lit up at the news and he hugged his father again as he glanced across at Catumanda. “Welcome to my father's home, druid. My name is Culwych, and I am head man here while my father is away.” He nodded to his sister who was still standing at his side. “This is my sister Nia, my mother is inside. Will you honour us and share a meal at our home?”

Ruffos roared with laughter and gave the boy a playful cuff with his giant palm. “In case you had forgotten, chieftain Culwych, I am home now. Take care of the horses and bring the salt into the dry while I settle our guest.”

Catumanda hopped down from the cart, rejoining Ruffos as the boy unharnessed the horses and led them away. Placing a friendly hand on Ruffos' shoulder the druid motioned to the boy with a flick of her head. “He is his father's son.”

Ruffos and Catumanda watched them go, brother and sister laughing together as they shared a joke, undoubtedly at their expense. “Aye, he is druid,” he smiled proudly as he indicated that Catumanda lead the way to the roundhouse with an outstretched arm.

The druid glanced at the big carter as they strolled across the courtyard. “Do you mind if I ask what happened to Culwych's leg?”

Ruffos pulled a pained expression and shrugged. “He fell from the cart when he was younger and the wheel ran over his knee. It was busted up pretty badly and then, to add to our ill luck, a bad spirit infected the wound. It seeped pus like a river and the boy burned up for days, but one of the local cunning women managed to drive it out.”

Catumanda watched as Ruffos glanced across to his son, and although the love and pride the man felt for him remained, the druid saw the flash of pain which crossed his features. It was obvious that despite the brave face he showed to the boy, he must struggle to accept the cruelty of fate. Culwych was already long past the age at which he should have been at foster, and it was clear to Catumanda that his physical impediment had failed to attract a client willing to train him in the ways of the warrior class, despite his father's wealth and standing in the community. The boy would couple below the level which would be expected, and despite the efforts of the wider clan on his behalf his life would be one of unfulfilled potential. The downward press of social mobility would weigh heavily on them all, a dark wolf which prowled permanently on the family horizon, ready and waiting to rush in and consume all their hopes for the future.

A dry laugh drew her thoughts back to the present, as a sturdy woman dressed in the simple but practical clothes of hard working country folk came forward to welcome the return of her *gwr*, the father of her children, and Catumanda smiled again as they embraced.

She was glad that she had taken the carter up on his invitation. Despite the calamity which had befallen the family the house was a place of warmth and love, and she shuddered at the thought of the likely alternative, a place at the hall of an 'important man' in bustling Tigguocobauc, listening to a sycophantic bard singing the great man's praises while the men of his cantref tried to outboast one another and earn their lord's *potlach*.

The introductions made, Ruffos formally invited Catumanda to enter his home and poured her what was sure to be the first of many cervesia that night.

CATUMANDA AND RUFFOS paused as they reached the high point of the saddleback and turned back the way they had come. Below them the valley head looked much as it did when they had arrived two short days ago: the deep greens of the valley bottom cut through by the beck, white smudges marking the places where the waters jumped and tumbled over the larger rocks and outcrops which littered its course; the roundhouse and stables rising almost organically from the narrow shelf. Despite the distance one thing *had* changed since the druid had arrived, and Catumanda snorted softly in sympathy as the big man at her side involuntarily gripped her sleeve in a display of gratitude and affection.

Far below them the object of the Ruffos' happiness could be seen, his long golden hair snaking away in the breeze as he ran out along the trackway which led from the settlement to the road connecting the valley to distant Tigguocobauc. Catumanda smiled and patted the man's hand as she turned to go. They had a long distance to travel and the gods were growing impatient with her dallying. The flight of the bittern had reassured her that the spirits had understood that she needed to visit her childhood home, before she could travel to the Spirit Isle and discover the meaning of the recurrent dreams which they were sending. It had, she was certain, flown north west before turning and flying away to the South. She had checked the position of the sun and she was sure that she was correct, but last night they had sent the most terrifying dreams yet and she had woken trembling and bathed in sweat. She really did need to move on. She angled off down the side of the next valley before pausing and looking back to her companion. "You should stay with your family. They need you there: you owe me nothing."

Ruffos pulled himself reluctantly away from the sight which he had thought never to see again and, clicking his tongue, urged the pack horse down to Catumanda's side. "You are wrong, druid," he gasped, the emotion of the moment obvious despite the big man's attempts to conceal it. Ruffos inhaled deeply and composed himself before continuing. “That thing that you did,” he hesitated, flicking his hands at Catumanda and unsure how to explain the 'thing' he had witnessed. “With your hands. That thing has lifted a veil from my family and clan, but most of all it has given my son the chance of a life which had been cruelly snatched away from him. If the spirits struck me down here and now, I could not die a happier or more contented man. If I can repay you in any way, even if it is only by carrying your food it would be shameful for me to simply wave you on your way.”

Catumanda smiled and indicated that the carter lead on. The *'thing with her hands'* which the man had referred to had occurred the evening they had first arrived. Following a meal of fresh bread, as fine a cheese as she could remember and strong dark cervesia, Catumanda had crossed the floor to the place where Nia had sat gently teasing her brother. Culwych blushed deeply as she sat between them, and the group laughed when Nia had made it known to all that her brother had developed quite an attraction for their visitor. The laughter had soon trailed away awkwardly as Catumanda had asked the boy if she could examine his bad knee. It was obviously a subject which was rarely mentioned in the family, and she had noticed that the boy's mother looked downcast and averted her eyes as she began to roll up the leg of her son's trews. Catumanda had felt the joint and chewed her lip in disappointment. She had hoped that the bone had been merely broken and badly reset, but the whole joint had clearly been badly crushed as the heavy wheel had rolled across it. She had wished that she had had more experience in healing, she had after all only been a druid for a matter of weeks, but her old master Abaris had always been pleased with her attempts, and she knew that she was now committed to try her best. To raise the subject and shine the light of hope on the family, only to immediately extinguish that light would be the ultimate betrayal of her hosts and Ruffos, and the boy, deserved better than that.

Catumanda had closed her eyes, channelling her consciousness towards the spirits which surrounded them, and soon the life forces which dwelt nearby had begun to flow through her. She had smiled as she recognised the tingling sensation at the front of her skull as the vitality of the spirits which inhabited all things began to enter her and flow down her body. It was the reason druids shaved the front of their scalp, and the portal began to channel more and more energy down through her. Holding her hands either side of the damaged joint Catumanda had moved them in a sweeping motion as the healing energies flowed out from her hands and into the damaged joint. Almost immediately the boy had jerked and cried out that his knee felt as though a naked flame were being held against it, and Catumanda had allowed herself a slight sigh of relief as she became convinced that she could help her friend's son. Within moments the boy had grown tearful and his mother had moved to comfort him, only to have him wave her away as he explained through emotion racked sobs that the pain and discomfort was leaving him. Soon Culwych was flexing his knee for the first time since the accident, and Catumanda had taken her leave and sat alone in the moonlight as the sounds of tear filled laughter broke the stillness of the night.

Ruffos spoke softly as he guided the horse down the narrow path. "The gods sent you to me, you know." Catumanda glanced across and raised her brow as Ruffos continued. "I know now that you were sent to help Culwych. His mother and I prayed daily and sacrificed what we could at the shrine at the head of the valley. The burn emerges there from the ground before it flows past the house and on to join the others to become the Trisantona. It is home to the spirit which protects us, and she answered our prayers by sending me a dream to buy salt from the Reaping."

Catumanda nodded knowingly. If anyone knew the power of dreams it was she. "It *is* possible. I too am guided by dreams."

Ruffos shook his head. "No, I am certain, druid. That was the first time that I have ever travelled that road. When it appeared, snaking off through the fields, I somehow knew that it was the trail that I should take, and then suddenly there you were." He laughed; "sitting on a fallen bough, tearing at a piece of deer meat."

Ruffos suddenly grew serious and placed a hand on Catumanda's arm. He chewed on his lower lip, and a troubled look swept across his features as he contemplated his next words. "The gods sent me another dream last night. In it, I travelled with you, until we reached a great sea," he paused, as if reluctant to complete the story of his vision, but eventually fixed the druid with a penetrating look, and continued. "As I watched helplessly, a great wind blew and you were swept up and carried out to sea by a white cloud."

Catumanda looked at her companion in amazement. "I too dream of the white cloud and the sea. The gods have been sending me dreams since I was a child, but they are never clear. It is as though they appear through a fog, glimpsed for a moment before they drift away into the swirling mist. It is the reason why I travel to my brothers on the Spirit Isle." Catumanda grinned as she began to realise the importance of her friend's revelation. She clapped the carter on the shoulder and moved on. "Come, we have a long journey ahead of us. You are right, the gods have brought us together for a reason. Culwych needed my help, and somehow, I will need yours to fulfil my destiny."

. . .

A HALF DAY's walk upriver to the West brought the pair to the place where the River Derwenta flowed down to join with the waters of the Trisantona as they mingled and journeyed on to the distant sea. Crossing by ferry they struck out north, following the course of the tributary towards the hills of the Brig Gwyn, whose softly undulating silhouette rose a little higher on the skyline with each mile tramped.

It was almost midsummer now, and the nights were short and warm. Catumanda and Ruffos relaxed beside the river as they shared the last of the fresh bread. They would seek out more on the morrow and it was always a time when the druid would reminisce on her childhood, before she left for the lands of the Trinobantes. She had accompanied her parents to the next valley, to the shrine at Nemeton for the midsummer celebrations. It had been the first time that she had left her home valley and she smiled as she recalled her father's light-hearted comment that day. The man was a simple miner, but the ways of the gods were sometimes mysterious and occasionally they would plant a word or action heard or seen in childhood deep within the memory like an image frozen in time. This casual quip was one such seed, and she had remembered it and the accompanying twinkle in her father's eyes always. She propped herself up on one elbow and shared the thought with her companion as they ate. "A very wise man once told me that you have strayed too far from home when the last of your home baked bread turns stale."

Ruffos laughed, and selected a stick from the pile they had collected earlier to feed the camp fire. With a grunt of effort he sent the stalk spinning through the air to land with a dull splash in the waters of the river. "If I had followed the advice of your wise man I should be a beggar. The man was a fool, who would say such nonsense?"

Catumanda, seizing the opportunity for fun, fixed the carter with an icy stare. "My father."

Ruffos' face dropped as he began to splutter an apology. To insult a clansman usually ended in bloodshed, but to insult a druid could result in a far worse end. The big man blanched as he realised that the future of his very soul could well hang on how he extricated himself from the depths of the hole which his big mouth had dug for him.

Seeing her friend's face Catumanda was unable to contain herself, and her own face creased into a grin. "My father was a simple man but he was no fool. If he had really believed that he would never have approached Abaris at the nemeton, nor fought so hard to have me accepted as an initiate by the brethren."

They shared a laugh as the tension evaporated, looking up together as a shooting star streaked across the night sky, its silvery trail gone in a heartbeat. Catumanda reached across and broke a piece from the cheese which they had brought along with them. Warming it in her palm, she sighed with pleasure as she worked the pale yellow ball into the bread with the heel of her hand. "This is the most fantastic tasting cheese that I have ever tasted!" she exclaimed, popping a morsel into her mouth. "Tell me again how it's made."

Ruffos chuckled and stretched out. Without exception, everybody liked Alwena's cheese. "She makes all kinds of cheeses with different herbs, but this is a simple cheese and I think that it is all the better for it," he sighed. He broke a piece from the wheel of cheese and held it nearer to the flickering light of the camp fire. "You see the small brown pieces?" Catumanda nodded as she peered forward and squinted at it. "Those are tiny pieces of onion. Everybody likes cheese and onion, right?"

Catumanda nodded enthusiastically. It was well known that every man, woman and child throughout the island of Albion, be they chieftain or slave, loved the unique combination of creamy cheese and the sharp bite of onion. Ruffos bit into the cheese, and the druid watched as he rolled it around his mouth, savouring the taste. "Well," he began, "Alwena gently cooks the peeled onion in a little beef fat until it is as soft as a baby's arse, and then just a little longer until it is a glistening golden-brown." Ruffos noticed that his friend was held in rapt attention and decided to gain a small measure of retribution on the druid. He lowered his voice and spoke in what he hoped was his most alluring manner. "Then, when it is cooled," he breathed, "she adds the onion and the juices to the curds and stirs them in."

Catumanda found that she was unconsciously reaching out to the cheese as she listened. Smiling, Ruffos slowly drew it beyond her reach until the druid almost fell forward onto her face. Both laughed as Catumanda realised that she was toppling over just in time to throw out a hand and save herself from pitching forward onto the grass. Ruffos pushed the cheese back between them and grinned. "That's it really: cheese and onion, Albion's finest!" he exclaimed, with a flourish, before adding, "I wouldn't eat too much though, especially a woman like yourself."

To Ruffos' delight Catumanda looked pained at the thought that the cheese might have to be consumed in small quantities. "Why is that then?"

The big man winked mischievously, overjoyed to be able to repay his friend in kind after falling for the earlier joke about her father. "Notorious it is for bringing out the dream horses."

. . .

THE PALE PINK feathers of light which heralded the onset of the new day were barely in the eastern sky before they had broken camp and resumed their journey. As they forged ahead a thin layer of mist hung suspended above the water meadow which girded the Derwenta, silvery-white like an old man's beard, and the friends marvelled at the sight of cows and horses, their legs hidden beneath the milky layer, apparently floating on the wispy air.

As the sun crept higher the mist pulled back to reveal the lush grasses of the riverside coated in a fine layer of dew, the webs of spiders massive and sparkling as they struggled to maintain their structure under the heavy load.

Midmorning they crossed the road which led directly into the Brig Gwyn. It was the route which Catumanda had intended to take, but the gods had already shown that they had provided Ruffos to aid her, and the carter had looked at her incredulously as he explained that he knew of a far more direct route through the rolling hills. "The valley of the Derwenta continues north into the heart of the Brig Gwyn, all the way to its source. It is not a wide pathway but there are only we two and a horse, how much room do we need?" He raised a brow and shot the druid a look. "Besides, if you want word of your return to travel ahead of you, I would think that taking the road which passes through Nemeton would be about the best way to ensure that it happens."

Catumanda nodded her head in agreement. It was important that she arrived at Eyam without the inhabitants in the area having been forewarned. She remembered that her clansman, Garo, kept flocks near the eastern end of the valley which contained the main settlement, and she knew that the man would be able to provide invaluable knowledge of the situation there and the well-being of her parents. At her side Ruffos was still happily rambling on. "It will be like an upended beehive at Nemeton at this time of year. You saw the numbers on the road back there, and there are a dozen roads which lead to the springs. It is the most popular place in the lands of the Coritani to welcome the solstice."

Catumanda nodded again, grateful for her new friend's advice. It *had* been a poor choice of route, but the uncomfortable truth was although it was true that she was returning home she barely knew the place. She had only ventured beyond the confines of her home valley once before she was taken away by Abaris to the distant lands of the Trinobantes. How was she expected to know any different? The springs which burbled forth from the rocks were so revered that the whole area had taken its name from the holy grove; there were certain to be people from Eyam celebrating the solstice at the place, maybe even her own parents she realised nervously.

"Of course," Ruffos continued as they walked. "If you could ride a horse things would be different." He paused and glanced across. "Why is that?"

Catumanda crinkled her brow. "Why can't druids ride?"

Ruffos plucked a stalk of grass from the byway, stripping the outer layer with a thumbnail. Popping it into his mouth he rolled it to one side before replying to her question. "Yes, why not? Surely it would help you to visit people and serve the gods and spirits better if you could move at more than walking pace?"

Catumanda shook her head as she explained. "It would be an insult to the animal to place the unclean parts of the human body onto it. What would Epona, the horse goddess, think if I did such a thing to one of her animals?"

Ruffos shrugged as he conceded the point. "It makes

sense when you put it that way. Don't they mind that others do?"

Catumanda chuckled at her friend's look of concern. "No, your soul is fine. The gods ask only that you treat your animals with respect. They understand that the relationship between beast and man is important to them both. Men use the great strength of the ox to pull their plough, the speed of the horse or the guarding ability of their dogs: wool from sheep to clothe themselves. In return the animals are provided with food, shelter and protection from wolves, bears and the like. Druids stand apart; we are as close to the gods and spirits as we are to our fellow man, we no longer need the help of animals to survive. The circle is broken for us, we must make our own way."

Ruffos suddenly broke into a smile, dropped the reins and loped ahead. With a bound which belied his great size he leapt to the top of a large white boulder which stood hard on to the path. Turning back he called to Catumanda to join him, reaching out an arm to steady the druid as she landed with a gasp at his side.

Ruffos pointed ahead to a great wall of rock which rose vertically from the green of the valley floor, its milky white face ushering travellers northwards along a leafy pass. "The Brig Gwyn, druid." He flashed her a grin. "Welcome home."

7

Connos and Solemis relaxed their grip on the reins and allowed the horses to pick their own way upwards. The day was fine, and the lands of the Mandubii stretched out around them in a sultry haze despite the early hour. Gaining the tree line they brought the heads of their mounts around and sat in silence as they drank in the view.

Far below them the small river which they had followed from the camp curled around to join with its cousin in the neighbouring vale to the West, now subsumed by the mass of the Senone clans as they paused before taking the final push down to the waters of the Souconna where the boats were waiting to carry them south.

Solemis glanced across at his father, smiling as he noticed the experienced warrior's eyes flicking all around the oppidum which stood atop its own hill almost on a level with them. Although concern still nagged him as to the reason he had been asked to take this trip into the hills the silence was becoming oppressive, and the young warrior decided to seize the opportunity to break it. "It looks formidable, father. Do you think that it could be stormed?"

Connos laughed as he realised how transparent his thoughts had been. "Oh, it could be stormed," he snorted. "Whether there would be any members of the attacking force left to tell the tale, might be another matter entirely."

They were studying the principal oppidum of the Mandubii, the hill fort of Alesia, perched atop its tear shaped hill to the South. A road snaked its way up to the massive timber gatehouse from the valley which contained the Senone camp, zigzagging its way across the bare flanks of the mount under the watchful gaze of the sentinels on the walkways above. Both men knew that the design had been intentional. Any approach to the oppidum would be slow and laborious, deadly to an attacker, as the roadway wove its way below the walls. As the cobbled path came within missile range of the defenders it switched back and forth as it threaded its way through the outer defences, forcing any attackers to bunch up in a confused mass as they repeatedly cut across each other. Similarly any attempt to storm the walls of the fortress from a different direction would be equally suicidal. The sides of the hill had been swept clean of all but scrubby vegetation, and even if an enemy managed to negotiate the steep climb whilst under attack from the defenders, he would come face to face with further obstacles before he could attempt to scale the walls.

Twin ramparts encircled the entire lip of the plateau, each bank towering twenty feet or more above the stake filled ditches which lay between them. Any assailant who had been fortunate to survive the rain of spears, arrows, and rocks which the defenders will have showered upon him would now be faced by the outer wall of the oppidum itself. Rising vertically from the very lip of the inner bank, the lower part of the wall had been dressed with a facing of smoothly worked stone to a height of fifteen feet. Surmounting this a timber palisade ran the complete circuit of Alesia, and Solemis could watch from his lofty vantage point as Mandubii warriors strolled the walkway in pairs.

Connos shook his head as he added to his earlier conclusion. "I understand that they have wells inside the walls to supply them with all the water that they need so no, I don't think that could be taken by storm. The only way that the oppidum would fall was if a besieging army could surround the whole hill for months on end and starve the defenders into submission. Even then..." he paused and pulled a face as his mind weighed up the chances of such a tactic succeeding. Eventually he shook his head in defeat. "No," he decided, "it couldn't be done. No army would be large enough to completely seal the defenders in. As soon as a few slipped away in the night and roused the warriors among the other Mandubii oppida and their allies they would have to break the siege or risk being attacked from the rear."

Solemis pulled a wry smile. "Unless they built their own defences in the valleys below. Then they could beat off the relieving force when it appears."

Connos laughed again and playfully whipped his son with his reins. It was a small gesture, but Solemis' spirits rose as he realised that the reason for their ride into the hills was benign. "That is true, but even if this enemy could spare the manpower to gather the material together and build the thing while still maintaining the siege, the warriors inside Alesia would sally and take them in the rear as soon as the relief force appeared. The attackers would be crushed like an egg in the grip of a giant."

The Horsetail chieftain looked out across the valley below. A haze of thick grey smoke hung over the vast encampment of the Senones and their allies, dwarfing the thin lines which rose from within the high walls of Alesia itself as the paltry summer breezes struggled in vain to move it on to the East.

Harsh bleats drew their attention back as hundreds of sheep suddenly appeared over a fold in the ground, blocking their intended route. The boy bringing up the rear looked horrified as he saw the two magnificently clad warriors before him, but Connos smiled and waved the lad on as he hauled the head of his mount around and urged the horse away to skirt the tree line near the summit. The sounds and smells of the huge encampment grew indistinct and finally left them as they walked their mounts into the next valley.

A wide path snaked between the trees and the steeper valley side, and looking ahead they could see that it traversed the slope at an oblique angle before ending at a small shepherd's shelter. The path was wide enough for them to ride abreast, and Connos indicated that his son bring his horse alongside with a flick of his head. For the first time ever Solemis felt that his father was struggling for the right words, and he waited patiently as they rode on. Finally the chieftain looked up and pulled a wry smile. "I have never talked to you about what happened to your mother." He paused, and grimaced slightly before going on. "They were very bad times and I know that I used my responsibilities within the wider clan to shield myself from the pain, but it was selfish to do. I failed you, and I apologise to you now." To Solemis' surprise his father suddenly laughed. "I should have known that if I failed to arrange a suitable pairing for you, that you would find one for yourself."

His face grew serious again as he went on. "You probably know that your mother died in childbirth, while you were at foster in Albion. The women told me that an arm appeared first, and although they tried all they knew to turn the boy around, by the time that he had been born the cord had wrapped itself around his neck and he had choked to death." Connos hesitated, but continued with a slight shake of his head as his voice dropped to a whisper. "They said that your mother looked fine at first considering the pain she had endured, and she spoke to them as she held his tiny body. Then they realised that she was still bleeding. The blood flow increased and nothing they tried would stop it. A girl was sent to fetch me and I arrived just as she began to lose consciousness." Connos paused, drawing in a breath as he sought to retain his composure. He turned and gave a weary shrug, and Solemis was shocked see for the first time that his father's eyes had reddened. "There's not much more to say. Although I left offerings for the gods and spirits, I felt that they had spoken clearly enough and I never seriously considered remarrying. I came close once," he smiled, suddenly brightening. "With a young woman of the Parisii, but her family were haughty and aloof. Her father, Gesatorix, demanded more cattle than the clan possessed as a dowry, so I thanked them for their interest and told them that I would leave the decision to the druids." He shot Solemis a smile. "That's a ploy worth remembering, son, especially when the druid in question is the brother of your chieftain. After that lucky escape I decided to be the best chieftain that I could be and waited until you returned from foster in Albion."

The horses edged to the right as they cut across the gradient of the valley sides. Far below a party of horsemen clattered into view from the direction of the hill fort, their playful whooping drifting up to the pair as it echoed along the flanks of the pass. Connos and Solemis laughed as they recognised the massive figure of Brennus leading the party, his dark cloak streaming in his wake. Solemis pointed across as they swept along. "A hunt! Is there any time when a man is happier?"

A sparkle of mischief entered his father's eye as he gave Solemis' shoulder a playful shove. "Maybe one: tell me about this girl, Aia."

Solemis looked at his father and it was obvious that he did not recognise the name. Connos chuckled and shook his head in mock disappointment. "You *do* know this girl's name I take it? You know, the one who is the very reason for your existence. The one who haunts your thoughts during the hours of darkness as you wait to gaze upon her face once again," he teased.

Solemis laughed as he felt his face redden but attempted to bluff it out nevertheless. "Yes, of course, we have spoken."

Connos snorted. The noise in the valley was growing louder as the hunters drew nearer, and glancing down Connos noticed that several other parties of riders were emerging from the tree line on the far side of the valley. "I will tell you what I know about her, and you can add to it if you feel that there is anything else that I need to know."

Solemis nodded as he attempted to suppress a smile. It was obvious to both men that he knew nothing about the woman other than the fact that he was besotted by her looks, and he listened eagerly as his father began to speak of her.

"Well, as you know, she is the daughter of Crixos, Brennus' man, so the daughter of a man whose star is ascendant. She is also betrothed," Connos continued, "as you would expect with a fine looking young woman of sixteen winters." Solemis' hopes sank at the words but, in reality, his father was right. If she was not already wed or promised to a man, there would be a line of suitors permanently camped outside her father's tent. He had no wealth or reputation as a warrior, how could he hope to wed such a woman?

His father smiled innocently. "So it was a great shame when the man to whom she was betrothed was a warrior in

Maros' war band and disappeared along with his chieftain." Solemis grinned at the unexpected good fortune as his father began to look past him at the events unfolding in the valley below. Narrowing his eyes Connos watched the horsemen intently, and his voice began to trail away as he concluded his thoughts. "Solemis, the gods can raise a man if they choose, as well as lay him low. Grasp every opportunity to gain a reputation on this journey and we will see what we can do about this woman."

Suddenly Connos reached down and frantically untied the bindings which secured his spears to the crupper. Kicking his horse into a gallop, he called back over his shoulder as Solemis looked on in startled bemusement. "Quickly, Brennus is under attack. Arm yourself boy."

Solemis snatched at the bindings securing his own spears and looked across as he urged his horse forward with his knees. As the horse gathered speed his mind took in the desperate situation unfolding in the valley below. To his right, twin outcrops of rock had brought the tree line down almost to the level of the road as they pinched at the valley sides. Dark clothed riders were holding the gap against the majority of Brennus' party who were already fighting desperately to come to the aid of their chieftain. Solemis looked quickly across to his left, and he watched as Brennus and the handful of men who accompanied him hauled on their reins and turned to face a tight knot of dark riders who had emerged from cover higher up the valley and were now sweeping down on the chieftain with a howl of victory.

Solemis reached the sheep herder's shelter and his horse picked up speed as the gradient decreased. Ahead of him Connos was bent forward as he urged his mount to greater speed but, flicking a look up, Solemis could see that neither of them would come to the aid of their leader before the attackers fell upon him and his small group. One rider had hung back from the attacking force and Solemis knew that this must be their leader. The man was looking from left to right as he weighed up the progress of the fighting at each end of the valley. He was obviously deciding which force would benefit most from his sword work and leadership and Solemis made the instant decision that this would be his opponent.

The unmistakable crash made by a collision of leather and steel brought his attention briefly back to his left, and he watched as his father loosed his gaesum and quickly drew his long sword as he entered the fray. The arrival of Connos had helped the enemy leader to make his decision, and Solemis watched as he dug his heels into the flanks of the big stallion and began to descend the valley side. A small stony trail led straight across to the scene of fighting, but quickly lifting his eyes Solemis saw that it was cut further ahead by a small rubble strewn burn and he hesitated as he weighed the options open to him. The trail was the shortest and most direct route to the fight but the chances of a stumble or, worse, a turned hock, would be high at the speed he would have to travel. Solemis turned the head of his horse aside, and leaning back into his saddle horns, gripped his reins tightly as it slithered on its hind quarters down to the valley floor in a cloud of ochre-coloured dust. Clambering back to its feet, the horse shook itself as the young Senone warrior tugged its head around and galloped north.

Solemis glanced to his right, checking on the whereabouts of the dark rider, and was dismayed by the progress which the warrior had made. Even with his horse now running at full speed on the gently undulating valley floor, he could see that the horseman would enter the fray long before he was in a position to intercept him.

He risked a quick glance ahead and was horrified to see that other than a group of milling horses there appeared to be no one left standing, and Solemis felt a hand of fear grip his chest as he realised that his father must also be lying among the bodies he could see littering the grass. Suddenly one of the enemy horsemen rose and dragged himself across to the position where the dark form of Brennus' horse lay. The man could only be going to finish off the Senone chieftain, and Solemis urged his mount on as he desperately sought to close the gap between them. The horse responded immediately, but despite his mount's heroic efforts he could already see that he would never close the distance quickly enough to enable him to use his spear in time.

The sound of fighting gave way to the thunder of hoof-beats to his rear, and Solemis stole a look back to see that Brennus' men had at last broken through the wall of mysterious horsemen and were pounding along the roadway towards him. He turned back just in time to see the wounded man drag himself upright and raise his sword as he supported himself against the carcass of Brennus' horse. Solemis held the spear shaft clear of his body and prepared to launch the missile as he calculated the distance to the target. Even a near miss should distract the warrior's attention long enough for him to close but he knew that, in reality, it would be a pointless gesture. The distance between them was still too great for him to have any chance of disrupting what must be Brennus' death blow.

Suddenly, as the warrior leaned forward to see his target, a leg swept in an arc from the far side of the stallion's hulk and a foot knocked the sword stroke sideways. A heartbeat later the long silver tongue of an oversized blade flicked out to take the attacker in the throat. As the would-be assassin slumped across the flank of the horse, Solemis saw the enemy leader hesitate as he calculated the time left to him before help arrived for the still living Senone chieftain. Despite the fact that a dozen or so of his men could be seen regrouping near the tree line, the man kicked in as he chose certain death over shame. He would reach the trapped form of Brennus before either Solemis or the remaining men of the hunting party could intervene; he would complete his task, despite the fact that it would cost him his life.

The dark rider cantered down onto the valley floor and guided his mount through the tangle of bodies and riderless horses which blocked his path. Solemis hefted his gaesum once again and sighted along it as the distance between them diminished a little more with every passing moment. A cry carried to him on the wind, and his heart leapt as he recognised the voice as that of his father. "Take the shot!"

Solemis inhaled deeply, releasing his breath slowly as he sought to match the rhythm of the galloping horse to his own body movements. Far ahead of him, the enemy warrior was just rounding the body of Brennus' stallion and raising his own spear as he prepared to stab down at his incapacitated victim.

Solemis closed his eyes for a brief moment and sent a plea to the warrior god Camulos, the ram horned one, to guide his arm. A calm descended upon the young Senone as the war god answered his cry for help, and with a grunt of effort his arm whipped forward and released. The gaesum flew, the long tail which marked its owner as a member of the Horsetail clan streaming back from the silvery blade like the mane of a war horse at full gallop, and Solemis held his breath as his hunter's mind calculated the spot where the two, missile and target, would converge.

Intent on his victim, the dark rider wound his body as he moved to strike. An instant later Solemis' spear punched into his temple and carried on through, spinning the man around and sweeping him from his horse in a dark spray of blood. Elated, Solemis kicked his mount on as a cry of wonder and joy came from the rest of the hunting party, now thundering closer to his rear.

Rounding the rump of the dead mount, Solemis reined in. Brennus swung his blade around as he turned to meet this new attacker, but suddenly threw his head back and laughed as he recognised Solemis as one of his own.

Solemis leapt from his horse and checked the nearest bodies for signs of life but there were none, and he looked back to the Senone chieftain as the rest of his party drew up in an excited gaggle. "You are well!" he exclaimed, with genuine relief.

The man was a fine leader with no obvious replacement. Despite his youth Solemis knew that Brennus' death here could have carried a serious threat to the entire resettlement; it would now seem that other people were also aware of his importance.

Brennus grinned across at his men, and they all laughed again before he looked back at his young savour with a grimace. "Of course I am not well, you fool. I have a dead horse laying on my leg!"

Devorix leaned into his staff for support as he scaled the bank. Ahead of him stood the nemeton which gathered the source of the River Sequana into its protective embrace, and he smiled to himself as his personal journey neared completion.

It had been several years since the druid had last visited the shrine of the goddess, and he paused and let his eyes wander across the ancient trunks and boughs of the grove before entering. A well trodden path meandered alongside the watercourse which led to the old familiar temple, awash as ever with the small trinkets and other votive offerings deposited there by the faithful, tokens of gratitude alongside pleas for aid. Small bowls of grain and wine, a stone with a hole. The roughly carved figure of a woman, her belly extended, left by the childless.

The old druid ran his eyes across the temple before moving forward. It had always been one of his favourite places of worship, simple yet accessible to the people and what, after all, was the point of the gods without them? One could not exist without the other any more than life could recreate itself from one body.

Roofless, the temple of Sequana was made from a circle of oak posts, each one lovingly carved to resemble the waters tumbling forth from the bare rock by unknown hands long ago. The spaces between these posts had been left open to the seasons and Devorix watched as a damselfly, its body as blue as woad, flicked through the interior on vaporous wings.

The pathway before him had been a carpet of bluebells the last time that he had visited, but the year was further advanced now and all that remained of their show were the bare stalks which pierced the underwood like the spears of a defending army.

A cry of recognition broke into his thoughts, and a warm laugh escaped him as he recognised the portly shape of Diocaros enter the clearing from a side path. The temple guardian, although no druid, was a popular and devout man, and Devorix had always greatly enjoyed their times together. They came together and embraced as old friends. "Devorix, I received your message and all has been prepared for you. Come," Diocaros said softly. "Do me the honour of sharing an evening with me before you journey onward."

8

The wind freshened to pluck at the tree canopy and the skies changed from blue to grey as the pair beat their way north. Late that day they reached the place where the Derwenta divided, and they left their few travelling companions to continue their journey on to Nemeton, west along the valley of the River Wye, the Winding River. Taking the fork which cut northward towards her home, now only a few hours away, they plunged into the shadows.

The narrow pathway held hard on to the river here as it tumbled southward through a landscape of rolling hills and tree lined valleys, oak, ash and elm. Soft grey light from the overcast skies penetrated to the forest floor at intervals, revealing a wash of bluebells and dog's mercury as a treecreeper, its long hooked bill searching out grubs, scurried across the knotted face of an ancient oak.

Soon they were at the place where the pathway crossed the pass which led westward to Eyam, and Catumanda stopped to tidy herself after the rigours of the long walk north. It would be the first time that members of her clan had laid eyes upon her in more than ten winters, and despite the fact that she now stood outside the superficial code of dress and appearance which people habitually used to gauge another's worth, she found to her surprise that a vestige of the custom still remained within her. Settling beside a deep pool, the druid scooped out handfuls of the icy water as she set about removing the worst of the grime and stains from her body and clothing.

The surface of the pool shone like ice as the sun broke through the cloud cover, bathing the clearing in its warmth, and Catumanda was reminded that the Derwenta, the Clear Water, had been aptly named by the ancestors. Ruffos chewed happily on a hard piece of bread as Catumanda smeared a small dollop of animal fat onto the front half of her scalp, carefully scraping away several days' growth with her razor sharp moon blade. Finally the druid vigorously buffed the silver moon shaped brooch and pendant which were a mark of the brethren with a small piece of wool which she kept for the purpose. The oils which they contained and the softness of the wool made it ideal for the task, and soon they were gleaming. Catumanda looked across to her friend and grinned. "Time to go calling, I think."

IT WAS LATE when the tired travellers, druid and carter, approached the roundhouse perched on a wide shelf of land above the beck. Catumanda paused and smiled as she recognised the home of her clansman from visits long ago.

She was pleased to see that it appeared that her uncle had prospered during the years she had been away. Several small storage houses had been added to one side of the main house, the roof of which had been newly thatched. Above them the last ragged clouds were being driven away to the north-east and the evening looked set fair. The surface layers of the roof still retained the pale yellow colour of the straw, and the western side now shone a burnished gold as the last rays of the setting sun shone directly down the valley.

Harsh barks broke into her thoughts, and she glanced up to see a pair of black and white dogs of the kind favoured by drovers and shepherds silhouetted at the top of the path. A man emerged from the barn, wiping his hands casually on his trews as he peered down the hill at them, and Catumanda felt a small kick in her stomach as she recognised Garo.

Ruffos reassured the pack horse, and Garo held out a hand to steady the excited dogs as the strangers approached. He smiled as they came up, and lowered his head in deference to the druid who stood before him. "Welcome to my home. I gladly offer you a roof for the night and food to drive away your hunger."

Catumanda smiled warmly and laid a hand on Garo's shoulder as she realised that she had not been recognised. It was a good sign. If she was unrecognisable now to close relations, it would be unlikely that others in the area would know her for who she was. "What, you have no cervesia to offer a weary clansman and her good friend, uncle?"

Garo lifted his head and the look of puzzlement writ large across his features suddenly turned to one of shock as he realised the identity of the young holy woman. The travellers laughed aloud as he managed to gasp out a question. "Catumanda?"

Catumanda grinned and drew her uncle to her, clapping him delightedly on the shoulder as she did so. Glancing up at the house she was amused to see that Aballa, her aunt, had been drawn from the building and now stood in the doorway, her hand cupped at her brow against the blinding sunlight as she peered down at them. She was obviously unsure what to make of the scene which had presented itself to her, and Catumanda laughed again as she watched the woman perform an erratic dance, unsure whether to come forward or retreat into the house and call the other men out to protect her *gwr* from attackers.

The young druid took a step back and regarded her uncle. The family peculiarities, lopsided ears and freckles were there, and she felt a ball of emotion build in her throat as she realised just how long it had been since she had gazed upon a man or woman who shared her own features, her own blood. Garo had now recovered enough to return her grin, and Ruffos calmed the jittery horse with his hand as the dogs circled the scene excitedly. Finally he indicated the house with a flick of his head. "Come and drink your fill clansman," he breathed, before glancing across to the big carter. "Come on up, friend. The sun is almost below the hill and I have just realised that I have developed a raging thirst."

RUFFOS TORE great clumps of grass from the riverside and lovingly ran them the length of the horse's flanks. The beast shook its head in appreciation as it drank its fill from the cool waters of the stream, and Catumanda nodded with approval as she wandered away and sought out the grassy hillock which rose from the floor of the valley. Settling herself, she smiled as her friend spoke soothingly to his animal and it whinnied in response. The size of the man was clearly matched by the innate goodness of his soul, and the druid was pleased to see that her friend walked the path of the virtuous.

She settled back and sighed softly as she began to turn over the news which she had received from Garo the previous evening. The situation at Eyam was even worse than she had expected, and for the first time since she had begun her journey from Camulodunon she felt a knot of anxiety tighten in her stomach as she began to regret her hasty departure. Abaris had expected her to go directly to the Spirit Isle, where she was to complete her training in that most divine and powerful of places. The brothers there would help her to make contact with her shadow guide, and together they would interpret the dreams which the gods were sending her each night. Fully prepared then for her life as a druid, Catumanda would have no cause to fear the power of man or spirit. Alas, she knew now, she was not yet that woman.

She had received the heart-rending news the previous evening that her father had died the first winter after she had left with Abaris. It would seem that he had drawn the displeasure of the head man upon him by the action of sending his daughter away without seeking permission. Garo had explained that this man, Piso, had turned the area into a virtual chiefdom of his own, ruling over the valley with the help of a score or more heavily armed men. He had accused Catumanda's father of deliberately weakening his future work force, forcing the man to do the work of two men as punishment. Already worked close to exhaustion, the extra labour had broken him and he had died soon after.

Several years later one brave man had been driven by desperation to travel to far off Tigguocobauc to expose the situation in Eyam, and ask for the protection of the chieftain of the Coritani himself. The chieftain had sent a force of warriors to investigate the complaint, but within days of their return to the distant oppidum the man and his entire clan had been found in their roundhouse with their throats cut. Since that day the people of the valley had laboured with the ever present fear of incurring the displeasure of this Piso.

Catumanda shifted slightly to a place where she had an uninterrupted view of the sky above her. Folding her legs before her, she straightened her back and assumed the tree position which she had practised with her master so many times. The druid took three deep breaths and cleared her mind as she began to imagine a treelike root growing down from the base of her spine, into the ground beneath her. The root sank deeper each time that she exhaled, and soon she felt that she was firmly connected to the earth's unfathomable depths. As the root sank ever deeper, Catumanda began to feel the power contained within the earth seep further into her body with each intake of breath. Slowly at first, the energy was soon coursing up and through her torso, a liquid, golden warmth akin to being gently lowered into the waters of a hot spring. As the warmth reached her head, Catumanda raised her arms and cupped them to form the branches of the sacred tree. The power from the earth now contained within her body swirled about her chest, as Catumanda began to visualise a gentle stream of flashes and stars descend from the sky and enter her shaven scalp, the window to her soul. Empowered now as the forces of the sky god and the earth mother boiled and mixed within her, Catumanda thanked them both for the gift of their energy and settled back to study the sky.

Breathing slowly and deeply the druid relaxed once more and allowed the clouds to slide slowly across her field of vision. The day was fine, all the wind driven madness of the previous day a memory, and the sky above was a brilliant vault of blue and white as the clouds rolled lazily away to the north-east. As the divine energies whirled within her Catumanda emptied her mind and stared ahead and soon, as she had hoped, the gods revealed to her the path she should take.

CATUMANDA EASED her way back onto the bench and took a long draught from her cervesia. Tensing, she belched happily and winked slyly at her companion. “That was easier than I dared hope. Let’s settle down and watch the entertainment.”

Despite the detour to the water meadow, the walk from Garo's farm to the main settlement at Eyam had taken them little more than an hour. Briefly leaderless, there had been a sullen reluctance on the part of the guards to admit the pair but, sensing their fear and uncertainty Catumanda had simply brushed past them and made herself at home. Piso had returned soon after, and the druid regarded the man as he sat at the top table with his cronies.

The contrast between the chieftain, his men, and the general population was stark everywhere, but something about the obvious chasm which separated the lives and aspirations of the people of Eyam and their leaders seemed to set this place apart. Suddenly it came to her, and she leaned across and confided her thoughts to Ruffos. “It's the colours.”

Ruffos glanced across, sucking the warm chicken juices from his fingers one by one as he did so. “What is, druid?”

Catumanda kept her gaze fixed on the head man as she contemplated her reply. Piso, despite the warm weather was cloaked in a fine mantle made from what appeared to be wolf skin, the iron grey contrasting tastefully with a shirt of the finest blue linen. Golden thread had been expertly stitched throughout the garment which reflected the pale light thrown out from the hearth as he moved. The whole effect reminded Catumanda of the wings of the kingfisher as they emerged from the water, the metallic sheen was, she had to admit, a thing of beauty. A fine golden torc encircled the man's neck, and a heavy brooch of the same metal adorned his shoulder. Catumanda nodded in satisfaction. A man should look his best on the day that he descends to *Annwn*, the underworld.

“The colours,” she continued finally. “It's the colours which mark out the haves from the have-nots.”

Ruffos nodded in agreement and shrugged. “And the size; the wealthy grow big on a diet of fresh meat and good bread, the poor are sometimes lucky to eat at all.”

Catumanda took a sip from her drink and continued gazing across to the top table. A serving woman was clearing the first course and forcing a sickly smile as Piso ran his hand beneath her skirts until, to the accompaniment of howls of laughter and ribald comments from his men, it was clear that it could travel no further upwards. Cradling her cervesia the druid shuddered with disgust as she dragged her thoughts back to the conversation with Ruffos. “That’s true,” she conceded, “but there is more to it than physical size alone. Here we sit in a world of colour. Colourful clothes, gold, silver, fine tableware and a great bronze cauldron to mix the drink at feast time. Outside, in Eyam, the people move through a world almost devoid of colour. Pale, grimy faces which rarely see the sun, clothes of earthy browns and tan: but it is the eyes which lack the most. The sparkle of life has been extinguished from them, the people live in a world without hope or dreams, and that is far worse than a lack of fine shirts and gold platters.” She paused as the women began to bring in the main meal. Today it was pork, the finest cuts, Piso's favourite so they were told and they should be grateful that they were there to share it. Naturally Piso was served first and a plate of solid gold was placed before him. As was the custom the choicest cut was reserved for the man's champion, and the grizzled warrior bowed respectfully as Piso handed it across. The man scanned the hall as he took the hind quarter then settled back, satisfied that no challenge to his position as head warrior was forthcoming.

A movement to her left caught Catumanda's eye, and she was surprised to see one of the women approach her table with what looked to be a rough wooden trencher filled with hard cheese and stale bread. The woman placed it before them, flicking a look of terror at the pair as she did so, and Catumanda softened her features, offering the woman a smile of reassurance as she turned and hastened away.

Piso was the first to break the pregnant silence which followed. Mopping his golden platter with a fresh gobbet of pork, he stared across to Catumanda and his face broke into a satisfied smile as he savoured his favourite dish. "You should have tried the pork, druid. It's delicious."

A ripple of nervous laughter ran along the benches opposite as the warriors, unexpectedly finding themselves caught between the rival power of chieftain and druid, shifted uneasily.

Catumanda shrugged and gnawed at the hard, cracked corner of a piece of cheese. "I have no need for anything finer. I thank you for your hospitality."

Piso smiled but the gesture carried no warmth, and it was obvious to Catumanda that the man must know her identity. Any remaining doubts were removed as the chieftain leaned forward and exclaimed dramatically. "Of course, this would have been a feast for you when you were just another runt in one of my huts, *Catumanda*."

If the chieftain had expected to unnerve the druid with his revelation, he was to be disappointed. Catumanda watched with a self-satisfied smirk as he scooped the last of the pork into his mouth and swallowed. She shrugged nonchalantly and took another sip from her cup. The poison would already be coursing through Piso's veins. Soon his extremities, his feet and hands, would start to feel numb and lifeless. Next the sensation would begin to move along his arms and legs and so on into his torso until he was unable to move at all. The gods flashed a picture of the plant which she had gathered from the water meadow that morning into her mind, and she sent an orison of thanks to them for their guidance. Water hemlock was a very unremarkable looking plant, not much more than an untidy weed, but its thick tapered roots were deadly. Mixed in the correct proportions by a person with knowledge and training in such things, a druid perhaps, the dosage could be administered in such a way that the victim would appear to be dead but still in fact very much alive, fully conscious and aware, his pupils fixed and dilated but unable to move even a single eyelash.

Piso chuckled, stroking his moustache as his amused gaze remained locked on his supposed victim. "Now," he began finally. "What shall I do with you? I imagine that you came to kill me, or did you come back to visit your father? Oh no!" he exclaimed, "I almost forgot. He died soon after you left us."

Catumanda took another sip from her cup and calmly replaced it on the table before answering. She was determined to conduct herself in a manner which befit a druid, whatever the provocation. "You worked my father to death for harbouring ambition for his child. I already know that."

Piso looked surprised and disappointed that his revelation had been unable to upset the young druid, but his expression changed to one of joy as he realised her most likely source of information. He walked across to the centre of the hall, and Catumanda noticed him grimace slightly as he did so, as if a sudden attack of wind or the painful stab of a stitch had taken him by surprise. "You must have visited Garo on your way here, he is a clansman of yours I believe!" he exclaimed. "That is excellent news, I need another farm to reward my followers. I shall pay him a visit tomorrow."

Piso's face creased into a smile of triumph but Catumanda's eyes were elsewhere. As she watched, the man began to spasmodically flex and straighten his fingers, and a quick glance down at his shoes confirmed that his toes were moving erratically beneath the soft leather. Catumanda knew that the time to strike back at her tormentor had arrived and she rose slowly to her feet. Slipping out from behind the table she crossed the room and placed her hand gently onto the chieftain's now sweating, puckered brow. The terror-stricken warriors nearest to Piso shuffled away from their leader as Catumanda spoke calmly and softly:

"Piso, you have squandered the time given to you.
The spirits have sent me to return your soul to them.
Be dead in legs.
Be dead in arms.
Be dead in body.
Return to Annwn.
Go now!"

Catumanda recrossed the floor of the hall and resumed her meal as a silence, heavy with expectation, descended on the room. Suddenly Piso attempted to move but Catumanda had timed her intervention to perfection as, with a gasp of horror, the man's legs gave way beneath him and he fell heavily to the floor. It was the signal for his men to scramble back from the table in terror, and Catumanda stifled a smile as she noticed several of them dart out through the doorway.

The druid tore another piece of the stale bread from the loaf before her with her teeth, swilling her mouth with cervesia to soften the hard crust and raising her cup in a toast to the now confused and terror stricken man who lay nearby. "Here's to your journey, Piso," she managed to say through a mouthful of mush. "Don't worry, I will make sure that your replacement will rule the people here with a benevolent hand. Better times are about to return to Eyam."

Catumanda noticed another of the warriors attempting to steal out of the doorway, and she called across to the man. "I would rather you stayed if you don't mind. Your leader here has only a short time remaining in this world and I am sure that you would not wish to miss the wake." The man froze and slowly returned to his place at the benches as Ruffos sauntered across and helped himself to another jug of cervesia.

On the floor at the centre of the house, Piso began to jerk violently and uncontrollably as the poison began to attack the very core of his being. The stifled sound of retching carried to Catumanda and she noticed that several of Piso's men had turned aside and were vomiting with fear. Slowly the paralysing effects of the hemlock converged inward until they reached the heart and lungs of the man. Piso gave a final shudder and lay as still and cold as any stone.

Catumanda straightened up and pushed her fist gently into her chest, belching as she rose from her bench and ambled across to the stricken man. As the warriors looked on, frozen in fear, she pushed at the chieftain with the outside of her foot. Satisfied that the man was paralysed, she bent forward and spread his eyelids with her forefinger and thumb as she looked deeply into the vacant stare which was all that Piso could now manage. Despite the lack of movement Catumanda could sense the depth of despair which inhabited the man's still fully conscious mind, and she gave the slightest of winks before rising to her feet and addressing those present. "Piso has left us and travelled onwards. Let us hope that the spirits will forgive him the errors which he made in this life and send his soul back to live among us when they consider the time to be right."

She walked across to them and struggled to suppress a smile as the burly warriors shrank back before her. "You all have one last duty to perform for your erstwhile leader. Take the body out immediately and place it on the platform of the dead. The Morrigan and her sisters wish to convey the spirit directly to *Annwn,* it would be disrespectful to keep them waiting."

It was the final act of terror for the warriors of Piso's cantref, and Catumanda could sense the moment when any lingering sense of sympathy or loyalty to their dead leader evaporated. All men, but perhaps warriors in particular, knew to fear the appearance of the Morrigan. Accompanied by her sisters Madness and Violence, the shape shifting goddesses often took the form of three huge crows, soaring above the battlefield as they waited to convey the souls of the dead to the underworld.

Catumanda and Ruffos followed on as the men carried the stiff and apparently lifeless form of Piso from the building. Making their way past the roundhouse, they took the stony path which led up to place of the dead. It was here that bodies of the higher class members of the community, head men and their families, bards and the men of the cantref, were exposed on high wooden platforms. Once the process of excarnation by carrion feeding birds was complete, the fleshless bones were removed and taken for burial inside stone lined vaults sunk into the hillside.

A buzz of excited voices carried up to them as they walked, and Catumanda glanced back to see that the inhabitants of Eyam were gathering to witness the culmination of the great event which had occurred in their midst. As she watched, Catumanda noticed a small wizened woman emerge from one of the shabbier dwellings and shuffle across to her friends, and her heart skipped a beat as she recognised her mother despite the passage of the years.

As they reached the platform a woven litter was produced and Piso placed inside. Several of his warriors heaved the litter onto the platform and, with a last glance at the body of their leader, returned to the group. Catumanda indicated that they leave and return to the base of the hill with a flick of her head as she climbed to a small crag which overlooked the site. Ruffos handed over her crane skin bag, and she rummaged inside until she found the tiny horn which she had fashioned at the riverside earlier that morning. Inhaling deeply the druid raised the horn to her mouth and blew a series of raucous, sky ripping croaks. *Craw...Craw...Craw.*

Almost immediately, three dark shadows detached themselves from the higher branches of a nearby oak and glided down to the platform on jet black wings. Even at a distance an audible gasp, a macabre mixture of wonder and fear, carried up to the pair from the crowd gathered at the base of the hill as the crows hopped across to begin their grisly work.

Perched high above the rooftops, Catumanda sighed and stared out across the place of her birth. It was no wonder that the gods had been so keen to aid her in her endeavour to rid the place of Piso. Great grey scars slashed the hillside from the workings at the mines, and heaps of ugly slag lay piled along a riverside devastated by the effects of the lead which leached into the waters. The area around the settlement had become a dead place, a wasteland where the spirits of the river, trees, animals and people had struggled to flourish. She glanced back down to the platform to ensure that her enemy remained paralysed, despite the ordeal he was enduring in his last moments. The largest crow had already removed Piso's right eye, and although it still remained attached to the man by a gory grey sinew, The Morrigan had already punctured the organ and was in the process of hungrily gobbling down the fluid which it contained.

Catumanda felt Ruffos sway slightly at her side, and she realised that it had been unfair of her to expect her friend to witness the depth of her vengeance, so she nodded in agreement when the big man suggested that she say a few words over the tormented man. Flames of hatred for Piso still burned within, but the three sisters of death themselves were before her and the perfect verse came instantly to her mind. Catumanda hauled herself to her feet. Slipping the crane skin bag over head, the druid held her hands over the scene as she repeated the words of a long-dead bard:

> *"Over his head is shrieking a lean hag,*
> *quickly hopping.*
> *Over the points of weapons and shields.*
> *She is the grey haired Morrigan."*

9

Aia smiled sweetly and slipped her arm through his as they walked. "How is Connos?"

Solemis had barely spoken since they had been formally introduced and, try as he might, the words just would not come. Of course, the fact that it appeared that every man and woman within sight was smiling in their direction as they passed by did little to help, neither did the fact that Aia's aunt was walking several paces behind them. "My father is fine. He will soon be back to his old self."

Another pregnant pause fell upon them, and Solemis winced at the stilted answer which was all that he had been able to think of. His mind raced as he tried in vain to conjure something further to add to his brief reply. Aia glanced up and Solemis' heart leapt as she flashed him an impish smile. "And your dog?"

His brow creased in confusion for a heartbeat before he realised what she was referring to. The only time they had previously met he had helped her brother win a rope pulling contest with Tarvos by giving the dog's balls a sharp tug. He grinned at the sight of the irate dog which flashed into his mind. "He is recovering too!" They both laughed together and Solemis could sense the tension of the moment drain away as they did so. He looked across to the heath which bordered the encampment and flicked his head. "Shall we walk across that way. I can almost feel the eyes boring into me here."

A supply of logs had been stacked at the edge of the camp to feed the evening fires, and they sat and watched as the wagons struggled across from the riverside with further loads. Aia shuffled across and sat close to him as her guardian settled down nearby. "My father was very impressed you know. He said that it was one of the finest throws that he had ever seen." Aia racked her mind as she probed for a subject which would get the handsome warrior to relax. She had had one lucky escape when her father had arranged a marriage to the oaf Acco: she was not about to let the hero of the day get away if she could help it. She tried again. "When will the skull be ready?"

Solemis brightened. This was a subject he felt comfortable with and he answered proudly. "Because we can't wait for the crows to pick it clean, Albiomaros is boiling it right now. Brennus says that I must attach it to my saddle while we are away to remind everyone why I am with them."

It was the most coherent sentence that she had managed to drag from the shy warrior in a full hour of coaxing, and she pressed ahead as she sensed him finally relax a touch. "Tell me more about Brennus. My father says that he is the greatest warrior that the tribe has ever had. What does he want you all to do?"

Solemis shrugged. "I have only spoken to him once, twice if you count the time that he was pinned to the ground by a horse. I do know that my father feels the same way about him, as do I. He is the greatest of the Senones. Brennus said that he had neglected his duty to the people and let our enemies get close. From now on there will be war bands of mounted warriors ranging ahead, to the flanks and bringing up the rear of the column. As a reward for saving his life I am to accompany your father's cantref as part of the largest war band. We are to go ahead of the people and ensure that the way forward is clear of enemies and that all the preparations made by the Greeks have been properly set in place." Solemis gathered his courage and turned his face to hers. "Despite his wounds my father asked Crixos, your father, that we become betrothed before he would let them remove him from the field of battle." He smiled at the memory. "Brennus laughed at the absurdity of the situation, two wounded men laying in a field surrounded by the bodies of men and horses calmly discussing marriage arrangements, and let Crixos know that it would please him also." He shrugged. "So here we are."

Aia stooped and picked a twig from the ground, idly shredding the bark with her thumb nail. Drawing her knees up she arranged her skirts and smiled again. "Tell me about the river and the boats. Are there as many as people say?"

Solemis puffed out his cheeks as he recalled the events of the previous day. He had been sent forward with her father and the new flying column of riders for the first time. Half a day's hard ride had brought them to the banks of the River Souconna, and a small self-satisfied smile tugged at the corners of his mouth as he recalled his first glimpse of the flotilla which would carry them all south. "We rode hard all morning, and just after the sun had climbed to its highest point we crested a slight rise and there they were, arrayed before us. The road fell way and ended at the river bank where a small drinking den had been thrown up by one of the locals to cater for the crews of the boats." He chuckled at the memory as he described the scene which had greeted them.

"It was only a ramshackle hut with a roof of woollen cloth to shade the drinkers, but it had obviously been doing a good trade for some time. The wide water meadow thereabouts was awash with boatmen who had started the day early, and Crixos ordered us to fan out and array ourselves along the skyline as he took his cantref and formed a wedge of horsemen at our midpoint."

Solemis was gratified to notice the excitement lighting up Aia's face as he continued his tale. "We sat there and waited, and eventually one of the cervesia sodden men noticed the fact that a war band had appeared not a hundred paces from them, and we all grinned as he shouted a warning to his friends and they scurried back to their boats like frightened mice. A mass of pale white faces appeared at the doorway of the hut as your father took the men of his cantref down into the valley to speak to the leaders of the rabble. Your brother, Caturix, edged his mount beside mine and we studied the boats together."

Aia smiled slyly. "Caturix and I are very close. I asked him to spy on you for me." She traced her fingertip across the rufous line of his moustache. "He likes you."

Solemis was elated at the revelation. Not only would it help him to become accepted by the members of Aia's clan, but he had quickly grown to like and enjoy the company of her brother. Caturix shared the easy-going nature of his friend Albiomaros without the bulk. Tall and lithe with a mass of the flaxen coloured hair which they had both clearly inherited from their mother, Aia's brother was a natural horseman and a popular member of the army. Solemis knew that his friendship had played a large part in his own rapid acceptance among the close-knit group, and he was grateful for it. She tugged at his moustache playfully. "You were going to tell me about the boats."

Solemis shook his head as he recalled the sight which had greeted them. “There were too many to count. The Souconna is wide there, very wide: a long bow shot?” he suggested with a shrug. Her eyes opened at the estimate. Aia's clan came from the upper reaches of the River Sequana and she could barely imagine a body of water to be so large. “There is a ferry to transport travellers to the far bank, but unless the ferryman is selling cervesia he is going hungry at the moment. There are so many boats waiting for the people there that a man could walk from bank to bank. Of course,” he continued smugly, “it still does not compare with the River Tamesis in Albion.”

Aia gasped in surprise. “You have been to Albion? Of course,” she said, “that is where your big friend comes from. Tell me more about it, does it really rain every day?”

Solemis laughed and shook his head as he thought back to the happy days which he had spent on what, to most people of Celtica, was a place of mystery and legend. “No, of course not,” he joked, “sometimes it snows!”

Aia dug him playfully in the ribs and pulled a hurt expression. “Don't make fun of me. So that is where you were at foster? It would explain the presence of your aptly named, tattooed friend.”

Solemis nodded. Albiomaros literally meant 'big man from Albion' and Connos' clan had called him it for so long now that he suspected that even he had forgotten the name which he had carried when he had left his distant home for foster among them. “Our clan have had fostering and clientage arrangements with the Trinobantes for generations, back to the time before they migrated to the island. My father was at foster there and his father before him.” Solemis put an arm around her and attempted to draw her to him as he continued with his description of Albion, but she quickly sidled away as a gentle cough from behind reminded her that they were not alone.

"The Trinobantes live in the area to the north of the Tamesis, the Dark River, the river which I told you about. From the low cliffs which line its northern bank the far shore is almost as far as the distance from Belgica to Albion itself. They do have summers." He smiled gently. "But they are not so long or hot as those in Celtica. There are no monsters there, the people are much like us. They drink, fight and raid their enemies. The chieftain distributes *potlach* to his followers and the people tend to their flocks and harvest their crops under his protection." He shrugged. "Much like everywhere else, I imagine."

A rumble came from behind them, and they turned as one just in time to see Aia's aunt upended as the poorly stacked logs rolled forward and deposited her on her back. Seizing her chance, Aia leaned forward and kissed him tenderly on the mouth as the woman's legs thrashed the air. As her guardian struggled to her feet, Aia slipped her hand down and lightly ran the tips of her fingers across his groin. Solemis gasped with pleasure and surprise as she gave it a final squeeze and moved across to help her aunt with a saucy backward glance. "Just checking that we feel the same way. I have enjoyed our talk and accept your proposal.

SOLEMIS AND CATURIX pulled their mounts to the side of the road and let themselves drop wearily from the saddle. Leading them stiff legged across a short grassy bank, they let the reins fall to the ground as the horses drank noisily from the icy brook. After several hours in the saddle the pair were unable to resist the urge to add a little more to the waters which burbled before them, and they moved downstream as they unfastened their breeches. Both men sighed with pleasure as the sparkling arcs gushed out to add their own tiny contribution to the flow which would eventually wend its way down to the great sea in the South. "That is...," Caturix began, before pausing as he squinted up at the ramparts of rock and snow which hazed the southern horizon. Screwing up his face he threw Solemis a sidelong glance as he readjusted his clothing. "What is it?"

Solemis shook himself, grinning as he wiped the splashes on his fingers against the side of his trews. "The roof of the world!"

"That's it; the roof of the world!" Caturix exclaimed, with a sweep of his arm. "My father, rightly, has no reputation as a bard in the clans, preferring to do his talking with the point of his lancea. But I find it difficult to argue with his description."

The young warriors were craning their necks as they took in the enormity of the peaks and dark shadowy hollows which bestrode their route like the giants of their legends. It was impossible not to pause and admire the silent grandeur of the Alpes at every opportunity. Each time that they had broken free from the covering of pines and beech which hugged the road their eyes had been drawn immediately upward. The tops of the mountains lay hidden beneath great sweeps of grey cloud, but the overpowering sense of age and permanence made each sighting seem as thrilling to the young Senone scouts as their very first.

Caturix walked around the clearing, flexing his legs and rolling his shoulders as he sought to restore the blood flow to tired limbs. Crossing back to his horse he groped about inside his travel bag and pulled out a hunk of cheese. Breaking it into two pieces he tossed one across to Solemis. "Do you think that the Greek gods live up there?"

They shared a look and laughed. Kyriakos, the fat little Greek who had persuaded their leaders to uproot the people and move to the new lands, had insisted that the gods of the Greeks took the form of men and women and lived in a great hall at the top of a mountain he called Olympus. The absurdity had swept the clans swifter than a summer grass fire and even the druids, who jealously guarded the secrets of the gods and spirits, had found it difficult to do anything other than pity the poor man for his beliefs.

The chief druid Devorix had visited the Horsetails soon after, and Solemis recalled his words that evening with a smile:

'the gods live in all things; they are in the stones and the water and the air. Why would so powerful a force wish to inhabit the frail body of a man or woman? Why would they wish to experience illness, death and decay when they can be free to soar with the winds or outlive the hills?'

The young Senones had been sent ahead of the main column by Crixos to scout the road ahead as it climbed towards their next goal, Genawa, the principal oppidum of the Allobroge. The steepening roadway was beginning to take its toll on the heavily laden horses, and Crixos had decided that several pairs of lightly armed riders would scout ahead on a rotating basis, swapping to their spare mounts as the main force came up. The summer months were drawing on, the days were growing noticeably shorter, and a sense of urgency had begun to haunt their every thought and action.

Once the tribe had reached the River Souconna and boarded the boats it had taken little more than a week to transport them to their next destination, the confluence of the river with the River Rodonus. Ranging ahead, Solemis and his column had arrived the previous afternoon and had been well received by the people of the Ambari at Lugdunon, the hill fort which controlled the important junction from its lofty perch above the rivers. Here the final payments were made to the boatmen and the people had disembarked, rested and ready to face the gruelling transit of the Alpes. The Greek trading city of Massalia lay to the South, near to the place where the river emptied into the Southern Sea, and the Ambari had grown rich on the trade which moved through their lands. Eager to help their trading partners, they had happily supplied the Senones with fresh supplies of meat and cervesia as they had passed through.

Thankfully there had been no further attacks on the people or their leader since the incident outside Alesia, but the dark clothed riders had clearly been far more than bandits. Darker in skin tone and hair colour than was usual in Celtica they were plainly far from their own land, and the discipline and forward planning which they had displayed during the ambush and fighting had marked them as an experienced war band to the experienced Senone warriors. The fact that each of the men who had died that day had been well provided with swords, daggers and even small axes of iron had only added to the impression. The leader, the man who had fallen to Solemis' spear, had worn a battle shirt of gilt iron beneath his outer clothing, and the Senones had marvelled at the piece which had been expertly shaped to resemble the torso of a heavily muscled man. As the warrior's vanquisher Brennus had rightly presented the breast plate to Solemis, and the young Horsetail had delighted every man present by making a gift of it to Crixos to help cement the hoped-for pact between their clans. Crixos wore it daily, and Solemis knew that the gift had done much to ease his acceptance among Aia's clan and the battle hardened warriors of her father's cantref.

Solemis moved upstream of the horses and plunged his head into the icy water. The day was hot and they had almost reached the rocky outcrop which was to be the limit of their reconnaissance. There they would rest while they waited for Crixos to bring up the rest of the column. Refreshed by the icy mountain water Solemis hauled himself to his feet, shaking the droplets from his face and hair as he looked across to Caturix. "Come on then, let's get going. Only a short while and we will be there."

To his surprise his friend had donned his bronze helm and was slipping his hand inside the grip of his shield as he moved towards the roadway. Throwing him a look of concern, Caturix indicated uphill with a flick of his head. "We have company."

SOLEMIS TOOK another pull of cervesia and replaced the stopper with a sigh. The drink was welcome after the long climb and although it was not quite as good as they brewed at home, the effects of the alcohol combined with the increasing altitude hit the spot. Soon he was as happy as he had been for days and he chatted amiably to the young Allobroge warrior who rode at his side. "How did you know that we were there?"

The warrior glanced across and laughed. He repeated the question to his companion and he too chuckled happily. "It is our responsibility to mark all which happens in the pass. We are almost there, you will soon see."

Solemis and Caturix had agreed to accompany the twin riders back to the outcrop where a welcoming party of Allobroge warriors were waiting to escort the weary Senones to Genawa, now only half a day away.

The pass began to twist and turn as it steepened, and Solemis watched as a pair of ravens soared high above them on their characteristic flicked back wings. Suddenly the birds dropped from the sky, tumbling over and over as they plummeted earthwards. With a dip of its wing one of the ravens slid across to its mate, and they clasped their feet together as they caught an up-current and spun back skywards. The men exchanged a grin at the birds' antics which seemed to embody the sense of space and freedom which permeated the pass. The warrior had been casting repeated glances towards the skull which hung from Solemis' saddle horn, and Solemis delighted him by unhooking the leather binding which held it in place and passing the trophy across. The cord had been looped through the holes in the skull which had been made by his gaesum as it had passed through, and Solemis listened proudly as Caturix described the throw which had killed the enemy leader as he prepared to finish off the helpless Brennus.

The roadway took a sharp turn to the left and, looking up, the Senones saw the creamy white outcrop of rock where they were to await Crixos looming above them. Coaxing their tired mounts up the final incline the pair were surprised to find themselves in a small grassy clearing. Away to their left a small fort had been constructed from timber, and Solemis guessed that it was from here that their escort had been sent out. The gates were open, and their Allobroge friends led them across and into the small encampment.

A short muscular man came from one of the small halls at the sound of the horses' arrival, and Solemis could immediately see that he commanded here. Darker in complexion than was normal among the Celts, the man was obviously an experienced and grizzled warrior. Even at a distance Solemis could see that his face and forearms carried numerous scars, and although he was not wearing armour the design of the gold torc which ringed his neck told all that this was a man of note. If the body and bearing of the Allobroge leader carried a look of menace, his disposition clearly indicated that those who came in friendship had little to fear. He strode across the courtyard, smiling as the riders dismounted and hobbled their horses. "Welcome to the lands of the Allobroge."

Solemis and Caturix self-consciously brushed the dust from their tunics as they moved to greet their host. The long hot summer months had turned the road into a virtual river of fine grey powder, and the length of their ride had coated them from head to foot. The slightest breath of wind had swept the dust across the road in clouds, and the pair had taken to covering their mouths and noses with their cloaks in an effort to keep the worst effects from their lungs. The Allobroge waved at them and laughed. "We are used to receiving travellers from the lowlands," he glanced around the fort. "That's why we are here. In the summer they are covered in dust and the spring and autumn, mud." He smiled once more as he introduced himself. "My name is Ullio and I command here."

Both Solemis and Caturix were the sons of chieftains, but Solemis had insisted that his friend assume the mantle of leader due to his greater age and experience. He was, after all, a guest among Crixos' war band and he was happy to follow.

"I am Caturix, son of Crixos and my friend is Solemis, son of Connos. We are happy to greet you Ullio of the Allobroge as friends of your people."

Ullio nodded and indicated that they follow him with a flick of his head. "I trust that the boys I sent down shared their cervesia with you?"

Caturix nodded happily. "It was very welcome. You have our thanks."

Ullio snorted. "I'll bet it was, it is a long journey from Genawa down to Lugdunon." He chuckled softly. "I should know, I have done it enough times. But you boys and your people, moving your entire tribe through Celtica and across the Alpes into the unknown." He whistled and shook his head. "Here; you deserve this." He reached across and scooped up a jug of cervesia from a table and handed it across. Solemis asked a question as he waited for his friend to quench his thirst. "How did you see us coming up? I thought that we were screened by the trees for most of the journey and I never saw this fort once."

Ullio laughed and walked across to the western side of the ramparts, beckoning them across with a sweep of his arm. Solemis caught the look of amusement light up the face of the Allobroge, and he turned and gasped in wonder at the sight before them. Solemis and Caturix gazed in awe as the lands of Celtica lay spread out below them. Caturix passed the jug across, and Solemis drank as Ullio moved beside them. Spreading his hands on the lip of the rampart he inhaled deeply and smiled. "What do you think?"

Ullio laughed as he realised that the pair were lost for words, and he began to describe the scene before them by tracing the line of the mighty river which snaked across from north to south. "There is the Souconna moving down to its junction with the Rodonus. At the point where the rivers meet you can occasionally make out the hill on which the oppidum of Lugdunon is built but today, as usual at this time of the year," he shrugged, "it is lost in the haze. Further west the land rises to the great hills and forests which contain the lands of the Arverni and down to the South we can almost see as far as the lands which owe allegiance to the Greeks at Massalia." He turned his back and leaned against the wooden wall as he indicated the rising land to the North. "Those lands are known as the Jora while to the South," he twisted and pointed with a sweep of his arm, "lie the peaks of the Alpes themselves, with the snow capped peak of The White Lady standing proud of her sisters."

The Senones shook their heads in amazement at the grandeur which surrounded them, and Ullio grinned as he indicated that they follow him to the furthest corner of the fort. In doing so they moved away from the ledge of pale coloured rock on which the fort was built. The drop here was precipitous and the friends edged warily towards the lip as they craned their necks and followed the line of the road back down the pass. Barely half a mile away Crixos was clearly visible, his muscular body armour shining brightly in the afternoon sun as he led the men of his cantref proudly on.

Ullio indicated the furthest reaches of the pass with a nod of his head and the pair looked across. "That is not the most memorable sight which you can see from my little eyrie," he breathed. "Look alongside the dark forest which juts in from the North, and give thanks to your gods that you lived your days at a time to witness such a thing."

Solemis and Caturix followed his directions and caught their breath. The forest stretched for miles, and perfectly outlined against the darker backdrop by the glow of the sun, the entire tribe of the Senones could be seen snaking through the pass.

Ullio continued as Solemis and Caturix struggled to control their emotions. "It is a sight which *I* never thought to see in my lifetime, how much greater must it seem to you. To gaze upon every man, woman and child. The young and the old, all that you hold most precious laid out before your eyes. How many people are there?"

Caturix glanced at Solemis for confirmation as he attempted to remember the figure which Brennus had given the boatmen weeks before. Finally it came to him and he replied without shifting his gaze from the meandering serpent in the pass below: "Eighty-thousand."

Ullio shook his head in wonder. "Eighty-thousand! Who

would think that the world could contain such a vast number of people?"

Ullio moved between them and placed a hand on each man's shoulder. "Remember this moment always. You see your world through the eyes of the gods."

10

The sun had barely risen when Catumanda paused at the head of the valley. Turning back she closed her eyes against its brilliance and let the warmth of the fiery orb seep into her skin. After a few moments, she shielded her eyes and gazed for what she was sure would be the very last time on the valley of her birth. The returning sun lay like a Bel Fire on the very pinnacle of the furthest spur of land, and the druid watched in wonder as the golden fingers of light probed deeper and deeper along the valley floor with each passing moment.

A full week had passed now since she had first arrived back in the valley, and the changes which she had caused to be made there were a source of great pride to her. Piso, the head man of Eyam, had been replaced and his soul returned to *Annwn* where it could recover from whatever had ailed it in this life and await its rebirth. Catumanda had temporarily ceased all work in the mines and set the men the task of clearing the settlement and the surrounding area of the heaps of slag and detritus which were the by-product of their labours. The thoughtlessly discarded body of mother earth had been taken back below the surface and returned to the older, worked out, seams in the hillside. Catumanda had performed cleansing rites at the worst affected locations, and left offerings of food and drink to assuage the spirits and ask their forgiveness for the years of wanton desecration and neglect during the time which had already begun to be referred to as 'the bad time' among the people of Eyam.

The druid was grateful if not wholly surprised considering the manner of Piso's death to have gained the full support of the warriors of the dead leader's cantref, and they had thrown themselves enthusiastically into the efforts to rejuvenate the area as they awaited the appointment of a new leader by the chieftain in Tigguocobauc. Catumanda had made it known that she would ensure that any druid passing through the area in the future would call in on the valley, to ensure that the spirits of both nature and people were never abused again.

She had been thrilled to lead the midsummer celebrations among her own clan and their neighbours, and had tried to persuade her mother to move down valley to live with her brother and his family but without success. Surrounded by her friends, she had proudly basked in the attention and respect which her daughter's dramatic homecoming had drawn to her. Satisfied now that she was safe and well, Catumanda and Ruffos had stolen away as the pale glow of the dawn touched the eastern skyline. The words which had needed to pass between mother and daughter had already been said, and in truth they were strangers to one another. She had left her childhood home a small frightened child and returned as a woman of power, a friend of the gods, and their lives had little in common. It was clear to each of them that she now stood outside the common bonds of family and clan which formed the structure of normal society. Druids of course did so, and it had always been the intention of her father that she escape a lifetime of back-breaking work underground or childrearing if he could make it so.

The druid pulled a thin smile as her friend laid a hand gently on her shoulder and smiled knowingly. Not so long ago the roles had been reversed, and it had been she who had persuaded the big man that it was time to move on from his own steading. Catumanda returned the smile, and with a last glance over her shoulder, put the valley and people behind her.

LATER THAT MORNING they crossed the last valley and gazed up at the creamy white scar which marked the entrance to the uplands men knew as the Brig Du, the Black Peak. The green line of the valley curved away to the West in a gentle gradient before it passed out of view, offering the easier, well trodden route, but Catumanda knew that she had dallied long enough on her journey already. The gods had indicated their approval of her actions in and around Eyam by lessening the intensity of the night terrors which plagued her. As if to spur her on to make good on lost time the dreams had returned with a vengeance once midsummer had passed. Each night she had awoken bathed in sweat, gasping at the visions which assailed her tired mind. She really must press on to the Spirit Isle, the brothers there would have the means to help her.

A smaller path branched away to the right, and Ruffos paused and pointed it out. "I have never been in these parts, but that will be the quickest way up onto the moors, druid."

The day was growing warm, and Catumanda unstopped her flask and took a swig as she looked across. Swilling the water around her mouth she swallowed and wiped her chin on the sleeve of her tunic. The pathway trailed across a small field and forded a beck, before winding its way up a narrow rubble-strewn pathway to the summit. "Will Clop make it up there?"

Ruffos smiled and gently stroked the pack horse's muzzle. The horse had originally been called something far more mundane but his daughter, Nia, had begun to call it Clop when she was little more than a bairn and the name had stuck. Having Clop along with him on his travels was akin to bringing along a small part of his family, and the name always transported him home when he heard others use it. "Don't you worry about Clop," he said. "He could carry us both up there if we needed him to!"

Ruffos clicked his tongue and led the horse across the meadow to the beck where it gratefully lowered its head and drank. Catumanda moved downstream a little and, removing her boots, lowered her feet into the chill waters. Ruffos continued to chatter as the druid swished her feet to and fro. "That is likely to be a salt traders' trail, they move salt from the West coast to the interior. It might be a bit rough going in parts, but it will be quicker than the normal route so that should prove ideal for us."

The druid glanced across and nodded. "Let's get going. The quicker we complete our journey the better."

Catumanda waded across the beck and rested on a boulder as she replaced her boots. A little way to their right, a small bush hung festooned with offerings to the spirits which lived in that place. At the base of a solid wall of milky white stone a small spring burbled forth from the darkness, and Catumanda jogged across and added a small offering of her own for their safe journey.

Soon they had wound their way up the path and spilled out onto a wide rock platform. To the right of them a dry channel led to the lip of the valley which was cupped into a shallow depression. They were now at the top of the vertical wall of rock from which the stream issued forth far below, and they had wondered then what forces could produce such a thing. Now that they were above it the signs were unmistakable. Ahead of them lay a steep sided passage which led up onto the high moor, and it was plain to them that it must have been scoured out by the force of water. Druids were the repository of the folk memories of the people back through time to the earliest days and, as they guided Clop across the treacherous series of slabs and fissures which led on up to the pass, Catumanda explained to her amazed friend how the landscape had been formed. "In the days before our ancestors travelled to these lands, this whole area was a place of ice. The people grew too numerous for the lands in the South and Bel, the Shining One, answered their pleas. He shone ever brighter in the sky until the ice retreated and the people could move north to live here. As the ice melted it streamed away to the sea in great torrents, drowning some lands but releasing others for the use of men. It was during this time that Albion became an island." Catumanda swept the area with her arm as she continued. "This is one of the channels through which the waters drained away. At the time they would have flowed through this chasm and on over the falls. As the ice melted the spirits which live here saw that the waters were washing away and they replaced them with the springs which you see today." She turned and smiled at the incredulous carter. "So you see, the gods and spirits work in harmony. Great Bel provided land for his people and the earth spirits provided enough water for them to prosper in that new land. It is the reason we honoured them before we climbed up here."

Movement among the grasses cut the druid's story short, and the pair watched as the huge buff form of a mountain hare darted down and disappeared into one of the crevices littering the floor. A moment later the dark shadow of an eagle swept across the scene, and the friends watched as the magnificent bird circled them, its head quartering the ground below as it sought its prey. Finally, with a screech of frustration, it dipped one wing and beat its way westwards. "Come on," Catumanda said. "It's a sign. We need to get on."

They followed the gorge north-westwards as the wind picked up, and the track soon became visible once more as it climbed away to the black, peaty surface of the Brig Du itself. Climbing up they were confronted by a landscape which rolled away in a series of dips and mounds, a dark sea speckled by patches of heather, moss, and tussocks of tall white cottongrass. The freshening breeze came down from the West and, higher now, the travellers watched as an unbroken line of leaden clouds swept down upon them. Soon the day turned to night and the first raindrops, as large and hard as peas, began to fall.

Pulling their cloaks about them, they hunched their shoulders, lowered their faces and forged ahead into the full fury of the storm.

It took them the rest of that day and a greater part of the next before they descended gratefully once again to lower lands. The winds howled, sweeping the rains across the moors in great white sheets which turned the pathway to rivulets and the moorland alongside into a porridge as black as jet. It took only a moment's lack of concentration or the blinding effects of the driving rain to stray from the path, with the reward being a knee deep immersion in the strength sapping ooze for man or beast.

Unable to sleep on the flooded ground, Catumanda had spent the night crouched over a flickering candle as she continued to carve powerful spells on the inner surface of

Piso's skull. A day had been time enough for the Morrigan and her sisters to strip the head of its mantle of flesh, and Catumanda had chopped the grisly trophy from the cadaver's spine with her moon blade. The head was the dwelling place of the immortal soul, but Catumanda had no desire to keep *this* soul in the world of men and had carefully removed the top half to act as a mortar. Imbued with marks of power, the skull of her father's killer would be perfect for the task.

As they trudged gratefully down the head of a small valley the clouds had finally lifted, and a shaft of watery sunlight pierced the gloom to reveal the pale grey glimmer of the western sea on the far horizon. Away to the left rose the mountainous peaks of Ordovicia, beyond which lay the wave lashed shores of the Spirit Isle. Their destination almost in sight, Catumanda and Ruffos found that their weariness evaporated along with the water from their rain lashed bodies and clothing.

Within the hour they were eating their first hot meal since they had left Eyam as their clothes steamed beside a raging hearth. Soon after they were aboard a boat which would take them as far as the coast as, freed of its burden, Clop happily shadowed the craft on the bank. By sunup the following day they were bidding the boatman farewell, the travellers striking out along the narrow coastal strip which skirted the mountainous chiefdom. The salty tang of the sea refreshed their spirits, as they followed a path which squeezed between the rolling breakers and the dark ramparts of the mountains which towered above the route.

Finally, as the day drew to its end in a chaotic smear of orange and reds, they crested a small rise as the road took a turn to the south. Catumanda and Ruffos exchanged a look and grinned. There before them, beyond the narrow strip of water, lay the forests of the Spirit Isle.

. . .

THE WIND HAD CONTINUED to freshen during the afternoon to such a degree that, despite the fact that it was the height of summer in the northern lands, a full scale gale seemed imminent. The gusting wind shook and picked at the walls of the small hut, forcing its way into and through the tiny gaps which marked the junction between the wattle and the sheer rock wall which lay behind. Catumanda inhaled slowly and deeply, drawing the pungent yellow smoke deep within her as she waited for the ceremony to begin. She blinked away the tears and peered about the hut once again, as the effects of the smoke began to seep into each and every sinew of her body.

The pelt of a great white bear dominated the floorspace, and arranged at regular intervals around this sat a succession of small bowls: earthenware, gold, silver, bronze. Although no fire danced in the central hearth, the air in the room was hot and dry; lit and warmed by a series of small individual fires, the flames licked hungrily at the bases of the elaborately decorated bowls which circled the tiny space. Each bowl, she knew, contained a mash of grains and herbs: wheat, fennel, chervil, garlic. Each ingredient had been a gift to men from the gods, and the smoke which rose from them would entice them to this place.

Beyond the womb-like atmosphere of the room the wind howled and moaned, plucking at the structure and threatening to drown out the efforts of the sibylla, the enchantress whose rhythmic beating of a small drum would help her to cross over into the spirit world and alert the inhabitants to her presence.

The wind seemed to redouble in strength as the door at the far end of the room opened briefly to admit several shadowy forms into the choking atmosphere, and although

Catumanda knew them to be druids like herself the effects of the week long fast, the measured beat of the drum and the choking effects of the smoke caused her to feel uneasy for the first time.

Their heads cowled the druids seemed to float through the room, and although they quickly passed from sight, Catumanda sensed they had taken up positions at each side of her. Firm hands gripped her arms as a hooded figure, his features unseen in the depths of the shadows, suddenly appeared before her causing her befuddled mind to start. The man lifted Catumanda's eyelid with his thumb and gently nodded to his companions. "She is ready."

The druid placed his hands on either side of Catumanda's head, careful not to smudge any of the sacred markings with which her face and torso had been daubed back in the nemeton. Not all spirits which dwelt in the body of the Earth were kindly disposed towards the living, and the markings would help to protect the brother from their malevolence. The man tipped Catumanda's head up and looked her directly in the eye. "Druid. We have prepared you as far as we are able, but only you can decide whether you wish to journey onward before you have become one with your spirit guide. Once you enter the Earth you cannot return until you have gained the knowledge which you seek." He held Catumanda's gaze to ensure that the young woman understood the dangers which she was about to face below ground. All experienced druids had contacted their spirit guide, and visited the gathering place of their ancestors. Either would be an invaluable source of help and advice now, but Catumanda knew that she had already tested the will of the gods with her detour to Eyam. The dreams were almost constant now, their shadowy images insistent and disturbing. She must forge ahead alone and trust to their protection, she would make contact with her spirit helpers another time. She forced her eyes to refocus despite the dreamy state which the combined effects of the gruel and smoke had inflicted upon her consciousness and returned the druid's gaze. "Yes, I am ready."

The druid gave a small nod of respect and took Catumanda by the elbow. Moving to the back of the hut he placed his hand gently on the young druid's head and guided her through a small crevice in the face of the rock.

Naked but for the crane skin bag at her side, Catumanda gave an involuntary shudder as the icy blackness enveloped her. A small amount of light filtered into the entrance of the grotto from the fissure to her rear, and she inhaled deeply as her eyes slowly became more accustomed to the murk. Before her lay a passably dry rubble strewn floor, beyond which three distinct tunnels crawled away into the leaden blackness.

Catumanda paused as she tried to recall the advice which she had been given in the days leading up to this journey. Without the aid of a spirit guide she would have to trust to her instincts and pray that the spirits were kind to her. She had sacrificed a lamb earlier that day and the auspices had been good, but she had been made aware by her concerned brethren that druids far more experienced than she had entered these caves never to return.

Catumanda closed her eyes and used her hands to feel the air about her. To her consternation she felt no reaction on her skin towards any of the tunnels before her. If the spirits were with her, she had hoped that they would help to direct her towards the correct route to her destination with the force of their energy. She cleared her mind and concentrated as she repeated the act, but again there was no tingling sensation to indicate which passage was the correct one for her to take. The rhythmic drumming from beyond the fissure crowded in on her thoughts, and Catumanda moved forward in an effort to clear her mind as she frantically sought an indication of the way ahead. As she did so, a slight sensation like the gentle caress of a child's hair moved across her hand. Catumanda stopped and squinted as she tried to pierce to gloom. A pale line of light bisected the space between her and the source of the energy, motes of dust swirling and dancing within. Catumanda crawled across in hope but was crestfallen to discover that no passageway opened up before her. Already disorientated by the combined effects of the gruel and the sacred smoke and growing increasingly desperate to complete her labour, she pummelled the stony ground with her fists in anger and frustration. Suddenly the floor of the cavern gave way beneath her blows, and as the tingling sensation, strong and pure, washed over her body, she gasped in relief as she realised that the way forward had finally been revealed to her.

The light from without was barely enough for the young druid to see the extent of the passageway as she cupped her hands and scooped out the grit and rubble of years, but she sensed the space which was opening up before her was tight, far smaller than the previous three she had seen. Catumanda looped her bag across her shoulders and lowered her head inside, groping forward with her outstretched hands as she did so. The passage felt smooth and rounded and Catumanda was sure that it must have been carved out of the rock by the water spirits long ago. Small rocks and stones littered the floor and she was certain that no man or woman had entered this particular part of the cave for a very long time. It was entirely possible, she reflected with a sense of awe, that she was the first to enter this place. As she crawled forward, deeper into the passageway, Catumanda began to feel the tunnel narrow as it twisted and turned in the blackness. No light entered this far into the Earth and she inched her way along in a darkness which was more total than any she had ever experienced on the surface.

Catumanda, her outstretched arms thrust before her, slowly squirmed deeper into the tunnel. Despite the smoothness of the passageway her breasts rubbed painfully, but suddenly the shaft rose slightly and she thrust her hand over a lip and into a wider space beyond. Running her hand around the opening ahead of her, Catumanda was sure that she could just manage to slide her body through and into the void but it would be, she knew, an act of faith in the good intentions of the spirit which had guided her here. She may still be able to wriggle back the way she had come and return to the cavern, but the energy source was strong and constant, enticing her forward.

One thing she did know for certain was that once she had passed across the lip which stood before her there would be no going back. Groping in the dark, her fingertips seemed to be telling her that the space beyond was slightly less constricted but also that it seemed to plane steeply away. If the slope ended in a narrow part of the passage or a sink hole she would never be able to push her way backwards up the incline. She would die a long, lonely and agonised death in the cold and utter darkness of mother Earth.

As the druid struggled to come to a decision a sudden feeling of intense fear threatened to overwhelm her, a terror which screamed in her mind and liquefied her innards. The calming effects of the gruel were beginning to wear off as the measured beating of the sibylla's drum became a memory, and Catumanda fought to retain her composure in the dark, airless, constricted throat of the passageway as the breath rasped from her in short, dog-like pants. It took every scrap of courage, but she balled her fists and pushed down the overwhelming terror that she would never escape this place, that the spirit which had lured her into this bottleneck had been malevolent and was even now preparing to snatch away her soul. Slowly, as the druid's self discipline reasserted itself, she cleared her mind and sought to make contact with her guide in a bid to allay her worst fears.

To her surprise she found that she was presented with the image of a young man. His hair was as dark and lustrous as any raven, but his natural beauty was marred by a latticework of angry red welts which crisscrossed his torso and legs, and as Catumanda watched, spellbound, he turned his deep dark eyes directly upon her. She was certain that it was sign from the gods that the man needed her help, and she had regained enough self control to realise that they would need her to survive this ordeal in order to carry out their wishes. She had been captivated by the depth of beauty and desperation writ large in the dark pools of the young man's eyes and, her decision reached, she clawed her way forward again. Soon she was balanced across the apex of the lip, the icy stone kissing her belly as she arched forward at the very fulcrum of balance. Splaying her legs against the smooth stone walls of the passageway she groped blindly forward in the crushing darkness.

Committed now, Catumanda slid her hands forward as she attempted to support the weight of her body, but as she did so her crane skin bag shot forward and crashed into her elbow, knocking it aside. Unsupported, the druid plunged forward into the abyss. A searing pain shot through her as her legs were flung up into the unforgiving rock above and she instinctively pulled them in. Immediately she was hurtling head first into the unknown. Whimpering with pain and terror she desperately flung her arms and legs wide as she attempted to slow or halt her headlong dash to oblivion, the nails tearing from her fingertips as she clawed desperately for a handhold.

Her spirits rose for a heartbeat as the shaft began to bottom out, her speed decreasing, but with a shocking suddenness her face slammed violently into the unyielding rock.

Trapped, inverted, in a world as black as jet, she remained conscious just long enough to spit a curse at the spirit which had drawn her here to her death.

11

Placing his hand lightly upon the soft downy muzzle of his mount, the warrior whispered encouragement as the horse threw its head and skittered nervously. Leaning forward he blew softly on its nose as his father had taught him to do so many years before, taking in the sweet smell of grass on its breath as the horse calmed.

Ranged around them, scores of concerned faces were turned their way, and the young Senone could read the fear in the eyes of the men as he smiled weakly back at them. Each man present knew that discovery and almost certain death lay only a snicker or a whinny away, but he still smiled instinctively as Albiomaros threw him a characteristic grin and a wink from his place in the line.

A rasping *caw* carried to the group, and they looked up as one as three enormous crows circled them high above before moving away to the South. It was a sign, they knew. Death was among them, perhaps the Morrigan and her black-hearted sisters Madness and Violence themselves, and as if in confirmation of their thoughts the scout ducked his head sharply and began to edge his way carefully back down the loose grey scree of the ridge. The man placed his hands and feet deliberately as he descended, spider-like, back to the floor of the ravine, and Solemis watched in approval as the Allobroge warrior leapt the last few feet and landed without a sound. Scampering across to Brennus he inclined his head respectfully and the warriors watched as he swept his arm, stabbing out to left and right as he made his report to the Senone chieftain who, his face a mask of concentration, nodded thoughtfully as he pulled at his moustache. The chieftain of the clans clapped the man on the shoulder, and he smiled and moved back across to the place where the Allobroge scouts had gathered as a pensive looking friend held out the reins of his mount.

Brennus grinned across to the waiting warriors and indicated that they mount up with a flick of his head. Each one of them knew the plan and they moved forward together, snaking their way out from the mouth of the small offshoot as they rejoined the main canyon. Once clear of the sheer walls the whoops and cries of the attacking force carried up to them from the valley below, and the formation wheeled together and took station on the towering bulk of their chieftain as they spilled out onto the plain.

Solemis quickly estimated the size of the attacking force as Albiomaros pushed his mount to his side. "Two hundred?"

Solemis shot his friend a smile and nodded. "About that; someone trying to make a name for himself."

The big Trinobante chuckled. "It is a shame we are so far away. I would have liked to see the look on his face when he notices that the door home had been slammed shut behind him!"

Solemis snorted and cast a glance to either side. Arrayed across the slope, a wall of riders now stood between the Helvetian raiders and safety and, with the trap now sprung,

Brennus abandoned the need for silence and called forward the men holding the carnyx. Solemis looked on proudly as the great bronze war horns of the Celtic people were thrust up into the cool Alpine air all along the line. Shoulder high to the tallest of men, each carnyx terminated in the gaping jaws of a fantastic creature, boars, dragons and eagles and Solemis watched as the familiar haunting cry broke from them. The rising and falling wail was added to by the staccato clatter of the loose wooden tongues which he had seen in the mouths of some of the carnyx, and amplified by the bowl of the valley side, the noise had an immediate effect on those below.

As the group of Helvetian riders checked their charge and began to mill in indecision, Solemis watched as the covers were thrown from the nearest wagons and groups of armed warriors began to tumble from their sides. Within moments, a solid wall of shields and lancea had replaced what had appeared to be the soft belly of the Senone column which stretched away for a dozen miles in each direction.

Brennus swept his sword in an arc above his head and called for the men at his side to follow him to victory as the cries of the war horns redoubled in intensity. Solemis urged his mount on with a squeeze of his knees and exchanged a grin with Albiomaros as they dashed forward into the valley. Hefting his shield in his left hand, Solemis gripped his lancea tightly as he transferred his gaesum throwing spear to his right and began to search for his target as the war stallion rapidly gathered speed on the grassy slope.

Ahead of them the Helvetii were recovering from their shock and beginning to reform on their leader. Solemis watched as the man, magnificent in a war shirt of the latest mail, wheeled his horse in a circle and quickly took stock of his position. Solemis risked a glance to either side and was gratified to see that mounted warriors were now converging on the enemy group from both ends of the column. The trap was sprung, and the Helvetian leader thrust his sword into the air and dug in his heels, his men reforming on him as he arrowed away, back up the slope towards a narrow pass which cut into the valley side.

Brennus wheeled the formation to the right, and Solemis could see that although they should intercept the enemy force before they reached the safety of the pass it would be a tightly run race. Surprised and disappointed, he wondered at the uncharacteristic oversight on the part of the Senone chieftain to leave even this small chance of escape open to the Helvetii. As the young Horsetail was about to look away, a party of Senone warriors walked their war horses casually out from the shadows and took up position across the head of the gulley. Solemis shouted in delight that this last slim chance of salvation was denied to the enemy and his gaze flicked across to his war leader, thundering on beneath his raven capped helm, in admiration.

The Helvetii plunged on regardless, desperate to use the power of their charge to punch through the encirclement, but Brennus was already upon them and Solemis drew back his arm and loosed the gaesum at the enemy chieftain. The spear flew true, its horsehair plume streaming comet-like in its wake, and Solemis felt a surge of elation as he realised that his first contribution to the fight would result in the death of the Helvetian leader. Suddenly the man to the chieftain's right glanced across, and sweeping his shield in a high arc, managed to get just enough contact on the plunging dart to deflect it up and over the head of its intended target. A wave of disappointment swept the young Senone before the blast of a carnyx at his side refocused his thoughts.

The Helvetii knew that even the slightest delay, the merest deflection from their path, would cause them to forego any chance of escape and they crouched low over their horses' necks and swept on.

Brennus crested a small rise and swung his broadsword at the head of the nearest enemy, as he smashed into the desperate riders and plunged into their midst. A heartbeat later Solemis became aware that he was roaring at the top of his voice, as he couched his lancea into his side and shifted his weight forward to resist the violent recoil of its strike. His warhorse flicked its bulk to one side as they reached the enemy and shot between them as he knew that it would; only men were mad enough to run full pelt into solid walls of brass, muscle and spears.

Despite the chaos which had enveloped his world, Solemis suddenly saw a giant Helvetian warrior snap into solid focus before him. Gritting his teeth with the effort his arm shot forward, and he watched in wonder as the silvery blade disappeared and buried itself deeply into the chest of the man. The violence of the strike sent a searing pain the length of his arm, and on into the muscles of his shoulder as the momentum of his stallion tore the lancea from his grasp. Solemis' mind just had time to fix an image of his victim, arms and head thrust upwards, a face contorted in agony, before he swept past, back into the maelstrom.

Once again his world became a blur of bronze, steel, leather and muscle as panic-stricken men and horses swirled around him in a madness of noise. Desperately transferring his remaining gaesum to his right hand Solemis stabbed at the shadowy figures which flashed before him, but each strike pierced only the dust filled air. And then suddenly he was through, and he hauled on his reins as he sought to turn his mount and rejoin the fray. Albiomaros appeared at his side laughing maniacally, the white of his teeth flashing like moons amid the blue swirls which decorated the Trinobante's face and body. He shouted above the din and held up the fingers of his right hand. "Three! How did you do?"

Solemis, despite the mayhem which surrounded them, shook his head at his best friend's happily grinning face. Albiomaros had not only taken the time to seek out a druid to anoint his face and body with a protective spell in woad, he had followed the way of his people by washing his hair and moustache in lime water. Fashioned into an elongated dome of almost rock hard spikes his hair now resembled a demented hedgehog, but the overall effect had been so intimidating that several children in the camp had simply run away at his approach, and people had gaped in awe as he passed them by. He shrugged and his face broke into a smile. "Just the one; he was huge though!" They shared a laugh and hefted their gaesum as they pulled the heads of their stallions around to renew their attack but, looking back, it was already clear that their part in the fight was over for that day.

The shrinking mass of Helvetian riders had been brought to bay near the head of the cut, and a roiling tide of Senone and Allobroge warriors was lapping at them, hacking into their ranks from every side. They could just make out the raven helm of Brennus amid the press, and Solemis indicated that his friend follow him to the top of a small hillock where they could witness the end.

A knot of riders had already collected there and Solemis called out joyfully as he noticed that Caturix was among them. Crixos' son threw him a grin and walked his mount across. Solemis anticipated the obvious question, and he pulled a face and raised a solitary finger in the air as his friend approached. Caturix' eyes widened in surprise. "You got among them? You lucky bastards!" He flicked a look across to Albiomaros and they laughed at his pained expression as the big man held up three fingers in reply. "We never got close, still," he hawked and spat, "the chase was good fun."

A roar came from the upper reaches of the gulley, and they glanced across to see what was obviously the head of the Helvetian war chief dancing a jig on the end of Brennus' distinctive broadsword. Albiomaros tugged at his ear as they watched the celebrations, before a thought occurred to him and he nudged Solemis with his elbow. "Let's go and find your huge opponent," he teased, "he should be easy to find."

The three of them led their horses back down into the gulley and halted as Solemis and Albiomaros tried to orientate themselves. An island of bodies lay where they had fallen as the charge of Brennus and his war band smashed into their flank. Casting a look up the defile, a lighter trail of bodies led away from them until the view ahead was obscured by a rocky outcrop. Already men were moving among them, stripping the dead of their war gear and dispatching the wounded to the Isles of the Dead.

Albiomaros called out, and Solemis looked back to see his friend hopping across between the fallen. "Here he is."

He looked up and whistled as he pulled the spear with its distinctive horsetail from the Helvetian warrior and held the gory blade aloft. "You weren't joking: he was a big bastard."

Caturix clapped Solemis on the shoulder and shot him a sly look. "Well done, little brother."

Solemis pulled a weary smile and arched his brow. Caturix had begun to call him little brother during the days they had spent scouting together on the way from Lugdunon because he was, as he explained, *'practically part of the clan already, from what my aunt tells me.'* Obviously Aia's quick grope at the woodpile had not been as stealthy as she had hoped, and her brother had delighted in reminding Solemis of the fact at every opportunity, especially after he had discovered how much it had irritated him.

Albiomaros tossed the spear across and pulled the Helvetian corpse up by his hair. “Do you want to take this?”

Solemis nodded and unsheathed his sword as he made his way across. Albiomaros held the head at arms length and Solemis felt the heavy blade bite through muscle and bone alike as he removed it from his opponent's torso with one powerful sweep.

“You'll be wanting this too.” Albiomaros reached down and retrieved a magnificent gold torc from where it had slipped to the ground from the severed neck. Tossing it across, he nodded appreciatively as Caturix snatched it from the air and fitted it around Solemis' own neck. “It suits you brother. Wear it with pride.”

Albiomaros pushed the warrior's headless body over with the sole of his boot, and let out a cry as a bright flash caught his eye. Reaching down he picked up the object and rubbed its surface on his sleeve before holding it out; narrowing his eyes and fixing his face with a scowl as he regarded his reflection. “What a fierce bastard I am, it is no wonder that the Helvetii were riding so hard to get away!” Grinning, he hopped across the body strewn floor of the gulley with great exaggerated strides, passing the hand mirror across to Solemis as he landed beside him with a thump. “I think that it would be wasted on us,” he said with laughter dancing in his eyes. “Do *you* know anyone who might appreciate such a beautiful thing?”

Caturix gave Solemis a playful dig and nodded in agreement. “She *would* love it.”

Solemis turned the mirror over in his hand as he admired the decorative design on the rear. Etched and chased into a series of swirls and circles, the body of the mirror was held by means of a handle of twisted bronze. Flipping it over, Solemis laughed in wonder as he saw his face clearly for the very first time. The waxy, golden surface of the bronze had been highly polished, and Solemis snorted as the faces of his two friends hovered into view at his shoulder. He had, like most people, only ever seen his reflection on the surface of still water and the detail revealed by the deep sheen was breathtaking, and, he had to admit to himself, a little disappointing. He had always imagined himself to be handsome in a rough, manly sort of way, but it would appear that the gods had not been so kind to him after all.

He saw Caturix' mouth move in the reflection as he spoke again. "My mother has one very like it, it is one of her most treasured possessions."

Solemis watched his friend's reflection as he reached out and took the handle. "Here, watch this."

Solemis reluctantly let go and looked on as Aia's brother held the mirror by its handle and, turning it once more onto its back, let it swing upside down. "What can you see now?"

Solemis and Albiomaros studied the patterns as Caturix smiled knowingly at their side. Eventually both men had to admit that they could see nothing obvious among the polished swirls and hatched etchings which littered the back of the mirror other than the familiar triskele, the looping triple spiral which adorned many items in the Celtic world and signified the interconnecting worlds of men, the afterlife and rebirth.

Caturix, delighted that he would get to reveal the secrets of the design to the friends, explained. "This small loop at the base of the handle is used to suspend the mirror when not in use, so obviously for the majority of the time people see it it is hanging this way, with the circle of the back of the mirror at the bottom." He threw them the faintest of smiles. "Now watch." Caturix moved his finger slowly through the patterns as he began to trace the outline of a feminine face framed by a series of long flowing trestles, and Solemis and Albiomaros laughed in wonder and admiration at the level of skill employed by the engraver. Solemis turned back to Caturix and grinned. "You are right, *brother;* she *will* love it."

THE SUN WAS BEGINNING to set as the three friends rode back towards the column from the scene of the day's triumph. Ahead of them, stretching away for miles in each direction, the still waters of Lake Lemannus shone a burnished gold as the fiery orb sank lower in the West. To the South lay the torn skyline which marked the peaks of the Alpes, their next destination, now only a few days away. Once there the Allobroge warriors would guide them to the mouth of the Beninus Pass and return to Genawa, laden with gifts for their help and tribute for their chieftain. Brennus had allowed the Allobroge scouts their pick from the spoils of victory, to honour their chieftain and reward him for the aid and goodwill which he had shown to the Senones during their transit of his lands. He had, after all, sent a messenger hurrying to warn Brennus the moment that he had received word of the whereabouts of the Helvetian war party, and his warriors had fought as well as any Senone in the skirmish.

Solemis watched as the first of the wagons wallowed down to the lakeside with all the steadiness of a ship in a swell. They carried the weapons and armour which had been stripped from the bloodstained bodies of the Helvetii and, flicking a look across, he could make out the party of druids who would officiate over the ritual destruction and deposition of the spoils of war by Brennus and the clan chieftains in the waters of the lake that evening. The Allobroge had clearly been gratified that the Senone chieftain had chosen to honour the goddess of their lake in thanks for the victory, and they had promised to sacrifice for the safe passage through the passes for his people in return.

The sky to their rear was already a black chaos of crows as the Morrigan led her sisters to the feast which men had provided, and bright petals of flame began to lick the air amid the corralled wagons as the people prepared to celebrate their victory. As the warriors began to return, elated from the fight, a ululating body of women came forward from the camp to welcome the return of their men.

Spying Aia and her mother among them, Albiomaros and Caturix hung back as Solemis led them home, the gore smeared head of his kill held proudly aloft on the point of his spear.

Aia came up and rested her head proudly on his thigh as the horse walked slowly on. He stroked her hair lovingly and, as she looked up, he bent low and they shared their first open kiss as the celebrations swirled around them.

DEVORIX RESTED his palm on the lip of the fissure and glanced back. Diocaros, his friend of many winters, pulled a wan smile and raised a hand in farewell from the shadow of the nemeton as the old druid grinned and nodded in reply. The portly guardian of the shrine had always suspected that he would be the last to lay his eyes on the old druid, and so it was.

Casting a final look back, beyond his friend to the canopy of greens and the cloud studded sky beyond, Devorix swept the area with a look for the last time. The summer was full and the spirits of the forest were drowsy, drunk on the time of plenty. Like all druids, Devorix knew the wild places for what they really were, a vast living thing of many parts, some large like the trees but others too small for the human eye to see. Only a man who had climbed to the very pinnacle of understanding could sense the mood of the forest, and he had been one such man. Buzzing with vitality and vigour in spring, roaring in autumn and curled around itself, sleeping away the dark and unproductive days of winter, the sylvan world reflected that of men in so many ways the old man reflected with a heavy sigh.

Turning back, he ducked inside and squeezed his way between the furrowed walls of rock towards the very wellspring of the Sequana. He would not return.

12

Euphoria threatened to overwhelm her senses as she stood and gazed out across a gently undulating field of pale yellow barley, its peaks and hollows splashed by islands of poppies the colour of blood. A soft breeze, warm and soothing, caressed her body as it washed across the barley in waves. Catumanda smiled as she reached down and brushed the palm of her hand across the tips of the ripened ears. She had always pictured *Annwn* this way, and felt a deep sense of joy that she had found it to be so. Turning slowly she saw that the field stretched away into the distance, a gently swaying sea of yellow beneath the perfect cerulean dome of the sky.

A flash of colour caught her eye, and the druid was surprised to see the figure of a man pushing his way through the stalks towards her. For a heartbeat she thought that she was being welcomed to the underworld by Cernunnos himself, but she quickly realised that she was mistaken. Cernunnos, Lord of Animals, took his form from the stag, that most noble of forest beasts. Tall and lithe, his head was always crowned by a magnificent set of antlers. The figure which was advancing on Catumanda was shorter and far more heavy set, and although his head was crowned by a set of stag horns they were far less impressive than she would have expected. As the man came closer, Catumanda became increasingly convinced that this was no god. Although squat and sturdily built, this was clearly a mortal like herself, despite the heavy set brow and wide fleshy nose. The man wore a cloak of deerskin and his wide friendly face was covered by what appeared to be an ochre coloured paste, cut by a band of white about the level of his eyes. Catumanda returned the smile and walked forward to greet the man she had decided must be a hunter.

"I am Catumanda. Are you here to welcome me to the underworld?"

To her surprise a deep roll of laughter came from the man, and her heart lifted as she recognised affection reflected in his gaze. As he came up he reached forward, slipping a hand inside her own as he began to lead the bemused druid towards a nearby hollow. Catumanda attempted to strike up a conversation, but the hunter strode resolutely on. "I died below ground. Were you killed on the hunt?"

Her guide turned his eyes upon her, and Catumanda was shocked to see that red, livid flames were flickering deep within them. She was about to attempt another question when the man placed the palm of his hand in the middle of Catumanda's back and pushed hard. Taken by surprise the druid shot forward, gasping in shock and horror as the ground before her opened up and swallowed her down.

CATUMANDA WAS COLD, colder than she had ever felt in her life.

As she began to regain consciousness she slowly became aware that she was not quite dead after all. Rolling her tongue around the inside of her mouth only resulted in the accumulation of a gummy paste of blood and small pieces of what she hoped was grit from the fall, and not the remains of her teeth. With the return to full awareness came a pain greater than she had ever known. Her skin had paid a terrible price as she had been funnelled down to this place, and a gasp of agony escaped her lips as she tried to move. To her intense disappointment she was still very much alive, and she felt hot tears of dismay run down the side of her bruised and battered head as the joys of *Annwn* faded.

She tried to turn aside to spit out the iron tasting pulp which was filling her mouth, but found that she appeared to be wedged tightly into the base of the shaft. Pursing her lips she squirted the foul tasting mixture along her chin, as her iron will began to reassert itself and she began to take stock of her situation. Her shoulders appeared to be jammed inside a choke point in the shaft but her head remained free, so it would seem that it must open up again on the other side. A small flame of hope flickered into life inside her, as she realised that there was a possibility that she could yet force her body through. Thinking clearly now despite the pain, Catumanda realised that she could use the echo made by her voice to help her determine the size of the cavity beyond, and she steeled herself as she let out a cry. The sound remained close to her head, almost as if she had placed it inside a bowl, and she bit down on her lip as she sought to overcome the crushing sense of disappointment. Realising now that there was no way forward and certain that it would be an impossible task to shuffle back up the shaft inverted, even if she could extricate herself from the place in which she was trapped, Catumanda felt the brief spark of hope wither and die.

Even if she had ever doubted its existence, which of

course she had not, her brief experience of the joys of *Annwn* had if anything left her eager to return, mad hunter or not. The knowledge of what lay before her when she departed this life, and the pain and cold which she now felt led the druid to a decision. The air deep inside the body of Mother Earth was already thin, barely enough to sustain life. She always carried candles inside her crane skin bag, they were an essential aid for many parts of her craft, and naturally, flints for lighting them. Catumanda reached across with her hand and rummaged inside her bag. If she was going to cross to *Annwn* here she wished to see the place of her passing. Man had always feared the darkness but, despite her earlier panic attack, Catumanda now felt at peace. She knew and had accepted that this was her time to return to the underworld and she would use the candles to hasten it if she could. Once alight the candles would quickly consume the air in her little chamber and she would, with luck, merely drift away as if in sleep.

Grasping a candle she laid it carefully on her upturned chest before reaching back inside to remove the bowl of Piso's skull which she wedged between her side and the wall of the shaft. Gasping with pain and exertion, Catumanda reached back inside the bag and scraped around in the corners as she sought out the strands of dried grass and other detritus which she knew always collected there, despite her best efforts at keeping it clean. Soon she had transferred the tinder dry scrapings to the bowl, and with a grunt of effort she managed to bring both hands together and strike the flints. The roof of the passage was just high enough to allow Catumanda to raise her head slightly and sight between her breasts as she did so, and she blinked as the sparks revealed her surroundings to her for the first time since she had left the first cavern.

She lay in a small chamber with her bloodied and lacerated legs pointing away from her at a steep angle. Luckily she had come to rest on her back, otherwise she would have been forced back on herself, in all probability breaking her spine and leaving her in indescribable pain. Despite this one piece of good fortune, the momentary glimpse of her surroundings confirmed to her that it would be an impossibility that she could harbour any hopes of pushing her way back up the way she had entered the chamber. The shaft was far too steep, and there was simply too little room to turn her body even if she managed to extricate herself from the choke point which held her shoulders in a vice-like grip.

Lowering her head again she concentrated on striking the flints above Piso's skull. Constricted by the walls of the tunnel it seemed to take an age for the tinder to catch, but to her intense relief it suddenly flared into life, bathing the area in light for what the druid realised must be the first time ever. Reaching up she took the candle from her chest and held the wick above the flames. She knew that she must move quickly or her one chance of a swift and easier death would slip away from her. The scrapings from her bag would burn for little more than a few moments, so she was overjoyed when the wick took the flame almost immediately.

As the light from the bowl began to dim and the darkness reclaimed the outer passageway, Catumanda carefully turned the candle in her hand and transferred it to her mouth. Twisting her head as far as she could she gently let it slip to the ground near her head. To her intense relief the candle came to rest wedged between the wall and a small loose rock, the precious flame well clear of the dust and grime of the floor which could have extinguished it in a heartbeat. The light from without had finally flickered and died, and Catumanda sent a small prayer of thanks to the gods that she had managed to complete her plan in the short space of time available to her.

The sudden return of light was painful after so long underground, and she turned her head away, squinting to protect her eyes from the glare. As they grew accustomed to the light Catumanda reeled as a fist of shock and disbelief gripped her. There, within an arm's reach of her face, lay the reason for her journey.

CATUMANDA CLOSED her eyes tightly and squeezed away the tears which were forming there. The sudden reintroduction of sight to her senses had shocked her more than she could have imagined, and she lay there afraid to look again in case they had played a cruel trick on her. Bracing herself for an agony of disappointment she slowly opened her eyes once more and attempted to focus on the images which had been revealed by the candlelight, and her heart raced as a series of indistinct images appeared before her. The scenes were covered by a fine layer of dust and were obviously very old, archaic even, and Catumanda blew on them in an attempt to reveal the finer details. Immediately the small space which enclosed her head disappeared in a billowing cloud of grey, gritty dust, filling her eyes and causing her to cough repeatedly. As she blinked away the grit from her eyes, the druid prayed with all her might to the gods and spirits that the delicate flame on the candle would survive the dust storm which had engulfed them both. There was no chance of relighting it should it succumb to either the dust or the effects of her choking cough, and she cursed herself for the fool that she was. To come so far and through so much to fail on the very cusp of discovery would very likely be the final act which would tip her mind over the edge into insanity.

As Catumanda lay with her eyes closed and attempted to regain control of her breathing, the red light which danced across the face of her eyelids slowly began to brighten and regain its former steadiness. Blinking away the final pieces of grit from her eyes, Catumanda squinted up at the wall before her. Thankfully most of the dust had now settled and, mindful now of the danger posed by even the slightest movement on her part, she attempted to retain her composure as the images were finally revealed.

A quick glance along the line of the wall told her that she was faced by five scenes. Four of these, to her utter joy, represented the first solid representations of the shadowy dreams which had plagued her sleeping hours since she had been a child. The fifth she noticed with a jolt, was clearly an image of the raven haired man in her earlier vision. Each picture was the work of a man, albeit one who had lived in the distant past. This fact was reinforced by the splayed outline of the man's huge hand which seemed to have been created by spitting or flicking an ochre coloured dye as it was held against the wall. Catumanda resisted the temptation to take in all of the images in one fevered sweep and concentrated on the first.

A young boy of perhaps six or seven winters sat with his back turned towards her on an arc of green dye. Although his face was not visible he seemed attentive and alert, as if he were watching or waiting for something. Catumanda realised that this boy, sat atop his hill, would mark the first step on her journey and she fixed the image in her mind.

Moving on, the following image was of a monster's skull. An elongated oval in shape, the heavy set structure reminded her of the skull of a bear which she had seen gracing the door frame of a roundhouse in Camulodunon, but this was clearly from a different beast. All the jawbones of such man-killers as bears and wolves that she had seen always contained rows of flat, grinding teeth behind the fangs for crunching the bones of their victims. This skull however contained only the wicked, knife-like, slashing and tearing teeth. She had seen the jawbone of a sea monster fishermen called a shark once, a curiosity brought by a traveller from the south-west, and she wondered if this dream was linked to a sea journey. Ruffos' dream had certainly indicated that she was to leave Albion and travel across the sea, and she feared that the monster must be part of this.

The following scene appeared to show the billowing white cloud of Ruffos' dream suspended above a smear of dark brown. Although the picture had faded over time, Catumanda thought that she could still make out a small eye at the front of the smear and wondered whether it was meant to represent a giant snake.

The next image was unmistakable and unforgettable. It had always been the final shadowy scene in her recurring nightmares, the clearest and most troublesome of all, and she grudgingly acknowledged it as one would an old enemy. It had always caused her to wake, sweating and panting in the early hours, and the sight of the flame topped mountain was finally revealed to her in all its detail. The huge brown peak flecked by patches of white rose high above small fields and smaller white houses. From the top of the mountain great gouts of flame and smoke rose high into the air as rivers of living fire streamed down its flanks. She had always thought that the scene represented the place of her passing but now, after her vision of the dark haired man had been confirmed here, she realised that she must have been mistaken.

Her gaze moved across to the fifth and final image and her heart leapt as she looked again on his dark features. The face was still slashed by red but Catumanda looked beyond this temporary disfigurement to the beauty which lay beyond. Buoyed up by the thought that this man must play a great part in the story of her life she attempted to wriggle a little further into the cavity to study his face in greater detail. As she did so her legs slipped down from the throat of the tunnel with a bone jarring crash. Immediately, the sharp daggers of pain which had burrowed deep into the small of her back disappeared as she was able to stretch her freezing and battered body. Weary, bloodied and chilled, Catumanda was slow to realise the importance of what had just occurred. It was as if the spirits which inhabited this place had shown her the way out now that she had uncovered their long hidden secret, and she moved her legs gingerly in an ever increasing circle, her hopes soaring as the movement revealed that the newly revealed passageway was easily large enough to accommodate her body.

With a final lingering look at the ancient markings, Catumanda hooked her feet either side of the new opening and began to prise herself clear of the blind corner into which she had tumbled. With a final heave she was free, and she flexed her body, grimacing as the blood flow was restored painfully into chilled, weary muscles. She must return to the surface soon she knew, otherwise she could still die of cold. The future which had been revealed to her would only be one possible future, nothing was ever certain in a life, and her mind was beginning to reel from the accumulated effects of the gruel which she had ingested, the weariness of her battered body and the mind numbing cold of the cave.

As movement returned to her she reached back and retrieved the candle from the hole. Holding it before her she pushed on, out of the space which she had thought to be her tomb.

. . .

To Catumanda's utter relief the passageway which led from the chamber slowly opened out ahead of her. The increase in space allowed her to continue burning the candle without fear, but she carefully shielded the flame with the cup of her hand as she inched her way along, checking it every few paces to ensure that it continued to burn with a healthy hue. She had been warned before she went below ground that the presence of bad spirits could sometimes be detected there by carefully watching the actions of a naked flame. If the flame suddenly flared or took on a bluish tinge it was a sure sign that malevolent spirits were close at hand. Miners had also advised the druids that often spirits lay close to the ground and sucked any air from that space as men rested there. It was imperative that anyone deep underground keep their head as high up in the tunnel as possible and only rest on high shelves. Miners who ignored this rule had drifted off to sleep and their friends had found it impossible to wake them again.

The sounds made by her scrambling progress soon began to echo back to her, and from its tone Catumanda could tell that a larger open space was just ahead. Soon she had squeezed through the narrow scar which marked the end of the passageway, and was staring in wonder at the scene which presented itself to her. Although the feeble light thrown out from the candle was barely sufficient to light her way ahead, Catumanda could see that this new chamber extended to the height of two tall men and seemed to stretch away into the darkness to each side of her. Slipping down onto the floor of the cavern she felt the mild tingling sensation in her left hand which she had experienced on first entering the cave system from the wicker hut, and she smiled happily at the realisation that the spirits were still at her side, helping to guide her back.

Very soon the passageway narrowed again and climbed

upwards as the sounds of the storm outside began to filter down to the weary druid. And then suddenly she was at the mouth of the cave and, squeezing past the last boulders which obstructed her passage, Catumanda emerged to find herself near a rain lashed beach. Despite the storm raging about her, she turned her face to the sky and drank in the sweet fresh air as she gave thanks to the spirits for her deliverance from the place which she had so long thought to be her tomb. Glancing up, she saw that the lights of the druids' buildings lay away to the right and she made her way towards them. The pathway, illuminated by the lightning bolts which flashed and crackled overhead, was wide and clear and she was soon on the outskirts of the settlement.

Catumanda made her way across to the cliff face and climbed the final incline to the place where she knew the hut containing the druids was located.

Although she had no idea how long she had remained unconscious underground, the rhythmic beat of drumming still carried to her from the tiny cabin as she approached the door. Reaching out, she threw it open with the last of her strength as a mighty gust of wind tore it from her grasp, ripping it from its hinges and casting it aside. At that very moment Toranos, God of Thunder, hurled a great lightning bolt which snaked across the sky as the night was split by a thunderous crash. For a single heartbeat all was as light as the brightest day, and Catumanda had the momentary glimpse of faces turned to her, their expressions frozen in a mask of horror. As the light extinguished itself there came a high pitched scream from within, and a soft thud carried to her as the thunder trailed away and the drumming came to an abrupt end.

13

Pulling at the reins he guided his horse across to the vantage point. A knot of riders had already gathered there, and Solemis came to a halt and dismounted among them as Albiomaros appeared at his side. Loosening their trews they took the opportunity to relieve the pressure on their bladders as they gazed back along the trail in wonder.

The Senone column had passed by now and the roadway which scarred the valley side like a dark grey stain was returning to its slumber. Eighty-thousand people with their accompanying animals and wagons had cut a swathe through a pass which rarely handled more than a hundred horses at any one time, and Solemis smiled to himself as he imagined the spirits which lived in this place breathing a sigh of relief that they had finally passed through. As he finished and adjusted his clothing, Solemis raised his eyes and drank in the scene.

Below them the wide valley stretched across to the indistinct peaks of the Jora. It was here that they had annihilated the Helvetian war party the previous month, and his hand moved instinctively to his neck as he caressed the heavy gold torc which he had won through force of arms that day. Between their lofty perch and the faraway peaks, the silver-blue ribbon of Lake Lemannus swept majestically away to distant Genawa. A high yelp drew their gaze upwards, and the Senones grinned and pointed as they watched the flight of a lone golden eagle, soaring and calling to its mate on powerful outstretched wings.

A clatter of hooves came from the road, and they turned as the last of the Allobroge warriors cantered back along the roadway. They had led Brennus and the people to the brink of the great Pass of Beninus and, laden with fine gifts, they were now starting out on their own long journey, back to the comforts of their distant oppidum. The warriors of the rear-guard quickly retrieved shields and spears from their stallions and rushed to line the roadside as their friends swept by, beating them together and calling their war cries as they passed. The Allobroge raised their own gaesum in salute as they thundered through in a cloud of grey dust, calling out their own battle cries and grinning insanely at their new allies.

Albiomaros stepped to his side and sniffed as the Allobroge riders swept around a bend and disappeared from view in a brawl of yapping madness. "That's that then."

Solemis turned to his friend and shot him a grin. He had spent his own formative years at foster among Albiomaros' people in far away Albion and he had enjoyed his years there immensely. The Trinobantes were a laconic people, not given to unnecessary displays of emotion, unlike the members of his own tribe who were sometimes a little excitable he had to admit to himself. He sometimes missed his days there and he was glad that his big friend, his blood genos, had decided to remain with the clan after the period of his own fosterage with the Senones had been completed.

A voice called to them from the roadway, and they looked across to see that Crixos and the others had already mounted up and were waiting for them. "When you two are finished admiring the view we will continue with the migration."

A rumble of laughter came from the group, and Solemis and Albiomaros each flashed a self-conscious smile as they remounted and walked their stallions across. As Crixos, straight faced, pulled the head of his horse around and led the men south, Solemis took a last look at the valley as he chuckled at the chieftain's deadpan comment and wondered. Perhaps Aia's father had been to foster in Albion too?

SOLEMIS CAUGHT the worried look which passed between Crixos and Caturix and felt a kick of anxiety. They were now in serious trouble and it was becoming obvious, even to the dimmest or most optimistic of the people that lives were going to be lost, quite possibly a very large number of lives, and soon.

The first flakes of snow had fallen among them the previous day, as the tail of the great column had laboured over the head of the pass and begun the slow descent to the Plain of Bodencus. At first the people had looked to the sky in disbelief and, despite the excitement of the children, a deep fear had gripped all but the most unimaginative adults.

The Pass of Beninus ran down in a series of tight switch-backs, and the wagons and people had folded back on them-selves as they moved down towards the distant plain. While this had helped with the warriors ability to defend them, their progress had been slowed to little more than a few miles per day. Now the weather had turned and, caught in the open, the entire migration was at serious risk of catastrophe. Unable to erect tents or shelters in the constricted pass, the Senones had spent the previous night huddled together beneath cloaks and blankets in what shelter they could find.

The flurry of snow had been brief, but the following morning they had awoken to a thick covering of hoarfrost. Their world had been swallowed by a veil of dense white vapour, which squatted in every valley and swallowed every peak. The roadway, which had been rutted and rock strewn already after the passage of so many feet, hooves and wheels, had been frozen into a latticework of troughs and razor sharp ridges by the action of the ice. Already one of the wagons had become trapped within a deep scar which had gone completely unseen beneath the light covering of snow, and despite the desperate actions of those nearby, it had tumbled over the edge taking its cargo of people with it. They had rushed to the lip and watched as the wagon had spun away, rapidly increasing in speed as it whipped and bounded over and over, scattering bloodied bodies across the mountainside like a farmer sowing a spring crop. The wagon had quickly been swallowed by the veil of mist, but the screams of the injured and the cries of broken children had drifted up and added their own horror to the melancholy scene.

All forward movement had ceased as rescuers had scrambled down to the injured, but pitifully few had returned with the living. Caturix had been one of those who had descended into the boulder field and, visibly upset, he had confided to his friends that his knife had eased the journey to the Isles of the Dead for more than one of the badly injured.

Soon after this disaster cries carried up to the men of the rearguard from further down the track, and the ghostly shapes of riders had slowly hardened into the forms of Brennus and several members of his cantref. The men watched sullenly as Crixos walked across to welcome their chieftain as he came up to them. Brennus dismounted and, letting his reins drop to the ground, nodded pensively as he walked across to the edge of the road. Crixos waited respectfully as Brennus stared down at the broken bodies which lay scattered about the mountainside. Finally the chieftain shook his head slowly and turned back: "ice?"

Crixos nodded in reply and kicked at the place where the wagon had slithered over the lip. "It got itself caught in a hidden rut and just took off. There was nothing anyone could do to halt its slide once it had gathered momentum on the slope, it would have just taken them with it."

Brennus ran his boot along the tracks which led over the edge and sighed at the amount of polished ice underfoot. He grimaced and cast a worried look around the pass, rubbing a hand slowly across his chin as he thought. Finally he walked across to the nearest wagon and levered himself onto the tailboard.

The people there shuffled up to make room for their chieftain, and Brennus called across to his men to distribute the fresh bread which he had brought up with him. Taking a loaf he tore a piece for himself and handed the rest to a nearby girl with a smile. Casting about, Brennus called out for everyone to come close as he casually broke his fast among the people of his tribe.

Solemis and Albiomaros walked across as people left their wagons and gathered around. Soon Brennus was surrounded by a sea of expectant faces and he cleared his throat and addressed them. "That was a bad start to the day, but what has gone by is in the past. We all knew that such things were likely before we set off from the North. If Toranos wishes to test the Senones he will not find us wanti-ng." He shrugged as the faces crowded in and raised his gaze to the sky. The clouds were becoming visible high overhead, and it was clear that the mist which had smothered them was slowly clearing away. Brennus looked back and spoke again. "Do we wait here until the sun breaks through and melts the ice? What happens if it is still too cold?"

He glanced around the crowd as they began to exchange looks of surprise and shock. Most people were not accustomed to being asked for their thoughts by chieftains and Solemis watched as many of them began to lower their gaze, but a few were made of sterner stuff and a woman raised her chin and spoke. "Just push on as quickly as we can. If the snow returns we will become trapped here and we will all die, but we all knew the risks when we left the north. If it is my fate to die here, that is a matter for the gods to decide." Brennus nodded his thanks and raised his brow as he looked for further contributions from the crowd. Once one person had spoken, others were emboldened and they added their thoughts to the debate. Slowly a clear consensus grew that the dangers of remaining on the mountain far outweighed those of pressing ahead, ice or no ice, and it was clear that the people were prepared to risk further losses for the survival of the tribe. Finally Brennus nodded and held his hand up for quiet. The crowd fell silent as they waited for their leader's ruling on how they would proceed, but as he opened his mouth to speak he was interrupted by Solemis who jumped and clicked his fingers as he cried out. "Salt!"

Something about the situation had disturbed a deep-seated memory, and he had been racking his mind ever since the accident. Solemis clapped his thigh gleefully as a scene from his time at foster in Albion finally forced its way to the fore. All faces were turned to him as Brennus looked across in surprise, but Solemis grinned back as he began to explain his outburst. "Salt melts ice and snow. I have seen it!"

Albiomaros at his side clapped him on the shoulder, and as Solemis turned to him they exclaimed together. *Searix!*

Both men laughed, and Solemis turned back towards a nonplussed Brennus to explain. "Searix was the name of a salt trader who was based at Camulodunon in Albion. I was at foster there and Albiomaros is from the oppidum. He was a friend of Andalos, Albiomaros' father, and he used to take us to visit the salt pans which line the coast there. Salt is freely available in those parts, and many traders carry a bag of spoiled salt, bloodstained and the like, to sprinkle beneath a wheel which has lost its grip due to ice." He shot Brennus a look of triumph as he continued. "If we remove the meats from the barrels and pack them in ice, we can use the salt to clear a path for the wagons. We will only have to do it once if each wagon keeps to the same path, there should be enough, and anyway," he paused and cast a glance skywards, "it does seem like the fog is lifting little by little." They all followed his gaze across to the West as the fang-like peak which the Allobroge had called The White Lady began to emerge from the gloom, its southern face bronzed by the midmorning sun.

Brennus smiled and nodded. "Everyone, do as he says." He slipped from the wagon and dusted the seat of his trews before glancing back with a grin. "Well done. A way off the mountain and double helpings of meat this evening. You are making quite a name for yourself, Solemis."

As evening fell the path began to broaden as the tail of the Senone column drew closer to the Plain of Bodencus. Leaving the road the wagons rolled across to the bank of a fast flowing gill and made camp as the warriors of the rear-guard walked their mounts across, stripping saddles and bridles from the animals as they prepared to corral them for the night. Solemis tore a handful of long grass from the bank, sweeping it along the sweat stained flanks of his horse as he reflected on the journey they had just made.

Almost a month had passed since they had crested the saddleback which marked the northern entry to the Beninus Pass and began to zigzag their way down towards the plain. The icy conditions underfoot had lasted for several days but good progress had been maintained due to the supply of salt. One of the craftsmen in the column had approached Crixos and offered to make up a team of men to pound some of the smaller stones which littered the roadside into a shingle, and this had been added to the salt to extend the supply and increase the grip beneath the wheels. The mixture had been a great success, and very soon they had moved down from the higher altitudes and put the snow line behind them.

Weariness, illness and plain bad luck had still added to the numbers of dead which the Senones would leave behind beneath small stone cairns to mark their passing, but this had been expected. The people, and Brennus, knew that they had Solemis and the salt traders of Albion to thank for the survival of so many of their number.

It was early autumn now, and the leaves on the trees which were beginning to appear in the more sheltered spots of the pass were tinged with reds and browns as the seasons rolled on. Solemis paused from his grooming and stared back up at the jagged peaks of the Alpes as the horse drank greedily from the cool waters. The ragged walls of rock stared back impassively, silent and massive, a brooding presence as permanent and awe inspiring as the gods themselves. But something *had* changed; not to the Alpes of course but within him, he now realised. Although it had gone unsaid, particularly among the warriors of the tribe, they had approached the mountains with a sense of fear and dread, almost as if they were challenging the gods by attempting such a feat. They had not only conquered those doubts, but Solemis himself had played a large part in that success. His reputation had soared to new heights in the mountains, both during the fight with the Helvetii and by his contribution to the successful transit of the pass.

Tomorrow, he and Albiomaros were to leave Crixos' band and rejoin the Horsetails near the spearhead of the column as they moved down into the lands of the Insubri. Tonight, he would drink cervesia with the men of Crixos' band and then, he smiled, maybe he would drink a little more.

CONNOS GUIDED his mount along the crest of the ridge and halted at his favourite viewpoint. Swinging himself from the saddle he looped the reins around a branch and walked across to the fallen trunk, lowering himself down upon it with a grunt of effort. The last few inches had been more of a half-controlled drop, and he laughed as he recognised that maybe the previous year had taken more out of his old hide than he cared to admit. Still, he mused as he reflected on the events of the great migration, it had been the making of his son. Solemis had left the lands of their ancestors little more than a boy, but less than a year later he had arrived at their new home a proven man and a warrior of reputation.

They had poured out from the Alpes and followed the headwaters of the River Bodencus towards the great oppidum of the Insubri at Mediolanum. At first they had been surprised that there had been no welcome from their fellow Celts, but as day followed day with no sign of a reaction from their supposed hosts a feeling of unease had begun to seep into the minds of the Senones. Outlying settlements had been either abandoned or populated by incredulous clan members who clearly had not been expecting almost eighty-thousand people to pass by their gate that autumn. Brennus had visited the clan chiefs of those which *had* remained, and it had soon become clear that the people had had no inkling that they were about to receive so many 'guests.' Their food supplies all but depleted, the situation again seemed grim, and Brennus had led a party directly to Mediolanum and had managed to negotiate the delivery of supplies from the astonished chieftain there with the promise of mediation between the Senone leader and the chieftains of the Taurini and Cenomani who bordered his lands to the South.

Even more worryingly, the representative of the Greek colony of Massalia at the oppidum had denied all knowledge of Greek involvement in the migration of the Senones. Fortunately the various tribes of Celts who inhabited the Plain of Bodencus had come together to supply the Senones with food as they passed through their lands to settle further south on the rich lands which lay between the mountains known as the Apeninnus and the Adriaticum Sea. It had been a small matter to eject the Etruscan and Umbrian peoples who lived on those lands, and Brennus had shared out the best lands of his new Chiefdom among those of his followers who he decided best merited them.

Connos reached forward and plucked up a small twig from among the leaf mould and idly stripped the bark back with his fingernail, flicking it at a stone as it came away. It had been, he decided, a good year. To cap it all the formal betrothal of his only son to the daughter of Crixos had taken place, and they were to wed in the spring. The union would not only add a fine young woman to the clan, but bring an important alliance between her people and those of her new *gwr*.

The chieftain of the Horsetails looked out across the valley and down towards the distant coast. The entire vale had been a reward to the clan for their loyalty and efforts on behalf of Brennus and the people during the migration, and Connos was in no doubt that the various contributions made by his son had been the primary cause of the honour.

Pausing only to mark the three nights of Samonios which ushered out the dark months of the year, the stone buildings of the previous owners had been cleared and roundhouses constructed in their place. Within weeks of their arrival the Horsetails were masters of their valley.

A soft footfall carried to Connos and he gave a gentle snort. He had told his champion, Cauros, that he was quite old enough to ride alone in the hills overlooking his own land, but he had half expected the man to follow along anyway. Connos started to turn, and he had just begun to flash a welcoming smile at his old friend as the sword cleaved his skull.

14

She giggled with delight as her friend reached the end of his tale again; turning to Ruffos, Catumanda threw him a cheeky smile. "Go on, one last time, just the bit at the end."

Ruffos sighed wearily. He had enjoyed the tale told by the druid from the hut that night as much as any, but even he was beginning to grow weary of retelling it to his friend. "You cook tonight?"

Catumanda chuckled and nodded as Ruffos resigned himself to the inevitable. "Vernogenos said that they were on the point of abandoning their vigil. You had been gone for several hours, and they were running short of chervil and garlic to burn which was always a sign that the druid was unlikely to return. Several men in the past had simply disappeared underground. Powerful spirits live in the Earth and you had gone below ground without the aid of a spirit guide." He looked across and crinkled his brow disapprovingly before continuing his tale. "Besides he said, they had been listening to the beating of a drum for hours on end and the poor old sibylla, whose best years were already long behind her, was practically passing out from her exertions."

Ruffos lowered his voice and made expansive sweeps with his hands as he approached the climax of the tale. In truth he enjoyed telling the story almost as much as hearing it himself, and he was already planning the embellishments which he would add for the benefit of his clansmen at home. Family gatherings always needed a fresh supply of stories and adventures, and he knew that the events which had already happened to them on their journey would not only increase his standing in the community, but ensure him a ready supply of cervesia for the remainder of his years. The gods truly had smiled upon him when they had guided him towards the Reaping that far off day.

He unstopped his water skin and took a long pull as Catumanda waited patiently at his side. With a gasp of satisfaction, he slowly and deliberately replaced the stopper and stuffed it back inside the pannier which hung at Clop's flank. Ruffos could not help but shoot his companion a quick glance as he did so, and laughed as he was rewarded with a light-hearted threat. "You *were* there when Piso met his unfortunate end?"

Ruffos moved his hand back to the pannier as if to take another drink but hesitated and smiled. "If you feed me to the Morrigan and her sisters you will never hear the end."

Ruffos patted the bag and prepared to conclude his tale, as the druid chuckled happily. Catumanda sent words of thanks to the gods each day that they had seen fit to provide the big man as a travelling companion for her on her quest. His companionship and knowledge of the ancient road systems of Albion had been invaluable, and now that the dreams which had plagued her since childhood had ceased, she felt that a great burden had been lifted from her. Perhaps for the first time, she reflected, she was actually enjoying the life which the gods had gifted her rather than merely living through it.

She began to realise that the older man had become a father figure to her, and she felt a stab of regret that she had not known her own father well. He, of course, had paid the ultimate price to gift his daughter the chance of a better life, but Catumanda now realised that the gods had also exacted a price from her also. At her side the carter continued with the tale of that evening, and she shrugged aside her sudden feelings of melancholy and forced a smile.

"The raging tempest outside was practically overhead, the vivid flashes of light dancing around the door and seeking out any holes in the body of the hut, sending skewers of light through the gloom like an arrow storm."

Catumanda smiled at the man's description. She could see that her friend was planning to feast heartily on the tale for many years to come and he had obviously been carefully honing his descriptions in readiness.

"Suddenly!" he exclaimed, "there came the loudest crash of thunder yet, gripping and shaking them violently as it sucked the very air from the room. Toranos hurled a great bolt through the sky turning night to day and, as they gasped before the might of the sky god, the door was torn from the hut and the naked, bloodied figure of the Morrigan herself stood before them as the thunder rolled away. Dumbstruck, they stared at the figure of the shapeshifting goddess in dread as a blood-curdling scream filled the cabin and the sibylla fell to the floor, dead: struck down by the power of the battle hag. The druids, thinking that they had offended the gods in some way, forced the terror induced rictus of a grin to their faces in welcome as they waited for her to speak. After what seemed an age, the grim silhouette framed in the doorway finally made its demands known to them as it uttered the words which nobody there would forget as long as they lived;

Bel's flames, what a night I have had! Pass me a

cervesia."

The travellers laughed aloud, and Ruffos threw his big arm around his friend and drew her affectionately to him. They would part at the coast she knew, the dreams had told them both so, but they had grown very fond of each other on the journey and they had outgrown the norms of behaviour. It was a crime punishable by death to touch a druid without their express permission, but they had grown as close as clansmen on the trip. Each step took them closer to the great southern sea and their inevitable parting, but they were both determined to enjoy each other's company in the little time which remained.

They had left the Spirit Isle soon after that eventful night. The brothers had tended to the scrapes and grazes which covered Catumanda's body from her time underground, and presented her with the Sacred Staff which marked the moment when she had fully graduated from initiate to druid. The staff was a defining feature of the brethren, and Catumanda admired it as they plodded steadily south. Formed from a single limb of oak, the druids' sacred tree, each staff contained a naturally occurring hole near the top, was stripped of its bark and polished constantly with the oils from its owner's skin. Used as a weapon, a wand and an everyday aid to walking, the staff was one of a druid's most prized possessions, almost a part of themselves. The druids on the Spirit Isle paid a handsome price for each example that men brought to them, and such was the fear and respect in which they were held by all that, although it *had* been known, it was rare that the holes could be mistaken for anything other than those formed naturally in the wood by spirits.

Desperation sometimes led men to produce their own examples but they were fools. Any druid could tell immediately that the hole had been made by the hand of men, however cunningly produced, and such men were simply never seen again. The tale had grown on the mainland that the brethren had eaten their bodies but kept their souls in a dank cave for eternity. It was a useful deterrent, and the druids were happy to encourage the belief even though the truth was in fact far more mundane. Any men attempting such a deception were passed directly to the slavers who plagued the coasts of Albion and the island of Ierne which stood opposite, with strict instructions that they were to be sold beyond the southern sea.

The daylight was dimming now, and the air was beginning to cool. Now that they had returned to the gentler lands in the South, the air was alive with the high pitched call of swifts and swallows. Soon the arrow winged birds would depart again as the summer drew on. The days were shortening quickly now, already the great festival of Lugh was a memory, and the fields of barley and spelt, so typical of the South, were a wash of pale yellow. Within days the people would fill these fields as they gathered in the harvest and gave thanks to the gods for their bounty. The first berries and fruits were ripening in the trees and hedgerows, and the hogs would be driven into the forests to gorge themselves on the acorns which the sacred oaks would provide.

Catumanda watched contentedly as the birds cut down to within a whisker of the barley ears in their search for the insects which the still evening air drew forth in abundance, and decided to call an early halt to the day. They had been travelling for several weeks since they left the Spirit Isle, and the end of their journey together was rapidly approaching. They came across a perfect clearing on the bowl of a south facing slope, and Catumanda lay back and reflected on their journey as Ruffos wandered away to collect material for the evening fire.

She had declined the offer of a sea passage to the South by one of the visiting traders, despite the fact that it offered by far the quickest route so late in the season. The first image which she had seen in the cave had clearly shown a boy seated on a hill and, as far as she was aware, hills generally confined themselves to land. Recrossing the strait to the mainland, the pair had hugged the coastline as they travelled south. After several days they had come to a wide valley which led into the interior, and they had turned inland and struck out through the steep sided passes which wound their way across the face of the land. Dark, lofty peaks lined their route, crowding in on them as they channelled the travellers away to the south-east.

Within days they had reached their first goal. Despite the desolation of the area through which they were moving, a well beaten path led from the valley floor to the boggy moor which capped the highlands there. Emerging onto the uplands, it had been but a short walk to the source of the River Sabrinna. Little more than a disparate collection of dark, peaty pools, the largest was marked by a small wooden platform which extended out into the waters. Her mother had given her a small collection of objects which had belonged to her father as keepsakes, and she had chosen a small knife from them and placed it below the waters as an offering to Sabrinna.

They had followed the waters of the goddess as she grew and gained in strength until they had exited the brooding, cloud capped mountains of Ordovicia and come out into the great forests which marched south to the lands of Siluria.

Following the river southwards they had come near to the place where the now mighty Sabrinna would disgorge her strength into the sea, before they had cut across country and followed the course of the River Parwydydd deep into the flatlands of the people known as the Durotriges. The land was a vast area of low lying swamp and marsh, so like the lands of the Reaping, and she had rediscovered her love of the vast blue skies and proud, independent people who inhibited them. Now they were in the gently hilly lands in the southern part of that chiefdom, and they had marvelled at the huge hill forts and ancient standing stones which littered the landscape.

Ruffos returned and broke her reverie as he deposited an armful of twigs and sticks with a clatter. "I hope that you have something good in mind for this evening's meal, druid." He grinned. "Fish would be nice."

Catumanda laughed and pulled the pannier across. Rummaging inside she produced a brace of gutted and salted trout with a flourish. "Oh well, as you insist. I do have a few left." The long riverside journey south had provided the druid with ample opportunity to prove that her success with a fishing line from Dorros and Attis's reed boat had been no fluke, and it had provided the majority of their food. Soaking the fish in river water to remove the salt and rehydrate the meat, Catumanda glanced up and winked at her friend. "Cheer up. We are near the great southern sea. We could be eating mackerel this time tomorrow!"

GULLS HAD RETURNED to the skies the following day, and both knew that the end to their time together was at hand. The road, wide and well travelled, angled away to the West as it made its way unerringly towards the ramparts of yet another hill fort which sprawled across a nearby summit. A smudge of grey lay over the unseen buildings from the home fires within, and they stopped and watched the ant-like figures of the inhabitants as they wove their way up the path towards their homes. The day was drawing on, and most sensible people were returning to their hearths and the company of friends and clansmen. Catumanda glanced at Ruffos and felt a tinge of guilt as she recognised the familiar look of melancholy flash across the face of her friend. Although she had tried to persuade the man to remain at home, the gods had sent the carter a dream which had told him to accompany the druid on her journey to the coast, and if any knew that the power of dreams could not be denied it was her.

Catumanda indicated that they leave the road with a flick of her head, and Ruffos clicked on the horse as they pushed through a gap in the hedgerow. The faint run of a fox or badger led them onward, curving away as it hugged the contours of a small hill.

Intent on placing travel-sore feet well clear of the rocks and pebbles which littered the path, Catumanda was unaware of the lone figure which crowned the high point until she had almost passed by. A slight movement caught her eye, and she glanced across and drew up in shock as the old familiar image presented itself to her. Ruffos came alongside her, and seeing the look on her face followed the druid's gaze up to the crown of the hill. He smiled and placed a hand on her shoulder as he too recognised the picture which presented itself 3to them from Catumanda's descriptions over the course of their summer together. “That is the boy, isn't it Catumanda?” he breathed.

Catumanda nodded in confirmation as she finally looked upon the scene which had haunted her nights for so many years. She had seen the image which now stood before her so many times over the course of her life, that to finally see it take on a hard physical form was breathtaking. The boy sat with his back to them, and it was obvious now that he was tending sheep. The dark droppings from the animals littered the ground all around, and for the first time ever she noticed that the boy sat with a shepherd's crook laid absent-mindedly across his lap.

Catumanda began to walk up the hillside towards the lad as if still in a dream, and as she approached a dog seemed to appear from nowhere and barked a warning. The boy turned sharply, scrambling to his feet as he recognised the druid for who she was as he brushed himself down and calmed the dog with an outstretched hand. Catumanda was relieved to find that the boy had an everyday human face and not the elongated, tooth filled head of some of her dreams. Although the images of the boy and the terrible head of the monster had been drawn separately in the cave, the shadowy nature of her recurrent dreams had often fused the two into one. They were clearly linked, and she must discover that connection before she could move forward with her work on behalf of the gods.

She smiled what she hoped was her friendliest smile, and leaning into her staff as the gradient increased to the final summit, finally spoke to her lifelong tormentor. “My name is Catumanda. Are you expecting me?”

To Catumanda's amusement the boy stared at her wide eyed, his mouth opening and closing like one of her recent riverine catches.

“Clearly, you were *not* expecting to see me,” she laughed gently.

Catumanda glanced at the dog who, sensing the druid's power, lowered its head and flicked its tail submissively. She gained the crest of the hill and indicated that the boy sit beside her. He did as she bid in awestruck silence, and the druid decided that it may be a good idea to talk of more mundane matters before she started to quiz the boy about razor-toothed monsters. “You have me at a disadvantage,” she smiled. “What is your name?”

The boy attempted to speak but all that came was a strangulated gasp. Catumanda waited patiently as the boy composed himself and finally answered. "Dun, druid. My name is Dun."

Catumanda smiled reassuringly and continued her questioning of the nerve-racked boy. "I can see why they called you Dun," she said, "I have not seen many people with hair as dark as yours since I left the lands of the Ordovicians and the Silures. Are you free or slave?"

The question finally broke through the boy's inherent shyness as it was meant to do. His eyebrows shot up as he realised that a druid had confused him with a slave and he pulled himself upright and answered proudly. "I am freeborn, druid, and I am entrusted with the care of my family's wealth." Dun reached down and thrust a horn in front of them. "One call will have the men of my clan here in moments."

Catumanda looked down into the valley and noticed the small collection of farm buildings for the first time. Four roundhouses sat in an ordered fashion around an open central area, the whole enclosed within a stout timber palisade. Pens for the sheep stood off to one side, and several pigs and dogs wandered to and fro across the yard in the soft evening light. It was, she thought, an almost perfect encapsulation of the values of self reliance and hard work which was the lot of the majority of the population. She indicated the settlement with a nod of her head. "Are you about to return to your home, freeborn Dun, or are you set to tend the flock for the night?"

The boy looked aghast as he realised the extent of his sudden outburst but the druid placed a hand on his shoulder and reassured him. "You have no need to fear me, Dun. I am a friend."

Dun raised his arm and waved down at the settlement below, and Catumanda noticed that several figures had emerged from the largest roundhouse and were staring intently in their direction. As they watched, another emerged from the house and began to distribute weapons among his clansmen as they started to hurry across to the gateway.

She raised herself from the grass and stretched her weary limbs. They had been on the road now for what seemed like an age and this looked as good a place as any in which to spend the coming night. Dun's rescue party would soon discover that the mystery figure on the hill was a druid and no threat to the boy or their sheep. Besides, no traveller was ever denied food and shelter among the inhabitants of Albion, and the settlement below carried an aura of homeliness which reminded her of Ruffos' home. As the men began to labour up the slope towards them Catumanda held a hand out and beckoned to the boy. "Shall we go? I should like to meet the clansmen of such a spirited young man."

THE TRIO BREASTED the slight rise and there, shining like a jewel in the late summer sunlight, lay the great expanse of the southern sea. Catumanda leaned into her staff as Ruffos came up alongside her and gently teased Clop's ear. The horse snorted with pleasure, shaking its head gently as he did so, and Catumanda smiled at the closeness of the pair. Ruffos had bought the horse as a foal many years previously and the pair were now as close as any friends, human or otherwise, could be.

Dun turned back as he realised that he was walking on alone and called out to hurry them along. "We are almost there, druid." He swept his arm along a small Combe which cut gently through the final ridge before the sea. "That will lead us down to the beach and we can walk along to the cove from there."

Catumanda nodded and walked on with mounting excitement as she was led to the Place of Monsters. As she had suspected, the previous evening had proven to be the perfect balm for their exhausted minds and bodies. Naturally Dun's family had been somewhat overawed having a druid house guest, but very soon the cervesia had begun to work its magic and the evening had been a great success. The boy's standing had immediately increased within the clan, and Catumanda had pondered on the similarity between Dun and herself. She had been a similar age when the dreams had first started, and she could but wonder if the gods had marked the young boy as a potential initiate.

They had entertained the clan members with the tale of their journey that summer, holding the people spellbound with their descriptions of the rugged beauty of their land of Albion. Catumanda had laughed along with the others as Ruffos had stood and recounted the tale of her dramatic return to the storm-lashed hut following her time underground and the death of the unfortunate sibylla.

Ruffos had been delighted to discover that the local cheese was excellent and had munched on it happily as the head man had explained its origin. The cheese came from a deep gorge which lay to the north of them called Chedwr. Cheeses were matured in great underground caves for several years until small salt crystals began to form within the body of them. Allied to the natural bite of the firm yellow cheese, the salt crystals added a satisfying tang to the overall taste, and Ruffos had been delighted when he had been presented with several cheeses as a parting gift. Sensing an opportunity for great profit, the trader had promised to accompany Dun on the return journey from the coast and had arranged to be introduced to the cheese makers before he finally set off for distant Tigguocobauc and home. He had confided in Catumanda that if this chedwr cheese proved as popular as he expected, he would make regular runs to the place and become a wealthy man.

Soon they had descended into the Combe, and Clop tossed his head and whinnied happily as the onshore breeze carried the zest of the nearby sea to their nostrils. The gradient increased sharply as they followed the dry watercourse which nestled at the base of the cut and, intent on picking their way through the maze of boulders which had been deposited there by innumerable spring floods, they found to their surprise that they were suddenly spilling out onto a wide beach. Dun hopped across the rubble strewn area at the base of the cliff and scrunched across the shingles as he ran laughing down to the shore.

Catumanda walked across the dark ragged line which marked the high water mark and inhaled deeply as she looked about. They were near the centre point of a wide bay, the arms of which curved away on each side enclosing them in a gigantic bowl. The eastern arm of the bay swept around to end in a series of high sea stacks but away to the West the land gently fell away, finally petering out in a low cliff, the rocks piled at its base testament to the power of the winter storms.

Beyond the entrance to the bay the sea shimmered and danced as a gentle westerly breeze plucked at the wave tops. Dun was racing along the firmer shingle which bordered the breakers, whooping with joy as he jumped to avoid the fizzing arcs of water which dashed across the beach.

Catumanda glanced at her friend and recognised the wistful longing to once again hear the laughter of his own children play across his features. Walking on alone she left Ruffos to his thoughts.

Ahead of her Dun was grinning and waving, and Catumanda hurried across as the end of her journey came in sight. “Here is the monster, druid. Just like I promised.”

Catumanda gasped at the image which presented itself to her. Etched onto a large slab of rock, perfect in every detail, was the giant head of the monster which had inhabited her dreams for so long. As long as a man, the egg-shaped head with its line of wickedly serrated fangs, lay before her in such detail that the animal could have only recently lay down and died there. Catumanda knelt beside the skull and traced its outline with her fingertips. It was all here. The heavy muzzle, the flared nostrils and the huge eye sockets of her dreams, the dreams which had left her sweating and shaking in the darkness of the last ten winters.

The shadows of Ruffos and Clop moved across the smooth surface of the stone, and Catumanda spoke to her friend as she continued to trace the outline with her hand. “Isn't it amazing? Truly, I cannot tell if it is bone or rock!”

Entranced, Catumanda continued to gaze on the skull for a few moments before she realised that her friend had not answered her. Glancing up she was surprised to see that he was staring away to the West, completely indifferent to the wonder which lay before them. Catumanda tried to attract her friend's attention once again. “Ruffos, look at this, it is fantastic. It is the reason we have travelled to this place.”

Finally the big man seemed to become aware of Catumanda's question, and without lowering his gaze he gasped a reply. “The clouds…”

Catumanda narrowed her eyes in confusion. “The clouds? What about the clouds?”

Ruffos finally managed to break the spell and, as he looked down, Catumanda was shocked to see the fear which had gripped her friend. “It is the clouds from my dream, the ones which carry you away across the sea. They are here.”

15

Pausing, he gazed down the valley. Spring had cloaked the land in soft shades of green and the distant line of blue which marked the shore of the Adriaticum sparkled in the forenoon sunshine.

To his rear the open tumulus stood awaiting its first occupant, and Solemis turned and descended into the shade of its embrace. Rows of amphorae lined the far wall, their contents, fine wines, dates and the juices of pressed olives from the new lands, towering above the squat bowls of silver and bronze containing the drinks of their homeland, cervesia and honeyed *medd*.

At its centre the space opened up in a stone lined circle, and Solemis stepped around the carefully arranged bones which were all that remained of his father's favourite war stallion. The warriors of Connos' cantref nodded respectfully as the new clan chief of the Horsetails made his way to the far end of the chamber, resting his hand on the lip of the shelf which would very soon contain the bones of his predecessor. Patting the shelf he turned and nodded to Cauros, still the champion of the Horsetails, that it was time to prepare him for the festivities which would mark the final rites of his father's passing to the lands of the ancestors.

Retracing his steps, Solemis emerged back into the full light of day and waited as Cauros retrieved his arms from the weapons stand. It had taken the new chieftain several weeks before he was finally convinced that he had managed to replace the big champion's desire to accompany Connos to the Isles of the Dead, with a burning desire for revenge against the killer of his chieftain and friend. Albiomaros had suggested that he promise the man the honour of being first to issue a challenge between the armies at the upcoming battle, and Solemis had watched gratified as the fire of vengeance immediately kindled in Cauros' eyes.

Solemis raised his arms as Cauros slipped the mail over his head and arms, rolling his shoulders as the heavy war shirt unfurled down his body with a metallic swish. The new chieftain drank in the beauty of the valley as his champion moved to secure the mail shoulder guards and fixed the heavy bronze sword belt about his waist. As Solemis' hand instinctively moved to rest on the hilt of his broadsword, Cauros carefully lowered the dome of polished bronze which had replaced his own battle helm at the moment of his acclamation. The conical helmet was capped by a finial of rings from which the plume of black horse hair which marked him as the Chieftain of the Horsetails shifted softly in the breeze. Beneath the heavily decorated band which ringed the lower edge of the piece, Solemis had had a sturdy peak incorporated into the design in the latest fashion along with a pair of wide, heavily ornamented, bronze cheek guards, and he raised his chin as his champion secured the bindings. He turned to Cauros and nodded his thanks, before motioning along the ridge line with a flick of his head. "It is time."

Solemis led Cauros past the gathering of mourners and

across to the site of the raised platform which contained all that remained of Connos' physical form. The vultures which had carried the flesh of the man to the sky gods were infrequent visitors now that the juicier parts of the chieftain had been excoriated from his frame, and only a single pair of the birds laboured into the air at their approach. High above several others circled on huge black wings, their curious low hanging head, neck and great size marking them apart from the svelte eagles of the Senone homelands.

Solemis climbed the short ladder to the platform and examined the bones of his father. None seemed to have been removed by the birds or other scavengers, and he marked the dark slash in the crown of the skull. Glancing across to Cauros he indicated the wound with a jerk of his head. "Fix the mark of my father's death wound, Cauros. Call it to mind when you take your vengeance."

Cauros stared hard at the jagged line of the sword strike and, glancing up, gave his friend's son a deliberate nod. Satisfied that they were of one mind, Solemis gripped the woven mat by the handle and stepped down from the platform. Suspended between the two men, son and champion, Connos, Chieftain of the Horsetails was carried to his howe.

There would be a riotous night of drinking and feasting as the new chieftain distributed *potlach.* Clansmen and friends from far and wide would congregate about the mound, swapping stories of the man and recalling his deeds as they paid a final visit to his bones. In the morning the mound would be closed up to await the day when Solemis would board the boat which would reunite father and son on the Isles of the Dead.

Then they would ride to war.

. . .

Brennus rode at the tip of a spearhead of warriors, down into the vale. The day was hot and the grasslands ranged before them were an indistinct haze of green, white and red as a sea of daisies swirled around scarlet islands of poppies. At the base of the vale a small stream, its waters shrunken back almost to a disparate collection of pools by the heat of the Etruscan summer snaked lazily down from the North, and Brennus led his *delegatio,* as the Etruscan envoy had repeatedly referred to his war band on as his mount picked its way through.

The Senone warlord looked across as he did so and smiled as he recognised his newest clan chief coming up. Flicking a look down at the holed skull which still bounced from the saddle horn at Solemis' knee, Brennus called across cheerfully. "Solemis, how is my old adversary?"

Solemis leaned forward and patted the skull as he shot back a grin. "No change, Brennus, he still has a splitting headache."

A rumble of laughter ran along the line of warriors as they approached the far bank, and Brennus returned the grin and fixed the young chieftain with a look. "What do you think?"

Solemis ran his gaze along the length of the stream bed as a brace of pigeons clattered out of the trees and passed away to the West. The water level would barely cause a charge to check its pacc. The rocks which lined the stream bed were a more serious obstacle and a few men would be lost there in a mad charge, but not enough to blunt the ferocity of their attack. "Its enough to slow the charge for a moment but not to check it."

Brennus nodded. "What if the Etruscans move forward and form their line on the far bank. Can we still force the position?"

Solemis fought back a smile as he replied. "That would

never happen, Brennus. At the first sign that the enemy were moving into the valley, you would order the Horsetails to lead the mounted warriors down to break up their charge before they could reform."

Brennus threw back his head and laughed as the men to either side chuckled happily. The horses climbed up onto the far bank and began their walk across to the waiting Etruscan legatus. Solemis was close enough to his chieftain to catch his muttered retort, and he swelled with pride as he caught the words. *"Yes, that is exactly what I would do."*

Casting a look ahead, the Celts could see the members of the Etruscan party exchange looks of bemusement at the light hearted manner of their approach and Brennus called over his shoulder to his men. "Serious faces now, boys. We have come to take their land from them, the least that we can do is look grateful."

The Senones dressed their line and came to a halt as Brennus and Crixos rode forward to negotiate with the Etruscan legate and his second. As the pair rode on Solemis, took the opportunity to study the people he had come to regard as the enemy.

Following the murder of Connos, Brennus had sent a strong party of warriors to support the Horsetails as they swept the surrounding hills and valleys, looking for any armed parties and gathering what information they could from the few Etruscans who remained in the area. Although the killers had long ago fled, careful and not so careful questioning of the local peasants had led Solemis to discover that the mysterious black riders which they had last seen making an attempt on the life of Brennus himself outside Alesia had tracked them south. The locals, having seen the strength in both arms and numbers of the Senone settlers, had mostly been keen to share what information they knew with their new masters, and the key part of that information was that all had confirmed that the men had been Etruscan *equites,* mounted soldiers of noble rank. One of the informants had sworn that the men had mentioned that they were eager to return to the city of Clevsin on the far side of the Apeninnus and, to Solemis' satisfaction, Brennus had identified the city as the focus of their forthcoming campaign. Riders had been sent to inform the clan chiefs that a punitive expedition would be mounted against the city immediately after the Bel Fires had been lit in the spring.

The army of the Senones had gathered in the hills near to the twin pools which were the source of the River Tiberis. Sacrifices had been made to their own gods and the goddess of the river and Brennus had led them south, following the course of the river as it slowly gathered strength. At the Etruscan city of Perusia they had struck out to the West and within the week they had pitched up before the walls of Clevsin.

Solemis's gaze wandered across to the city as his leaders reined in several paces before the Etruscans. Both the walls which enclosed the city and the buildings within seemed to be constructed from the same buttery coloured stone which formed the mountains they had recently traversed. The roofs of the buildings were uniformly capped by tiles of terracotta and, shimmering as they were in the heat haze of the southern spring, Solemis found that despite his hatred for its inhabitants the city itself was a wonder to behold.

He lowered his eyes and ran them along the ranks of the Etruscan army which had drawn up in battle array, one hundred paces to the rear of the place where the leaders were deep in conversation. The centre of the enemy line was formed of a solid square of bronze and leather clad warriors and he noticed to his surprise that, unlike their own armies, the older and more experienced warriors seemed to be at the rear of the formation. Most were armed with spears of varying length but a few here and there carried swords of iron or bronze while several seemed to be equipped with light axes, possibly for throwing. This was, he knew, the famous *phalanx* which they had discussed with their northern neighbours, the Boii, over the winter. The dense formation formed the basis of the southern armies and while formidable and difficult to defeat if they stood shoulder to shoulder, their interdependence became their weakness if the formation could be smashed open by a determined and well led charge.

The flanks of the enemy force seemed to consist of lightly armed spearmen and archers and Solemis guessed that these would belong to the lower classes of citizen, those men who were without the means to supply themselves with arms and armour of the quality required to fight in the main phalanx.

To the rear of the army of Clevsin several hundred of the mounted warriors he now knew to be called equites were divided equally between the two flanks, and Solemis found that he was looking from face to face in an effort to recognise an individual from the confused skirmish in the valley behind Alesia.

His thoughts were interrupted as Brennus twisted in his saddle and called across in his direction. "Solemis!"

Exchanging a look of surprise with Cauros and Albiomaros, the young chieftain urged his horse up the rise and drew rein alongside his leader. There was a palpable air of disdain carrying to him from the Etruscan leaders, and Solemis shot them only a cursory glance as he nodded in deference towards Brennus. The look, however brief, had been enough to see that both Etruscans wore similar muscled breast plates to the one which he had presented to Crixos. He had taken it from the body of the leader of the band of men who had attempted to kill Brennus the previous summer, and they now knew that those men had come from this city. It seemed that the men opposite had realised the same detail.

Brennus smiled as Solemis came up, and indicated the skull which was secured to his saddle horn. "I was just telling our new friends here how surprised we had been to meet a few of their horsemen a very long way from home last summer." He tapped the skull with the toe of his boot and glanced back at the legate. "It would seem that Solemis has been riding around with the skull of one of your clansmen all this time." The Etruscan leader shot Solemis a look of pure hatred as his companion translated Brennus' words to him. His face paled as he looked from Solemis to the skull and back again. The man's nostrils flared as he fought to keep his composure under Brennus' deliberate provocation, and Solemis met the man's stare as he spat his own condition for peace. "I may be persuaded to part with my trophy in return for the killer of my father, stalked and struck from behind by a coward!"

Brennus snorted and a brief flash of puzzlement crossed Solemis' mind as he noticed Crixos shift uneasily in his saddle. A look of disbelief swept the faces opposite them as the legate glanced back at Brennus to gauge his reaction to Solemis' demand. Seeing their amused expressions his eyes narrowed as he snapped a reply. "What gives barbarians, animals from the forests, the right to think that you can ride here, falsely accuse us of cowardice and demand that we leave our own lands, the lands of our ancestors?"

Brennus raised his chin and inhaled deeply as the insult was conveyed to him by an increasingly nervous looking interpreter. "So, these are your lands? By what right do you hold them?"

The Etruscan snarled a reply. "I hold these lands from my

father and his father before him, back through time to the founder of my clan."

Brennus nodded sagely, and Solemis noticed the corner of his mouth curl in amusement as the big chieftain formulated his reply. "Tell me, Etruscan. How did the founder of your clan gain these lands?"

The legate visibly swelled with pride at the question, and he answered in a tone heavy with menace. "He fought for and was granted possession of these lands by the gods as a reward for his victories!"

Brennus smirked, as the enraged Etruscan fell neatly into his trap. Leaning forward in his saddle he fixed the man with a chilling stare and replied calmly.

"In that case, *I* challenge *you* to fight for it."

THE WAIL and blast of the carnyx trailed away in the sultry air, as Solemis and his Horsetails looked along the line of the Senone army and waited for their man to appear. Despite their fears, the Etruscans had held their position lining the gentle ridge before the city walls, and Brennus had ordered the Celts down into the shallow vale before them. The move had had the effect of halving the distance which the warriors would need to cover to come to grips with the enemy and, despite the disadvantage that an attack uphill would bring at least, Brennus had argued, the momentum of the attack would not be interrupted by the need to negotiate the rock strewn watercourse.

A small knoll stood hard on to the western bank of the stream, and Solemis had been ordered to draw up the mounted warriors of his clan here. The position offered an elevated and uninterrupted view of the entire battlefield, and

Brennus had handed Solemis the responsibility of covering the entire right flank of the army.

Away to his left Solemis, watched with indescribable pride as the champion of the Horsetails emerged from the centre of the line and made his way up the gentle slope towards the centre of the Etruscan phalanx. Cauros halted fifty paces from the enemy spear points and brandished his shield and gaesum as he called out his ritual challenge. Solemis and the men of the hero's clan were too far away to clearly hear the address, but snippets carried to them in the light breeze and they already knew of the man's lineage and bravery. They did, after all, share common ancestors, and the glory and honour which Cauros was drawing to himself reflected on the clan as a whole.

Solemis listened with pride as Albiomaros spoke a line from the works of an ancient bard:

> *"Then the madness of battle came upon him.*
> *You would have thought that every hair was*
> *being driven into his head,*
> *that every hair was tipped with a spark of*
> *fire!"*

As Cauros strutted the length of the Etruscan line, issuing his challenge and seeking to belittle his opponents, Solemis reflected on the effort it had taken them to persuade Brennus to allow the rite. The chieftain's initial thoughts had been to dispense with the custom of ritual challenges between the armies and order a quick advance to the far side of the stream. Once in position they would bellow their war cries to the accompaniment of the braying sound of the carnyx before breaking into a head-long charge. Solemis had pleaded with the chieftain to allow the challenge to go ahead. Explaining the promise he had made to the man as they stood over the body of Connos, he had managed to persuade the reluctant chieftain, and add greatly to the reputation of Cauros, by incorporating the challenge into Brennus' plan of attack. That scene was playing out before them now, and a flash of bronze rippled along the front of the Senone line as the carnyx were thrust into the air once more. It was the signal for the last part of his plan, and Solemis watched as the twin forms of his dogs, Tarvos and Suros, were brought proud of the battle line.

Cauros brandished his arms for the last time and broke into a run, directly at the hedge of spears which lined the ridge. The haunting blare of the carnyx all around them and the goading of their handlers had driven the dogs to a fever pitch of excitement, and Solemis watched with mixed feelings as the dogs strained at their leashes as they prepared to attack. The dogs had been *potlach* to him from the old chieftain of the tribe, Catubaros. He had taken them when it seemed nobody else could see a use for them, and Solemis had used the experiences with hunting dogs during his time at foster in Albion to train the pair in the arts of hunting and warfare.

Ahead of them Cauros broke his stride to hurl his gaesum at the enemy formation, before hunkering into his shield once more and thundering on. It was the signal to unleash the dogs, and Solemis watched with pride as Suros and Tarvos raced away up the grassy slope with long, galloping strides.

A final roar rose from the Senone line as the warriors broke ranks and surged forward, their boar standards and war horns puncturing the air above them, and Solemis watched the Etruscan lines waver as the men there braced themselves to meet the onslaught.

A dozen paces from the enemy spear tips Suros and Tarvos galloped past Cauros and, hurtling beneath the level of the deadly weapons, smashed into the Etruscan front rank. The line shivered as the dogs hit, throwing the defence into disarray at the vital moment, and the Horsetails watched with pride as Cauros, their champion, swept aside the wavering spears with his broad shield and plunged into their midst. The Etruscan formation bowed inward as man and hounds cut a swathe through them, and Solemis watched as Brennus bounded ahead of the Celtic mass and, drawing back his arm, sent his own gaesum arcing into the enemy. It was the signal for the whole of the charging mass to unleash a volley, and the Horsetails watched from their elevated position as the deadly darts fell in a concentrated area around the breach. In an instant all semblance of a cohesive defence disappeared as Brennus led the wedge of sword wielding warriors deep within their ranks and widened the breach. A call came from Solemis' right, and he tore his gaze away from the carnage which had been the Etruscan phalanx. "Their horsemen are moving, Solemis!"

The equites of the Etruscan left were moving down the flanks as they came to the aid of their centre, and Solemis kicked in and urged his horse forward as he led the counter. Hastily calculating the distance between the Etruscan force and the flanks of the attacking Celts, Solemis led the Horsetails into and along a sunken hollow which snaked away to the East. He had spotted the depression the moment that they had gained their start position on the knoll earlier in the day, and had fixed it in his mind as a possible route forward. Although they would be intermittently visible to the enemy riders as the lip of the depression rose and fell, Solemis had weighed up the risk and decided that the chance to outflank the Etruscan force was just too good to miss.

A stunted cypress, its gnarled trunk stooping with age, marked the point at which he would swing the formation south, and Solemis thundered up and over the edge there as he bore down on the Etruscan flank. He had timed his charge to perfection, and the noise of battle redoubled as they emerged a hundred paces from the wheeling enemy equites. Solemis charged ahead screaming his battle cry as the Horsetails swept onto the plain to his rear. He had a momentary glimpse of an Etruscan face turned in his direction, its features a mask of surprise and horror, before he hit them with a bone jarring crash.

Before his opponent could drag his own spear across Solemis had skewered him and urged his mount on into the press of riders. Solemis worked his way through the Etruscan riders as their forward momentum slowed and they reacted to this new threat which had suddenly appeared in their midst. He had learnt a valuable lesson during the fight against the Helvetii the previous summer and, only a little older but greatly more experienced now, Solemis jabbed his spear in short, controlled thrusts as each target presented itself. He had lost his gaesum immediately in the short fight in the Alpes as he had allowed the heavy blade to pass deep within his victim. It had left him unarmed and surrounded by enemies in the moments it had taken him to draw his sword and he had realised afterwards that, although the gods had been with him that day, he could not trust to their benevolence in every fight.

The Etruscan charge was broken now and they wheeled about and defended themselves as more and more Horsetails and allied clans entered the fray. Solemis glanced across and saw a rider wearing a magnificent helm of bronze twisting in his saddle as he surveyed the fighting. The man's face was all but enclosed by twin sheets of the ochre coloured metal, which wrapped around his face to leave only the centre part of his face and eyes visible. The helm was crowned by a high crest of alternating red and black horsehair which, added to the quality of the warrior's gleaming war shirt, greaves and weapons, told Solemis that here was the leader of the Etruscan horsemen.

Hauling on his reins he attempted to force his stallion through the press towards the man, but he was quickly spotted and several enemy riders moved across to bar his way. Hurling his gaesum in their direction Solemis drew his sword and forced his way through the scrum.

As the enemy began to waver a roar came from the centre of the field, and Solemis looked across to see that the Etruscan phalanx had broken and its members were streaming away, back towards the safety of the city.

A shouted command came from the crested warrior, and Solemis watched in frustration as the enemy group reformed and retreated to the South. Broken by the ferocity of the Horsetail attack and with their army in headlong retreat, the equites disengaged with expert precision and galloped away after the departing leader.

His whole being fizzing with the elation of victory, Solemis screamed at his men to reform on him as he led them in a wild chase after the fleeing horsemen.

16

The druid rose slowly to her feet and shielded her eyes as she gazed across at the nearby headland. There, moving slowly along the summit of the ridge, billowed the greasy white cloud of her dream. The gods had sown the spectral cloud in the unconscious mind of Ruffos also, and the pair walked forward together as they waited for it to clear the promontory. After what seemed a lifetime of waiting for the gods to reveal their secrets, the previous two days had seen the mysteries which had tormented her nights tumble as rapidly as leaves in an autumn gale.

The boy, Dun, appeared at her side and Catumanda indicated that he move away with a jerk of her head. "You should leave us now, Dun. I have no idea what this thing is and it may be dangerous."

To her surprise the boy brayed with laughter at the worried expressions on the faces of those before him. When he had recovered he grinned at them and pointed at the dark shape which was just emerging beyond the point. "That is not a cloud druid, that is a southern trader. It will be on its way to the great trading settlement at Isarno."

Catumanda squinted into the distance as she sought to see what a southern trader looked like. The afternoon sun reflected from the surface of the sea like shards of broken ice, and the druid found it impossible to see clearly through her tear filled eyes. Finally the hull cleared the headland and pointed its bows to the East, and Catumanda laughed in wonder as she turned her face to Ruffos. “What a day this has been! I have heard of these clouds, they are called sails. My master, Abaris, encountered them on his travels in southern Celtica. He visited a Greek town there known as Massalia, and I remember now that he described these ships to me.” She shook her head. “What a fool I am; I thought that the line beneath the cloud on the cave wall was a giant serpent but look,” she pointed at the front of the ship, “they have an eye painted on the bow!”

Ruffos and Dun shielded their eyes and exchanged a grin before Ruffos turned to Catumanda and, lowering his voice to little more than a whisper, smiled sadly. “This is where we part then my friend.”

The realisation drew the humour from the moment, and Dun showed a maturity beyond his years as he silently took himself off to skim stones in the surf. Ruffos delved into the pannier which hung at Clop's side and produced a cheese of Chedwr as a parting gift. “Here, take this,” he smiled. “Every time that you smell rank old cheese you will think of Ruffos and old Clop here.”

Catumanda took the cheese, but found that words were unnecessary. The friends embraced in a final farewell and, calling to Dun, Ruffos led the boy and horse back across the beach and up into the Combe.

The druid watched as they picked their way back along its rubble strewn course, the boy leaping happily from one rock to the next. Glancing across to check on the progress of the trading ship, she looked back to discover that they had disappeared as completely as if they had never been.

Catumanda adjusted her crane skin bag as she felt a knot of emotion tighten in her throat. She had promised to call on the big man and his family one day if the gods had it in their minds that she return to Albion, and it was a promise that she fervently hoped that she could keep.

Feeling suddenly very alone, the young druid sighed and set off along the coastal path which led eastwards.

CATUMANDA GAINED the crest of the hill and looked out across the scene which unfolded before her. Below, a great spit of land ran parallel to the coast before curving back, hook-like, towards the mainland. Almost completely enclosed between the peninsula and the mainland lay a great body of water edged on the far side by marsh and forest, while away to the right the wind puckered sea drew away to a great island, its green capped cliffs edged in white.

To her great relief the trading ship was clearly visible near the beach in the inner bay, and Catumanda hastened down towards the twin earthworks which marked the limit of the bargaining place beyond. The warriors collecting tolls from the merchants nodded respectfully and waved her through as she approached, and Catumanda immediately skirted the barrows which capped the ridge line and took the path which led down towards the ship, her tall mast still clearly visible as she rolled gently at anchor. The beach which ran eastwards to the sandy spit was clearly the main market place here, and Catumanda hurried past the stalls and mats of the merchants as she dropped down onto the strand.

As she approached the ship she spotted a group of men whose short stature, black hair and swarthy skin tone marked them out immediately from the generally fair and ruddy local populace. Dressed in the pale linen clothes and leather sleeveless over-shirts common among seafarers everywhere, Catumanda was immediately struck by the dark, tight curls of the spokesman's beard. Up close now she was surprised to discover that the trader's hair and beard glistened with what appeared to be a delicately scented oil. No man on Albion would do such an effeminate thing, and she found that she was struggling to suppress a snigger.

A tall blond man sporting a magnificent, manly, flowing moustache was deep in conversation with him while the men who Catumanda took to be the members of his cantref stood resolutely behind their leader. Each of the men wore patterned trousers gathered at the ankle in the Celtic fashion and plain red tunics of the highest quality, while the torcs which ringed each man's neck and the swirling blue patterns which adorned their arms clearly indicated to all who saw them that they were high class warriors.

The warriors glanced her way and nodded respectfully as she approached, and Catumanda paused at their leader's side and waited patiently for a natural break in the conversation. The southerner flicked a questioning look in her direction, and the warrior finally realised that they had company. A look of surprise swept the warrior's features as he finally saw that a druid had appeared among them, but he quickly recovered his composure and smiled in greeting. "Druid! can I be of assistance in any way?"

Catumanda returned the smile and indicated the crew member with a small nod. "Yes, I think that you can. My name is Catumanda and I need to arrange passage on this ship. Would you explain that to this man and ask what payment his master would require?"

The warrior snorted and leaned across conspiratorially.

"Believe me Catumanda, he knows no master," he smiled. "The Greek is called Hesperos and he owns this ship and, for a short while at least, the cargo it contains. My name is Bellovesos and I am here on behalf of my chieftain, Britomaros. I am negotiating a price for the complete cargo, but he knows how to drive a hard bargain. I am trying to get him to accept a cargo of slaves in return for his wine, but he insists that he will only accept tin." Bellovesos held up a hand to the ship master and spoke briefly to him in a language which Catumanda assumed must be Greek. The man shrugged as if disinterested, and Bellovesos indicated that Catumanda step to one side, out of Hesperos' earshot. "Forgive me, Catumanda, but Hesperos knows a little of our tongue. Must you travel on this particular ship? It is returning directly south and I have a feeling that this Greek drives his crew as hard as his trading deals. There are other ships which I can recommend above this one if you need to travel across to Celtica."

Catumanda shook her head. "No, it must be this ship. I have been guided here by our gods to do their work." She smiled and continued. "They have even provided a man who can speak both the Greek tongue and our own to smooth my passage."

Bellovesos pulled a face and nodded on agreement. "It may be as you say. It is unlikely that any other ships will come to our shore from the South this year, they should already be long gone. Apparently they were blown far to the West by a sudden squall, and then had to beat their way back along our coast in an almost dead calm." The warrior smiled. "I have assured them that the season of storms is almost upon us, it should help me to broker a quick and advantageous deal. Now I can see that our gods delayed them until your arrival here, that much is obvious. I will negotiate a passage on your behalf Catumanda. Have no fear, they will not leave these shores without you whatever the cost."

The druid returned the smile and indicated the summit of the hill which rose to their rear, where an ancient barrow broke the contours of its highest point, a dark cap against the blue sky beyond. "Bellovesos, would you be kind enough to loan me one of your men for a short time? I have a small matter which I would like to attend to before I depart, and I would hate to miss the ship after all of our efforts."

Bellovesos called one of his men across and returned to his bargaining. The warrior came over and smiled warmly at her as he introduced himself. Young, tough and self confident, Catumanda found that she took an instant liking to the man. "My name is Galba," he chirped happily. "Where would you like to go Druid?"

Catumanda indicated the summit of the ridge, and Galba chatted away as they crossed the trading settlement. "All these forges and workshops you can see around you use the iron which the gods have provided in this place. Lumps of ironstone the size of your head can be found throughout the cliff face and on the beaches below, and the iron workers collect them up and work them in this area." He indicated their surroundings with a sweep of his hand. "It's where the place gets its name from of course, Isarno. It's safer to work iron here," he continued, "it's on the lee of the hill so winds are cut down and there are few buildings to burn down. Not that it has never happened of course," he laughed. "Sparks and embers can travel a long way!"

Catumanda laughed along with the young warrior. She suddenly realised that this may very well be the last time that she would get to spend time with a man from her home island, and she knew that the gods had shown her favour in their choice once again. Galba was typical of the young warriors of Albion, and she had met enough now to know instinctively the man's likely qualities, both good and not so good. Straightforward, honest and forever cheerful, they sometimes gave the impression that they were little more than a drunken, disorganised rabble. However, the druid knew that the irreverent surface masked a core of solid iron, and if a warrior of Albion ever decided that a thing was unfair or unjust he would call on his friends and stand his ground against all comers, irrespective of the odds ranged against him.

They were soon at the high point, and Galba planted himself on a small tussock and gazed out over the inner bay as Catumanda rested beside the mound, crossed her legs, straightened her back and assumed the tree of power position. Closing her eyes Catumanda breathed slowly and deeply three times as her mind cleared, and her soul sought out the connection with mother earth. Almost immediately she sensed the root from the base of her spine extending into the ground a little further with each exhalation and soon the warm liquidity of the earth mother's milk was coursing into her body.

THE BOWS LIFTED AND PLUNGED, flinging a fine spray back along the flanks of the ship she now knew to be the *Alexa* as she left the shelter of the bay and set her course for the South and home. Standing alone amidships, the young druid watched as the creamy white headlands receded a little more each time the great curved stern post fell away. Soon they were abreast the towering cliffs of the large island which stood off the coast hereabouts, a line of tall pyramidal sea stacks trailing away from its lee like the jagged tail of a monstrous sea serpent.

Glancing back once again to the mainland, she discovered that she could no longer distinguish the barrow perched atop Isarno where she had drawn strength for what she knew may be the final time from the land of her birth. The sun sat low on the headlands to the West, and the crew members paused at their work to admire the soup of reds and yellows as the sky there changed hue from moment to moment.

A shouted instruction drifted down the deck, and she glanced at the crewman who had appeared at her side. The man nodded apologetically before hastening away with a fear filled backward glance, and Catumanda knew that she must make the effort to learn the unfamiliar language of the Greeks if she was to allay the fears of some of the crew. Seafarers were among the most superstitious of men, and the druid was fully aware that most had an irrational fear of the presence of women aboard their vessel. Unless she could develop a relationship with them, and soon, she could very easily be blamed for any misfortune which may strike the ship during its long voyage. If that *did* happen she could find herself pitched into the sea whether her passage had been paid for or not.

She knew that most of the crew had been set against giving her passage on the ship, but Bellovesos had been as good as his word and had abandoned any further attempts at negotiation. To Hesperos' surprise and delight he had paid the extortionate price which the ship master had demanded for his amphorae of southern wine and, safely stowed beneath the square housing amidships, the hold of the *Alexa* now fairly groaned under the weight of tin ingots.

With a final glance away to the North at the sun washed cliffs of her rapidly receding homeland, Catumanda settled herself onto the hatch cover and began to listen.

. . .

SHE REMAINED at her place amidships, barely moving at all for the first three days of the voyage as she studied every movement and utterance made by the crew. Before the light had finally faded beyond the earth's rim on the evening of the first day at sea, she had already marked the nature and name of each man. Besides the master and owner of the *Alexa,* a crew of four manned the ship.

Markos was the eldest among them and was clearly the most senior crew member after Hesperos himself. His sun darkened skin and powerful frame told the story of a life spent around ships and the sea, and Catumanda had noted that Markos was the only other man aboard the *Alexa* to whom the owner would relinquish control of the big twin paddle blades which steered the ship. The man's ready smile was allied to a natural air of authority, and Catumanda knew that his was a friendship which she must do her best to cultivate in the coming weeks.

Tall, slim and wiry, Arion appeared close in age to Markos and the pair were obviously great friends despite their difference in rank. Unlike the rest of the crew, Arion appeared to take great care over his appearance despite the fact that they would be away from land for weeks at a time, and Catumanda had admired the man's silver beard rings and red chiton, the heavyweight work shirt favoured by the crew. Arion's slighter frame and longer reach seemed to have led him to specialise in working aloft, and he spent a greater part of his day either in the upper reaches of the main mast or perched precariously at the tip of the shorter mast which protruded ahead of the ship.

Hektor was a good deal younger than Markos and Arion, Catumanda estimated only several winters older than herself, and although he seemed to be popular among the crew he was careful to avoid any contact with their passenger. Each time that Catumanda had caught the man looking her way he had quickly averted his gaze, and the druid's attempts at enlisting the help of the gods and spirits had led her to the disconcerting realisation that the further from land that the ship sailed the weaker their powers seemed to become. Alone among the members of *Alexa*'s crew, Hektor clearly still resented her presence there, and Catumanda set herself the task of discovering the cause of the man's hostility.

The youngest member of the crew was little more than a boy. Philippos was a lad of ten or eleven winters and as fast as a lizard. Ever cheerful, the skinny body which seemed to hang stick-like below a crazy mop of dark curly hair was just beginning to lose its childhood plumpness despite his apparently insatiable appetite.

As the evening of the third day at sea approached Arion called down from the masthead and pointed off to the East. Within the hour the coast of Celtica hove into view, and Hesperos steered a steady course to the south-west as the *Alexa* ran parallel to the wave lashed cliffs of a great headland. Soon the scarred and jagged coast was left behind, and the ship came about and pointed her bows to the South. High above the sky shaded from blue to a deep lavender as the first stars of the night flickered into view, and Catumanda watched as the men shortened sail and took the way off the ship. The sea was calm enough to light a fire on board, and Philippos set to work as Arion secured a leather pail of sea water to the base of the mast as an added precaution against disaster.

A small hearth of smoke blackened stone had been constructed on the main deck, and the druid watched as Philippos attempted to set the fire. Despite having been stored below decks the wood was clearly damp, and Catumanda watched as the boy worked furiously with a small hand bow as he attempted to light the kindling. The boy glanced across and panted in mock exhaustion as he noticed the amusement in the druid's eyes. It was a small but very human gesture, and Catumanda was emboldened to offer her help as it became obvious that the boy at least held no fear for the strange foreign holy woman in their midst. She moved across, placing a hand on the boy's shoulder as she reached inside her tunic and drew her moon blade. Reaching inside the stone hearth she selected a stout stick and shaved the end with her blade until it resembled a long autumn pine cone. Finally, taking a small ironstone from her bag she struck the rock with her blade several times. Immediately sparks jumped the gap and the wood shavings began to smoulder.

Philippos exclaimed with delight as he carefully husbanded the flames, blowing delicately as the first wispy tendrils curled up into the cool evening air. Within moments small petals of flame struggled up from the shavings, and the boy shielded them with his body as the kindling finally caught.

As Catumanda retreated back to her place near the deck rail, she glanced across to the steering platform and was rewarded with a slight nod of thanks from Hesperos. It was, she reflected, virtually the first communication which the man had had with his guest since they had left the shores of Albion, and she hoped that her small act would bear greater fruit.

Philippos had spent most of that day casting a long line from the side of the ship and soon the *Alexa* was enveloped in the mouth-watering smells of a thick fish stew as the results of his labour simmered gently in the pot.

As the last of the light faded in the West, Markos relieved Hesperos of the steering duty and the crew came together and formed a circle on the deck as the owner doled out the broth to the hungry men. To the great surprise of Catumanda and of every man present, the Greek master handed the first bowl to the druid before moving on without comment. Catumanda was thrilled that she had made a small amount of progress in her efforts to become more accepted by the Greek crew, and she decided that she would attempt to join the conversation that night if the right opportunity presented itself.

She had listened to the day-to-day conversations of the crew ever since they had left the shores of Albion, and she felt certain that she was now ready to take her first faltering steps at conversing in the strange sounding tongue. The soup was hot and delicious, and she spooned it gratefully and concentrated as the conversation swirled around her. Very soon the chance came, and she smiled to herself that her old adversary had provided it as she somehow knew that he would. Catumanda cleared her throat and kept her gaze fixed on the bowl before her as she casually replied to the crewman's jibe in halting Greek. "My name is Catumanda, Hektor. It would please me if you would use it."

She dipped her spoon into her soup, blowing on the contents as she flicked a look up at the circle of dumbstruck faces which surrounded her. Pulling a large piece of fish from the spoon with her teeth, she rolled the scalding chunk around her mouth and panted quickly as she sought to cool it enough to swallow. Her mouth clear, she glanced up as her spoon chased another nugget around the bowl. "By the way," she asked, her expression a mask of innocence. "What is a fantasma?"

17

Brennus kicked the lamp angrily across the room and balled his fists. “You fool, Solemis!”

The young chieftain felt himself flush as the other clan chiefs in the room lowered their gaze at the awkwardness of the moment. Brennus gritted his teeth and let out a growl of frustration, blowing out as he sought to regain his composure. Finally he shook his head, slumping down into the chair as he pulled a weary smile at the humiliated Horsetail. Cupping his hand he spoke softly to him. “You see this? That was us. Inside here…” he swirled the finger of his other hand inside the cup, “nestled the Etruscans’ balls. All we had to do, sorry…” he corrected himself. “All that *you* had to do, was come between the phalanx and the walls of Clevsin and we would have squeezed those balls until they begged for mercy. We could have been inside their city, and I could have been inside several of their women,” he raised a brow and shot them all a watery smile as his usual humour attempted to resurface, “if you hadn't gone chasing off.”

An uncomfortable silence descended on the room as Brennus took another swig from the flask of wine which he had liberated from a portly, richly dressed Etruscan body. To Solemis' surprise Crixos broke the hush. "He did well, Brennus. You know how difficult to control our boys are once they get going. We rely on the battle-fury of our men, not the discipline of the enemy." He shrugged. "Usually it is to our advantage, but sometimes we lose an opportunity due to it. The fact that the Horsetails broke the charge of the equites was more important than annihilating their forces."

Solemis shot Crixos a look of gratitude. It was the first time that he had ever heard the man question a judgement made by the chieftain, and it was the moment when he knew that he would be fully accepted as an important ally of his clan once the marriage to Aia went ahead. Brennus looked up in surprise and took another slug from the flask. As he contemplated Crixos' words another clan leader added his own thoughts. "Crixos is right, Brennus. The Horsetails honoured the memory of Connos here today. Not only did his son break their counter attack but their clan champion," he shot Solemis a smile, "and Solemis' great ugly dogs, were responsible for breaking their formation. The man died the death of a hero, and I for one will pay for a bard to recount the tale before the benches."

A murmur of agreement came from the gathering, and Solemis gave a small nod of appreciation to the man for his words of support. Brennus glanced around the room and let out a long, drawn out, sigh. Pushing the chair back onto its rear legs he crossed his boots on the table top before him. "You are all right of course." A tired smile suddenly painted the chieftain's face as he accepted their arguments. "Without Solemis's idea to use Cauros and the dogs the attack may not have gone so easily." He looked across at Solemis. "Did you find his body?"

Solemis nodded grimly. "What was left of it, he had been

hacked at by several attackers for some time." He lifted his chin as he continued proudly. "But we did note that every wound was on the front of his body."

Brennus nodded. "No man here doubted that fact. What about your dogs?"

Solemis grimaced. Although he had tried to tell himself that they were just dogs, he had still found their deaths hard to accept. Unlike men who made their own choices in life, Tarvos and Suros had trusted him implicitly and he had ordered them to certain death. "We recognised Suros by his collar and we found the front part of Tarvos still attached to an Etruscan."

Brennus raised his brow at the description. "Still attached? How?"

Solemis answered proudly as the men in the room listened with fascination. "We found what remained of his head with its jaws still locked in the groin of one of their spearmen."

MARCUS FABIUS AMBUSTUS, *Pontifex Maximus*, *paterfamilias* of the Fabii idly fingered his beard as he reflected on another successful advancement for his *gens*. In truth it had taken little effort on his part to persuade the men of the senate to appoint his sons as ambassadors to the Etruscan City of Clevsin, Clusium as it was known among the Romans, when the appeal for help had arrived earlier that week. He cast a satisfied look around the room as he thought. No, they were fine boys, a credit to both himself and Rome, politically and militarily successful, steadily ascending the rungs of the *cursus honorum* as their breeding dictated. It was, he congratulated himself, as fine an evening as he had enjoyed for many a day. The boys would depart at first light and an evening's entertainment at his official residence, the *Domus Publica*, was the very least that he should provide.

Ahead of them the *poeta* raised his voice for emphasis as the first ever recitation of his new work reached its climax.

"And thus it was that, emboldened by years filled only with victories, the men of the Fabii fell to the snare set by the brigands of Etruria.

Despairing of ever removing the threat posed to their city in open conflict, the Etruscan contrived a different stratagem.

A herd was driven onto the plain before the fortified camp and in such disorder that, already contemptuous of the martial prowess of the Veientines, the men of Fabius, noble descendants of Hercules, sallied forth as to a raid.

The herders ran before this manly assault whilst the men set to guard them fled from the Romans as if from fire.

Emboldened by their easy victory and mindful of their superiority at every clash of arms, the Fabii were drawn further and further from the safety of their redoubt by the abundance of cattle, so easily obtained.

The road ahead narrowed but the sons of Hercules came on, scornful of a people who had proven time after time that it was not within their power to resist even this single gens of the people of Rome."

The Pontifex glanced across to his sons, and saw the light of battle shining from their eyes as the deeds of their ancestors unfurled before them. Quintus and Caeso were no strangers to the press of shields and Numerius had, in his youth, led the successful campaign which had ended in the capture and sack of the Volscian City of Anxur, bringing even greater glory to their name and not a little profit to the *familia* vaults. An extravagant cry drew his thoughts back to the recitation, and he settled back to listen as the poet reached the bloody conclusion to his tale.

"ALAS! They had given little thought to the cunning of the enemy and came on in little order. Once through the constriction they scattered across the plain as they sought to drive the herds to their encampment, when suddenly the sound of a war horn split the air and the borders came alive with rank upon rank of their enemies.

In disarray the Fabii fell back, but as Roman disciplina returned formed a square. Shoulder to shoulder, back to back, they fought against the overwhelming numbers of Veientines who stood as thickly as corn at the harvest.

Seeing the numbers ranged against them their leader, Caeso-"

the poeta nodded graciously to his namesake who inclined his head in recognition:

> *"-abandoned the square and formed a wedge, driving through the packed ranks and regaining what they thought would be the safety of the heights, only to find that a further force of Veientines had taken advantage of their absence and occupied it in force"*

The poeta lowered his voice as he neared the conclusion of his piece.

> *"There fell the flower of Rome, outnumbered and surrounded. It is known that of the three centuries and six of the sons of Fabius who had left Rome through the Carmental Gate that sun filled morning long before, carrying fire and violence to the Etruscans with the aid of no other, all perished, cut down to a man."*

The poeta paused and furrowed his brow as he allowed a few moments for the men present to reflect on the actions of their ancestors, before adding a note of cheer to his voice once more.

> *"But not quite all trod Elysian Fields. One boy remained. Too young to accompany his peers to war, though he had chafed for that honour, he had remained in Rome with the women of his gens. Hercules noted the*

quality of his descendants and ensured that from this one small cub the pride would grow again. To the great satisfaction and delight of the Romans and in honour of the fallen, a new praenomen, Numerious, was added to those others."

He nodded in turn at those present who bore the *familia* names:

"Marcus, Caeso and Quintus, so that men would call to mind the sacrifice made by them for the glory of Rome, and reflect on the quality of their lineage."

The Pontifex Maximus joined the applause as the poet bowed respectfully before his audience at the conclusion of his piece. Reaching beneath a cushion, Marcus retrieved a bag of coins and tossed them to the expectant performer who smiled happily as he was escorted from the room. Quintus replaced his cup on the table before him and looked across. "Not bad, not bad at all, father. It's still a shame about the ending though!" The group smiled as he continued. "Perhaps it was not the best send off you could have given us on the eve of our departure for Etruria!"

Caeso shoved his brother with his foot. "Maybe now is not the time to discuss that, brother."

Licinia, Numerius' wife replaced her cup and gathered the folds of her stola. "Caeso is quite right. It is time that we left the men to discuss more weighty affairs." She swept the group with a mischievous smile. "Let us retire ladies, where we can discuss more interesting things."

The women rose and went across to kiss Marcus lightly

on the cheek before departing in a waft of scent. The old Pontifex beamed at them as they went and he congratulated himself on the choices he had made when he had arranged marriages for the boys. Of course, he reflected ruefully, he had had the help and advice of Cornelia then and, although it had been almost ten years since she had died, it was at times such as this that he missed her the most.

The doors to the *triclinium* closed softly, and the men made themselves comfortable as servants came forward to recharge their cups. Marcus studied the wall paintings which ran around the room as a slave rearranged his pillows.

There were many *triclinia* in the Domus Publica and more than a few of them were far grander than the one in which were currently sat, but this had always been his favourite for intimate gatherings, especially those which consisted of the members of his gens. Unlike the grander rooms with their riotous images and mosaics of Bacchus and Pan, the room which they had always called the 'familia room' was small and intimate. It had been Cornelia who had discovered the room when it was little more than a storeroom and she had immediately seen its potential. Like the more formal triclinia, the room opened out directly onto the *peristylium* with its exotic plants, magnificent colonnades and statues of the gods, but there the similarity ended. His wife had noticed that, although small, the view from the threshold of the room was simply breathtaking, taking in a magnificent panorama of the city but focusing particularly finely on the quadriga of Jupiter. Perched high on its temple atop the Capitoline hill, the chariot drawn image of the father of the gods basked in the glow of the setting sun from late afternoon until the orb finally set in the West, the perfect time to relax and entertain after a day of toil and duty in the city.

Stripping the room, she had instructed one of the leading

artisans to oversee its complete refurbishment. The floor had been tastefully tiled and the walls stripped back, before the damp lime plaster had been repainted in a series of frescoes which told the story of the gens. Beginning with an image depicting simple shepherds on the scrubby hills which would become the city, the scenes encircled the room as they told the tale of the triumphal rise of the Fabii. It was the story of Rome itself, and each member of the familia were intensely proud of the part they had played in its rise to greatness.

The ceiling was dominated by a central image of Hercules himself, around which were painted representations of the god's twelve labours. It was an intimate and tasteful place for the familia to dine, and the evenings were greatly treasured by them. It was, Marcus reflected, the perfect way in which to honour the memory of Cornelia.

The cups charged, the Pontifex ordered the servants to depart and regarded his sons. "I have asked you all here this evening not only to toast your success in the North, but also to share the knowledge of the events which have led us to this place." He sipped from his cup as the brothers shared a look. "What do you *think* that you know at the moment? Numerius; you are the general among us."

Numerius pulled a face. "Thousands of shaggy Gauls have pitched up outside Clusium and routed their army. It's easily done," he glanced at his brothers as a smile played across his features. "Even Marcus Furius Camillus managed to take Veii and it only took him, what, nine years was it?"

Caeso interjected. "I think that you will find that it was a full decade, brother."

Numerius nodded his thanks and shrugged. "Thank you; I stand corrected, it was indeed ten years. It was unfortunate that he used the wealth he gained from the sack of the city to give so much work to his cronies on the new temple he had promised to house the goddess Juno, and forgot his promise to pay one-tenth to thc mighty Apollo. Why should the plebs have to make up the shortfall out of their own purses, while Camillus and his high-born friends hoard their own considerable wealth? What's more," he continued fervently, "it was Camillus who persuaded the senators not to move the excess population of Rome into the empty houses of Veii, just to keep the rental income high from the wretched *insulae* owned by the patricians, cramming the poor into squalid rooms three, four and even five stories high. Veii is barely more than ten miles to the north of Rome, it could have housed a free and prosperous population of brothers, the twin cities of Rome, a Remus to stand alongside the Romulus of Rome herself, if it were not for the greed of Camillus and his like."

A gentle round of applause washed around the room at the end of Numerius' impassioned speech. The Fabii had for the last century taken the side of the plebians in the ongoing battle between the classes of Rome, and the wars of the last decade between the city and their Aequi and Volsci neighbours had cost the people dearly. Eventually the wars had been brought to a successful conclusion, but the appointment of Camillus as dictator had ushered in a period fraught with danger for the Fabii and their allies. Quintus popped another grape into his mouth as he joined in the discussion. "Is the great dictator still skulking down in Ardea?"

Numerius shrugged. "So I hear; a stinking little place, it suits him. He should not have cheated the people of Rome, he deserved his banishment."

The brothers murmured in agreement. The days of Camillus' rule had been uncomfortable ones for many, but good Roman law had prevailed in the end and the tyrant had been deposed.

Their father had kept his council during the conversation

as he sipped from his cup, but he finally judged the time was ripe to begin his explanation of the factors which had driven recent events. “It's good that you have brought up the person of our old friend the dictator. It would seem that we have the man to thank for the situation which you are tasked by the senate to mediate tomorrow.” The brothers were instantly intrigued as Marcus continued. “I have been spending my time since you were appointed to the post of ambassadors trying to discover what I could about the situation in the North, and it would seem that we owe the presence of these barbarians to the ongoing ambition of our old friend Camillus. I have discovered that the reason why Camillus was so reluctant to share the spoils from the fall of Veii with Apollo and his priests was because he already had other plans for the treasure.”

The brothers shared a look of curiosity as they waited for their father to explain his findings. The Pontifex smiled smugly. He had been anticipating this moment ever since he had uncovered the plots which Camillus had been hatching in the North. He had had to pull in a few old favours, and meet with several people he would rather have avoided but he had no regrets; the revelations had been worth the effort. “Camillus was intent on widening the war, both in the South and the North. He had been secretly channelling payments, quite large payments at that, to certain chieftains in the barbaricum by way of an intermediary from Sikelia, a merchant called Kyriakos. This Greek was duped by Camillus into believing that the payments were coming from his own countrymen in Syracuse, and he managed to persuade large numbers of Gauls to migrate through the passes of the Alpes to join their brothers in Cisalpine Gaul. Obviously the arrival of thousands upon thousands of Gauls on their northern frontier would have upset the delicate balance between the Gauls already there, the Greeks down the coast in Massalia who would shoulder the blame, and the northern cities of the Etruscan League."

Numerius gasped at the audacity of the plan as the brothers shared a look of wonder. "The wily old bastard! Perhaps we underestimated the man. Naturally," he continued, as a mind trained in strategy worked through the ramifications, "while the Etruscans were busy in the North, Camillus could gobble up a few of their southern cities, maybe even advance our borders north of the Ciminian Forest."

Caeso pulled a face. "This is terrible; I am beginning to like the man!"

They all gave an ironic snort. Far too much had passed between the rival factions for a reconciliation to be that easy. Quintus waited for the resulting laughter to subside and shot his father another question. "So why have the barbarians turned up here in the South? It's a bloody mess. They have settled across the salt route down through the valley of the Tiberis, and several of my clients, good friends, are facing ruin."

Marcus smoothed his beard and fixed them with a stare. It was the same look they remembered from childhood if they had failed to live up to their father's high expectations and they quietened immediately. "My sources tell me that the Etruscans discovered the plot, and sent a body of equites north to make an attempt on the life of the leader of the Gauls before they had travelled too far south. Leaderless, there was at least a chance that the barbarians would return to their lands, but the attempt was unsuccessful. The survivors shadowed the Gauls and attempted to enlist the help of other barbarian tribes, but they were largely unsuccessful and they duly arrived on our side of the Alpes last autumn." He shrugged. “All they could do was pay the Gauls already there to move them further down the valley of the Bodencus and hope that they attacked the Umbrians instead, but it would seem that they were to be disappointed.”

The mood in the room had grown increasingly sombre as the Pontifex's tale unfolded, and the enormity of the task which awaited them at Clusium began to become apparent to the brothers. Numerius leaned forward on his lectus and shared a look of concern with his siblings before looking across to his father. “This is all very tragic father and I can see how it reflects badly on Camillus and the Etruscans, but surely any turmoil in the North can only serve to strengthen Rome's position. I still fail to see why you pushed so hard for the Fabii to sort out this mess.”

Marcus leaned forward, his features suddenly contorted into a rictus of hate. “As Pontifex Maximus and high priest of the Collegium Pontificum, it falls to me to safeguard the honour and dignity of the gods. Rome will rise or fall by the will of the gods, not by the actions of dictators. I am told that these Gauls have occupied the headwaters of the goddess Tiberis, the sacred river which runs past Rome herself, and are sacrificing to their barbaric gods at the twin springs there. It cannot continue or Rome itself will fall. They have sullied the waters which feed our city,” he spluttered as he sought to describe the abomination which the gods in their wisdom had seen fit to inflict upon them, “this...this...terror Gallicus!”

He clenched his fists to emphasise the importance of his final instruction to his sons. “These barbarians must be beaten and pushed back beyond the Apeninnus. I don't care what it takes to achieve this goal, but they must be utterly destroyed.”

18

It was a further two days before Hektor garnered his courage and approached the druid for the help which they both knew he needed. Following the revelation that she had all but learnt their language unaided, Catumanda had used the time well.

Hesperos, the owner of the *Alexa*, had had the druid in plain sight from his position on the steering platform ever since they had sailed, and he had clearly formed a shrewd idea of what to expect. A deep rumble of laughter had issued from the stout man at the expressions of amazement on the faces of his crew as the druid had calmly joined their post meal conversation, and he had shown his own lack of surprise as he had thrown in the comment: "Catumanda, I suggest that if you ever attempt to study a language in secret in the future that you practice your words without moving your lips!" He had then delighted the druid by asking the young boy, Philippos, to teach her the intricacies of their language as he went about his work. As the boy's work seemed to consist mainly of fishing from the side of the ship this was hardly too taxing, and Catumanda had happily taken the opportunity to reacquaint herself with a fishing line.

Catumanda smiled pleasantly when Hektor finally plucked up the courage and shuffled across to her as the crew relaxed following their midday meal. Clearing his throat, he spoke in a self conscious murmur. "Catumanda, I am sorry if I seemed to resent your presence aboard the ship. I am weighed down by a great burden, and I thought that you might bring bad luck on board from Pretannica."

Catumanda shrugged and answered in the language which still seemed to fit about her tongue like a new pair of shoes, a thing to be brought out and admired, but not yet fully comfortable. Philippos had told the druid that the Greeks referred to the island of Albion as the Pretannic Isles and the people as the Pretanni, the painted ones, due to the habit of the leading men and warriors to daub their skin, and Catumanda waited patiently as the Greek crew member fought a final battle with his conscience as he prepared to unburden himself. Finally, sensing the man's fear, she laid a reassuring hand on his arm. "I will read the entrails of one of the birds if Hesperos agrees."

Catumanda pushed herself up from the deck and rested her hand against the guard rail as she walked towards the steering platform. Drawing herself up upon the raised section of deck, she chuckled as Hesperos pointed at the big twin steering oars and threw her a question. "And what are these?"

Catumanda pulled a wry smile and answered immediately. "Those are known as pedalia, kubernetes."

Philippos had explained that most Greek ships needed a man at each steering oar, but due to the small size of the *Alexa* one strong man was deemed sufficient. As a result, both Hesperos and Markos had developed upper bodies which would not have shamed a bull and their shoulders and arms were corded with wiry muscle. It was a different kind of power to her own but, to her surprise and despite the sweet smelling beards, Catumanda found that she was attracted to them both.

Hesperos' face lit up with delight at her fluent reply, and he laughed in surprise and acknowledgement at her skill. Kubernetes was their name for helmsman, and the Greek was clearly impressed with her progress in learning the tongue which they proudly claimed to be the first and only language of civilisation. "Very good! I shall have to make sure that Philippos receives an extra portion of food this evening for his efforts in teaching our barbarian the only language of cultured men," he said with a gleam in his eye.

Catumanda ignored the jibe and indicated the pen which had been erected to keep a number of small goats, lambs and chickens to provide fresh meat for the crew on the return journey. "I would like to help Hektor. May I take one of the hens for sacrifice?"

Hesperos paled immediately and swallowed hard. Leaning forward he lowered his voice and answered in a worried tone. "I will not allow anything to jeopardise the safety of my ship and cargo. If Hektor has an appointment with Hades he can travel alone."

Catumanda shook her head. "If Hektor pays you for the bird and asks for my divination, then any messages from the gods will be for him and him alone." Arion stood nearby and the druid turned her head to one side so that the man could not hear her next sentence. "Hektor's mind is clearly troubled. If I can help to allay his fears he will be a more efficient member of your crew. I am no seafarer, but I do know that your god Poseidon is quick to punish sloppy seamanship."

Hesperos looked along the deck and Catumanda could see that he was studying Hektor. Finally he sighed and nodded thoughtfully. “It is as you say druid. Hektor's mind is often elsewhere, and that could cost me my ship. Send him to me and I will sell him a hen. We will do this thing immediately if you are agreeable?”

THE CREW HAD SHORTENED SAIL, and the *Alexa* wallowed in the swell as they gathered amidships to witness the ritual. Catumanda had used her moon blade to shave the front part of her scalp, and she marked her face with the correct pattern of swirls and dots to attract the spirits to this place for the divination as the crew had looked on anxiously. It was the first time that most of them had seen the blade, which was clearly a weapon of great power, and Catumanda had caught several of the men exchange worried glances after their earlier reluctance to grant her passage. The looks had been as nothing compared to the unease which had swept the crew the moment that Catumanda had retrieved all that remained of her old adversary, Piso. The druid had completed carving the symbols of power, both inside and around the rim of what was clearly the top of a man's skull while she had prepared for her ordeal on the Spirit Isle, and the brothers there had skilfully inlaid them with gold which shone dully in the watery sunlight of the northern autumn.

Following Catumanda's instructions, Hesperos had allowed Hektor to choose which hen to sacrifice from among the stack of cages, and the man now came down the deck towards them holding the fated bird by its legs. Drawing up before Catumanda, he repeated the request as he had been instructed. “Druid, I have a sacrifice which I wish to dedicate to the spirits. In return I ask that you interpret any messages from them on my behalf.”

Hektor passed across a piece of silver in payment, and the

druid slipped it into the pouch which hung at her waist. Catumanda took the bird and held it aloft by its head. As the hen kicked and struggled she called on the spirits to reveal their secrets, and reaching inside her tunic she drew her moon blade once again and removed the hen's head with one smooth sweep of her arm. Despite the solemnity of the occasion, Catumanda could not help but smile inwardly as she noticed Arion step smartly back as the bird's lifeblood swept across the deck in a crimson arc. The Trinobantes had a good word for those who seemed to take extreme pride in their appearance, coxcomb. Today's work shirt was a crisp white affair, and she could only imagine the horror with which this coxcomb would react if a line of chicken blood suddenly sprayed across it.

Catumanda ran the gory neck of the bird down the front of Hektor's face to reinforce his connection with the sacrifice, before lowering herself to the sun whitened deck as she slashed open the bird's chest. Carefully balancing herself on the gently rolling boards, she spread the hen's flesh and noted the way that the viscera spilled out. Catumanda crouched and scurried crab-like around the tiny corpse until she was satisfied that she had gleaned every scrap of information from them. Finally, taking up her blade once more, she carefully removed the bird's liver and placed it inside the bowl. This was the most important part of the ritual, and the druid stared intently as the crew members looked on uneasily. The liver was the wellspring of the lifeblood which coursed through every living thing and, as such, was the source of the power which drove the physical body in the same way that the head was home to the spiritual being.

Most druids carried a small bronze platter which helped them to map out the signs and peculiarities contained within the liver, but Catumanda was travelling light. She had asked

Ruffos to care for it while she was away, but she knew the markings by heart and she dipped her finger into the blood and began to sketch out the design on the sun whitened planking of the *Alexa*'s deck. As she studied the markings, the message they contained slowly resolved themselves until she was confident that she had understood all there was to see. Inexperience caused her to shoot the expectant crew a look of alarm, but she quickly recovered her poise and smiled at the man who stood before her, pensively chewing on his lower lip. "Do you know a woman called Aikaterine?"

A wave of joy mixed with incredulity washed across the man's face as he nodded enthusiastically. "Yes…yes…she is my wife!"

Catumanda grinned up at Hektor as she wiped the blood from her fingers with a small cloth. "She wishes to know if it is still your intention to name your newborn son Thestor?"

Hektor gasped and gripped the sleeve of his neighbour as tears of happiness came to his eyes. Finally he managed to answer the druid in a voice made thick with emotion. "Tell her, yes. I still wish to honour the memory of my father thus."

Catumanda wiped the markings from the deck with a sweep of her hand and rose to her feet. "I am sorry Hektor, I cannot. Divination is not a two way conversation, but there are other ways which I can use." Catumanda took the man by the shoulders as his friends began to move forward and offer their congratulations. "I promise you that I will find a way to deliver the message to your wife. Your son will carry your father's name."

THE NIGHT WAS UNNATURALLY CALM as the *Alexa* nudged her way slowly south. Several days had passed since they had put the rocky headlands of Celtica behind them, and now each man knew that they were deep within the region known as the Bay of Storms. Despite the lateness of the hour the crew had gathered about the cargo hatch as they drank in the beauty of the evening. The sea was as smooth as any pond; looking back the way they had come, Catumanda marvelled at the luminescent wake which trailed away to the horizon as straight and bright as a shooting star.

High above them a gibbous moon shone brightly down on ragged tufts of clouds, their rims edged with silver as they calmly rolled away to the north-west. Each of them sat lost in their own dreamy world as they stared out at the great celestial dome of the night sky, every constellation, Kassiopeia, Perseus, Andromeda, a gift to the Greeks from their gods to enable them to navigate safely home however far their ships wandered.

Markos was kubernetes, and he suddenly called out to them from the steering platform and pointed outboard. Slipping down from the raised hatch cover, Catumanda and Philippos joined the others as they hauled themselves up onto the deck rail and clung to the shroud lines.

At first there was nothing to be seen, and they were about to lambaste the helmsman for dragging them back from their warm thoughts of home when a large dark shape broke the surface not half a mile away. As the shadowy shape fell back into the sea in a welter of spray, the backs of several others broke the glassy surface before slipping smoothly back into the depths.

At her side, Philippos instinctively clutched the druid's sleeve in fear as he gasped out a word, *"Ketea!"*

Catumanda laid a comforting hand on the boy's shoulder and glanced up at Arion and Hektor for support, but despite the fact that the moon had washed all the colour from the world she could see that the men too had paled before the sight of this Ketea. Catumanda looked down at the boy and smiled reassuringly. "You seem to have neglected this part of my Greek lessons."

Philippos seemed unconvinced. "The appearance of even one *Ketos* is a bad omen, Catumanda. More than one, Ketea, is a very bad thing."

The men watched in silence, and Catumanda could tell from their nervous expressions that the crew were hoping desperately that the Ketea would pass them by. Just at the point where it appeared that the gods would answer their prayers, the nearest Ketos sheared away from the pack and drove in at them.

As they strained their senses, the stillness of the night carried the sound of staccato clicks and whistles to their ears, and the Greeks tensed as the group turned in to follow their leader. Catumanda smiled up at the men in the shroud lines, but she could clearly see the look of terror on their faces. "What is wrong? They are only sea wolves. They visit our coasts at home and they never attack men, even if they are in the water."

Arion and Hektor seemed not to hear her attempt at reassurance, as they half stumbled down from the deck rail and retreated to what they obviously hoped was the safety of the cargo hatch, right at the centre of the ship. At her side Philippos tugged at her sleeve. "Come druid. Let us join them until the Ketea leave us."

The big animals had reached the *Alexa* now and they circled the ship, calling to each other across the rippling bow wave. Catumanda decided to show her new friends that the creatures meant them no harm, and she quickly slipped out of her clothing and dropped overboard before their horrified faces. To her surprise the waters of the great southern sea felt warm against her skin, and she trod water as she waited for the first of the great beasts to examine this strange new creature among them.

Despite her confidence that the Ketea meant them no harm, Catumanda still felt a knot of anxiety tighten within her as a long dark shadow suddenly broke the surface little more than an arm-length away. There came the sudden harsh report of air as the sea wolf cleared its blow hole, and Catumanda blinked away the misting of water vapour which drifted across her face. Other dark shapes loomed before her on the surface of the moon-silvered sea, and the occasional clicks and whistles increased in frequency to become a dizzying chatter of chirrups and calls. They were clearly discussing her, and Catumanda cautiously reached forward and ran her hand along the dark smooth dome of the Ketos to show that she meant them no harm. The animal rolled gently to one side, revealing its white belly and the side markings which shone like ice in the moonlight, and Catumanda found that she was looking directly into the deep obsidian depths of the creature's eye. The whistles and calls from the Ketea died away suddenly, and Catumanda could feel the silent gaze of a dozen pairs of eyes upon her as man and beast held their collective breath and watched and waited. The silence stretched as druid and sea wolf regarded each other across the swell. Suddenly the great animal blew a loud blast from its blowhole and, taken unawares, the woman snatched back her hand with a start. Catumanda was moved to laughter as she recognised an unmistakeable glint of amusement in the creature's eye, and the Ketos nudged its great snout firmly into her body as if to reinforce the joke it had played on her. A final chirrup, and it sank back beneath the surface as an excited chatter began among both the Ketea and the watching men above as the spell was broken. A distinctive bird-like call rose and fell several times from astern of the *Alexa* as the leader moved away, and the more general chatter fell in pitch and intensity as the rest of the pack listened to their instructions.

As they moved away, Catumanda watched as the dark shapes circled the ship one last time before following their leader northwards. She listened as the reports from the wolves' blowholes trailed away, reluctant to leave the scene of their encounter, until she was left alone in the warm sea.

SHE SHARED out the last of the chedwr as the sun struggled into the eastern sky in an almost reluctant display of pale greys and pinks. The crew had grudgingly admitted some time ago that the sharp tang of the hard yellow cheese held some attraction for them, but they had insisted that Greek cheese was far tastier as the druid knew that they would.

As they lay sprawled amidships and gnawed on the now hard and split remnants of the final morsels of Ruffos's parting gift, Markos explained their fear of the Ketos. "Centuries ago there lived a proud and boastful *anassa*," he paused to explain the new word to the northerner by smiling and making the outline of a woman with his hands to the delight of the crew, "the wife of the basileus, called Kasseopeia. She was very beautiful but also vain, and she let it be known that the beauty which her daughter Andromeda had inherited from her eclipsed even that of the nymph daughters of the titan, Nerius, a sea god. Poseidon heard of this boast and, greatly offended, let it be known that he would send the sea monster Ketos to destroy their city. The basileus consulted an oracle who advised him that the only way to appease Poseidon was to sacrifice his daughter, and although she was left chained to a sea rock the great hero Perseus confronted Ketos with the head of Medusa."

Catumanda glanced around the circle of enraptured Greeks who were nodding in agreement at every point. Markos pulled on his skin of wine and swallowed noisily before resuming his tale. "To look upon the head of Medusa was fatal and the Ketos was turned to stone but, outraged at this insult, Poseidon was not to be thwarted. He plucked Kasseopeia from the earth and sat her on a throne in the heavens where she remains to this day."

Markos sat back at the conclusion of his explanation as his fellow Greeks murmured their agreement. Catumanda swallowed her chedwr, still unconvinced. "But how are the sea wolves connected to this tale of gods and heroes? They meant us no harm, if they had I should not be sitting here among you now."

Markos shook his head. "We call all monsters of the deep Ketos; they are harbingers of ill fortune to all men who ply the sea in their frail craft. I have lived my entire life within a mile of the sea, as have all the men you see before you and we know this to be so." His expression grew serious and he gave a fatalistic shrug. "You will see druid, it gave us the word which we use for any great disaster, *katastrophe.* We can expect the Bay of Storms to reveal its true nature to us sooner rather than later I think."

19

Solemis and Albiomaros walked their mounts free of the tree line and drew rein as the other scouts filed out behind them. Albiomaros glanced across to his friend and raised a brow. "Reinforcements?"

Solemis laughed. "I hope so. If that is the best they can do, we will be home soon!"

The valley sloped gently away before them down to the roadway, a roadway which had until the previous week contained nothing but frightened people heading south. This day however the flow had been temporarily reversed, and the valley echoed to the sound of a column of mounted men making their way towards the distant city of Clevsin. Solemis ran his gaze along the heavily armed force, mentally quartering them as he tallied their numbers. Albiomaros had beaten him to it. "About a hundred, it's difficult to be sure with this heat haze."

Solemis snorted and called out to his men. "Do you all agree?"

A good natured chorus confirmed that they did, and

Solemis shared in the laughter which followed. The week which had passed since the battle outside the city had seen the Horsetails range far and wide across the fertile plains and hills of Etruria. Living off the land they had swept to the south of the city, rounding up cattle and sheep to provide food for the besieging army of the Senones and driving them back to the main roadway where they would be collected and driven north.

The detachment had proven to be the ideal way to forge the members of his clan into a disciplined fighting force, and he had been pleased with the progress they had made in such a short time. It was, he knew, a form of fighting which ran contrary to all they had aspired to in the forests of Celtica. There the ideal warrior was a lone hero, meeting his enemy face to face and vanquishing him under the admiring gaze of his clansmen; but they were no longer in Celtica, and although the mass charge so characteristic of home was too deeply ingrained to change in the wider ranks of the army, the mounted clans such as the Horsetails would need to adapt if they were to prosper here.

Solemis looked again along the line of his clansmen and smiled happily. To their credit they had accepted the change readily, and he knew that the victory which they had accomplished together against the Etruscan equites had helped greatly. He was now a proven chieftain who had brought victory and reputation to the clan as a whole, and most of the men now saw Cauros' sacrifice as the magnificent final act of the chieftainship of Solemis' father, Connos.

Albiomaros spoke again. “What do you want to do?”

Solemis threw his friend a wicked grin. “Hit them with a flank attack of course. Are you set?”

A momentary look of horror swept across the big man’s

face, before his shoulders slumped as he realised that he had fallen for his chieftain's joke. The other scouts laughed as Albiomaros pulled a wry smile and replied with a quip of his own. "I meant after we had chased them away. What shall we do then?"

Solemis snorted and wheeled his stallion to face northwards. Inhaling deeply he looked away towards the distant city. "They will reach our outlying positions soon. They are too few to be mounting an attack and they are riding openly towards Crixos and his clan." He pulled the head of his mount back to the West and clicked him on. "Let them go, Brennus can see to them. We will finish our sweep around the hills opposite and head back before nightfall. We can discover who they were and what they wanted then."

NUMERIUS SLOWED his horse to walking pace and approached the Gaulish warriors. A line of barbarians had quickly formed as they approached the outskirts of their camp, and the Roman ambassadors and their three *turmae,* ninety men in all, approached them with some trepidation. Numerius could see immediately that the tales he had been told of the great stature and shaggy appearance of these men from the North were no exaggeration, and he sent a small invocation winging its way to Hercules that these giants were aware that their position as ambassadors made them inviolate, even in heated situations such as these.

The plain and the hillside away to his right were awash with Gauls, but Numerius found some comfort in the fact that they looked very much like any other army from a distance. The camp had a sense of order and a rugged discipline which told his experienced eye that they were far more than a seething mass of disorganised rabble.

Ahead of him the barbarian line drew apart, and a mounted warrior who was obviously a man of some importance made his way through. To the Roman's surprise the weapons and attire of the Gauls were of a high standard throughout the army, and he hoped that his father had not made the mistake of underestimating them. The leader of the group wore a muscled breast plate which must have been looted from an Etruscan he decided, but the warrior's choice of tunic beneath it would not have looked out of place on a wealthy Roman. A deep blue the garment had been edged with what appeared to be gold thread, the swirling patterns of which were clearly a barbarian design, so that at least had not begun its life on an Etruscan loom.

Numerius grudgingly admitted that the man's helm was very likely to be superior to his own. Cast in sturdy iron, the helm incorporated a thick rim to help protect the wearer from an overhead sword stroke which tapered to end in a wide, heavily decorated neck guard at the rear. Heavily embossed cheek guards enclosed a large part of the wearer's face and offered a high degree of protection to the sides.

Really, the Roman decided, had it not been for the quite horrible checked trousers, the ridiculous tufts of fair hair and long flowing moustaches which every man here seemed to sport, many of them could have passed as a respectable Sabine or Umbrian if not quite a citizen of Rome. Their swords he noted with the practised eye of an experienced soldier, were particularly impressive in length, decoration and sophistication.

Caeso and Quintus rode to his side as the Gaul, flanked by his retainers, reined in and waited for them to come up to him. The Romans came to a halt several paces away from the Gaulish noble, and Numerius nodded in greeting as he announced the reason for their delegation. “I offer you greetings from the senate and people of Rome. My name is Numerius Fabius Ambustus and these are my brothers," he indicated to each side with a flamboyant wave of his hand, "Caeso Fabius Ambustus and Quintus Fabius Ambustus."

Numerius waited for his opposite number to reply, but the Gaul remained silent as he took in the arms and armour of the delegation. Finally, as what the Romans had expected to be a brief pause to enable the Gaul to introduce himself began to stretch uncomfortably, the man replied. "My name is Crixos," he shrugged nonchalantly; "just Crixos. I am afraid that the road is closed at the moment so you will have to go back." He made a show of leaning to one side in his saddle and looking back along the line of the mounted Roman escort. Shifting back he leaned forward conspiratorially. "I should leave here quickly if I were you, and take those pretty boys with you. I heard that there were men," he glanced back over the Roman's shoulder and smiled sarcastically, "big men, fighting around here. You could all get hurt."

Numerius' mouth opened and closed as his mind searched for a reply to the insult. He exchanged a look of shock with his brothers before, clearing his throat, his *disciplina* reasserted itself. "We are here at the request of the leading men of Clevsin. They wish us to help broker an agreement between their people and your own, that you may live together in peace."

Crixos shrugged with disinterest and picked at a finger nail, but Numerius had now recovered from the unexpected insults and his Roman sense of superiority flared within him. "I demand that you allow me safe passage to the city. The laws of all *civilised* nations," he spat, "recognise the rights of ambassadors to pass where and when they will, unimpeded by combatants!" Crixos' face brightened and he threw out his arms. "Why didn't you say that you were here under the laws of all *civilised* nations!" he cried as a rumble of laughter rolled along the Senone spearmen to his rear. Crixos guided his mount to the roadside and waved the Roman delegation on. "Make way for *civilised* men lads!" he cried out to the men barring the road. "What have I told you all before? Don't you know that it is the right of ambassadors to pass where and when they will, unimpeded by combatants?"

The Fabii brothers, their features contorted into masks of hate by their treatment at the hands of the Senone chieftain led on, as the Senone spear wall opened up to let them pass. Crixos' son, Caturix, had been at his father's side during the exchange and he edged his mount up as the Roman column passed by and the soldiers and warriors exchanged looks of mutual contempt. "Was that wise, father?"

Crixos looked across and pulled a innocent smile. "Was what wise?"

"Insulting their ambassadors and then letting them take eighty armed men through to the enemy. You know that they will probably join them now."

Crixos chuckled as he watched the last of the Romans clear the defences and canter away towards the pale stone walls of Clevsin. He threw an arm around his son and pulled him in. "If these Romans are starting to concern themselves in our affairs we will have to fight them one day, probably soon." He hawked and spat after the disappearing column. "They will not have sent second rate warriors here first impressions count, and despite what I said those boys looked as hard as iron. If we can kill a group like that in isolation, we won't have to fight them later when they will have their friends with them."

. . .

SOLEMIS AND CATURIX leaned forwards and refilled their cups from the bowl before them. Kicking back they drained the cervesia and sighed. “This is a good way to spend the day.”

Solemis looked out across the rolling fields towards the city and let out a small belch. “This is a beautiful country. It's a shame that Catubaros never got the chance to see the place that we moved to.”

Caturix nibbled along the length of the pork rib and tossed it onto the rapidly growing pile before them. The hill-side was filled with the comforting sounds of an army at rest. A hubbub rose into the clear blue skies as the Senone warriors sat in groups and swapped stories of war and women against a background of the metallic sounds of iron striking bronze as the spoils from the battle, breast plates, helms and greaves were adjusted to fit their new owners.

“Yes, but just think, the old chieftain is dining now with Sequana, not trying to find enough meat on these bones to last through to the next meal.”

They shared a laugh, and Solemis looked back to the low rectangular house which Brennus had made his own while they waited for the zilach, the ruler of the city, to decide when he was going to fight for his land. Both sides knew that they could not remain holed up within the walls of Clevsin forever, and the arrival of the ambassadors from Rome the previous day had indicated to the Senone leaders that matters were hopefully coming to a head.

“I wish that I was inside. Do you think that we will fight again?”

Caturix snorted. “I should think that it is a certainty. If you had seen the look on their faces yesterday after my father had spoken to them, I am surprised that they even went through the formality of meeting with Brennus.”

The Roman soldiers of the escort party had insisted on keeping their mounts with them and their leader had declined the offer of cervesia with a curt shake of his head. Solemis found that he was in agreement with his friend's assessment. These men were only following protocol; swords and spears would settle this dispute. A flurry of movement to his left reanimated the Roman escort as the ambassadors swept out through the doorway. The three men remounted and rode away with faces like thunder. Solemis tossed his cup away and hauled himself to his feet, watching as the Romans cantered back across the meadow.

"It looks as though you were right." He held out a hand and helped Caturix up; "it is time to check the edge on your weapons."

NUMERIUS SPLASHED THROUGH WHAT, in wetter months, would have been a ford in the River Clanis and slowed his horse to a trot. This late in the summer the flow had dried almost to a trickle, and the ships which travelled from the city down to its junction with the Tiberis were absent. Whether they would return after the winter rains had fallen in the distant Apeninnus and replenished their flow was now largely in the hands of foreigners, Romans and Gauls, and the chances of that Numerius decided with a smile, were not looking very good.

His brothers came abreast as he pointed the head of his mount towards the great wooden gates of Clevsin, still half a mile distant. Quintus shot him a smile. "I would call that a highly successful day's work."

The Fabii laughed as one as the horses walked on. Quintus continued, his face beaming. "Did you see the look on Brennus's face when I called him a barbarian? He obviously realised that it was an insult, but he clearly didn't have a clue what it meant."

Their laughter rolled across the hillside as Numerius shook his head in mock despair. "Well, he will find out pretty soon I imagine, and then there will be no chance of peace between the city and these Gauls." He smirked. "As you say, a highly successful day's work."

Caeso added his voice to the conversation. "I shall enjoy watching our enemies tear themselves asunder. It will be like a day at the arena." He shot his brothers a look of mischief. "Who is up for a wager?"

They laughed again at Numerius's reply. "I'll wager that these Gauls are in for a nasty shock. Not even the Etruscans can break before a horde of savages twice in one month, it's very bad for morale."

He urged his horse forward as the gates of the city creaked open on their great hinges to admit the mission. "Come on," he called back. "Let us go and break the bad news to them."

Solemis slipped into the room and slid along the back wall as he moved to stand in the only space remaining. He had taken the Horsetails out for a final sweep along the road he now knew to be called the Via Cassia, and although he still felt a little uneasy riding along the hard, unforgiving stone roadways here in the South he had to admit that they were a speedy and efficient means of moving around.

The Via Cassia led from Clevsin south to Rome itself, and he had taken it upon himself to ensure that no further Roman forces were in the area, preparing to mount a surprise flank attack when the armies were engaged in the morning: to his relief, his fears had been unfounded. Albiomaros had led a similar force to the North, and he had reported back that the roads and fields there too were empty. It seemed the cities of Etruria were content to leave their cousins to their fate.

Brennus was sat on the edge of a large table, swinging his legs absentmindedly as the last of the clan chiefs filled their cups and waited for him to begin. Spotting Solemis in the corner he threw the young Horsetail a nod and began his address. "Ah, Solemis has made it, excellent!" He paused and smiled at the room. "We can restart the war!"

A rumble of good-natured laughter filled the small room as the men glanced across. Crixos sauntered over and handed the chieftain a large cup of wine. Draining it in one, Brennus wiped his mouth on the sleeve of his tunic and belched. "Now *that's* how a barbarian *should* behave!" he exclaimed with a grin. Refreshed he waited for the men to settle, and the clan chiefs came instantly to attention as he began to outline his plans for the forthcoming battle. "Right, most of you know what went on here earlier but," he shot Solemis a wink, "for those of you who were out admiring the countryside, I will run through where I think we are at this moment. The Romans have no right to be involved in this dispute, and I told them so in no uncertain terms. They, for their part, are clearly on the side of the Etruscans, and mentioned to me that we might like to withdraw back across the Apeninnus and leave their sacred spring alone. I of course, thanked them for their offer but respectfully declined."

A rumble of laughter rolled around the room at their chieftains dry wit. They had all heard of the welcome given to the ambassadors by Crixos, and already knew to a man that the fighting could resume at any moment and they were thankful for it. It was inconceivable that the men from Rome would come north at their neighbour's apparent behest and ask them to leave their lands to make way for Senone settlers.

Since they had come to the South, they had learnt from their Celtic neighbours the Boii that Rome had been expanding northwards into Etruscan territory for decades. The city of Veii had been taken after a war lasting ten years and the male population put to the sword. The city had lain empty ever since, the women and children herded south to eke out the remainder of their days in slavery. Rome was clearly a burgeoning power, and would need to be confronted if their own farms and oppida were to remain safe, whichever side of the mountains they stood.

Brennus continued with his address. "We have beaten them once and we know how they like to fight. I travelled to many oppida over the course of last winter, and all the chieftains that I consulted about the fighting style of armies here, from the Boii and the Cenomani here in the South to the Insubri and Taurini up in the Bodencus Valley, agreed that the formation which we encountered in our first battle is invariably the fighting style which they will use time and again." Brennus cleared the table with a sweep of his hand and placed a loaf at the centre. "As you are all aware, this is the basis of the formation which they call the phalanx. Typically they are spearmen, but some of them will carry a heavy axe which they use to break the enemy front ranks. For some reason," he continued with a look of puzzlement, "they use the youngest, least experienced men in the front ranks and their best warriors in the rear." As the chiefs exchanged looks of surprise Brennus shook his head. "Apparently the idea is for the most experienced men to keep the phalanx as tight and compact as possible but," he swept them with a look of bemusement, "how they gain honour and reputation is beyond me." A murmur of agreement came from the equally shocked chieftains. Brennus tore a loaf in half and placed each block at either end of the first with a handful of olives flanking them. "Here on the ends are the light spearmen and archers who attempt to pick men off on their unprotected sides with arrows and javelins, backed up by their horsemen, the equites."

Brennus flicked a look up at Solemis. "Thanks to the actions of Solemis and his Horsetails we were spared their attentions in the first battle, but they are generally used to pursue defeated opponents as they attempt to flee the field." He glanced up with a smile. "So we will not be meeting them tomorrow, either."

The men in the room looked across to Solemis and the young chieftain felt a surge of pride when he saw the respect in their eyes. The previous summer he had been the inexperienced young son of a chieftain. The gods had provided him with opportunities to forge a reputation within the tribe and he had eagerly taken each one. Now he was the leader of his own clan and a respected war lord. Soon the city would fall and the Senones could move across to the rich lands. His marriage to Aia was set for the time of plenty, as the people knew the time after the harvest, and the resulting sons would cement the alliance between Crixos's clan and his own.

Brennus walked across to the amphora resting near the doorway and refilled his cup. Turning he stood foursquare and pursed his lips as he regarded the men before him. Clearly he had something unusual to share with them, and they exchanged brief glances as they waited for their leader to begin.

"This is the plan which I want us to execute when they come out." He fixed the clan chiefs with a look as if evaluating each man in turn before settling his gaze on Solemis. He shared a glance with Crixos at his side who gave a slight, almost imperceptible nod that he agreed with his chieftain's choice.

"Listen carefully, because I want to kill their leaders and end this once and for all," he growled. "To do that we need to punch through to their hiding place at the rear as quickly as possible, and that calls for a change of tactics on our part. These tactics are risky, but I know the quality of our clans and the chieftains who lead them. Kill the zilach and we can plunder the city and begin to share out the land; fail and it will be *our* heads decorating the walls."

20

The mist had risen during the early hours. Brands had been placed in the valley at sundown, to give warning of a surprise attack by the forces of the city under the cover of darkness. Celts of course would never countenance such a thing. Spirits of all kinds roamed the land when Belenus the shining one took his rest, and many of them would eagerly seize the opportunity to snatch away the soul of a dying warrior, but the customs and beliefs of the southerners were still a mystery to them and no chances had been taken.

As the time neared for the sun to edge its way clear of the eastern peaks, the gossamer strands had begun to haze the banks of the Clanis. Strengthening its grip in the valley the milky veil had slowly flowed out to envelop the surrounding fields, snuffing out the torches with almost godly indifference. Blinded, Brennus had ordered the chieftains of the clans to roust their men early and assemble at their assigned positions in the battle line.

Solemis felt the first trace of warmth caress his back: twisting around, he squinted at the eastern skyline. As he had expected the pale bow of the returning sun had finally crested the hills, and its warmth and light began to rush along the plain towards them like an incoming tide. Albiomaros nudged him with his elbow and indicated the centre of the shield hedge. "Here comes the first to die."

The battle line parted as the distinctive russet clad figure of the chief druid emerged leading the Etruscan by a thin woven halter. Solemis snorted as he saw the layers of arrogance displayed by the captive peel away bit by bit as he began to realise that he was not about to be ransomed after all. "He should have kept quiet. The more important he made himself out to be, the more likely he was to be the chosen sacrifice."

The druid led the man to a point where they would be visible by the best part of the army and roughly swung the captive around to face the rising sun. Even at some distance, Solemis could see the fear which now furrowed the Etruscan's features as he saw Brennus, a battle chieftain dressed for war, emerge from the ranks and make his way down to them. The big man had already donned his raven helm and the wings of the bird moved gently in time with his footsteps as he came up to the pair. As the Celtic host looked on in silence the druid increased his grip on the halter and drew the Etruscan upright. Brennus cried out an invocation to the great war god Camulos as he thrust his lancea skyward. The heavy blade flamed as it caught the rays of the returning sun before, with the speed of a snake strike, the Senone war leader brought the point down and punched it into the captive's belly. The Etruscan gasped in shock and horror as the blade sliced obliquely down, pulping his innards as it passed through, deep within his groin. The strike was expertly judged to cause the maximum amount of pain while leaving the liver intact, and the army watched in anticipation as the sacrificial victim doubled up in agony and crumpled to the ground.

Brennus retreated several paces and, turning, raised his gory spear as the war cries of the Senones rolled out across the valley. Turning back he became merely one more warrior among many as he waited for Camulos to reveal the omens to the priest.

A nervous flicker ran along the line as the warriors waited for the druid to read the auguries for the day ahead. Solemis glanced back at Brennus and smiled at their leader's proud posture; only the absent-minded tugging at his moustache betrayed the anxiety which boiled within him.

The druid was moving around the man now, crouching and scuttling as he studied the victim's wild, agonised thrashings. Finally the holy man seemed satisfied that he had gleaned what information he could from the movements of the sacrifice, and he moved forward and pulled the man roughly onto his back. Bending forward there was a flash as light reflected from highly polished metal, and the druid leaned across his victim and opened his belly with a practised slash from his moon blade. The Etruscan was still watching in horror as the priest reached inside his belly and scooped out the shiny blue loops of gut, and the druid was muttering unconcernedly as the gods finally released the man from his torment and he lowered his head for the final time.

Reaching inside the hollow cavity which had a short time ago been a living, breathing man, the druid made a cut with his blade and removed the liver. Placing it inside a bronze platter he proceeded to cut and examine the organ as the impatient warriors looked on. A heavy silence had fallen on the army as they awaited the judgement of Camulos. Solemis knew that the large, bluish organ was the source of the blood which filled the body, the very wellspring of divine power within each and every man. The critical moment of the divination had been reached, and he chewed at his lower lip as he waited for the druid to conclude his deliberations.

The hush which had fallen on the assembled host was suddenly shattered as the druid looked up at Brennus and grinned. Solemis saw the priest mouth words at the chieftain, but they were lost in a storm of noise as the Celtic army took their lead from the man's expression and all the anxieties of the moment were released in an outpouring of joy. Within moments, carnyx were wooding the air above them, and the haunting wail of the great bronze horns rolled across the valley.

The omens were good, and as if to confirm the will of the gods, the air above them was torn by the strident rasp of a crow. Lifting their gaze the Senones watched jubilantly as three enormous crows passed over them to settle in the canopy of a large cypress. As the army cheered the arrival of the Morrigan and her sisters, their eyes were drawn on towards the place where the city of Clevsin still lay beneath a mantle of grey.

Solemis narrowed his eyes as his mind sought to understand the picture which was slowly unfolding before him. The fog which had dogged their night was lifting quickly now as the sun rose higher, and its upper levels now glistened as thousands of points of light sparkled on its surface like a thousand stars. A murmur rolled along the line as the warriors noticed the phenomenon, and Solemis looked back just in time to see the mist thin to reveal the blades of Etruscan spears. He shared a look with Albiomaros and grinned. "Heft your shield, genos. They are out."

. . .

NUMERIUS, Quintus and Caeso stood at the head of the Roman horsemen and waited impatiently for the great doors of the city of Clevsin to swing inward. The soldiers of Etruria pressed in on them to all sides, and it was apparent from their expressions that they were feeling as bemused as they that a Roman *turmae* were to take the field alongside them.

The Fabii had walked the streets of the city the previous day as they discussed the options which were remaining for them, if they were to stand any hope of fulfilling their father's wishes to free the headwaters of the Tiberis from the stain of barbarian occupation. They had all agreed that the Gauls could not have picked a worse time to spill over the Apeninnus and stir up trouble on Rome's northern border. The dictator, Camillus, had only been banished from Rome a very few years and he had taken a number of experienced soldiers with him. Sensing weakness the tribes to the south and east of Rome, the Volsci and the Aequi, had renewed their long standing wars against the Romans whose armies were now heavily engaged on both fronts. Once again it had fallen on the Fabii to quell unrest in Etruria, and it was not without some satisfaction that the brothers had taken up the mantle of honour bequeathed them by their ancestors. Still, he reflected with a snort of disbelief, he had never thought to see his gens attempting to save the necks of Etruscans, not even in his most grape addled moments.

The order was given, and the torches and braziers which lined the main thoroughfare leading to the gate were extinguished as the great doors swung open on newly greased hinges. The plan was a simple one and, he had to admit grudgingly, excellent. Once the sentinels on the city walls had confirmed that the usual fogs and mists had begun to thicken about the course of the river, the army had assembled and waited for it to cloak the valley. Soon the torches set up by the enemy in the lowlands had been extinguished one after another, and the order had been given to move out of the city and form up in silent ranks. The equites were to remain within the walls of the city until the advance commenced, their sheer size and potential for noise excluding them from the initial attack, while their greater speed would enable them to quickly close with the barbarians as soon as contact was made.

Numentius had gratefully accepted the zilach's offer that he and his men observe the battle from the ridge line which bordered the field. Barred from taking an active part in the attack by their official position as ambassadors, the Romans were eagerly looking forward to, what was in effect, a great gladiatorial display for their entertainment. The ridge skirted the walls of the city and ran down to a deep gully, enclosing the battlefield in the sweep of its great arm.

Several of the Etruscan leaders had told him of the barbarian charge against their left flank in the initial encounter between them, and the Roman hoped that the decisive fighting at that point would lead the enemy to try their luck there once again.

Soon they were out through the big doors and silently descending the valley towards the water meadow at its base. The fog was thick now, but it seemed to have taken an age to form; even late in the summer the hours of darkness left little time to manoeuvre an army into position, but finally they were set.

The zilach arrived at his position, and the great phalanx of the army of Clevsin silently raised their spears and prepared to commence the advance. Ahead of them the first pale light of the new day clipped the hills to the East, the long rolling crests of the Apeninnus barely distinguishable from the dark clouds above them.

As Numentius exchanged a grin with his brothers and prepared to advance against the slumbering army of barbarians, a great cry rent the air ahead quickly followed by the braying din of war horns.

The Roman cursed; the ploy had failed.

THE ARMY WATCHED as Brennus strode down into the valley and issued his war chant. The Etruscan phalanx was barely a spear throw away, and the contemptuous display from the chieftain served only to rouse the Celtic army to greater levels of defiance. As the champions moved proud of the war line and began to cry their challenges at the oncoming enemy, Solemis took the final opportunity to rally his own friends and clansmen.

"Today is the day that our clan has waited for, everything depends on us. If we can hold our position here the army of the Senones will win its greatest victory." He paused and fixed the grim faced warriors with his stare. "The field before us has been carefully chosen. The river and copse will anchor the end of our line and channel the enemy towards us. This is not horse country so we fight on foot, but cannot be outflanked. You all know the plan; we hold them here and withdraw steadily at my command. We have been chosen from all the clans on this field because of the discipline we have shown on our raids, and the ferocity of our attack in the first battle. Win here today and the name of the Horsetails will echo through the halls of Celtica, from the Apeninnus all the way home to the Sequana. Men not yet born will marvel at the words of the bards as they sit at their cervesia, and curse the gods that they live in more peaceful times."

The heavy tramp of thousands of feet marching in unison was growing by the moment, and Solemis judged that the time to take his position at their head had arrived. Away to his right the main battle line ebbed and flowed as the warriors fought to rein in their war lust. Above them the carnyx blared and howled as the men awaited Brennus' charge.

Solemis turned back to face the oncoming Etruscans and raised his shield and spear as he bellowed their own battle cry: *"Horsetails!"*

The cry was taken up to his rear, and Solemis fizzed with pride and excitement as the wave of sound enveloped him. Flicking a look back to the centre, Solemis was just in time to see Brennus launch the first gaesum deep into the Etruscan phalanx and set off down the slope screaming contempt. The Senone army cascaded down the slope in his wake, and Solemis watched in awe as the air above them darkened with spears. Moments later the armies crashed together with the sound of rolling thunder and the Etruscan phalanx shook visibly under the onslaught, the shock of the charge rippling through the body of men like surface waves on a lake.

To his immediate front the ground was more broken, and the arrival of the spearmen there was delayed. Solemis wavered, and panic gripped him with an icy fist as he struggled to hold back the warriors. The Etruscans were losing their formation as they traversed the boulder field which lined a small tributary of the Clanis, and a charge into them now would in all probability break them and drive them from the field. It was, he knew, the very opposite of what Brennus and Crixos had planned to occur on their left wing, but every sinew of his being strained to do just that. Several of his men were already moving ahead of his position as their war cries and challenges pulled them towards the enemy. Many of them were on the very cusp of charging down the slope, and Solemis turned towards them and screamed a desperate command. *"Get back into line!"*

Several of the warriors proved deaf to his cries, gripped as they were by their war fury, and Solemis stamped across and struck them with his shield, shepherding them back up the slope. *"Get back and wait for my command!"*

The men glared at him, and Solemis saw the anger flare in their eyes as they snapped a look at their assailant. Albiomaros had led the group, and he shrugged off Solemis's first shield strike and took another pace forward. Solemis knew that the moment had arrived when he must choose between friendship and the demands and responsibilities of a clan chieftain. The big Trinobante, his blood genos, looked magnificent as a man of Albion dressed for battle, his body and face whorls of sinuous blue markings, his hair and moustache thick with lime. Although the challenge to his leadership was unplanned by his friend, Solemis knew instinctively that he must act quickly and decisively. The men had followed his example as a natural leader, and one glance told Solemis that every clansman was waiting to see the outcome of the confrontation. Dropping his shield, Solemis swept his leg around in a powerful sweep which crashed into Albiomaros's legs behind the knee. Taken unawares the warrior crashed to the ground with cry of outrage. As he lifted his shoulders to rise Solemis was on him, treading on his spear arm and bringing the point of his own gaesum around to prick his best friend's throat. The Trinobante stiffened as he felt the blade nick his skin, and Solemis craned forward and snarled as he fixed him with a stare. *"I said get back and wait for my command!"*

Their eyes locked and Solemis saw the rage which boiled within his friend suddenly fade and die as Albiomaros regained his composure. He gave a curt nod, once, that he understood and flicked a look down at Solemis' spear. The chieftain moved it away and held out a hand. As he pulled him to his feet Solemis levelled his voice and repeated his order. *"Wait for my command."*

Albiomaros felt his neck and glanced down at the blood on his fingertips. To Solemis's disappointment he locked eyes and spoke under his breath. "This is not over."

Solemis's heart sank, but it was a problem for another time. The delay, however short, had been enough, and the Etruscan leading ranks had managed to cross the worst of the rubble and were desperately bunching together once more. He knew that it was time. Scooping up his shield, Solemis screamed his war cry and broke into a run.

AT THE CREST of the shallow ridge, Crixos watched the attack develop with mounting frustration. A metallic taste came to his mouth and the chieftain vaguely realised that he had been gnawing idly at his lip.

Brennus's plan had seemed to make sense when he had outlined it to the gathering of clan chiefs the previous day, but he was perturbed to discover that now the battle was a reality he was having second thoughts. Although fine in theory, the plan seemed to discard all of the traditional strengths of the Celtic armies: physical size, power, aggression, and place its trust in their greatest weakness, discipline.

He cast a glance along the line of warriors and recognised that the pensive expressions on each and every one of them must reflect his own. Some of the finest warriors on the field were here at his side, while the weakened Senone army fought for its existence at the bottom of the field. He ran his eyes along the front as the noise of battle redoubled in intensity.

At the centre, Brennus's raven helm occasionally hove into view beyond the waving mass of brightly coloured pennants and war horns as the chieftain stabbed and slashed his way forward with his big longsword. The line here was steady and, although worryingly thin, the Celtic army seemed to have the measure of their opponents and were holding their own.

As far as he could see, the gully which marked the right hand edge of the battlefield was clear of enemy warriors as they had expected it to be. The mist which had veiled the field had largely burned away as the sun had risen, but it persisted in low lying nooks and hollows and he had sent a pair of men down to the ravine to keep a watch on this important route. Narrow, rubble strewn and screened by a dense thicket which stretched away to the North, it had been the primary reason why the fight was taking place here today. Several rows of sharpened stakes had been set into the floor and sides of the defile to deter any attempts at outflanking the Senone army at that point, and although they appeared to have succeeded, he needed to be sure. When he moved he needed to move fast, and no time had been allowed in the plan for a fighting advance.

Away to his left Solemis's Horsetails seemed to have overcome their initial hesitance and were attacking vigorously. Crixos snorted as he recognised the chalky spikes which marked the place where Solemis's great friend Albiomaros was fighting. Solemis would lead from the front; he was a fine young man with far greater potential than his daughter's previous intended *gwr,* Acco. Despite his anxieties for the day, his mind wandered back to the dark field outside the Belgic settlement. He had had to lead Catubaros's fool of a son Maros and his cantref into the trap, and he had hesitated for a moment before he had left them there to die as he debated whether to tell Acco to follow him to safety. Something had told him to leave the man to his fate, and it was clear now that it had been the voice of the gods. Aia was far more useful to his clan as a Horsetail, the *gwraig* of a young and promising chieftain. It had been unfortunate that Connos had had to die to smooth the path for the young couple, but it was clear that he was doing the bidding of the gods, he had merely supplied the means.

A great roar rolled up the incline from the fighting below, and Crixos snapped out of his reverie. A glance to his left told him that the Horsetails were now fighting against overwhelming odds, as the Etruscans ghosted through the swirling mist and crossed the dry riverbed in force. Very soon they would begin to fall back under the onslaught, and Crixos sent a plea to Camulos that the Etruscan zilach would respond to the progress his army was making at that point as any good general should.

If he didn't, he reflected gloomily, they could very well be dead men.

21

"L*and, Hesperos!"* The crew members turned their heads as one, craning their necks to where the lithe, green shirted form of Arion clasped the masthead. Slinging an arm around the upright he grinned down at his crew mates, clenching his fist in triumph as he picked out Catumanda and threw her a wink. "You were right, fantasma. You averted the wrath of the Ketea!"

It had been some time since any of them had used that word to describe the druid, and the crew laughed and glanced fondly in her direction as they congratulated each other on their safe transit of the Bay of Storms. Catumanda pulled a wry smile in return, and she watched the men who she had come to regard as her friends excitedly flock to the raised bow in an effort to glimpse the first land which they had drawn near for over a week. Abaris, her old master, had counselled that the powers which the gods had bestowed upon her sometimes carried a great burden and this, she knew, was one such time.

Ever at her side, Philippos smiled up at her, his features a happy mixture of affection and pride that *his* friend had bravely swum with the Ketea and brought them safely through.

Catumanda returned the smile and tousled the boy's hair playfully. Despite the assurance which she had given to Hesperos, the sacrifice of the hen the previous week had revealed to her more than the existence of Hektor's newborn child, and she resolved to try to save the boy when the time came.

Catumanda looked back to the bows of the *Alexa* and watched as the men scaled the upright in an animated brawl, noisily jostling one another as they clung precariously above the fizzing bow wave. She was glad for their happiness, for she alone knew that the shroud of death cloaked them still.

DESPITE THE DISTANCE the smells of the land carried to them on the gentle offshore breeze, and for the first time the tough seamen came to realise that the sweet, resinous aroma of juniper and pine meant more to the men of the *Alexa* than they could possibly have imagined before their trip to the wild northern lands. Each man turned his face to the East and inhaled deeply as the smells rekindled memories of home and family. The carefree hours of childhood as they chased their cousins among the needle clad slopes; the rhythmic song of the cicada drifting across from the olive grove as they lay out beneath a mantle of stars during the heat of the summer months.

Markos had revealed to Catumanda one evening as they had taken in the beauty of the night sky, that this had been far more than their first trip to the land they knew as Pretannia. It had been, he confided with obvious pride, the very first time that the *Alexa* had put her nose through the narrow strip of sea known as the Pillars of Hercules.

To have navigated to the far north and returned unerringly with their precious cargo had been a great feat of navigation, and the crew were justifiably proud of their achievement.

Markos was kubernetes, and Catumanda watched as he held a steady course to the South. Hesperos paced the deck, checking all was well with his charge as the crew lolled amid-ships. Hektor was the first to break the spell as he regarded the owner with a friendly smile. "Are we going to put in, Hesperos?"

The owner placed a hand on Hektor's shoulder as he passed and snorted. "That would be a nice idea, if we could be certain of the reception we would receive."

Arion added his voice to the conversation. "There must be dozens of small settlements on this coast? It would be nice to taste roast flesh and drink fresh *woinos* again. We should have saved an amphora for the return journey like Markos said. The barbarians guzzle it down like that disgusting cervesia they serve up. It was a waste."

Hesperos stopped, resting his arm on the deck rail as he regarded the distant jagged line which marked the coast of the land the Greeks had named Iberia. He hawked and spat at the gulls which bobbed in their lee, and the pale yellow eyes of the birds stared back menacingly. Catumanda could see that he was turning over the pros and cons in his mind. Finally he sighed and turned back to the expectant men. "We cannot risk stopping, as much as I would like to. Even if we could find a small settlement where we could be sure that there were no tax collectors, our cargo is too valuable to risk." He smiled mischievously and looked across to Arion as he continued. "There are only five of us if we include the boy and the friend you just described as a barbarian." Catumanda laughed as Arion's expression changed to one of horror. The man attempted to apologise, but quickly realised that there was little he could say.

Catumanda shook her head as the others looked on gleefully. "I shall take it as a sign that I have been accepted into your brotherhood if it slipped your mind that you had a cervesia guzzler aboard, and humbly accept the status of honorary Greek." She bowed and grinned. "At least for the remainder of this voyage!"

Hesperos' expression grew serious once again as the laughter rolled away and he swept the sea with his gaze. "The gods have held their hands over us so far on this enterprise, but we would be wrong to test the limits of their benevolence. We are late in the year as it is, and the first storm of the season must surely break upon us soon. We should pass back through the Pillars of Hercules before we begin to think about putting in to shore, and even then we need to steer well clear of any Carthaginian ships or settlements."

Catumanda had a hazy idea that the empire of Carthage lay to the south of Celtica, and an uneasy feeling crept upon her as she began to suspect that the voyage of the *Alexa* may have been more than a simple trading expedition. She made to question the owner, but the words caught in her throat as she realised that their fates were already written. What had gone before was irrelevant, and all that remained for these men now was to decide the manner in which they would face that end when the time came.

THAT EVENING they unrolled their bedding on the deck for the first time on the return trip. The offshore breeze which had rekindled their memories of home had also carried the sleep inhibiting heat of the land to the crew of the *Alexa,* and the small deck house had quickly become unbearable as the travel weary men tossed and turned in the airless space.

Catumanda had been the first to abandon them and make her bed beneath the star speckled sky as the heat had radiated from the panelled walls, smothering her with an almost physical force which seemed to lay on her frame and pluck the very breath from her lungs. The overwhelming feeling of being trapped had returned to her, and the memory of the tunnels beneath the Spirit Isle were still too fresh in the druid's mind for her to remain a moment longer.

Sleep had come to Catumanda, but with it the return of the dream horses which had plagued her early life. It had been several months now since the climactic events that night on the Spirit Isle and she had relished her nights of sleep, free from the shadowy images which flickered into her unconscious mind. This night they returned and she awoke with a start, panting, heart racing, as the old familiar feelings gripped her once again.

Catumanda settled back and exhaled slowly as she swept a runnel of perspiration from the side of her face. She cast a glance around the deck at the prone figures of her companions and pursed her lips sadly as she recalled the fate which awaited them. The dark form of Hesperos stood outlined against the indigo of the night sky, his sturdy arms resting on the shallow roof of the deck house. Somewhere in the bows she knew that Arion would be settled against the big upturned prow as his eyes scanned the gloom ahead. Even this far from land any number of things could appear with little or no warning ahead of the ship, endangering the safety of both it and its occupants. The wide bulk and rising stem of the *Alexa* would render smaller ships or fishing boats invisible to the kubernetes from his position at the stern once they came within a mile of her prow. Trees and other debris washed out by rivers and even whales would be invisible well within that distance, and although each man regarded the duty of lookout as a chore, each one of them knew the value of a good pair of eyes and a quick brain.

Catumanda settled back on the gently rolling deck and cupped her hands beneath her head as her mind replayed the details of her latest vision. She had been sat on a fallen tree stump watching the people weaving their way around the Bel Tree, each one attached to the hoary oak by their gaily coloured thread, and she had recognised the place immediately as Camulodunon, the oppidum of the Trinobantes. As they had danced she had begun to slowly rise into the air until they appeared to swirl below her in a maelstrom of tumbling figures. Slowly the realisation came to her that it was not she who was rising but they who were falling away from her, deeper and deeper into an inky blackness, and she called out in terror as one of the revellers looked up directly at her and she saw the fear and hopelessness in his eyes. At the moment that she had recognised the face of Hektor below her she had awoken, bathed in sweat.

As the images drifted from her mind like summer smoke, Catumanda realised that all hope of sleep was now gone. Scrambling up from the deck, the druid walked back towards the dark outline of Hesperos. As she came nearer the shadow slowly resolved itself until, with a final duck beneath the big tiller, she came up to the man whose face lit up with a smile of welcome. "Still too hot for you, barbarian?"

Catumanda returned his smile. Even though she knew that the man was only speaking half in jest, she certainly felt little need to be offended by the term. Philippos had explained that the Greeks regarded any who spoke a tongue other than Greek as uncivilised, gibbering idiots, and therefore it was no slight on her ancestry in particular. She had always found arrogance in the insecure, and Catumanda wondered what these Greeks were so afraid of. Her years of training had developed an insatiable appetite for knowledge, and the druid rested against the deck rail as she asked Hesperos if he would explain to this barbarian a little of what made his homeland so special.

The big Greek beamed at the opportunity, spreading his hands wide as he launched into a eulogy for his native land and people. "Greece is the home of all civilisation, druid. Zeus, father of gods and men, chose to assemble all the great minds of the world in one place: philosophers, historians, playwrights and call it Magna Graecia. He provided the people of Athenai with the greatest seamen and the city of Sparta with the greatest warriors to protect and enrich them, and in return the Greeks built great temples of stone in their honour." He clapped Catumanda playfully on the back as he continued. "Even the might of the eastern despots in Persia broke against the walls of timber and muscle thrown up against them by the twin cities."

Catumanda nodded that she understood, but decided to push the man further. The gods she knew, even these unfamiliar Greek deities, rarely elevated one people permanently above all others. They moved through all men to a greater or lesser degree and disliked stability above all. "So Athenai and Sparta now rule Magna Graecia in perfect harmony then?"

Catumanda watched as Hesperos hawked and spat over the side and knew that she had finally unearthed the root cause for all their bluster about 'barbarians' and painted men. "Sparta, may Zeus punish them for their greed, decided that they wanted to take all the spoils of victory and conquered Athenai. They burned my home town of Peiraieus and ruined my family. We escaped with barely the old *Alexa* here to our name and settled on Sikelia."

Catumanda pulled a wry smile as the reasons for the voyage to Albion became clear. "So this trip is meant to restore your family wealth. That is why we are steering well clear of land."

Hesperos smiled grimly. "We should not be here at all, Catumanda. The Pillars of Hercules are controlled by our enemy in Carthage, we would all be slain if we were found here."

Catumanda nodded that she understood completely. "That is why you will not put in to shore, and why you are so late in the year. You hope to slip through unnoticed, outside of the usual trading season."

Hesperos shrugged, and they both looked up as harsh cries cut through the air from a cloud of gulls above. Catumanda followed their progress as they bore away to the north-east. "It would seem that our friends are in a hurry to be away from here."

She glanced back at the Greek and was struck by the look of despair which had washed across his features. Hesperos indicated away to the south-west with a flick of his head. "There is the cause of their flight, Catumanda." He threw the young woman a grim smile. "Great Poseidon never sends the Ketea to visit seamen unless he intends to dine with them soon."

22

Drawing back his arm, Solemis sighted as he roared the Horsetails on. The sun had risen to burn off the worst of the mist and the Celts were faced by a line of heavy bronze shields, the grotesquely painted discs a wall of shimmering amber. Ahead of him the front rank of the phalanx visibly braced themselves for the shock of contact with these giants from the North, nervous faces peeking from behind the rims of their defences. As the Senone chieftain came within twenty paces of the spear points, he unwound his body and loosed the gaesum. The dart flew true, the horsehair plume ghosting in its wake like a leaden cloud, and a heartbeat later the man immediately to his front was thrown backwards as his face was transformed into a gory pulp.

Before the Etruscan in the second rank could step forward to seal the breach, Solemis had batted aside his spear with his heavy shield and plunged into their ranks. Solemis stabbed desperately to left and right as the enemy recovered and attempted to overwhelm the intruder, but within a heartbeat the men of his clan arrived in a deafening crash of wood on bronze, sweeping the front ranks of the phalanx back and gathering in their chieftain.

A flash of white at the corner of his vision told him that Albiomaros was there, and Solemis' heart leapt that his greatest friend fought at his side. The sheer force of their initial contact had thrown the enemy back, but they were outnumbered three to one, and the depth of the phalanx absorbed the raw power of the charge and began to recover. Unable to retreat due to the press of their numbers, the young Etruscans in the front ranks fought for their lives in a savage scrum of heaving, stabbing madmen.

The snarling face of a lynx, its lips drawn back to reveal dagger-like teeth rose up before him and Solemis pushed back against it, working his stabbing spear beneath the shield's rim. Throwing his shoulder into his own shield he heaved against the leather backing, lunging forward again with his lancea as the gap widened. He was dismayed to find that the thick leather war shirt of his opponent deflected his blade with ease and he twisted his grip, stabbing upwards in a frenzy. Taken by surprise the Etruscan was too slow to withdraw his head, and the blade slid into the gap beneath his bronze faceplate and disappeared from view. The man clasped his throat and fell away taking the spear with him as Solemis stepped back from the press, and his sword hissed from its scabbard as Albiomaros stepped forward to take his place.

His friend's action had given the chieftain a moment to check on the progress of the fighting, and he threw his head to left and right as he gauged the moment to begin the fighting withdrawal on which so much depended.

The earlier miasma had all but cleared away, and Solemis took in the situation in a single sweep. If anything, he decided, the initial contact between the forces had been *too* successful. The Horsetails had driven the Etruscan phalanx back up the opposite bank of the rivulet by the sheer force of their charge. Flicking a look across the heads of their opponents, Solemis could see that more men were arriving with every passing moment to bolster their already overwhelming numbers. He had to retreat to the opposite bank and let the run of the slope work in their favour, or the position could very well collapse. He looked back and was relieved to see the clan carnyx at his shoulder. He grabbed the trumpeter's tunic and shouted into his ear above the din of battle. "Cotos: make the signal!"

Cotos nodded that he understood and raced back to higher ground. Solemis stole a look as he hoisted the great bronze war horn into the air and spat to clear his mouth. As the three short notes filled the air, the young chieftain looked back to the front and gasped at the scene. In the short time which it had taken him to issue the order to Cotos, the Horsetails had been pushed back into the rock strewn bed of the stream. Using the advantage of height which the bank afforded them, Etruscan hoplites were stabbing down at the Celts, forcing them to raise their shields to ward off the blows while lightly armed skirmishers moved down into the riverbed to attack their undefended sides.

Immediately ahead, an Etruscan wearing a helm plumed with eagle feathers slid into the shallows and levelled his spear at Albiomaros. Already heavily engaged with two hoplites the Trinobante was oblivious to the threat, and Solemis launched himself across the bed with a roar. The cry caused the man to look his way in alarm, and although it had been all that he could have done to save his friend's life it had been enough. As the men of his clan began to respond to the urgent notes of the war horn, streaming away across the riverbed to reform on the opposite bank, the Etruscan swung his spear around to face the new threat. Solemis hesitated as his mind weighed up the chances making the near bank with his retreating clansmen. The Etruscan spearman was already advancing towards him, the iron point of his weapon dangerously close, and the young chieftain knew that he must attack to stand any chance of survival. Even if he could outpace his opponent, there was nothing to stop the man throwing the spear at his unprotected back and besides, he grinned wolfishly, he was the clan chief of the Horsetails. He would never run from the enemy.

Solemis roared his defiance and accelerated across the broken ground as his clansmen streamed back. He had a momentary glimpse of Albiomaros' face as a he sped by, his mouth hanging open in shock and confusion, before he crashed into the Etruscan and sent the man spinning to the ground. Solemis landed heavily upon him a moment later, and he struggled to bring his sword into play as the man bucked and squirmed beneath him. The length of the Celtic longsword for once became a hindrance, as Solemis tried desperately to pull his arm back far enough to stab down with the blade. Gritting his teeth with the effort he glanced at the face below him and saw the desperation in his opponent's dark eyes. The boy was no older than he was, twenty winters at most, and despite the quality of his arms Solemis knew instinctively that this was his first taste of close order battle.

All around him now a forest of Etruscan legs were splashing down into the shallows, and Solemis knew that he must end this fight quickly. Once the rear ranks gained the riverbed he would be noticed, and it would a moment's work to run him through. Releasing his sword, Solemis drove the heavy peak of his helm into the nose guard below him as his hand fumbled at his belt for his dagger. The handle was surmounted by twin representations of the Wheel of Toranos, and his fingers found them easily and slid down onto the hilt. The boy's struggles were growing weaker as Solemis' helm made a horror of his face, and the Celt felt almost thankful as he brought the blade up and sawed into his neck, releasing his opponent from his agony.

Solemis lay panting from the exertion of the fight as his mind raced. He must move now, but he knew that as soon as he stood it would become obvious to those around him that he was an enemy warrior and an important one at that. His helm alone would mark him as one of the Celtic leaders, its fabulous ornamentation and horsehair plume unique among the clan. The quality of his weapons and armour were the equal of any on the field of battle and his prized golden torc, the one which he had taken as a trophy from the neck of the Helvetian warrior in the Alpes, would render him instantly recognisable to those around him.

The sudden realisation came upon him that he would meet his end on this patch of stones, that this was the time when he would travel on to the Isles of the Dead. He would never run from an enemy, and he could not hope to survive a fight here alone. His decision to stand and fight made, he felt an unexpected euphoria sweep over him as he realised that the gods had handed him the opportunity to die the death of a hero under the admiring gaze of the warriors of his clan.

He glanced to his right and saw to his joy that his sword still lay close by. Moving his hand slowly across until he could close his fingers around the hilt once more he drew it gratefully to him. Suddenly he realised that something had changed, and his mind focused back on the turmoil which surrounded him. To a man, the Etruscan hoplites wore bronze greaves; shaped plates which protected the fronts of their shins from low spear thrusts. During the fight with the now dead man beneath him, the greaves had been moving forward in an ordered line. Suddenly, he realised, the flow had been reversed. As Solemis prepared to spring to his feet and attack the retreating Etruscans, a hand gripped the neck of his battle shirt and hauled him to his feet. Spears were whispering overhead to skewer the hoplites, who were now frantically trying to scale the far bank as Solemis took in his surroundings. A salient had formed around him as the Horsetails moved back down to pluck their chieftain from certain death. Like a storm-driven wave as it dashed itself against a beach, the warriors had flowed through the hoplite ranks and were now beginning to ebb away, back to the safety of the near bank.

Solemis twisted to see who was holding him and looked straight into the familiar features of Albiomaros. The big man shook his head as he lowered him to his feet. "Three notes on the carnyx means withdraw, not run forward you silly bastard."

NUMERIUS NARROWED his eyes and shot his brother a quizzical look. "Quintus, explain to me what *you* think the zilach is doing."

The Roman raised his chin and swept the battlefront with his critical gaze. After a short deliberation he turned back to Numerius and raised a brow as he answered with barely concealed amusement. "He appears to be moving the light skirmishers from the left flank where they are covering the gully, and moving them across to support the right hand side of the phalanx where the barbarian wing is withdrawing in good order."

Numerius pulled a face and nodded his agreement. "I have to say that I concur, Quintus. Your assessment is a good example of what separates the Roman military mind from the

Etruscan, and it is the reason why the gods have chosen our city to rise to pre-eminence among its peers."

He glanced across to Caeso. "What do you say, brother? Shall we trot across and tell the old man that he is a fool?"

Caeso stroked the neck of his mount as the otherworldly clack of a wooden tongue sounded from a distant carnyx causing it to skitter. He shot them an amused smile. "It sounds like that war horn has been at the Etruscan wine." They all shared a laugh as he added with a chuckle. "It can be rather rough!"

The Roman ambassador peered across the field and shrugged as he answered his brother's question. "To my mind the two sides seem well matched. Why not let them fight each other to a standstill and then return with an army of our own. You know the Etruscan cities, they never seem to support each other, however grave the situation."

Numerius flicked a look up at the barbarian reserve perched at the crest of the valley, and began to entertain the thought that it may not be a reserve after all. Inhaling deeply, his gaze roamed across the battlefront as he decided his course of action. Finally, after considering his brothers' advice, he made his decision. "I agree, this is fascinating; let's watch the fun. Despite the strange patterned trousers and the fact that they sport more hair and jewellery than a high class whore, it's clear that these Gauls are not the mindless savages we have been led to believe."

Caeso beamed as he added to Numerius' description of the barbarians. "And they have finer moustaches than some of the *low* class whores!"

The brothers shared a laugh, and the fighting in the valley ebbed and flowed before them as Numerius reached his conclusion. "The Etruscans will never run these people off their land, so there is no point in offering them our support. I will explain to father that it will take Roman arms to drive back the barbarians from the sacred spring, and the promise of another Etruscan city to add to the conquest of Veii should be enough to sway the senate." He threw them a grin. "Who knows, I may even offer to lead the expedition myself!"

As his brothers chuckled at his side, Numerius mused softly. "If the Gaul's are about to spring the surprise on Zilach Porsenna that I think they are, this could be very entertaining."

CATURIX SUDDENLY SAT bolt upright in his saddle and gripped Crixos' sleeve. "They are moving, father!"

The chieftain's head snapped back, and his shoulders sagged in relief as he saw that it was true. The light spear-men, lacking any form of protective armour, were fast and agile. Lethal against a broken or disorganised enemy, they were able to stand off and rain javelins on their foe once the heavier hoplites had brought them to bay. Now, as they looked on from their vantage point across the valley, the Etruscan skirmishers were streaming across the rear of the main fighting towards the beleaguered Horsetails. It was the moment that they had planned and hoped for, and Crixos waited impatiently for the enemy to reach the point where he would order his men forward and launch the attack.

He had been watching the left flank of Brennus' army fight a desperately one-sided battle as it steadily retreated up the valley side. Solemis's clansmen and their allies had almost reached the choke point where the great curve of the River Clanis bit into the battlefield; it was their final redoubt and he had been on the point of abandoning Brennus's plan and leading his own clan across to shore up the front there. He was confident that the Horsetails would never break and run, but the numbers facing them were such that there was a very real possibility that they could be overrun, despite their undoubted bravery. If that *did* happen, the Etruscans would scythe around the rear of the main army and roll along its flank like a tidal bore, sweeping all before it.

He looked along the line and smiled as he recognised the eagerness in the faces of his own clansmen and the men of the clans which owed him their allegiance. They were some of the finest warriors in the army, and it had been a measure of the confidence, both in their own abilities and that of their chieftain, that they had grudgingly followed Brennus' orders and remained aloof from the battle when every fibre screamed at them to enter the fray. He wondered for a moment whether the spirits of the ancestors were watching over them in this foreign land, or did they still wander the forests of the North? His own father he had to admit had been a bit of a bastard towards him, but he *had* been a warrior of renown, and that was all that the bards were interested in. Crixos pulled a wry smile.

If this all goes wrong, I may very well get the chance to explain to him what the plan was and why his clan held back from the fight sooner than either of us expected!

He turned in his saddle and addressed his clansmen. "This looks like it boys. As soon as they pass behind the grove we get down there as fast as we can." He hauled on the reins and walked his mount along the front of the line. "You all know what to do. Get in fast, hit them hard; chop off the head and the body will fall."

Caturix cut in. "The leading men are there, father."

Crixos nodded to him and jerked his head. "Off you go then. We will wait until the tail disappears and we will follow on. Get those stakes down but watch out for the archers."

Caturix and half a dozen riders kicked their war horses

clear of the line and thundered away towards the gully as Crixos turned for a last, long look at the progress of the battle. At the centre Brennus was comfortably containing the Etruscan phalanx, despite his reduced numbers. Crixos snorted and shook his head as he noted the raven helm of his chieftain at the place of honour, in the centre, at the front, and he sent a brief plea to Camulos that he resist the temptation to add the big man to his own war band this day.

High above, vultures were beginning to gather for the feast to come, soaring effortlessly on their great, ragged wings. Away to the North a cloud of crows were blackening the canopy of a copse of cypress.

Solemis' Horsetails had anchored their line against the river and were now holding firm. The constricted space was acting as intended he noticed with satisfaction, thickening the Celtic line and reducing the number of Etruscan spears which could be brought to bear against them. The light skirmishers which were streaming across to add their weight to the push now had no place to go. They would arrive, having denuded the opposite wing of cover, and merely bunch at the back of the phalanx. The ploy had worked perfectly, and Crixos made a fist as he champed at the bit waiting for the signal from the gully that all was prepared. Suddenly it came, and he kicked in as all the pent up nerves of the morning were released. *"Let's go!"*

Sweeping across the rear of the fighting, Crixos led his clan down into the stream bed and on into the mouth of the defile. Caturix and his men were awaiting them with fixed grins, and he knew without pausing that they had prepared the route ahead. At a glance the gully looked impassable, a solid wall of sharpened stakes pointing towards the city, but the central pair in each row had been deliberately cut shorter than their counterparts. Although they looked to be the same size they were barely sunk into the floor of the passageway, and Caturix and his men had swiftly hurled them aside.

Crixos slowed his stallion as he began to guide the beast between the remaining posts and brambles. Immediately he entered the shelter of the defile the din of battle decreased markedly, and he cursed the amount of noise made by the column as they made their way through. This was the most dangerous part of the attack, and he anxiously scanned the broken line which marked the lip of the cut as he rode. Even the appearance of a single archer now could wreak havoc on the slow moving and tightly packed horsemen, and a call to his comrades would result not only in the failure of the attack but very likely the annihilation of the Crow clan.

After what seemed a lifetime Crixos reached the cleft which led up to the plain and he hauled at his reins, urging the horse up through the thicket with his knees. Reaching across he swept his sword from its scabbard and plunged on. A flash of colour caught his eye as he climbed the bank, and he brought his blade up ready to strike. Glancing down he had the momentary image of an archer squatting behind a bush, his bow laid innocently at his side. As he came abreast he hesitated for a heartbeat, his sword poised and ready to cut down, and he saw the look of surprise and horror in the man's upturned face as scores of heavily armed Celts swarmed around him. The pause had been enough to save the man's life and as he swept up and over the lip out onto the plain Crixos, despite the situation, found that he was laughing and a thought bobbed into his mind.

There are some places where a man deserves a little peace!

Crixos burst free of the gully and swept on. Ahead of him scores of archers were facing the battle in the valley, and he quickly debated whether to veer through them while they were unaware of his presence or strike out towards the zilach and his bodyguards. It was a situation that had been unforeseen during the planning for the attack, and although he knew that the archers could cause terrible casualties among his men when they finally did spot them and loosed into their flank, he knew that Camulos was with them. The war god had opened the way for them and the time to strike at the head of the snake had arrived.

Crixos glanced to his right as he drove his stallion towards the knot of Etruscan leaders. The large group of mounted equites that he had seen from the opposite side of the valley were still in place and he swallowed his disappointment. He had hoped that they would move away with the skirmishers once the main thrust of the Etruscan attack had been lured across by the Horsetails but he now recognised that they were, in fact, the Roman ambassadors and their party. He cursed; after the deliberate insults which he had inflicted on them, he knew that they would attack his flank at once if they recognised him for who he was but it could not be helped. He would have to deal with them once they arrived.

Thankfully the cypress grove had screened their advance down into the valley from the regular Etruscan equites, who had come from the city and formed up on the roadway once the fighting had started. They were now too distant to intervene before Crixos and his Celts closed with the zilach and his party; he would have to kill Porsenna and then place his trust in Camulos that the rest of his men came up quickly in support. It took time for a thousand riders to negotiate the winding track at the foot of the gully, time that he doubted the avenging Etruscans would grant him.

The Zilach Porsenna and his party had taken up position on a small shelf cut into the rising ground of the valley side, where they could look out across the heaving mass at the base of the slope. Huddled beneath brightly coloured banners and pennants, the Etruscan leaders were shading their eyes against the brilliance of the rising sun as they attempted to gauge the progress of the fighting on their right flank. It was all that the Senones had wished for, and Crixos craned forward over the neck of his war horse as he urged the beast to close the gap before the alarm was raised. One of Porsenna's screen of bodyguards glanced to his left and, even at the distance of a short bow shot, Crixos could make out the look of puzzlement cross his features. It could only be a moment before the man recognised the charging riders for who they were; he might miss one pair of red checked trousers but he was unlikely to miss upwards of a thousand he smiled wolfishly, and Crixos watched in amusement as the soldier's expression became a mask of horror as he realised the identity of the men bearing down on him.

Their charge unmasked, Crixos screamed his war cry and urged his men on as the Etruscan bodyguard hurried to come between the Celts and their zilach. Caturix and his friend Doros edged their mounts abreast of his own, and Crixos proudly joined in as they screamed their challenges and raised their longswords, ready to strike the first blows.

More and more bodyguards were scrambling across and attempting to form a cohesive wall of spears before their leader, who for the first time looked across and visibly gaped in horror as the wall of muscle and iron swept down on him but, Crixos knew, they were far too late. With a final invocation to Camulos the Gauls smashed into the makeshift barrier and crashed through, spraying broken bodies and spear shafts in a bloody tide before them.

Reality seemed to slow for a moment as the images of first contact seared themselves into the mind of the Celtic leader. Shattered bodies, their limbs twisted into impossible shapes by the impact of a horse going at full gallop whirled through the air. The decapitated head of an Etruscan noble, still wearing its handsomely plumed helmet, seemed to shoot vertically up into the air and disappear from view, as bizarre a sight as the old chieftain had witnessed in all his years of fighting. Doros had been unhorsed and his body described a perfect flip as it sailed over the heads of the desperate defenders. And then, just as suddenly the spell was broken, and reality crashed back with a roar.

Crixos slashed and fought his way across to the man who must be his target. The eldest man present he also wore the most outlandish and impractical armour, and although he had never laid eyes on this zilach, Crixos knew that he could rely on the reactions of those around Porsenna to unwittingly confirm his identity. As expected the Etruscan nobles rallied around the old man, and Crixos yelled with joy as his target was confirmed.

The momentum of their charge had carried the Gauls deep into the ranks of the stunned Etruscans, and Crixos was brought up only feet away from his prey. Forcing his stallion forward into the crush he hacked down with his sword to left and right as he batted away the spear thrusts of his enemies with his long shield. Glancing up he saw Porsenna draw his own blade as the Etruscan leader prepared to sell his life dearly, and a flash of respect flared in the Celt at the dignity shown by the old man in what he now felt sure were his final moments in the world of men.

23

The crew of the *Alexa* were just beginning to stir from their slumber as Catumanda walked the deck towards the great upturned prow. Away to the south-west a terraced wall of charcoal grey clouds rolled down on the tiny ship, its fringes lit by dancing flickering shards, a progress made all the more disconcerting by the silence which accompanied it as the world seemed to catch its breath. A sudden flash pulsed in the distant sky, illuminating the trim figure of Arion at his station at the guard rail and Catumanda made her way across. Reaching up she grasped the big fore stay and exchanged a look of resignation with the red shirted seaman.

Catumanda felt a hand tug at her sleeve and, looking down, she saw the fear-etched features of young Philippos staring back at her. The druid attempted what she hoped would be a reassuring smile, as the gaunt figures of Hektor and Markos paced silently across and joined them at the rail. Philippos was the first to break the silence, but the emotion in his voice caused it to trail away to a whisper. The boy cleared his throat, and Catumanda was aware of the conflict raging within him as he fought to act like the man he now realised that he would never get the opportunity to become. He smiled thinly as he gripped the druid's sleeve. "You should have left with the Ketea, Catumanda. They would have carried you home to the Pretannic Isles."

Catumanda shook her head and returned the smile. "That is not my destiny, Philippos." She leaned forward and whispered to the boy. "When the time comes I want you to remain at my side." Catumanda gripped Philippos by the shoulders and held his gaze until she was sure that he had understood the importance of her words. The boy gave a slight nod, and Catumanda held the look a moment longer for emphasis before she returned the nod and looked away.

Hesperos had recovered from his shock at seeing the storm bearing down upon them and was hurrying down the deck towards his men. He opened his arms in a quizzical gesture as he began to rally his crew to face the trials ahead. "Well? Do we want to survive this and become rich, fat landsmen or not?"

At the sound of their leader's voice the crew reluctantly shifted their gaze away from the boiling ranks of leaden clouds which were bearing down upon them, and Catumanda watched in wonder as their old sense of discipline reasserted itself.

Markos was the first to respond. "That would be nice, Hesperos. That is what you promised us after all!"

A nervous laugh rose from the throats of the crew as their senior members exchanged a grin. The owner clapped Markos on the shoulder as he replied with a wink. "And you know that I always do my best to keep my promises, my old friend."

The first gusts of wind caressed the ship, and Hesperos sniffed the air like a dog seeking the scent of its quarry. He came across and, smiling warmly, shook each man by the hand. "Let us see what Poseidon has in store for us. If we can outrun this tempest then we will have a fine tale to tell our grandchildren. If we are fated to be entertained in Poseidon's hall this night, then I can think of no men I would rather share a table with."

Arion had left his station at the prow and he indicated the hold with a nod of his head. "Should we ditch some of the cargo, Hesperos? It could make all the difference."

The owner grinned mischievously. "Your share you mean? That is very noble of you Arion."

The men snorted despite their fears as their leader looked back to the south-east. He shook his head. "It is a good idea, but the storm is too close. If this bitch catches us with our hatch cover off, we'll be gone in an instant."

The first rumble of thunder reached their ears, and as the crew turned and followed Hesperos' gaze, they were shocked to discover how close the storm front had advanced towards them in so short a time. Catumanda noticed the experienced seamen exchange a glance which seemed to confirm their leader's opinion of the rapidly approaching monster. It was going to be a bitch, almost certainly the last they would ever experience.

Hesperos clapped his hands and the spell was broken. He turned back towards the stern and called on his close friend to follow him. "Markos; come and take one of the pedalia and I will take the other. If we can run before this we may still have a chance."

The first raindrops began to spatter the deck, and within moments they had doubled in intensity as the leading edge of the storm front came up. As the wind began to rise, Hesperos raised his voice and called across to the men. "Arion, Hektor; lower the sail quickly, or the wind will either have us over on our side or snap the mast. Either way it will be the end." He glanced down at Philippos, and Catumanda could sense the regret within the Greek that he had brought the young lad into danger. "Philippos, look after our barbarian," he smiled. "Lash yourselves to the mast and hang on tight!"

As Hesperos turned to go he winked at the druid, who acknowledged with a solemn nod that she had understood the man completely. He had of course been asking her to save the boy if possible, but one glance at Philippos confirmed that the words had had their intended effect. The boy fairly glowed with pride at the confidence placed in him by his leader, and the self belief it had imbued in the boy could make all the difference very soon.

The wind had risen as they spoke, and the first waves were beginning to worry the *Alexa* as the pair made their way unsteadily across to the big rope locker. Further aft, Hektor and Arion were frantically playing out the halyards and already the big spar was nearing the deck. Catumanda and Philippos delved into the locker and tossed four ropes across to the base of the mast, hurrying after them as the spar reached the deck and the men hurried forward and began to secure the sail. The wind howled and sang through the shrouds and braces as the crewmen stowed the spar and began to tie themselves off with a speed borne by years at sea, and Catumanda stole a look to the stern as the ship began to come about.

Hesperos and Markos were both lashed securely to the handles on the big pedalia, and both men were hauling them to their chest, the strain writ large on their faces as they struggled to bring the head of the ship around before the full force of the storm broke upon them. Both men knew that the only chance they had of surviving the next few hours lay in running before the waves. Unable to use the sail in such conditions and with only four oars, two of which would need to be manned by a boy and a barbarian holy woman, there was no alternative. If their strength could see them through, the waves would push the ship before them until either the storm blew itself out or they were driven ashore and any shore, even one controlled by the barbarians in Carthage, offered a chance to live to see another day.

Catumanda squinted upwards, watching in fascination as serried black ramparts engulfed the tiny ship, drawing about them like a monstrous cloak as it moved rapidly across to extinguish the stars. Immediately overhead a great arm of lightning snaked through the boiling mass of cloud, instantly accompanied by a crash of thunder so powerful that it seemed to reach down and clasp the crew in an attempt to force the very breath from their bodies. Catumanda searched the sky in the hope of catching a glimpse of Toranos, god of the sky. He was surely here, the druid could feel the power of his presence in the very air about her, but all she saw was a brace of gulls, braver or more foolhardy than their fellows, illuminated for an instant as they flashed through the sky at a ridiculous pace. A hand clutched roughly at her tunic and pulled her into the mast. “Hold on!”

Catumanda wrapped her arms around the thick pine column and looked out across Hektor's shoulder just in time to see the wave strike the ship. A black green wall of water broke against the stern quarter and plunged on, dragging the side deck rail down with it as it rolled by. The *Alexa* heeled over, and Catumanda saw the fear in Hektor's eyes as the unmistakable rumble and groans made by a shifting cargo carried up from the hold beneath them. Just as it seemed that the ship would never right herself the wave washed away forward, and the deck rail reappeared as the *Alexa* rolled back to an even keel and shook the water from her back like a rain lashed dog.

The men clustered around the mast looked to one another for a few moments, before breaking into spontaneous laughter as they realised how close they had come to death. Catumanda glanced back towards the stern and was relieved to see that both kubernetes were still at their positions. Hesperos caught her eye, and the big Greek caused the druid to let out a nervous laugh as he pursed his lips and blew out in exaggerated relief.

The ship had just managed to complete her turn as the storm waves reached them, and now the men held on as the power of Poseidon drove the ship forward. Soon the pattern was set, and the crew hung on and prayed to their gods that the strength of the kubernetes would outlast the relentless march of mountainous waves. As the scene was lit by the flash and fizz of lightning bolts, they would look on in awe as the stern of the *Alexa* sank steadily down into a trough as black as Hades. Further and further it fell, until they knew that the ship and all aboard her must slide back and roll stem over stern as they plunged to the very seabed. Out beyond the trough, a wall of water would rise, solid, polished black, until the horizon simply disappeared however frantically Toranos threw his bolts. At the very moment that it appeared to the watching crew that this wall of death must come on and engulf them all, a small nick would appear in its face which would quickly widen until the whole wave tore itself apart and rushed forward, driving under their stern, lifting the ship and flinging her forward as fast as an arrow.

Despite the ferocity of the storm, once the turn had been completed safely the confidence that they may survive the ordeal rose a little more with the passing of each wave. The brief lull between each mountain of water allowed the kubernetes in particular to briefly rest their tired minds and bodies as each pause in their headlong dash came around. Catumanda looked on sadly as she realised that the men were beginning to believe that they would come safely home.

Suddenly the clouds parted to admit a gossamer-like moonlight which painted the boiling surface of the ocean with its hue and there, silhouetted against the slate grey clouds, the killer stalked them as stealthily as any assassin. Catumanda watched, spellbound, as the wave rose higher and higher, a solid wall of water glistening like jet. As the roar of the monster carried to the crew of the *Alexa* they turned and looked as one, all their hopes breaking as they recognised their end. The wave came on with no sign that it would tear itself asunder, the smoking white crest gleaming in triumph over the puny figures below. Finally the roller did rip itself apart in a flume of hissing spray, but for the men on the *Alexa* it was already too late. Philippos's courage finally deserted him, and he buried his face in the folds of the druids cloak as the air screamed around them. Catumanda instinctively clutched the boy to her, looking on sadly as Hesperos and Markos at the stern reached out and grasped forearms in a final act of friendship.

A heartbeat later the full force of the breaking wave swept across the deck of the little ship. Catumanda lowered her head and gripped the mast in a futile effort to fend off the power of Poseidon as the torrent cascaded towards them. An instant later, the booms and crashes which surrounded her were engulfed by a thick heavy roar as the waters swept over her. An irresistible force uncurled her fingers from their handhold as the wave lifted her from her feet and carried her off towards the bows, and it was only the fact that she was still attached to the mast by her man-made umbilicus which kept her from being swept into the raging waters beyond the ship. For what seemed an age the crew swung to and fro in the torrent like reeds in a rain swollen river until, just as it seemed as if the waters would never recede and their lungs would burst, they were laid gently back onto the deck.

Catumanda opened her eyes and gulped down air as she watched the last of the seawater sluice away through the deck rail opposite. To her amazement she had managed to keep a desperate grip on Philippos throughout the ordeal, and the boy attempted a grateful smile as he retched the seawater from his lungs.

Catumanda looked across to Hektor and Arion and was surprised to find the pair desperately attempting to untie the knots which had saved their lives only moments before, their expressions a worrying mix of terror and desperation. As the men continued to struggle with the water-sodden knots, Catumanda looked back along the ship to find the cause of their concern and immediately knew that the end of the *Alexa* and her plucky crew was at hand. Immediately before her the hatch board which sealed the raised opening to the cargo hold had been swept aside and the gaping maw which it revealed was, she knew, the entrance to the realm of Hades for Hesperos and his crew.

The *Alexa* slewed suddenly to the right, and raising her gaze to the steering platform, Catumanda was shocked to see that the big handles which controlled the pedalia were hard over with no sign of either Hesperos or Markos. It was obviously the reason for the panic stricken efforts at rope untying to her left, but the druid knew that they would be too late to avert the inevitable. She looked out beyond the stern of the ship as the next roller barrelled towards them, a surging, roaring wall of death and destruction.

The ship had now turned beam on to the waves, and all hope left the crew as they looked up in awe at the wall of water which towered above them. Slowly, almost apologetically, the ship began her final slide, sideways, down into the blackness of the valley which had opened up before the next onrushing wave.

As she watched in horror the druid saw a hand grip the deck rail at the stern, and a leg hooked itself inboard as the figure of Hesperos rose, wraith like, from the abyss. Catumanda noticed for the first time that the rope was still attached to the steering handle and that it now led across the deck before disappearing overboard, and she realised what had caused the ship to heel hard over in its final act. The big wave had lifted both kubernetes and deposited them overboard as it had threatened to do to her. Similarly, the ropes had held, and the weight of the men had hauled the pedalia around and fixed it on its new course, dooming them all.

The milky light from the moon paled and then vanished completely as Toranos drew a veil and turned away from the events which were drawing to their conclusion below.

Unseen, the wave broke over them, and Catumanda could just make out the swirling eddy as the water cascaded down into the hold. The wave continued along the deck of the *Alexa*, forcing her down, her timbers groaning and sighing as the ship began her final plunge beneath the surface.

Catumanda gripped her staff and tightened the crane skin bag as she drew her moon blade. With one sweep of her hand the razor sharp blade sliced through the rope which bound her to the dying vessel, and a heartbeat later Philippos was also free.

With a hold full of tin ingots and seawater the ship sank below the surface in moments, and the druid pulled the boy to her as she kicked out for the storm tossed waves above. The moonlight returned as the pair neared the surface, and Catumanda took a last look below as the ship sank rapidly from view and almost gasped as she realised that the gods had already revealed the scene which greeted her.

Below her, the crew of the *Alexa* were revolving slowly around the mast as, still attached by their ropes, they were dragged into the depths by the now indistinct form of their ship. Suddenly Hektor looked up, and Catumanda recognised the same look of hopelessness and despair which had fixed the man's features in the dream only a few nights previously. Catumanda held the dying man's gaze and nodded deliberately. She thought that she had detected a spark of recognition flicker into the seaman's eyes before he was lost to the depths, that an understanding had passed between them in the man's final moments. She would keep her vow to him. She *would* ensure that the son he would never now see would bear the name Thestor.

24

Solemis was nearing the end. The Etruscan hoplites before him took several paces back and twisted their upper bodies as fresh men slipped through to renew the assault. Tiredness was beginning to overcome him now and he felt like he had been fighting all morning but, despite the almost overwhelming urge to look, he just could not afford to take his eyes from the phalanx to check the position of the sun. Only the shortening shadows cast by his clansmen and their weapons told the young chieftain that time had passed at all, and he had not already slipped through the barrier into the underworld where time had no place and an hour could last a hundred years.

His eyes locked with those of the man who would be his next opponent and he noticed the fear come into them: another boy. Solemis threw him a cruel wink and jerked his head, inviting him on. The Etruscan swallowed and flicked an anxious look down at the ribbon of bloodied bodies which lay between them, and they both knew that the boy would soon be joining them.

Solemis gripped the shaft of his lancea and blinked away

the stinging perspiration from his eyes as the enemy began to shuffle nervously forward. The young Horsetails chieftain recognised that it was good tactics on the part of the southerners to rotate the men in the forward lines, but it was not *their* way. The leading members of the clans, the senior warriors, fought in the front rank always, where their experience, strength and sense of honour dictated that they should; the chieftain always fought in the place of greatest honour, at the centre of the front rank. The chieftain fought for victory, and the clansmen fought for his recognition and the honour of receiving *potlach* before the people of the clan at the victory feast.

It was the traditional form of warfare in the north, where battles seldom lasted long and were often decided by combat between champions in the dead land between the armies. Here in the South it would seem that contact between the rival hosts was maintained until one side broke and ran, and Solemis knew that if Camulos granted them victory today their methods of warfare would need to adapt if the clans were to survive here in the new lands.

The phalanx came on, and Solemis watched for the moment when his opponent would glance down as he attempted to pick his way through the pitiful maze of the fallen. *There!*

He shot forward and skewered the hoplite in the upper thigh with the blade of his lancea, and was back in position before his opponent had time to react. To a man the Etruscan soldiers wore fine war shirts of bronze or toughened hide, full faced bronze helmets and greaves to protect their lower legs, but their habit of leaving the area between their short leather skirts and knees completely unprotected had quickly been seized upon by the Celts. Even the briefest glimpse of this area beneath the large bronze disc of their shield was instantly speared by the experienced warriors in the Senone wall. Invariably the hoplite would fall to the ground, hampering those around him and blocking the path forward for those following on behind. Once the attack faltered and the phalanx withdrew to regroup, the Celts would move forward to deliver the killing blow before the watching eyes of the next wave, causing their spirits to plummet even further.

Solemis looked on as the boy fell forward clutching his wound, his screams adding to the mayhem all around. To the rear Cotos was redoubling his efforts on the carnyx with the advent of each new attack, and despite his own weariness, Solemis snorted as he imagined the state of exhaustion which the horn blower must be approaching.

A hoplite to the left moved in and stabbed with his spear; Solemis parried the thrust with his shield and leapt forward. Shoulder-barging his assailant aside, he swept the blade of his lancea around and into the tough leather covering the man's side as his hand slid along the shaft, gripping the lancea near the blade as he worked it between the fastenings in the Etruscan's war shirt. The cords give way under the pressure, and Solemis thrust the blade, dagger-like, deeply into his opponent's side and withdrew. As the man fell away, the Celt swung his spear in an arc and danced back into the protection of the wall of shields to his rear.

Suddenly the raucous blast made by a dozen carnyx swept across the combatants, and a rousing cheer rolled across from Solemis's right. The Etruscans exchanged fearful glances and backed cautiously away as they prepared to face a new threat, and the Horsetails risked a glance across and gasped with delight as a boiling, roistering wave of Senone warriors bore down on the Etruscan flank.

As the danger before them receded Albiomaros came

across and stood beside his chieftain, and the blood genos watched together in disbelief and disgust as the rear ranks of the phalanx, the most experienced men, men who had yet to come to grips with their enemy broke and ran, casting aside their weapons and discarding their armour as they fled back towards the city.

The surge of Celts hit the disorganised Etruscan wing and poured through, slashing and stabbing as it drove the survivors into the river beyond. In the blink of an eye the Etruscan hoplites, their victory incontestable only moments before, had been utterly defeated and swept from the field. Solemis exchanged looks of wonder with the men of his clan, and together they broke into gales of laughter at the sudden change in their fortunes as they realised that they would live to see the sun set that evening after all.

The young Horsetail glanced back towards the river and saw that Sedullos, another of the clan chieftains, was striding through the carnage which littered the slope, his face painted with a grin. He went forward to greet him and they clasped forearms in the warrior greeting.

Sedullos blew out his cheeks and whistled as he ran his eyes over the field and on down to the watercourse at its base. Solemis' gaze followed suit, and he looked on in pride as he realised the scale of their achievement. They had retreated steadily from the place where they had first encountered the Etruscan phalanx in a series of holding actions. Looking back down the slope now, he could see that each position they had halted and defended was marked by a thick line of bloodied corpses, the grim tidal marks of a monstrous beach. Several crows were already beginning to worry the outlying bodies, and more were arriving in a cawing mass with each passing moment.

Sedullos nodded knowingly and threw the young chieftain

a look of respect. “The Horsetails did well.” He paused and ran his gaze across the field of death. “Very well.”

Solemis tried to answer but found to his surprise that not much more than a strangled croak escaped his lips.

Sedullos laughed and unstopped the flask at his side, handing it over with a grin. “It's thirsty work; it doesn't look as though you boys were given many opportunities to take drinks!”

Solemis nodded his thanks and looked back across to the centre of the battlefield. The clans with Brennus had moved forward and were now pursuing the tattered remnants of the Etruscan phalanx back across the field towards the city, and he craned his neck to check the position of Crixos' mounted force.

Sedullos clapped him on the shoulder. “You'll not find them there. It looked like Crixos and his clansmen killed Porsenna and all the leading men from where we were fighting.”

Solemis broke into a smile of wonder. “You are sure?”

Sedullos took a swig from the flask and nodded enthusiastically. “We saw them burst from cover and ride them down. It was all over before any help could arrive.” He hawked and spat some of the dust of the day as he continued. “As soon as the enemy saw the flags beaten down a shiver seemed to run through the entire formation and the next moment they took off.” He jerked his head towards the river where the Etruscan survivors were being disarmed by his men: “a bit like your lot.” The older chieftain drained his wine and called for another. “You can get yourself across there and congratulate Aia's father if you like, I will take care of things here.” He winked mischievously; “he is about to give you his only daughter after all.”

Solemis snorted but shook his head. “Crixos can wait, he

can bask in glory without my help. My clansmen need food and drink; my duty is here."

NUMERIUS exclaimed with delight as the barbarian horse galloped down from the ridge line opposite and disappeared behind the cypress grove. "Here they come!" He shot his brothers a look of glee and craned forward in the saddle as he waited to see where the attack would finally fall. They *must* be heading for the gully, everything that had transpired so far indicated that it *must* be the place.

Quintus glanced across. "Shall we warn them?"

Numerius laughed. "I should think not. They are about to get what they deserve. Besides," he added, "this is fascinating, even *better* than a day at the arena."

Caeso added his own comment. "What about the equites? They will have been screened from the barbarian movements by the trees. Shall I send a rider across and warn them?"

Numerius gasped at the suggestion. "No, we bloody well shan't. If they choose to station themselves in such a place that they cannot see the enemy, and are too far away to do much good even if they *could,* they don't really deserve our help."

The Roman looked back across the field of battle. The light spearmen had traversed the rear of the main phalanx and were beginning to drop down the bank to bring support to their right wing. A quick glance back to his left showed that the archers had moved forward and were attempting to support their main advance which seemed to have become bogged down in the riverbed. The gully to their rear lay completely undefended, and Numerius watched with relish as he waited for the Gauls to emerge there as he felt sure that they would.

Quintus chuckled and pointed out the lone figure of an archer as he hastened away from the rest of the company, already tugging anxiously at his breeches. “He's in for a shock if your expectation is correct, Numerius.”

They watched as the man disappeared from view, and Caeso grinned and glanced across to his brothers. “That's what's known in plebeian circles as 'dying for a shit!'”

The Romans exchanged a wicked laugh as the tip of the leading Celtic helm finally broke cover. As they watched with mounting excitement, Gaulish horsemen burst forth from the lip of the ravine and poured across the valley side like water from an upturned barrel. The Celtic riders put back their heels and thundered on, and as the leading riders came abreast of their position Quintus craned forward in his saddle and gasped. “Brother; that is the bastard who insulted us when we first arrived!”

Numerius furrowed his brow as he tried to make out the features of the leading Gaul, and his eyes shot open as he too recognised Crixos for who he was. He hefted his spear and called to the men of the *turmae*. “Romans! I don't care about the fate of the zilach, but I want the head of the leading Gaul. Cut the man off from the support of his men for long enough and there will be a purse of silver in it for each of you.”

The Roman ambassadors urged their horses into a gallop, and a roar came from the ranks as they were finally released to take part in the action. Arrowing off across the run of the slope, it was quickly obvious that they stood no chance of cutting out the leading Gauls before they reached the Etruscan leaders who were just beginning to respond to the threat. Glancing across to his right, Numerius noticed with disgust that the Etruscan equites were at last waking up to the danger and were beginning to tumble down in a disorganised charge, but they would be far too late to intervene. The experienced Roman knew that Porsenna was about to discover that the gods had decreed that his unenviable fate was to be the last zilach of Clevsin.

Ahead of him Numerius saw that the barbarian charge had reached the Etruscan position and driven deeply into the ranks of the hastily arranged defence, and although the forward momentum was dulled for a heartbeat the remainder of the Gauls quickly came up and overwhelmed the command party. There was the momentary image of a barbarian horseman spinning through the air, end over end like a Cretan acrobat, before the pennants and flags of Clevsin were beaten down and he knew that the zilach was dead.

Numerius glanced across at the Etruscan horse and saw that they were coming down fast, and he screamed desperately at his own mount as he urged it on. The horsemen of Etruria were too late to save the day, but he would need to cut across their line of advance if he was to reach the arrogant Gaulish leader before he was swept away in the chaos. Already the rear elements of the Etruscan phalanx had noticed the disaster which had engulfed their commanders, and the first of them were abandoning the fight to flee for the safety of the city walls. It would take moments for the news to travel through the Etruscan army and then the trickle to the rear would grow into a flood. He knew from bitter experience that the moment an army lost its confidence and aggression the day was irretrievable. They would break and run, discarding their weapons and armour in a mad panic as they sought to save their lives, and no amount of threats or cajoling on the part of their leaders could reverse the situation.

Numerius gritted his teeth and kept his eyes locked on the head of the man he suddenly remembered had called himself Crixos. Gaulish horsemen were milling around as Crixos dismounted and re-emerged moments later with the head of Porsenna fixed to his spear point. A great cry of acclamation rose from the swirl of riders, and Numerius looked on in respect and surprise as, the primary objective of their attack realised, the oncoming barbarian column instinctively switched the line of their attack. Galloping across, the great column of Gauls swept down in a well led and aggressive counter attack on the Etruscan equites whose own attack, the Roman noted with dismay, had begun to falter the moment that the banners had been overrun.

Although clearly competent and a foe worthy of Numerius's respect, the Gaulish horsemen had emerged disorganised from the confines of the gully; the need to seize the element of surprise which they had worked so hard over the course of the day to achieve had dictated that they attack the zilach and his party immediately, but that same necessity had dictated that they must arrive piecemeal. Large gaps had appeared in the barbarian line as friends and clansmen naturally bunched together for mutual support, and Numerius thundered through such a gap as he closed with their leader. As he came up, the Roman began to become entangled by the first of the Etruscan spearmen as they fled the field but he stabbed and slashed at his erstwhile allies, trampling them beneath the hooves of his stallion in his desperation to force a way through to his quarry.

Caught up in the thrill of the moment, the Gauls were crowding their chieftain as he proudly raised the head of Porsenna aloft. Drunk on victory, the horsemen nearest to Crixos were gazing up at the gruesome trophy and acclaiming their leader as the man who had won the day.

Seizing his chance Numerius swept in. As Quintus and Caeso pushed into the throng, stabbing and slashing a path through to the Celt with their Greek spears, Numerius drew his short sword and prepared to attack. Immediately ahead of him Crixos' war horse was circling as the chieftain bellowed the news of his triumph over the heads of the retreating Etruscans. Warning cries from his men finally caused the Gaul to lower his eyes just as the Roman reached him, but mighty Hercules had smiled on his descendant, the timing was perfect, and Numerius had the immense satisfaction of knowing that his abuser had both seen and recognised the man who was about to take his life. The Roman drew back his arm and thrust the blade into Crixos's unprotected neck, and blood misted the air between them as the momentum carried the Roman past.

Elated by his victory Numerius failed to even see the avenging sword strike which stove in the side of his helmet, and it was only reactions honed over more than a decade of fighting against the enemies of Rome that saved him from being swept from his horse. He started as a hand gripped his arm and tugged him onward, and he realised to his horror that he now existed in a world of darkness, that he had been blinded by the blow. Fingers were forcing their way beneath the bronze of his helm, prising the life saving armour up, and Numerius struggled as he frantically sought to fight off his assailant but his efforts were in vain. As another figure moved in to grip his right hand side, Numerius began to lose all hope. Suddenly the helmet was wrenched clear, and light overwhelmed him as the sounds of battle redoubled. A face was before him, and he blinked as he attempted to focus. He knew this face, knew it well, but although the mouth was moving Numerius's addled mind could make no sense of the sounds which came from it. His senses returned in a rush; it was Quintus, his brother, repeatedly shouting his own name at him as his iron will began to reassert itself and he snapped a demand. "Quintus, the head! We need to take that bastard's head!"

Numerius pulled at his reins as he attempted to return to Crixos' body, but his brothers wedged him firmly between them as Quintus cried out above the din. "Numerius, forget it. Leave head hunting to the barbarians. We need to get away from here while we still can. The Etruscans have broken, they have lost the day!"

Looking up Numerius saw that they had become an island of horsemen stranded within a sea of running, terror stricken men. Glancing back, he saw that hundreds of Gauls bent on vengeance for the death of their chieftain were beating a bloody path towards his tiny party through this tide of humanity, and even in its still bleary state his mind recognised the good sense of his brother's shouted words. He nodded in agreement as Caeso gripped his reins and pulled the head of his horse towards the South.

DESPITE HIS EXHAUSTION Brennus grinned a welcome as Solemis approached. He regarded the young chieftain and gave a nod of approval. "You did very well today. Connos would have been proud of the Horsetails, and of the leadership shown by his son and successor."

Solemis nodded his thanks as he snatched up a skin of cervesia and took a long pull. Wiping his moustache on his sleeve, he looked across the battlefield towards the city of Clevsin. Thousands of mounted Senones were riding around the walls of the city, and most seemed to be carrying an Etruscan head on the tip of his spear. The head of Porsenna, complete with its ceremonial helm, sat perched on its own spear nearby, and Solemis gave it a cursory glance as he waited for the chieftain of the tribe to tell him the reason for his summons. Clearly there was something still on Brennus' mind despite his great victory here today, and Solemis hoped that it would not entail another detachment from the army.

Despite the honour which they had won since they had crossed the Apeninnus in the spring, the men were weary and keen to see their loved ones once again. The festival of Samhaine was almost upon them, and he would like the opportunity to display the evidence of the many great victories gained by the tribe and clan in the year which had passed since the ancestors had last crossed from the underworld and visited the world of men.

Brennus picked up a pebble from the ground and tossed it at Porsenna. His aim was good and the stone bounced off the old zilach's magnificent helmet with a metallic clang. He sniffed and looked back. "Crixos is dead."

Solemis' mouth gaped in shock and his shoulders sagged a little, drawing a weary chuckle from his chieftain. "Don't worry. The clan has already acclaimed Caturix as his successor, so I am sure that your marriage plans are even safer than before."

Solemis made to protest, but he knew that Brennus had read his tired thoughts exactly. He pulled a wry smile, but his chieftain's face told him that his mind had already reverted to the reason for his summons. He fixed Solemis with an icy stare. "The Roman ambassadors killed him, after he had dispatched our friend over there. Caturix managed to get a blow in against the killer, but the tide of battle was already sweeping him away and he couldn't follow if up with a death blow." Brennus shook his head as he thought back to the events of the morning. "You should have seen them, Solemis. As soon as the pennants fell, a wave of panic swept through the entire phalanx and they just threw down their weapons and bolted for the city. Despite the best efforts of Caturix and his clansmen to avenge their chieftain it was like trying to wade through a rip tide. Etruscans were streaming past and around them, but we are certain that it was a Roman who took Crixos's life. Caturix had done enough damage to the man's helmet that his companions had to prise it off so that he could see. They saw clearly that it was the ambassador, Numerius, who struck the blow."

Brennus pinged another pebble off the late zilach's helmet and leaned forward to scoop up some more. "I am sorry; I know that your boys fought hard today but I would ask that you perform one more duty on behalf of the people before we go home for the winter. I cannot send Caturix because he is obliged to take vengeance for his father, but you are the ideal man for the task. You are linked to the clan, but until you marry Aia you are not tied by blood to them and are not honour bound to take a blood price from these Romans. I have spoken of this with Caturix, and he agrees that a cool head is needed if we are to turn this to our advantage. He has already returned to our lands with the body of his father, but he told me to tell you that you would show honour to both himself and his clan if you would accept this charge."

Solemis pulled himself erect and nodded deliberately. "Naturally I will go. I will take twenty men with me; that will ensure our safety from bandits and the like but will be few enough to show them how confident we are in our strength." He glanced down and pulled a wry smile. "I may need time to clean myself up a little before I depart."

Brennus snorted. Both men were covered in mud and gore from the fighting. Solemis' right hand and arm were sticky with blood where he had repeatedly stabbed at his opponents with his spear, sword and dagger. His left eye was all but closed and it felt as large and shiny as an apple. He suspected that it was the result of a punch by the boss of a shield but, in truth, he had not noticed it during the grappling and had no idea when it had occurred.

Brennus grinned happily at the young chieftain's self-assured reply, fingering his dagger he beckoned the Horsetail across. Wiping the tip of his blade backwards and forwards on the leg of his trews, he stood and held it towards him. "Spit on the end."

Confused, Solemis did as he was instructed, and Brennus reached out and placed the palm of his hand gently on the side of the young chieftain's face, his outstretched fingers and thumb splaying to open the swollen eye. His own face a mask of concentration the chieftain raised the knife and it flicked out, once, twice. Immediately Solemis felt a hot gush, as a vile mixture of blood and mucus drained from the swelling and washed down his cheek.

Brennus took a pace back and examined his handiwork. He nodded, satisfied. "That should do it. The spit helps the wound to heal somehow." He shrugged. "It must be the work of the gods." With a final look and a nod of approval he sat back down and began to outline the demands he wished to be made on the city of Rome, as Solemis patted his lacerated cheek with his sleeve. "Tell them that it is expressly against the laws of all *civilised* nations that ambassadors side with one party against another in a dispute, much less take up arms. Tell them that we demand suitable compensation," he paused and flicked the air with his hand, "think of a suitable amount for a chieftain and double it, and that they hand over these Fabii brothers to me so that I can administer justice." He looked up and grinned. "You can spin it out a bit, but you get the gist. What do you think?"

Solemis looked up, still blinking as his vision began to clear.

"They will never agree to it. They may agree to compensation, but they will never hand over three men of rank to us. You heard what they call us, they think that we are mindless savages."

Brennus laughed happily. "Excellent; that's what I thought too. When they reject our demands, tell them that we will come to give them a taste of northern justice in the spring."

25

Darkness was descending as the toga clad citizens of the republic swept back through the *Porta Fontinalis* and disbursed to the homes and taverns of the city. It had been a long day of politicking, but the three men who watched the returning centuries were quietly confident that they had each carried their respective day. Away to their left the presiding magistrate, unmistakable in his purple-bordered toga, had vacated the curule chair and, flanked by the *lictores* with their distinctive *fasces* held before them, had begun to follow on.

Quintus turned to his brothers with a smile of satisfaction. "That should be that then."

Numerius inclined his head graciously as the magistrate passed them and turned to look out across the scene of his greatest triumph. The lowering sun was beginning to dip beneath the western hills in a splash of scarlet, and Numerius drank in the grandeur of the sarcophagi, the family tombs which lined the road, as the dying day painted their walls, columns and imagery the colour of blood. The *Campus Martius* was emptying rapidly now that the voting had been concluded, and the great sweep of the Tiberis which marked the field's western limit shone in the harsh autumnal light. He turned back to his brothers with a smile. "As you so eloquently say *tribunus*, that should very well be that." They shared a chuckle at the sound of the unfamiliar title, but each of them knew the result of the election which they had just witnessed.

The day had started early, but most of the preparation for their success had been laid in the days and weeks beforehand by their father, Marcus. As Pontifex Maximus he was a man of considerable influence, and it had been a small matter for their paterfamilias to call in a few favours to ensure that his three returning sons were successfully elected to the rank of military tribune. Perhaps the most difficult moment had come at the conventions that morning. As a speaker was in full flow, extolling the virtues of the Fabii and pointing out their efforts against the northern barbarians in the name of Rome, a sudden peal of thunder had shaken the forum and several birds had fallen from a clear sky. The augurs present had begun to cry out that the gods were showing their disfavour of the brothers, and citizens had begun to cast nervous glances before several burly thugs had moved in to silence the unhelpful charlatans and help them on their way. Unusually, the Pontifex Maximus himself had been present, and he had been able to interpret the sign as one of favour for the candidates. Moving quickly to the podium he had called for their attention as the low rumble rolled away:

'My friends, how can the sound of thunder carry from a clear, blue sky? Of course it cannot; that was nothing less than the club of Hercules beating the celestial vault to indicate approval for the election of his gens, for the men who you see before you are the direct descendants of the god, as you are all well aware.'

The following vote had been a formality, and the citizens

had organised into their voting centuries and proceeded from the city to the Field of Mars for the final vote. Now the jars containing the pebbles which men used to indicate their preference were being escorted back to the city, where the count would be made and the result announced.

The Fabii paused and looked for a final time along the line of the roadway as it marched away to the distant bridge across the Tiberis. Caeso said the words which each man was thinking. "Was it really just a week ago that we clattered across that bridge and brought the news back to Rome of the rout of the Clusines?"

Numerius stroked his chin and sniffed as he gazed back along the road. On the far side of the river the road divided; one road led towards the distant line of the Apeninnus and thence on to the shores of the Adriaticum. Traffic from that direction had slowed to a trickle over the course of the previous year, as the shadow cast by the land hungry Gauls had lengthened with each passing month. The northern branch was none other than that of the Via Cassia, the very road which ran beneath the walls of poor tormented Clusium, the very road in fact which they had taken to flee south from the avenging barbarian horde only days before. A cloud as dark as Pluto lay over the hills there, and Numerius pursed his lips as he imagined the suffering which was being enacted beneath its dark ramparts. With a final, subdued, glance to the north the brothers pulled at their reins and urged their horses back towards the city.

Numerius ran his eyes along the line of the defences as he approached the gate. He was determined to treat the responsibilities which his new title brought with it with the seriousness which they deserved. The Servian Wall which encircled the city was in a poor state of repair. Several wars, both civil and against foreign enemies had taken their toll in the two centuries of their existence. It would be his first duty to see to their repair once his election to *tribunus militum* had been confirmed in the morning. Unlike other Romans, he had already witnessed the Gauls at first hand. The fools in the senate could hide behind words and feelings of superiority if they liked, but the security of Rome now fell upon the shoulders of the Fabii. The brothers had seen these barbarians in action and they had been impressed, both by their acumen and their ferocity.

Away to his right the great colonnade and portico of the Temple of Jupiter Optimus Maximus atop the Capitoline Hill had taken on the sheen of burnished bronze as the last of the day melted away. Numerius closed his eyes for a brief moment as he passed into the shadow of the wall and appealed to the father of the gods:

Jupiter, Greatest and Best; grant me one year of grace and I can make these walls impenetrable.

SOLEMIS SADDLED his horse and fished around in the purse which hung at his waist. Swinging himself up he tossed another silver coin to the delighted farmer and bade him farewell.

They had spent the night in the old man's ramshackle barn, and although the walls and roof seemed to be more hole than wood it had been comfortable nevertheless. The old crone had supplied them with a large iron pot brimming with a vegetable stew, and although there had been little wine, the bread had been plentiful and wholesome. They had deserved the silver for their hospitality and, in truth, Brennus had supplied them with so many of the silver coins that he was glad to lighten the load by paying over the odds for food and lodgings. Winter was fast approaching, and the payment could very well make the difference between starvation and survival for the old couple. He could see that the back-breaking lot of the farmer was as hard here as in the northern lands, harder perhaps. The people here seemed not to live in clans, and he wondered why they would do such a thing. Each family prospered or starved independently, and the old seemed to struggle to provide for themselves as their neighbours no doubt totted up the worth of their land holdings with avaricious eyes.

The column was already formed up and waiting for him as he steered his mount off of the track and back onto the road the Etruscans and Romans called the Via Cassia. The metalled roadway was wide enough for two riders to ride abreast, and Solemis fell in beside Albiomaros as they pointed the horses back to the South.

He had humbled himself for the good of the clan, and apologised for his actions towards the big man at the start of the fight before the assembled warriors. Hoping to make amends, he had declared that his blood genos was his choice for champion of the Horsetails. The clan had been without a champion since the heroic death of Cauros in the first Battle of Clevsin, and Solemis had invited any challengers to come forward and fight the new champion for the honour. Albiomaros had drawn himself up to his not inconsiderable height, and puffed out his chest as he proudly awaited the challenge that no one really expected to follow. The new champion had looted a helmet from an Etruscan hoplite at the start of the battle, and he had worn it still. Fashioned into the face of an owl the bronze helmet sported a vicious dagger for a beak, and Albiomaros had used it extensively during the day to stab at the faces of his opponents as they came to grips. His own face and chest had become coated with the blood and gore from his victims and, added to the background of blue spells with which he decorated his body before each battle, he had appeared to all as a scion of the Morrigan herself. Unsurprisingly no challenge had been forthcoming, and Solemis had formally declared his friend to be the new champion of the clan on the field of battle to wild acclamation.

They passed through the hillier country by midmorning, and the road dropped down to a softer land of gently rolling fields. The Via Cassia still arrowed away to the South, its tree lined flanks heavy with yellowing leaves. The farms were further apart here, and the buildings which capped the ridges larger and grander. The harvest was in, and the fields were a swathe of ochre coloured stubble as they dismounted and retrieved the bread and beans from the pack horses. As they settled down in the shade of the trees, the harsh crack of the lash carried to them across the fields. Several of the men had gone to the opposite side of the road to relieve themselves before they ate, and they returned clearly troubled by what they had witnessed there. Solemis had asked Cotos to bring the carnyx along to add a sense of what he knew the Greeks called *'drama'* to their appearance when they pitched up before the city, and the man hurried across now with a frown. "Solemis, there is a slave being used to pull a plough in the field opposite; he looks like a Celt."

The young chieftain tossed his food to one side and levered himself up. Crossing the road he pulled at his moustache as he looked out across the farmland. A big man wearing what looked to be a bundle of rags loosely tied around his midriff was indeed hitched to a plough, and Solemis watched as the overseer cracked a whip about his ear as he drove the man on. Tall and broad of shoulder, heavy blonde braids swung beside his face as he laboured under the hot sun and, as Solemis shaded his eyes, he thought that he could still make out a fine moustache. The man was clearly a

Celtic warrior, and before he was really conscious of making a decision Solemis found that he was striding across the field towards the group.

As he approached them the men paused at their work and turned his way, and Solemis flicked open the leather bands which secured the hilt of his sword in its scabbard. He cast a look at the wicked looking goad and regretted for a heartbeat that he had not retrieved his shield from the pack animal, but the sound of his clansmen walking their horses to his rear dispelled his fears and he marched resolutely on.

Solemis ignored the bemused overseer and marched directly up to the Gaul. “You are a warrior; which nation?”

The man looked shamefaced but cleared his throat and replied. “Aedui, master.”

Solemis’s eyes widened in shock, and he took a pace back as his eyes weighed up the man before him. His experienced gaze quickly noted the old scars of battle on the torso and right forearm, and he jerked his head to indicate that the Aeduan turn around. As he had suspected, the man's back was completely free from the scars of battle although the longer, thinner marks of the lash had scored him badly. This man was an experienced warrior who had never turned his back and run from a fight, and yet here he was being used as beast of burden. He composed himself, lowering his voice to a growl as he fixed the man with a penetrating stare. “I am not your master, never use that term again. Why are you not dead?”

The Aeduan moved his head to one side and parted his hair to reveal the hard puckered smile of an old scar. “I was knocked unconscious during a raid on my steading; I awoke in chains at spear point.”

Solemis nodded and glanced towards the other slaves who were cowering behind the overseer. Smaller and darker he dismissed them as worthless. “Why do the others have their hair shorn like spring sheep, while you do not…?" He raised his brow letting the question hang in the air, and the Aeduan showed that he was aware enough to supply the answer he sought. "Berikos, my name is Berikos. They told me to keep my hair long because they said it made me look like a woman." He shrugged, and the corners of his mouth turned up into a hint of a smile as laughter danced in his eyes. "I begged them to let me shave my warrior moustache because it added to my shame, so they insisted that I keep it."

Solemis chuckled at the man's guile. It was a good answer. There was clearly a spark of honour left in the great Aeduan despite his misfortune, and he found that he was beginning to warm to him. Berikos raised his chin and Solemis was pleased to see that the light of hubris was beginning to rekindle in his eyes. The overseer had recovered from the shock of being suddenly confronted by a war band of barbarians in the middle of Etruria, and was now jabbering away in Etruscan. Solemis turned to Albiomaros. "Genos: ask our friend there to be quiet."

The Horsetail champion's features broke into a smile as a fist shot forward to connect with the man's chin with an audible *crack!*

As the Etruscan was sent spinning away, Solemis turned back to the Aeduan who was now grinning like a fool. "Why did your clansmen not came after you?"

The smile fell from his features, to be replaced by a haughty look of pride. "My clansmen fought to the death; I am the last to board the boat to the Isles."

NUMERIUS PAUSED at the top of the steps and drank in the view. Spread out before him lay the city of Rome, the place of his birth, in all its metropolitan splendour. Across the open expanse of the Forum Romanum the temples to the gods marched away, each seemingly finer than the next; Caster, Vesta, Alius Locutius, Vulcan, the House of the Vestals nestling at the foot of the Palatine.

Atop their huge columns the statues of the gods and great men of the past, gleaming dully in bronze or gilt, looked down on the beating heart of the Republic. Beggars were not permitted here and the forum contained only the better sort of citizen, the *nobilitas* and the more industrious members of the plebs, those who had risen above the common herd by sweat of brow or sharpness of mind. The forum was ringed by their small shops and stalls, selling goods from across the known world and beyond. Stonemasons rubbed shoulders with fine jewellers, mosaic makers with wine merchants, money lenders and lawyers. Above them all buzzed the hubbub of men and women eating, drinking, bargaining and politicking.

As he dropped down the steps to the waiting horsemen, he acknowledged the smiles of his brothers and hauled himself up into the saddle. A small group of citizens had gathered to watch as the delegation moved away, and the crowd broke into laughter as one of their number called on *Fortuna* to attend them on their dangerous assignation.

The barbarian delegation had arrived unexpectedly at the city gates several days before. As the Senones had not established formal diplomatic relations with the Republic, the Senate had been unable to entertain their request for an audience inside the walls of the city, and they had been directed to the residence which was maintained on the Campus Martius at public expense for just this purpose while the response to their demands was debated in the chamber.

Even with his experience of the arrogance and temerity of the Gauls, Numerius had gasped as loud as any when the sum demanded for the slaying of one of their chieftains had been conveyed to the house. As for the demand that he and his brothers be handed over for the administration of barbarian 'justice,' well that was just preposterous! Several of their political rivals had spluttered with delight as they voiced their support, and he knew that their father, the Pontifex, had duly marked them out for future retaliation.

Moving through the crowds, Numerius glanced back at the Temple of Jupiter before it was lost from view as they rounded the base of the Capitoline and struck out for the gate:

Very well, Jupiter; I shall not get my year. Test me and you shall not find me wanting for ability. Place me in command of the forces of the city and I will devastate these barbarians and dedicate my victory to you.

THE DOOR to the *latrina* swung open and the massive forms of Albiomaros and Berikos came through in an animated brawl. At first they failed to see their chieftain in the shadows at the edge of the small open area of the peristylium, and Solemis suddenly found to his surprise that he felt a measure of resentment at their carefree relationship. The big men had been inseparable ever since they had freed the Aeduan, and Solemis snorted guiltily as he recognised how absurd he would sound if he ever shared his thoughts with either man.

Albiomaros had been his closest friend ever since they had met as boys in far off Albion, and Berikos had witnessed the death of his entire clan and been carried away to endure a life of slavery. They had all witnessed the depths of his humiliation under the Etruscans; that he had managed to keep a tiny flicker of pride and self respect burning within him under such daily torment spoke wonders for the character of the big man, and Solemis knew that the doubts which had plagued him ever since he left the rest of the army paled beside such things.

He knew that Brennus' choice of envoy had caused some surprise and even a little dissension among the older chieftains of the clans, and he sometimes wondered himself if the responsibilities which were being thrust upon him *were* coming too quickly. Perhaps it had been a mistake to learn the language of the Romans, but he found that such things came easily to him and he knew that the knowledge would benefit them greatly during scouting forays. If few others had the foresight that was hardly his concern.

In little more than a year he had risen from being the young son of one of the lesser known clan chieftains to the leader of the Horsetails. He had been entrusted with the command of an entire flank of the army in battle against a dangerous foe, and now he was camped before the walls of the mighty Roman Republic and making outrageous demands on them at the head of a force consisting of twenty men. If Toranos struck him down here and now, he would have achieved more than most men would manage in a dozen lifetimes.

Another figure exited the latrina, and Solemis glanced up to see that Cotos had sauntered out into the weak autumnal sunshine. Albiomaros and Berikos pulled themselves upright and nodded happily to the carnyx player as he passed them by with a grin. Cotos winked in their direction and waved a *spongia.* "I may as well take a few, they are bloody great. You need a fresh mouth when you blow a carnyx, and my teeth have never felt so clean. Mind you though," he said, as he ran his tongue back and forth across the front of his teeth, "that vinegar stuff is a bit strong!"

Solemis spluttered as he realised what the joke had been. He looked across to the big pair and saw that they were on the point of collapse, mouths open, their breath coming in short pants as they fought a desperate battle for self control. Finally Albiomaros managed to nod in acknowledgement and a high-pitched, strangulated reply crept from his lips. "That's what friends are for Cotos. Glad we could help."

Solemis shook his head in dismay. He remembered that Cotos had volunteered to keep watch when they had first arrived at the *domus,* and he had missed the tour of the building by the *dispensator*. Although most of this domus was not to their liking, they had all enjoyed the use of the latrina with its communal seating plan and the ingenious method of cleaning oneself involving a sea sponge tied to a small stick.

Solemis twisted to call after Cotos and let him in on the joke, but found that Druteos was approaching from the main atrium; one look at his clansman's face was enough to tell the chieftain that the time for joviality was over.

SOLEMIS REGAINED the roadway and turned the head of his mount towards the walls of the city. The great doors had been symbolically closed to them, and his gaze ran along the crenelated upper level of the bulwark as the citizens within stood and stared at a Gaulish chieftain in his battle finery.

A gusting breeze blew across the Field of Mars, sweeping a wave of crisp brown leaves across the way. Suddenly Albiomaros' horse bucked and reared as it shook its head vigorously, and the Trinobante slid a hand down to the animal's neck as he attempted to calm it. The big war stallion shook its head in irritation, and Albiomaros moved his hand up to caress its ear as he calmly spoke to it. As Solemis watched, a look of puzzlement crossed his big friend's features, and he reached inside the cup of the horse's ear with his fingertips.

Withdrawing something, Albiomaros's expression turned to one of shock as he held the object out to his chieftain. "It's an oak leaf, a big one!"

Solemis was about to shrug and urge his mount on when he realised the importance of his friend's words. Both men shared a look of wonder and they instinctively glanced down at the angry red scar which bisected their left hands. Albiomaros was the first to find his tongue. "It's another sign, Solemis."

They looked beyond the waiting Romans to the walls of the city, and Solemis nodded his agreement as he replied to his friend using his birth name. "It *is* a sign, Acco. A great episode in our life stories will take place here."

Albiomaros's face lit up. "Perhaps Catumanda is here!"

Solemis laughed as he remembered their childhood friend, the missing member of their fraternity, the remaining blood genos.

"Catumanda will be a woman now, possibly even a full druid. Women don't roam the world looking for adventure; she will be lying on a hillside in Albion watching the clouds for a sign, or fixing up potions for some barren old hag with a face like the rear end of a horse!"

The friends shared a laugh as the waiting Romans exchanged looks of bewilderment at their antics. Solemis noted their puzzlement and chuckled to himself. Clearly they were more accustomed to foreign delegations treating occasions such as this with a bit more of what they termed *gravitas.*

He composed himself and urged his stallion on once more as Albiomaros and Cotos moved to his flanks. Albiomaros made one last comment before they came within earshot of the Roman delegation. "You are right genos, poor Catumanda; a woman is never happy unless she lays her head in the same place each night. Still, she did say that she dreamt that we would meet again in a wondrous place," he ran his eyes back along the walls and took in the Temple of Jupiter perched atop the Capitoline, "and you have to admit; this *is* a wondrous place."

Glancing up at the massive defences and the blood red rooftops beyond, Solemis nodded in agreement as he walked his mount on. Reining in half a dozen paces from the waiting Romans, he acknowledged them with a confident nod as Albiomaros and Cotos hung back. He recognised the three leading members of the Roman delegation at once, they were, after all, the reason he had travelled to this place, and he understood immediately that the leaders of the city wished to show them the utmost disrespect. In truth he had expected no less; they had already been informed that the Fabii, far from being censured by the senate for breaking what they themselves regarded as the Laws of Nations, had been elected by the people to higher office. The idea that they would then hand these men over to him for trial was obviously ridiculous, and he had met the revelation with relief as he had realised that his principle instruction from Brennus had already been fulfilled.

Whatever happens, Solemis; make sure that you don't return with the bastards.

Albiomaros had forgone his recently acquired owl helm and had reverted to the customs of the Trinobantes for the meeting with the delegation from the city, and Solemis smiled inwardly as he noted a ripple of excited chatter run through the distant spectators as he came into view.

The dispensator had readily obtained a supply of lime from a builder in the city; woad had caused him more of a problem but, although the colour of the paste which the man had eventually delivered was somewhat lighter than usual he had insisted that it was due to the fact that the oak trees in the South were unlike those in the northern lands. Albiomaros had been content nevertheless. Without a druid to work his spells the markings would lack power and were merely *'to show these Romans what a real barbarian looks like.'*

Solemis looked from one brother to the next and addressed the Romans individually. "Numerius Fabius Ambustus, tribunus militum. Quintus Fabius Ambustus, tribunus militum. Caeso Fabius Ambustus, tribunus militum." He shot them a wry smile. "I offer you my congratulations on scaling another rung on the cursus honorum. Have you brought everything that you need for the journey?"

The brothers exchanged a brief look of disbelief before breaking into gentle laughter. Numerius regarded his adversary with a new-found sense of respect, before showing the Gaul that Roman intelligence was no less efficient than barbarian. "You are well informed Solemis, Chieftain of the Horsetail clan. I am afraid that we will not be accompanying you, despite the tempting offer. As you appear to have discovered, our newly acquired responsibilities tie us to the confines of the city."

Solemis gave a curt nod and stretched his neck to peer beyond the Roman equites which formed the guard party. "I see no wagons containing Crixos' blood price."

Numerius brightened. "Now *that* matter *is* open to negotiation. I could supply you with," he paused and glanced at his brothers who sat impassively at his side, "half of the amount you requested? In return your army will withdraw beyond the line of the Apeninnus and relinquish control of the springs from which the goddess Tiberis springs forth to water our land." He glanced across to the nearby river and cocked his head. "If you listen closely you will hear that this is also the wish of the goddess. As you know Solemis, a people who ignore the will of the gods are a people who invite destruction upon themselves."

Solemis leaned forward in his saddle and fixed Numerius with a stare. "A people who allow themselves to be fooled into discounting a roll of thunder from a clear sky and a rain of dead birds do, as you say, invite calamity."

He leaned back and threw an instruction over his shoulder as the colour drained from Roman faces. "Cotos, let the people lining the ramparts hear the sound of the battle swine."

Cotos raised the carnyx to his lips as a ripple of wind-blown leaves came between the Celts and Romans. The war horn climbed into the cool autumn air, and the snarling face of the boar looked out on the Walls of Servian for the first time. Cotos blew a long mournful howl which rolled around the Campus Martius as the watching citizens fell silent.

Solemis began to turn the head of his stallion away as he threw a comment to Albiomaros. "Come genos. We are done here." He glanced down as a sudden gust plucked the crest from a mound of leafage and swirled it about the hocks of his mount. Solemis looked back at the Romans as the final note faded, his voice a snarl. "Mark the sound of our war horns. When the snows retreat and the Bel Fires burn, look to the North!"

AFTERWORD

If the words 'historic' and 'cataclysmic' are often overused today, there can be little doubt that the fall of the city of Rome to the Senone army under the leadership of Brennus, 'Raven', around the year 390 BC fully justifies both descriptions. Far more than the Spartan defence of Thermopylae less than a century earlier, the event can truly be called a pivotal moment in the history of Europe, the repercussions from which live with us to this day. It was the single most important event which propelled Rome from being one of a number of such states on the Italian peninsula to the great empire she would later become, as first the leaders of the Republic and later the Emperors sought to push the 'others,' the 'barbarians,' further and further away from the walls of the city.

The original Servian Walls were named after the king of Rome at the time of their construction in the sixth century BC, Servius Tullius. The present day walls which still carry the name are thought to have replaced this earlier wall around the time of these events, quite possibly as a result of the fall of the city to Brennus and his Senones.

That this defeat occurred at the hands of invaders from

the North should no longer surprise us. Militarily the people of the Mediterranean world had much to learn from their Northern neighbours; many of the characteristically 'Roman' items carried by later legionaries were direct copies of those introduced to the South during Brennus's war and later conflicts. Sub-rectangular shields, linked mail shirts, the long 'spatha' sword used by the Roman cavalry, and even the distinctive 'coolus' type helmet were in fact imports from the sophisticated and thriving civilisation of the Celtic north.

Known as Gauls to the Romans and Keltoi by the Greeks, the people we today call Celts inhabited a vast swathe of central Europe stretching from the Atlantic to the Balkans. Bounded to the North by the Germanic tribes of the Belgae and others, their southern limit was in fact the mountains of the Apennines in Italy itself. The Plain of Lombardy was heavily settled by Celts and many names in the region trace their origin back to them. The city of Genoa shares the same Celtic word root with Geneva, both meaning 'port,' Turin was the oppidum of a Celtic tribe, the Taurini; Mediolanum, Milan, was founded by the Celtic Insubres around 600 BC. In our story Solemis's Horsetails settle in the foothills overlooking the present day town of Senigallia, the town of the Senones/Gauls, fully one-third of the way down the Adriatic coast of the peninsula.

This first volume in the Conqueror of Rome series was necessarily the tale of the migration of the tribe from the region of present day north central France, and the initial conflict with the Etruscan city of Clevsin. It seems fairly certain that the Fabii brothers were sent by Rome in response to a plea for aid from the city, and that they broke the laws of neutrality by taking up arms against the Gauls. Although our scanty sources tell us that it was Quintus who killed a Gaulish chieftain during the battle I had the deed done by his brother,

Numerius, as the probable leader of the mission and principal character on the Roman side of our tale.

While some modern historians have questioned why Rome would aid their traditional enemies, I have had them do so at the instigation of their father, Marcus. He *was* the Pontifex Maximus at that time, and both Romans and Celts/Gauls believed that sacred spirits lived in springs and rivers. As Pontifex, Marcus was the head of the priesthood of Rome in much the same way that the present day Pope is the Pontiff of the Catholic Church. The source of the Tiber was close to the lands being settled by the Senones and it is entirely possible that this situation could have arisen.

Almost every druid that I have ever seen depicted has been male, but there seems no logical reason why this should be so. The Irish mythological hero Cuchulain was said to have received training in the arts of war from the female druid Scarthach, and what little we do know of the pagan religions of pre Christian northern Europe tell us that women played at least an equal part, and often the greater part, in many rituals. The mysteries of the craft were seen as 'unmanly' in the later Viking age, and there seems no reason not to extend the custom back into the deeper past. It also gave me the ideal opportunity to introduce a strong female character into the story which I was keen to do.

The role of women in Celtic society was much greater than in the South, it was in fact one of the features which the Romans found so barbaric. Women could divorce their husbands and continued to hold property in their own name after marriage, even rising to leadership of the tribe, with the examples of Boudica and Cartimandua the most familiar to us today. Both women ruled large areas of Britain simultaneously 'by right' in the first century and there must have been many others.

Britain and Ireland were well known to the people of the Mediterranean world by the sixth century BC. Tin was important in the production of bronze, and there was a long established trading centre at a place known as *Ictis* which may have been the island of St Michael's Mount in present day Cornwall. I took the liberty of moving it along the coast to Hengestbury Head in Dorset, another known trading centre in antiquity, and renaming it Isarnos due to the iron which is found there. This brought it much closer to the Jurassic Coast with its well preserved fossils from the time of the dinosaurs, Dun's 'Place of Monsters.'

Julius Caesar tells us that the Belgae were proud of their Germanic heritage and that they had settled the coastal areas of what is now England before his time. Many of the British tribes share common names with those across the channel, Atrebates, Parisii and even the tribe which retained the name of the Belgae itself. There is strong evidence that several rulers held lands on both sides of the channel, and coin finds in southern England support Caesar's claim that many men who fought against his forces in Gaul came from the island.

Clientage was a pillar of the clan based system of obligations in the North, and I chose to set the opening scene of the novel the day before Albiomaros/Acco left his home in Albion to travel across the sea to foster with the Senones, Solemis's tribe in Celtica. Solemis of course was already at foster with the Trinobantes in a reciprocal arrangement, and it enabled me to introduce the three main characters in the first book before their later adventures and explain their connection. By the act of fostering children, a web of interdependence was built up between clans and tribes which was essential at times of conflict in a society where raiding and warfare were endemic. It was the duty of the clan Chieftain to spread wealth throughout his people by means of *potlach* so the demand for high status goods was continual. A successful chieftain attracted a large retinue of warriors which added to his prestige but called for ever greater amounts of *potlach,* and a vicious cycle was produced where supply and demand fed upon one another continually.

If you enjoyed my tale please take a few moments to leave a review on Amazon or elsewhere. We all like to read reviews of books and it can really help to bring an author's work to a wider audience.

In book two, the overconfident army of Rome is swept away by the barbarian horde and the *Battle Swine* of the Horsetails returns in triumph to the Walls of Servian.

Cliff May
East Anglia
November 2014

CHARACTERS

ABALLA – A member of Catumanda's clan.

ABARIS – Chief druid of the Trinobantes. Catumanda's master.

ACCO – A member of Maros' war-band-betrothed to Aia.

AIA – Daughter of Crixos, later betrothed to Solemis.

AIKATERINE – Wife of Hektor.

ALBIOMAROS/ACCO – 'Big man from Albion.' Solemis' blood genos.

ALWENA – Wife of the trader, Ruffos.

ANDALOS – A Trinobante, father of Albiomaros.

ARION – Greek crewman on the *Alexa*.

ATTIS – A hunter in the Reaping.

BELLOVESOS – Warrior of the Belgae in Albion.

BERIKOS – Aeduan warrior freed from slavery by Solemis.

BRENNUS – War leader, later chieftain of the Senones.

BRITOMAROS – Chieftain of the Belgae in Albion.

CAESO FABIUS AMBUSTUS – Tribunus Militum of Rome.

CATUBAROS – Chieftain of the Senones.

CATUMANDA – A druid. One of the blood genos.

CATURIX – Son of Crixos, later clan chieftain.

CAUROS – Champion of the Horsetails.

COTOS – Carnyx warrior of the Horsetails.

CONNOS – Chieftain of the Horsetails, Solemis' father.

CRIXOS – Clan chieftain, father to Aia, Caturix and Matunos.

CULWYCH – Son of the carter, Ruffos.

CYNOBELIN – King of the continental Belgae.

DEVORIX – Chief druid of the Senones, brother of Catubaros.

DIOCAROS – A temple guardian.

DIONYSIUS – Basileus of Syracuse.

DOROS – A clansman of Crixos.

DORROS – A hunter in the Reaping.

DRUTEOS – A Horsetail warrior.

DUN – A shepherd boy/guide for Catumanda.

GALBA – Belgic warrior at Isarnos.

GARO – A clansman of Catumanda.

GESATORIX – Chieftain of the Parisii, killed by Brennus.

HEKTOR – Crewman on the *Alexa.*

HESPEROS – Owner and captain of the Greek trader, *Alexa.*

KYRIAKOS – A Greek merchant.

LICINIA – Wife of N Fabius Ambustus.

MARCUS FABIUS AMBUSTUS – Pontifex Maximus. Paterfamilias of the Fabii.

MARCUS FURIUS CAMILLUS – General, dictator and political opponent of the Fabii. In exile due to charges of embezzlement.

MARKOS – A crewman on the *Alexa.*

MAROS – Son of Catubaros, chieftain of the Senones.

MATUNOS – Younger son of Crixos.

NIA – Young daughter of the trader, Ruffos.

NUMERIUS FABIUS AMBUSTUS – Tribunus Militum. Conqueror of the Volscian city of Anxur.

PHILIPPOS – Boy on the *Alexa.*

PISO – Chief at Eyam. Poisoned by Catumanda.

PORSENNA – Zilach of Clevsin.

QUINTUS FABIUS AMBUSTUS – Tribunus Militum.

RUFFOS – Friend and guide of Catumanda.

SEARIX – A salt trader on Albion.

SEBASTOS – A Roman surrogate.

SEDULLOS – A clan chieftain of the Senones.

SOLEMIS – Blood Genos to Albiomaros and Catumanda, later clan chieftain of the Horsetails.

SUROS – 'Runner,' a war dog.

TARVOS – 'Bull,' a war dog.

THESTOR – Son of Hektor.

ULLIO – War chief of the Allobroge at Genawa.

UROGENOS – A Bellovaci warrior killed by Brennus.

VERNOGENOS – A druid on the Spirit Isle.

PLACES/LOCATIONS

AETNA – Mount Etna, Sicily.

ALPES – A word of pre Indo-European origin, *ALB*, 'high place'-The Alps.

ADRIATICUM SEA – Adriatic Sea.

AGEDINCUM – Sens, 'town of the Senones,' France.

ALBION/PRETANNIA – Britain.

ALESIA – Venarey-les-Laumes, France.

ANXUR – Terracina, Latina, Italy.

APENINNUS MONS – Apennine Mountains.

ARDEA – Province of Rome, Italy.

ATHENAI – Athens, Greece.

BENINUS PASS – Great St Bernard Pass.

PLAIN OF BODENCUS – Plain of Lombardy, Italy.

RIVER BODENCUS – River Po, Italy.

BRIG DU – Black Peak, Derbyshire, England.

BRIG GWYN – White Peak, Derbyshire, England.

CAMULODUNON – 'The Hill Fort of Camulos.' Colchester, Essex, England.

CELTICA/KELTICA/GAUL – Roughly the area corresponding to present day France, southern Germany, Switzerland and northern Italy.

CHEDWR – Cheddar Gorge, Somerset, England.

CIMINIAN FOREST – Silva Ciminia. A dense primeval forest which straddled the border lands between Rome and Etruria.

RIVER CLANIS – River Chiana, Tuscany, Italy.

CLEVSIN/CLUSIUM – Chiusi, Tuscany, Italy.

RIVER DERWENTA – River Derwent, the 'Clear Water,' England.

EYAM – Eyam, Derbyshire, England.

GENAWA – Geneva, Switzerland.

IBERIA – The Iberian peninsula, present day Portugal and Spain.

IERNE – Ireland.

ISARNO – Hengestbury Head, Dorset, England.

ISLE OF EELS – Ely, Cambridgeshire, England.

JORA – Jura Mountains.

LAKE LEMANNUS – Lake Genenva.

LUGDUNON – 'The Hill Fort of Lug', Lyon, France.

MASSALIA – Marseilles, France.

MEDIOLANUM – Milan, Italy.

MEDIOMATRICUM – Metz, France.

NEMETON – Buxton, Derbyshire, England.

RIVER PARWYDYDD – River Parrett, Somerset, England.

PEIRAIEUS – Piraeus, Greece.

PERUSIA – Perugia, Umbria, Italy.

PILLARS OF HERCULES – Straits of Gibraltar.

PLACE OF MONSTERS – Jurassic Coast, Dorset, England.

THE REAPING – The Fens/The Wash, eastern England.

RIVER RODONUS – 'The Running River,' River Rhone, France.

RIVER SABRINNA – A goddess-River Severn, Wales/England.

THE SPIRIT ISLE – Anglesey, Wales.

RIVER SEQUANA – A goddess-River Seine, France.

SIKELIA – Sicily.

RIVER SOUCONNA – A goddess-River Saone, France.

SPARTA – Sparti, Greece.

SYRACUSE – Syracuse, Sicily.

RIVER TAMESIS – 'The Dark River,' River Thames.

RIVER TIBERIS – A goddess-River Tiber.

TIGGUOCOBAUC – 'Place of Caves,' Nottingham, England.

RIVER TRISANTONA – 'The Strongly Flooding,' River Trent, England.

VEII – Isola Farnese, Province of Rome, Italy.

RIVER WYE – 'The Winding One,' River Wye, England.

THE WHITE LADY – Mont Blanc, France.

ABOUT THE AUTHOR

I am writer of historical fiction, working primarily in the early Middle Ages. I have always had a love of history which led to an early career in conservation work. Using the knowledge and expertise gained we later moved as a family through a succession of dilapidated houses which I single-handedly renovated. These ranged from a Victorian townhouse to a Fourteenth Century hall, and I added childcare to my knowledge of medieval oak frame repair, wattle and daub and lime plastering. I have crewed the replica of Captain Cook's ship, Endeavour, sleeping in a hammock and sweating in the sails and travelled the world, visiting such historic sites as the Little Big Horn, Leif Erikson's Icelandic birthplace and the bullet scarred walls of Berlin's Reichstag.

Now I write, only a stone's throw from the Anglian ship burial site at Sutton Hoo in East Anglia.

ALSO BY C.R.MAY

NEMESIS

SORROW HILL

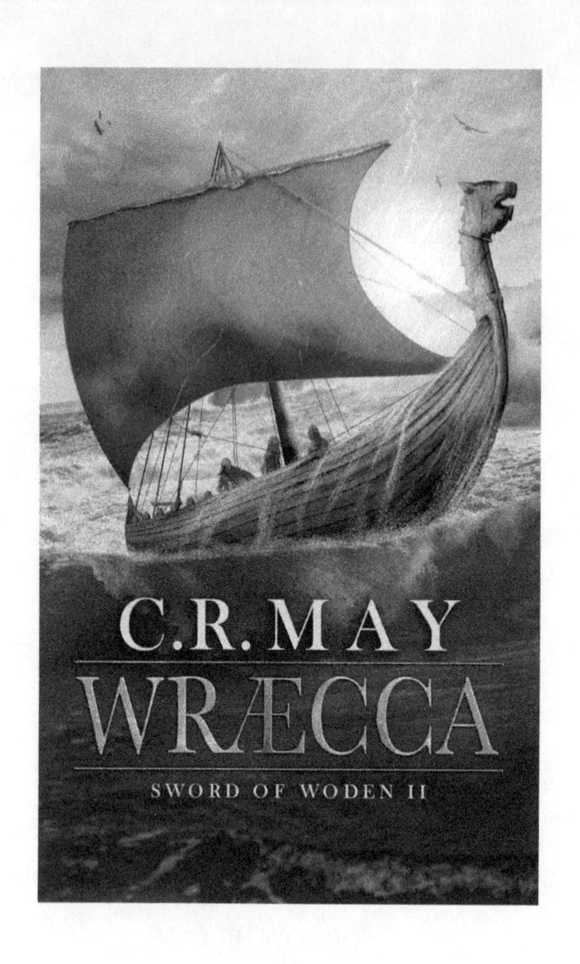

WRÆCCA

MONSTERS

DAYRAVEN

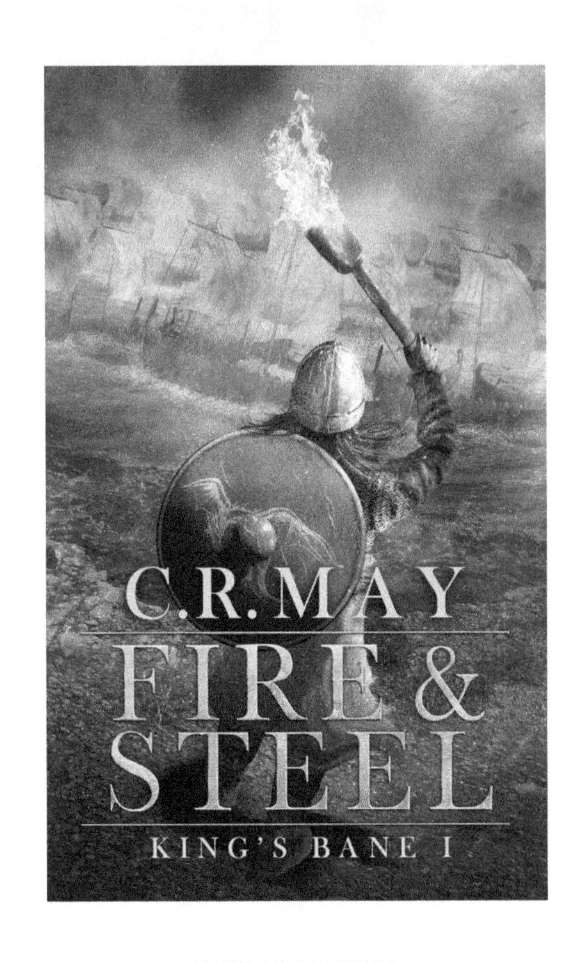

FIRE AND STEEL

GODS OF WAR

THE SCATHING

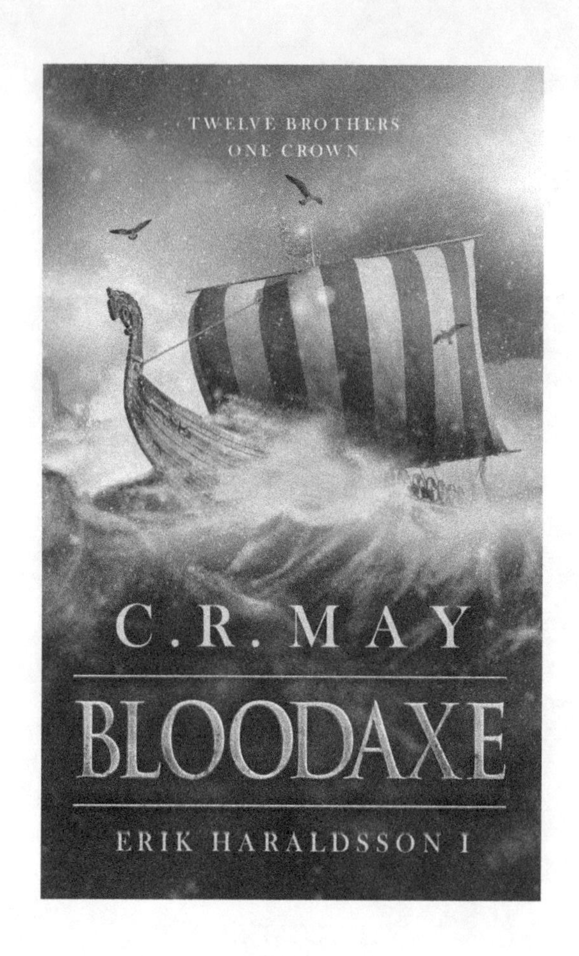
TWELVE BROTHERS
ONE CROWN
C.R. MAY
BLOODAXE
ERIK HARALDSSON I

BLOODAXE

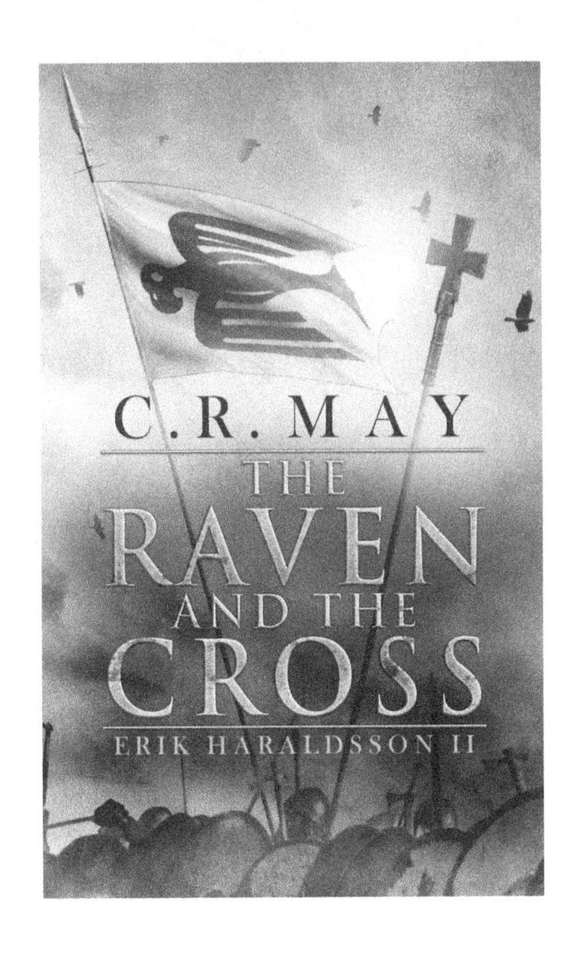

THE RAVEN AND THE CROSS

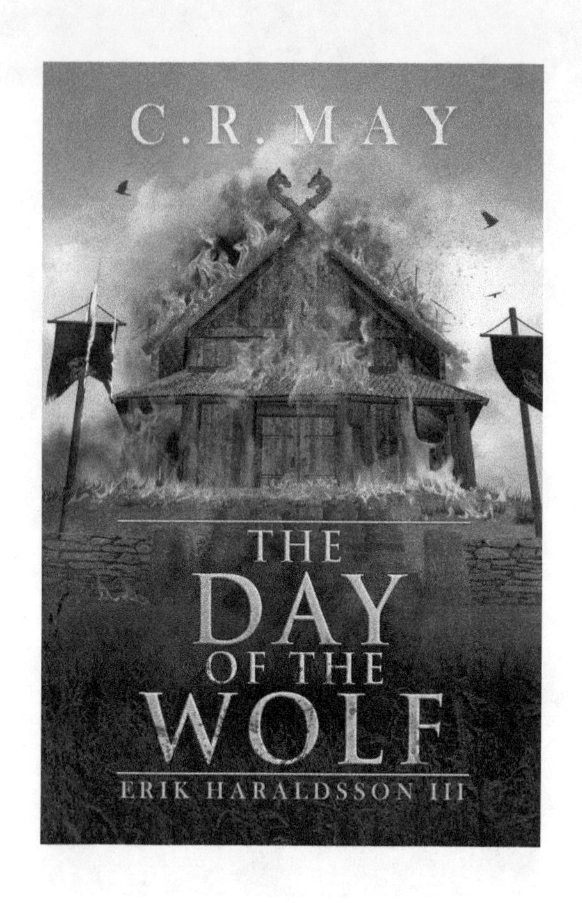

THE DAY OF THE WOLF

SPEAR HAVOC

CPSIA information can be obtained
at www.ICGtesting.com
Printed in the USA
BVHW031345030221
599282BV00007B/114